THE THIRTEENTH LAW

Chapter One

"Security, report to level seven! Repeat, report to lev..."
Abruptly, Officer Jalice Royst was grabbed from behind. Hands
clasping her neck and mouth. A savage kick to her left calf muscle
sent her down to her knees.

"Get out the rope!", a young female whispered.

Polished grey, and blue walls of steel reflected her futile struggle.
Biting one of her attackers only brought more fury down upon her.

Three pairs of hands pinned the young woman down, making
movement next to impossible. But the captive sentinel nevertheless
struggled. Fear of being injured, or worse, fueled her resistance. But
she was overpowered.

The lookout began watching, on alert for any other D.O.s
(detainment officers) that could be lurking about.

"Get her tied!", an anxious sounding, young woman commanded.
A slender neck craned around the far corner. The other lookout, a
burly youngster, guarded the rear. Sweating profusely, a dark ham of a
hand swiped away the perspiration.

"How does it look?", she asked, helping the others accost Royst.
"Are we clear?"

"So far, so good, Tahina", a girl in faded, grey prisoner's garb
whispered. She spoke in whispers. They may not have been seen, yet,
but they could be heard. There had to be audio surveillance around
and about. Even relic starships like this had to have them.

Once Officer Royst was bound and gagged, Tahina, leader of this
small team of Duriyans, began searching their captive thoroughly. Not
a transponder, nor a useable weapon on her. The communicator was
dead, broken in the scuffle.

"Grab her, and let's go", she said sharply. She kept them moving,
hoping, and for a moment, calm and lucid. Way too much was at
stake, and the slightest misstep would damn them all.

Jojas, she thought, for all our sakes, don't sluck this up.

In the sky bright illumination, silhouettes played cautiously.

"Where to, Boss lady?", one of the guys, named Hudd asked Tahina, snidely, as he took hold of their hostage. The snarky undertone rankled Tahina, but she had no time to be bothered. *These fools may not like me, but Jojas and the other leaders do,* she thought. Each team had a specific target. Jojas and his crew would take out the gravity controls. Iajim and his gang would attempt to hack into the main computer systems, and get this hunk of a decrepit ship turned around. Tahina's squad would go after the communications, and generally disrupt the flow of things. Another girl, whose name she couldn't remember, was to find the munitions rooms (as the D. O's were heavily armed, they knew they had rifles available) and take what they could. Best case scenario, they'd negotiate their way back to their home world. Worst case scenario went unspoken. But it was felt, nevertheless.

"Where else?", she retorted, keeping it short.

Suddenly, alarms began blaring, shrieking through the S.S. Titanus.

"Security on all decks! Prisoners escaping! Repeat... prisoners escaping! ..."

Harsh yellow and orange light flooded the halls, its intensity blinding, disorienting. Pulsating flashes sickened even the hardest of stomachs. Royst made a vomiting noise, a trail of spit leaked from the filth stained cloth that silenced her.

An intense dread fell over Tahina. But she kept wearing a mask of cold iron and deceptive indifference. *Can't allow them to fall weak! Can't allow myself to fall...*

Before anyone asked, she whispered, "We move forward".

The warnings fell dead. From somewhere, smoke began billowing into the steel hallways. Tahina, with outstretched arms, halted everyone.

Hudd pointed up. "Through the vents". The short, husky teen that held Royst deliberately pushed her in the smoke's direction. Tahina shot him a wild eyed look of delirium.

"To see if it's a knockout gas", he replied, his tone inflecting the absent *genius.* The lookout fought through the attacking lights, which had begun to subside. She gave an indication that it was still all clear.

Wall consoles a few steps ahead erupted, spitting out sparks and embers. A bad omen, for sure. Yet they pressed onwards. Ahead, not too far distant, there was a hyper lift. *If only,* Tahina thought.

Another eruption. This time, a maintenance sub router console was melting, the sparks twisting and dying on the floor. Metal frame tarnished and deformed, faded red light bled from between the still legible black lettering on the keypad.

Choking clouds formed, and they became nauseated with each step. She hated fires. Soot, the stench that lingered forever. The memories of the night that led her here began replaying before her. The hunger, the looks of desperation. The crippling hopelessness that led her to act. Everyone that was held prisoner and shunted off world on this voyage of the oppressed was here for those reasons. Those reasons made her and those with her, with Iajim and Jojas and what's her name do what they were doing now.

Enduring the smoke and flame and desperation. Deja vu', indeed.

She shook off the memory. That was then, this is today. *Today we fight for...* she thought, before the bright flash of a laser shone before them. Their lookout's head snapped back, a loud, final gasp. Smoke fled from where her face had been. The corpse crumpled and rolled onto the ground. The others backed away, too stunned to even think of going further.

As the rest of her team crouched, Officer Royst mumbled triumphantly. Saki. Her name was Sakime', better known as Saki. She came from a province not far from her own Shakur province. She didn't know her before this, but she was brave. Brave, and her life was worth infinitely more than this sack of human feces they held tied up. More than the line of D.O.s that were lining up before them, weapons trained and they were obviously more than willing to kill a few more people.

It had come to this. That moment of kill or be killed. *Can I take a life?* she was thinking anxiously while the plan was being laid out.

"Either them, or us, Tahina", Jojas said firmly, his strong, steady palms on her shoulders. The rough fabric of her drab, grey prisoner coveralls stuck out in between long brown fingers. "We come first."

"That was your warning, your *only* warning", a burly, harsh looking man in the hated red and golden camo uniform bellowed over the smoke of death and hissing of malfunctioning, interconnecting systems that ground the starship to an abrupt, unwelcome halt.

"Surrender, release your hostage..."

"Or you'll mow all of us down ?!", she screamed, her rage had taken her over. Three. Three of them versus six fully armed and ready to kill animals. Without another word, they rushed forward.

Duriyans, to their credit, never fled in the face of adversity. A proud people from a world settled in the former fringes of the human diaspora known as the Far Worlds. One of many worlds that broke away after the costly, brutal wars for independence and sovereign government. Duriyans were known for their strong nationalist tendencies and an almost overbearing pride. And they fought like hellions.

The looks on the faces opposing them ranged from naked incredulity to open hatred to shocked outrage. *These kids simply aren't afraid to die.* That they also held back, out of fear of accidentally shooting Royst, gave the surviving trio a minor edge. They exploited it to the max.

However ferocious they fought, with staggering blows and brutal kicks, they were only three. Their oppressors recovered themselves, and began to deal them a cruel retribution.

First to go down was Hudd then the short big boy. Hudd fell before the desperate flash of a hastily drawn laser. His bloodcurdling scream traveled down the hallway, into the pit of her soul. Tahina had her hands around the throat of the Commander. The big man, helmet now on the floor, was a grizzled, middle aged man toying with a child like she was a life- sized rag doll. Her punches may've bruised, and her claws cut and disfigured, but he could barely hold his laughter. From her right, in her eye's corner, she saw them gang up on him, kicking and hitting and flailing away with the butt of pistols, and then a steel truncheon. He fought as hard, as long as he could. But Big Man went down in a fury of violence that would give her nightmares for nights to come. The sickening crack on the back of a skull fractured, and from the wound, blood spitting and painting the cold floor.

Don't give in, she thought with deep desperation. *Don't ...*

She was pushed back, and Officer Royst repaid her by kicking her from behind. She shedded tears as she fell, as a paralyzing shock of taser volts stabbed her left side.

She fell in the still leaking pool of blood. "Murderers..." she murmured.

As everything faded to black, she heard the one in charge. That slobby, pus bag towered above her, his size twelve foot nudging the side where she was taser shocked, and spoke into his communicator. "Level seven is secure."

"How many are left?", queried a hushed voice on the other end. Sounds of massive systems failure, an eruption in the background made the speaker almost intelligible.

"Just one", was the equally terse reply. The hardened toe of his left boot lifted out of the blood. He pressed it on Tahina's other side, leaving a grotesque mark as a symbol of contempt.

A harried voice replied, "Level five is secure, so too the holding bay. Riots have been quelled." After a few minutes, the message spread all over via the inter-communicators the security force utilized.

As Royst was being untied, her superior looked at her, amused. She felt a blanket of shame come over her.. "Consider yourself lucky, Ms. Royst. You avoided the bloodbath on levels four, six and ten." The grim mirth was undercut by the announcement overhead:

"Begin separating the living from the dead".

It was hardly a minute past nine A.M., Earth Standard Time.

By now, she knew better than to look for anything besides a weak sun lurking in an endless blanket of grey, too shy to show itself in full. Drab, and without the nurturing influence of sunlight, it was no wonder that life never came into its own here, on a world so dead, so lackluster, human involvement notwithstanding.

Nevertheless, this new assignment made her the ruler of "The Gate to Oblivion". That had to count for something.

After all, who else under the employ of IREL Unlimited, or any other conglomeration for that matter, could lay claim to being chosen to spearhead a new field of intergalactic endeavor?

Warden Ednisa Quinn had scarcely begun decorating her new office when a red glow came alive in the middle of the gigantic glass and real oak desk that dominated her office. The communique circle, a feature she had built in, custom made, was only for emergencies, red taking highest priority. She hoped she could ignore it, maybe it was a misplaced I-Mail. However, after a few minutes, the flash of red grew stronger. To avoid the screeching alarm (she regretted asking for such a thing, but never found time to have it removed), she went over, holding a box haphazard.

"Never a moment's peace", she complained. The golden and black name plate went on the desk, the other contents to the side. Glancing out her spacious bay window, the languid gray gave her a momentary sensation of ill feeling. She had been on many worlds, saw and walked in too many dawns and early mornings to count, but she still couldn't adjust to the dullness of morning here on Asylon.

Ednisa Quinn sighed heavily and sat in the banker's chair, staring at the increasing intensity of the red beacon and decided to get it over with.

"Start with the bad, so you can rise past it to reach the good ". A proverb from Polim Tef, her home world.

"Answer", she said with an almost sultry contralto.

From her desk a robotic voice squeaked, as a monitor rose from the left side of her desk. It was a feature she had to have installed.

The screen came alive with the large furrowed brows of Captain Aduk, his face scarred, with a sagging left cheek. He looked bereft of sleep for days. Eyes were a hardened red and cracked, his forehead polished with sweat.

"May I help you?", Warden Quinn asked, already annoyed with him.

"Y-Yes", he stammered, collecting himself. "I'm calling for Warden Quinn".

"I am she", Ednisa Quinn responded confidently. More confident than anything the Captain could recall in recent years.

His bushy brows furrowed, joined by confusion. "You?!" He couldn't help but be surprised.

"Yes, me! Were you expecting a man?!", she yelled, exasperated. *The twenty eighth century, and people still think...* She let it die. Obviously, there was something of importance that had occurred. Something that would affect her work, and she couldn't stand for that to happen. So, she would play diplomat. *For now.*

"Not particularly", Captain Aduk responded, somewhat hostile. "A man or woman makes no difference, I just didn't expect someone looking like *you*". *Presuming, arrogant wench! How dare you judge me! Especially after the hell we've been through here!*

Truly, she was a beautiful woman, statuesque (just a tad over six foot two), shapely and with a sheened, chocolate complexion that recalled the most gorgeous of models, which, incidentally, she had been in her youth.

"I'll take the compliment, but give me the news", she said coldly.

Captain Aduk told her everything in a detailed report. She made him repeat it twice. Out of frustration, he asked her, "Why are you asking me to repeat myself?"

"So that you don't miss, or mess up a detail", she said flatly. "The corporate office will need an accounting for this."

A riot broke out, in which prisoners en route to Asylon attempted to take over the vessel. Quelled, but not without casualties.

Final tally: out of two hundred prisoners en route, twenty- two are confirmed dead, forty injured, maybe permanently. The remaining hundred and thirty- eight secured,heavily drugged and shackled. *As they should've before they left Duriy,* she reflected. As for the crew of the S.S. Titanus, five officers were seriously injured, two were killed, and the ship itself took some damage to non- vital, minor operational systems. But the incident and the repairs would delay the ETA by two days. A learning curve to be studied, and subsequent counter measures would be enforced.

The notion seemed silly at first, to use old star trawlers to transport human cargo across the galaxy. After all, it was known that they were criminals. However, the prospect of the ship being stopped and raided by pirates, notably that band of asteroid dwelling thugs called the Karuki, had tempered her earlier reservations. They weren't known to attack derelicts. *Besides,* she mused silently, *who was she to question the great mind of Heram Bevel?* Shaking her head, she realized Capt. Aduk was staring at her. This amused her slightly.

"The leaders, she queried, have you singled them out?"

His startled look indicated no. But she pushed further until he answered with a henpecked "W- what are you ....?"

"Of this little putsch. Have you separated them from the others, if they're still alive, that is."

"Yes, yes", he spoke too quick to be reassuring. *Who does she think she is?!*

She let it go, but she would review the ship's memory base when they arrived.

"Thank you, Captain. Inform me the minute you are over Asylon."

The screen went black before he could issue a response.

She swiveled around to again look out the bay window; such a grand overview it provided her.

Just some seven stories down, lay a patch of sickly grass that was lined with long, wooden benches and picnic tables that would serve as the courtyard for the Asylon Project. A pilot program in the burgeoning field of intergalactic prisons. This venture would begin with a juvenile and young adult facility. Here, the most unruly would be brought here from their respective home worlds, for crimes too heinous, or for the fact that many worlds in the human diaspora didn't have either the will or the necessary wherewithal to deal with increasingly dangerous, desperate and violent populations. Far world planets such as Duriy, and hell spots like the Karuki belt were proof as to how far, even in such advanced times as this, humanity could still regress to the level of mud throwers.

She decided to talk a walk.

"Stepping out dearie?", her wizened receptionist asked her.

"Yes, I am, for a brief tour", Quinn said, making sure the wrinkles were out of her neatly pressed one suit uniform. All tan, resembling a brigadier commander's, sans the rank insignia. "I have my communicator on me."

Ms. Roshin said nothing more, only sighing in relief that that impossible woman was gone.

Some two centuries ago, this was the not just an ore and mineral processing foundry, it was part of a waystation from one half of the galaxy to the next. The building still reeked of chemical residue and polluted water fumes. No amount of bleach vapors would remove the stench of history. A few of the guards (Corrective Officers, they were called), waved. The first wave would be a skeleton crew. The others in place by the time the first batch of moral degenerates arrived.

In true corporate fashion, everything had to be "hit the ground running" style, which causes more problems than it solves. However, as she turned a corner to speak briefly to the head of the Infirmary ward, she recalled some advice her late father gave her. "Always be flexible, because things rarely go according to plan".

Before heading back, she inspected, for as how many times since she arrived three months prior, the loading depot. The Docking Centrix, located in the middle of what was a virtual ghost town, was far too risky to chance. True, very few ships arrived here, even when it was called Evir and was a miner's planet. But an escapee had far too much leeway, too much ground to evade capture, even temporarily. This area, besides the building itself, was the largest part of the complex. It's circumference matched the massive length of the artificial mesa plateaus terraformed on Pluto and a few actual planets. In height, it was less than half the size of the docking centrix, adding in the control tower, where everything could be handled with precision. The technology was state of the art, with the finest surveillance money could supply.

When she returned, the foul aroma of chemical doused sediment and tainted metal had begun its daily ritual of making her nauseous. She took a pill with her coffee, to dim the effects. No other calls, no other emergencies. Finally, a quiet day.

It didn't take long for monotony to set it. Again, she left out.

She spent another hour and a half inspecting each high tower, one for each corner of the prison's diamond. The high energy laser grid was running perfectly, almost obscured by the dense grey morning. For good measure, old fashioned barb wiring looped and coiled about crumbling concrete. Another order to reinforce the roofing would be put in. And languish in Maintenance Dept. datafile.

Just this once, she thought, with unusual childlike giddiness. She went up to the top of the tower. And for what amounted to less than five minutes, she stood in the dank, drab, eternally oppressive Asylon morn.

Beyond the high, grey brick walls, she could see the housing complexes for the guards who had already begun. As well as those to come. And her penthouse suite.

But sightseeing and daydreams had to wait. An investigation needed to begin. Mr. Bevel would accept nothing less than the most thorough detailing of what went wrong, went right, and what was needed to ensure total success going forward. That was the IREL way.

She made her way down, and was back in her office no more than a quarter of an hour later.

No calls, or I-mails from home office, which was a good thing. Sitting at her desk, the preliminary report took less time to compose than she expected. Until she could corroborate all the facts Captain Aduk had supplied her (via interviews with the crew, reviewing the data banks, if they were operable. Damage could've occurred during the melee, or the ship's aging systems could be suffering malfunctions. A million plus one things can go wrong), all she had was a report that was no more than a half screen. As the prisoners were being brought in via a private contractor, informing the families of the deceased fell upon their heads, not hers nor IREL Unlimited.

In another three hours, she had a new training class. And her Chief of Guards would be arriving late this afternoon, or early tomorrow. She needed to consult with Ms. Roshin as to which.

Right now, though, Warden Quinn needed a brief diversion. Activating the Data stream, multicolored pixels came alive, forming images and speaking as though they were in the office:

"Live from Duriy, this is Jet Symmons..."

"Quarter", Quinn yelled. The damned thing could never pick up anything lower than a scream. One image became four.

"The strongman of Sefu Trius, Nazrym Hagit has proclaimed an immediate..."

"The emergency meeting of the GCW (Galactic Community of Worlds) has run into gridlock over the timetable of readmission of the Far World planet states into...."

"The Ominous specter of Trans Stellar Slavery " is the op-ed piece of today's "Our Galaxy in Review". I'm your host Baldwin Wright Hurston. Joining me on the panel are Professor Aldwin Jaru, of the Galactic Justice Studies Department at Siktu University, Mr. Selwyn Sefyn of "Interstellar Press", and finally, an Attorney for Galactic Trust, and a liaison to the GCW Cabinet of Justice Enforcement, Mr. Anwar Anwari." Short applause.

"Thank you, gentlemen, for being here today."

A chorus of polite, obligatory salutations punctuated a lively, somewhat heated debate. The slick tongued Anwari parried and sparred against the trio of obviously liberal pundits. The plain faced, unimpressive man of Indian descent contrasted the handsome men of onyx. But she felt foolish, allowing looks to come into a debate. Especially when the merits of her livelihood were being weighed for public opinion.

She cut the news off, disgusted. Another public show of sympathy for criminals, she thought. Had they seen what happened on Duriy? What was going on in the Karuk Belt?

Of Sefu Trius, though, she had some sympathy; after all, Hagit was a tyrant. And would gladly murder his own parents to stay in power. But otherwise ...

She pressed onto the console. Yet again, the secretary, Ms. Anna Roshin, answered meekly.

"Suspend all calls, except from Home Office for the next hour. I have an investigation to complete."

She heard the beleagured woman sigh. She spent the next few hours soaking up the news, to get a glimmer of insight on the thought processes of a rapidly changing humanity.

Home.

Long shadows from the globular domes were like slim fingers. The sky was a faded, milky azure. Stained glass windows, the centerpiece of the pagoda like structures glittered, a beacon in the middle of a hazy, humid afternoon. The bronze gates, dented in some areas due to age and consistent usage, bore a placard that read, gold lettering standing out from the solid blue background, "The University of Duriy. For all those who seek a place amongst the stars, this is home."

Home.

Tahina was home. On nice summer days, when school let out early, she loved to sit on the steps of the University she'd hoped to attend in the fall. Today, sitting on a blue squared pillow, she sat crossed legged under a cyfus tree, in her long cream sundress, drinking tea, holding a trio of books. The zen economy of branch and leaf offered a sliver of shade, but the afternoon was so nice.

She alternated between the poetry of Dez Vulker, Astro Science Mechanics and Herbs and roots of Duriy Cuisine. She loved reading; she did it for hours, much to her mother's chagrin. A violent shudder ran through her at that moment. *How she hated that woman!*

A woman who was a demanding, irresponsible, drunken, Dujin addicted failure. Who neglected not only three children, but herself, most of all. Her younger siblings could scarcely remember, since they were so young. But long ago, their mother was one of the prettiest, most admired women on their part of the planet. Maybe she was being hyperbolic, but the woman was admired, even envied for her sense of style, stunning looks and can do demeanor. Well, that last one was Daddy. But it rubbed off on his wife and oldest daughter.

Then, he died. And her mother's fall began shortly thereafter. First Tahina mourned. Then she sympathized, doing everything in her meager power to help her mother, while keeping herself and the twins, Rom and Kela, somewhat protected, somewhat nurtured. Finally, she began to feel derision and disrespect. Her nature didn't allow empathy for those who persisted in failing themselves.

Yes, the hate was deeper now; what happened to make her despise her, beyond the usual? Hating.... she held her head, as if to purge herself of negativity. Today was too nice to allow herself to fall further in that familiar train of thought.

Yes, too nice, and like today, her tomorrow was too bright to dwell on the dark shadows of her soon to be yesterdays. She would take the twins with her on the pathway to a better life.

Ascending the stairs, which curved at the street and joined into the middle, leading into the main of the campus was the entrance of heaven. She had the grades, the ability and the desire. All she needed now was the....

Abruptly, she felt a nudge on the right. Achingly, her eyes began opening.

She was aroused to her stark reality. The left side of her was sore, and her mouth was salty. Vision blurred, and she couldn't move her arms freely. Wrists and elbows shackled, held together by a steel restraining bar which was fastened to a neck collar. After some minutes, she forced herself to a sitting position. The vision in her green eyes were clearing, though what surrounded her made a surge of dread run through her.

"You're awake", a boy, almost as dark as her replied. He was shackled the same way.

She saw the blood marks on the grey coveralls she wore, then looked around at the restrained bodies and despondent faces. A couple of them were weeping bitterly.

The holding pen in the gallows of the Titanus was surrounded with armed D. O's and crewmen, itching for an excuse.

Tahina turned her head again, taking a sober count of how many were missing. The gravity of their failure had begun to take its full measure.

Her group... gone, except her. The blood caked footprint mocking her, she turned to face the young man next to her.

The boy besides her, named Iajim, was badly beaten. His dark face bruised, blood dried and caked all around his left temple, the eye closed, and puffed. Like her, the shame of defeat crystallized in his open eye.

"Some ...of yours?", she let the question die. *Damn these restraints!* she thought wildly. They prevented her from taking her own... she let that thought die where it stood.

"Only me, and two others, he admitted. His team had twelve people. They caught us on level ten." A trickle of blood stopped, dried at the tip of his chin.

She shifted slightly, as if hoping it would lessen the pain. It didn't. She was hesitant to ask what she *really* wanted to know. "What about... I can't recall... "

Iajim cut her off, brusquely. It startled her, causing her to think the anger was aimed at her. "She, he began, betrayed us. Hejimma sold us out. She's probably in that sluckhead captain's quarters."

"How do you know this?" She couldn't accept this revelation of betrayal, let alone believe one of their own...

"As they were beating me, I overheard them speak about it. Those with her, he said sadly, lived long enough to curse her name."

Tahina felt herself sinking to the lowest depths of despair. Then she found the grim courage to give her feelings words.

"Did ... he ... die?", she forced herself to ask him.

Hard silence, then a nod of acknowledgement. He couldn't bear to look into those tear laden, grief stricken green eyes.

Tahina stared downwards, tears freefalling to the floor. But she said nothing. Accepting no comfort, nor even raised an eye to view the descent into Asylon's orbit, when a holo- screen projection came alive to torment the survivors. Her mind was preoccupied with lost love, forfeited freedom and the bitter sting of betrayal. She would never forget Hejimma for as long as she lived.

Chapter Two

Mournos.

That name had always given Ednisa Quinn a chill. Two decades hadn't changed that, and nothing ever would. That an exoplanet in the Taurus Maxim system could be the financial heart of the Human Diaspora and be so morbid in name was a paradox she never reconciled. When she lived within its pyramidic domed biosphere, the place was just spooky. The spirits of the original inhabitants, the venture capitalists that founded IREL and their legions of lawyers, accountants and sycophants haunted the place, so various old legends went. The shadows that wandered freely in the daytime were said to be their horrid souls, wandering in between the realms of heaven, hell and purgatory. *An old tale to be dismissed,* she thought when she first heard it. But from time to time, she wondered.

Her hover cab stopped just at the parking helix, with less than ten minutes to spare.

There were some changes since she was last here. The Bevel Tower Seven had finally reached its completion, now a towering behemoth some seventy eight stories erect; all iron, all glass, all reminiscent of the phallic monoliths that still stood on Earth. She would try to make a point to visit, assuming she survived her meeting before the Directorship.

Other skyscraper buildings fingered the red skies above and the connector tubes that linked monolith to monolith, while shadows, living and dead, were everywhere. Moving, silent, and in some undefined way, unnatural. As she reached the lobby of the Capital Uber Building, nostalgia tugged at her. When *she* went from building to building, working her way to where she was now.

Glass and ice clear diamond tiled flooring and ornate carved marble statues in the lobby made the place look and feel like a mausoleum. And before her stood the crypt keeper.

"Gus!", she said cheerfully enough. "How are you? I haven't seen you in ages! A wizened desk guard heartily grinned. "Gettin' along for an old man! You're gorgeous as always!"

This made a faint blush appear on her cheeks. She always liked sincere compliments.

"My thanks", she replied. She always liked the old coot. He reminded her of what her father could've been like, had he made it to old age.

A few ex co-workers, recognizing her, spoke warmly as they were leaving out. IREL always kept their people coming and going.

"Here for the board?", He asked her, not holding back his concern. So many who went before them did so for the final time.

"Yes, and I'll be fine", she squeezed his gnarled, brown leathery hand. She sounded reassured. Perhaps more for his sake than her own. As she entered the hyperlift, she heard "Give 'em hell!", in a rasping voice. She smiled, hoping she wouldn't be the one receiving it. *So, so much like Dad,* she thought, steeling herself for what she had to face.

Bevel's boardroom, in her mind, was a feudal king's court. The differences were a giant oakwood U shaped table dominating the room, and they were upwards forty stories. Medieval courts, at least, were far less cruel. So the stories went. A deep, shuddering chill ran through her when the hyperlift stopped at floor Thirty -Nine.

No one greeted her, and the entrance was left wide open. *Ill omened?* Like the knight eager to slay the dragon, she entered, heart in throat. She glided through the vestibule and entered the King Bevel's Court. Of the faces staring icily at her, she was only concerned with two. Naturally old man Bevel's, who looked more guant than ever, yet even more dangerous than she remembered. And that man to the left of him. The lawyer from Galactic Trust.... *what was he doing here?*

That said, she knew she would be unwise to discount the others. Their treachery in IREL affairs were renown in corporate circles. She had to tread the razor tightrope very deliberately.

Taking the dais (known to some as the chopping block), she felt them. She felt the intense stares of the Board members that made up the Directorship. The men and women who were the eyes, ears, and if necessary, hands of the body that was IREL. In the heart of the U sat the brain, the King himself, Heram Bevel.

Ednisa marveled at how a man well over one hundred years kept the workload he did, the hectic schedule. Even with a multitude of assistants and sycophants, the man kept up a hands on approach that was archaic in some ways, but highly successfully in many more. His deep, brown eyes, held in that almost mummified face, were sharp and alert. Alert and intense, they penetrated with a level gaze that even the most hardened wouldn't fail to find intimidating.

Before she could begin, Mr. Bevel fired the first salvo.

"Warden Quinn, Mr. Bevel began, his voice creaking, thank you for your presence."

"I'm honored, sir, I truly am", she replied, restraining the gush factor.

"Now begin". The terse reversal was off putting, but she delivered her report.

The first forty- five days of operating Asylon was a learning curve; one teachable moment after the next. Immediately after their arrival, the Duriyan kids proved to be a formidable obstacle to overcome. Defiant, intelligent, destructive, and creative, they defaced property, fought guards (six had quit the first week, citing unforeseen occupational hazards) and had managed to maneuver around the prison's biometric scanning system, The Eye. They *heavily damaged it* to the point that it would be months before it was fully operational again. State of the art surveillance provided no true, adequate countermeasure against human ingenuity and wily desperation.

"Despite these setbacks, have there been any more deaths since their arrival?", a voice she couldn't identify inquired. "No", was the curt reply. Thankfully, no follow up questions arose, so she resumed her report.

Despite these difficulties, Warden Quinn maintained control over the fledgling project. Several factors, one expected, the other a complete surprise, accounted for this.

For one, Warden Quinn had the Chief of Guards, Turlak, on her team. Big, strong, with admirable cunning and frightening brutality, his presence garnered a begrudged respect from the Duriyans, and when sending more than one of them to the infirmary ward (they tried to jump him), he forced them to revise their tactics of resistance.

His was the appearance of a lifelong militia man (until recently, no formal intergalactic armed forces. Each world maintained a domestic militia) who had only recently begun to let himself go, the cruel scars that forever tarnished his deep brown face gave him a ripped leather mask that never smiled. Though his uniform may have been a sloppy fit (rarely had she seen him in the "standard". Neat, clean and professional looking. It irked her beyond belief), it was no deterrent to quick, brutish reflexes and adroitness of martial art skill that, after the failed group attack, made all the male convicts think hard and twice about another attempt. The females avoided him altogether. The harshest of stares came his way well after he turned the corner. He did his best to empower the C.E.Os (Correctional Enforcement Officers, or just C.Os) as he was able, and his leadership was given more value than even Warden Quinn's, a prospect that she admittedly (to herself) was uneasy with, though she masked it with cool professionalism. If she had to be, she could be as frigid as possible.

She didn't fail to notice how quiet the room had become. *It seems I have their rapt attention, or they're waiting for me to make a mistake,* she thought warily.

And what was the second factor, the one that caught her and her staff by surprise?

The arrival of the Karuki. They were more vocal, more vicious, and even more obnoxious than their Duriyan counterparts. Naturally, the two ethnicities hated one another. Karuki were nomadic, spreading their cultural norms and biases among the Far Worlds. They were, as a rule, tall, lanky, and spoke in thick, heavily accented sentences that made them sound uneducated. An unfounded notion, because many of them, even ones involved in piracy, were very intelligent and well read. Those who employed them commented that they had a strong work ethic. And, despite the constant moving about, they had strong family and community bonds.

Duriyans also claimed each other, and defended each other, The prison dorms were quickly quartered off. "Little Duriy" , "Karuk" . And neither let the other trespass. Male or female. Especially the females.

Excepting cultural and some physical differences, both groups of teens looked alike, their dark and strong features only slight in variance. "Their similarities, remarked Turlak, should be enough for them to unite and overthrow the whole damn thing". It wasn't. "Fortunately, all of them combined don't have enough cells to make one brain."

An impatient member of the board, a woman Quinn knew of and despised heartily, asked "How was the problem resolved? This Turlak seems a wise man. "

Quinn offered a plastic smile, knowing the comment was an indirect dig at her. Politely, she continued.

A program of dissension was implemented. The guards could act as intermediaries instead of targets. Largely, it was working, albeit with some setbacks. A female officer was beaten, stripped nude by two fighting girls. The combatants ceased their fist fight and turned on her. The display showed both Quinn and Turlak they needed to clamp down harder, keep improving their tactics. So, a series of psychological skirmishes (gossip, nurturing the apparent dislike and distrust the Duriyans and Karuks had for one another) was launched, and largely it was a successful operation.

The question of how many of each group presently at the facility arose. She gave them the numbers. Then the question of available spaces came up.

"At present, Asylon can hold up to five hundred. We have it at half capacity. "

"The more extreme among both groups, how are they handled?", asked someone near Mr. Bevel. A man this time, with a strong baritone.

The room felt a little heated, and she had the urge to wipe perspiration away from her forehead. She resisted, thinking *this is just about over. An impromptu questioning session.*

"Asylon has a designated area for such…people. The Quarantine Zone. In times past, it was known as solitary confinement."

"Is it working?"

She mulled the answer carefully, since there was just *one* person currently in quarantine. And that occurred shortly before she left for Mournos. She needed an answer to placate, not inadvertently cause yet another, second investigation. That report she gathered and sent regarding the Duriyan "uprising" on the S.S. Titanus was a waking nightmare; to this day she cursed at Captain Aduk every time his grizzled face popped up in memory.

"The data is still being gathered regarding its effectiveness. The full results will be made known by the time of the next meeting before the board."

This seemed to satisfy them, and she continued her reporting unimpeded. She concluded to a brief, polite applause.

Now the real questioning begins, she thought in anticipation.

She well prepared herself, having rehearsed with her secretary. *The poor woman,* she chuckled inwardly.

Most were about logistical matters, such as damages and upkeep. Then Mr. Anwari stepped further into view and inquired pointedly:

"How soon will the first wave be available for leasing? "

She felt confusion on her face, not liking the uncertainty it awoke in her. And this lawyer aroused it, in a sly manner, in a way that initiated a long running hate you-hate you even more relationship. A question.

A question seemingly so left field, her first response was "Come again?"

With practiced deliberation, Mr. Anwari repeated his query. And again, Quinn was at a loss. "Mr.... "

"Mr. Anwar Rajesh Anwari, Esq.", he replied confidently.

Of course.

"Mr. Anwari, Esq"., she said, attempting to inject humor, your line of questioning. What exactly does that...."

The old man cut her off. She was offended, but she dared not show it.

A clearing of the throat, then Mr. Bevel spoke. "What he means is that there are clients waiting. We need a timetable as when to expect a workforce to be available from your facility."

Suddenly the gaze of fifteen pairs of eyes felt a wearisome burden to carry. She lacked a convincing answer for this; her job was only to...

"We're waiting, Warden Quinn", the old man said quietly. She noticed a distinct absence of either compassion or pleasantry. Before her facade of semi- competence could erode further, she came up with:

"I estimate anytime from ninety to one hundred and twenty days, sir", she said, for an answer. How she wanted, more than anything, to be outside, in that crimson afternoon. *To be an insignificant ant trotting around in the connector tubes, rather would I be than here!*

"That's fairly reasonable", Mr. Bevel spoke amid a flurry of polite clamor.

Quinn sighed deeply within herself. She saved herself, for the moment.

Even that upstart Anwari seemed satisfied with her rapidly scrambled response. She seethed at this curveball he had pitched, but, as the old saying went, she knocked it out of the park. She needed to find out about him, but for now she'd savor surviving this meeting with the Directorship. Then a polite round of applause signaled adjournment.

Then, to nobody's delight, Mr. Bevel began droning on about his family's legacy, as he did at every meeting. It was one of those things he did, simply because he could do it. Through the lens of family pride and nostalgia, he not too subtly reminded his captive underlings that "Since the race for space *truly* began, the Bevels have been at the helm, our ebon fingers on the pulse of history." This point was particularly important, as he explained how people of Nubic (derived from the ancient Imperial name Nubia) had been discriminated against and persecuted. Yet, in the end, these people were the ones to conquer the vastness of the galaxy.

He went to speak about the Space Rush, The Independence Wars, and other things one could study from a textbook (bibliophiles still exist!), historical data stream, or a holographix channel.

Mr. Bevel fancied himself a historian, albeit a personally biased one. He spoke at length, enjoying the obviously captive audience about him.

Like everyone else, Quinn eagerly waited for him to finish. And like everyone else, she had the good sense to be nodding deferentially and clap enthusiastically when he concluded. *Make it sound as sincere as possible,* she thought, her palms smashing against each other, until they were deep pink.

"We are entering a new age, a new era where everything is truly possible", he concluded, a sudden cloud casting a shadow over his being. For some reason, Quinn felt very uneasy. Perhaps the sheening red in the background gave off an aura of menace. It was a horizon she'd seen many times before, yet never had it held such ill portent. Until now.

It took her a week.

By the third night in the Quiet Zone, Tahina no longer wanted to kill herself. Laying on the iron mattress, near fetal, alone with her thoughts and nightmares. The walls, a cube of greyness whose hybrid stone and metal mesh wire held onto the pungency of cleaning fluid and the stink of metal ore, kept her holding her head, folding her arms alternately in discomfort. Grey became the bane of her young existence. Even the Asylon issued jumpsuit, with ID numbering on the back and right breast, was a dull, sickly, monotonous drab grey.

So were the skies. So too the walls of the women's dorm. And so was the cafeteria, where prisoners were forced to eat under the constant eye of the C.E.O.s. Since the disabling of the EYE, the patrols were doubled down, and no place in Asylon lacked an armed presence. While she could imagine the scrutiny was far worse for the males, she detested having eyes, human or otherwise, follow her about, especially in the showering rooms. Twice, she'd gotten into skirmishes, the first between her and a guard, the next being a mini brawl in the showers between Duriyans and the newly arrived Karuks. It took two teams of C.E.O.'s to break up the naked combatants. They were made to stand on opposite sides, backs turned from one another, palms on the wall, heads down. Under heavier scrutiny, first Karuks, then the Duriyan (who voiced their displeasure vehemently as they were in the showers FIRST) females, were made to shower hurriedly. They would have to towel off while they walked to their dorm, holding their clothes. The humiliation was just one of many injustices they were forced to endure.

Yet, these incidents, along with other offenses (what the oppressors called her acts of defiance) weren't enough to earn her this unwanted stay in purgatory. It was the battle in the courtyard that landed her here. Alone. No others were singled out. Just her. That slug worm Turlak and the Wicked witch of Asylon Quinn had finally gotten her.

The whole thing wasn't her fault. Not entirely.

A month after arriving here, she'd earned a reputation and a few nicknames: The green eyed devil. Lady Lucifer. And, most derisively (from her fellow Duriyans), Brain. The first two were remarkably redundant, the last being a shot at her obviously exceptional intellectual capacity, her penchant for expository conversation (when she chose to speak) and, despite the harrowing new circumstances she found herself in, an unquenchable desire to learn. If only her dark moods and abrasiveness didn't get in the way.

Sullen and unapproachable, she was also probably the only person to curse Warden Quinn to her face. Trying to slam her into the grey concrete wall, Quinn's Jujitsu skills, height advantage and that sewer slug Turlak got in the way. As they restrained and lead her away, she unleashed a volley of obscenities at the Warden, causing Quinn to label her a "demonic bitch". Later, Quinn felt shamed by her outburst. Perversely, the girl took pride in that. After everything she'd been through, and was still being subjected to, she had little to have pride in.

However, others took note.

Despite a feral, superior demeanor, a few other Duriyan girls looked at her as their leader, one who could devise and carry out stratagems against their foes. Ironically, her most effective quality was also the one that, back home, would be reason to ostracize her. Being highly intelligent and verbose, she also had to let everyone else know it. Repeatedly.

Along with Iajim, her male counterpart, they effectively ruined the EYE. And did serious damage to the electrical wall grid that powered the C.O. Break area and the Showering Areas. The swearing that went on that day...

For her part, her fearless demeanor and effective tactical prowess against both the C.O.s and Karuks alike earned her their grudging respect. But unlike Iajim, who did his sabotage in the grimy, sludge gritted shadows, she made herself an obvious target. As if she was daring them to do something, almost anything, that she couldn't withstand. She didn't care that the razor was cutting her deep. She was bereft of care.

Then the Quiet Zone happened.

It was during the afternoon of a rather troubling day. There'd been a fight between a Duriyan boy and a Karuk. The Karuk boy was beaten badly, which caused some of his brethren to intercede. Then Duriyans joined the fray. After the battle was ended, the whole male dormitory was locked down the rest of the day. Reportedly, the Karuk died of his injuries.

So instead of going into the cafeteria, to have jackasses stand over her, watching her eat the half cooked, nearly indigestible slop they served them (no one in their right mind, or even diseased mind could call that trash food), she took off for the only freedoms allowed them. Either the courtyard, or the library. She went to get some stale air.

Sitting on top of a metal picnic table, she had her hands clasped, almost in a prayer, between her legs. The afternoon sun was the same as the morning sun; forever hidden but eternally teased. The grass was feeble and spotted with brown specks. She wondered, more than once, why they chose an environmental wasteland to house such a den of moral bankruptcy. The prison, just from the look of the haphazardly placed brick and makeshift siding, and the age crusted steel pillars in the "Restricted Zone (she had managed, with Iajim and another girl, Sali, to sneak around. Just in time, as Warden Quinn and Turlak (that sluckworm !!) really clamped down on the "No intermingling of genders" policy) ". The place was only a refurbished step up from a condemned warehouse depot. Which Duriy had plenty of.

Her thoughts turning to home, she mourned what fate most likely had befallen her younger brother and sister. State Care, since their "mother" was most definitely in no shape to provide for them. She didn't have her around to cover up her negligence. Their neighbors might've taken them in, they may've run off into the bushlands. That frightened her, since that tract of desolation was known for some of the worse sins known to Humankind.

"Jojas, you damn fool! Why did I let you talk me into this?! Why did you go ahead and let yourself get killed? ", she whined, stifling a cry. Then, she let it pour out.

He was the one who urged her to come with him and some others to "Take what's ours. Rightfully ours." The slightly muscular, tough featured youth had a feral charisma and was quick on his feet, both in the literal and figurative senses. Like her, he had big dreams that would lift him out of the dire poverty that crippled their home world for generations now. And like her, and Duriyan youth in general, he viewed himself as one of the "New Wave" that would restore Duriy to its former plateau of glory. "Make Duriy Strong Once More" had been a popular slogan that sounded good, yet remained empty words in the hearts and souls of many. However, a new, bolder generation was rising, a generation more than willing to take decisive action.

On the surface, they seemed an odd coupling. But after close observation, one could see how well they complimented each other. Hard chocolate melded with smooth cocoa, introvert and extrovert, quiet meditation and boisterous calisthenics. A leader, he wasn't hard to follow. Even that last time. Though the wound was still raw, she continued thinking on the circumstances that landed them into, in Dez Vulker's words, "The sewer of Mankind".

It was the fourth day of the food riots. All over Duriy the unrest was of a magnitude unheard of; people were tired of going hungry. Famine had grown past emergency levels; in more distant, secluded areas, people were disappearing.

Tahina thought her mother was one of them, at first. The last of the state approved rations would've vanished with her mother. For Dujin, most likely. As a precaution, Tahina hid them in her book sack, giving it to her younger siblings.

"Stretch this out", she told them. It was a medium sized package, weighing no more than four lbs. Hard silver foil packaging. ERE: DRY BEEF AND POTATO POWDER. JUST ADD HOT WATER was written in hard blue wording on the metallic silver backdrop.

The Duriyan evening was beginning. As the skies dimmed, a golden crimson horizon turned purplish black. The limitation of movement was also beginning, because the planet wide curfew was now in effect for a second night in a row. Everyone everywhere was in a panic; desperation was strangling the populace. Otherworldly assistance was extremely slow in arrival. "Slower than a moon sloth", was the contemptuous proverb. Throngs of hungry, weakened, sad Duriyans looked above, hoping that relief would come, and arrive soon. A hope that was tragically held in vain.

It was almost three days since she ate anything. Hunger pangs were worse than the monthly cramps she endured, but there were things far worse than her own inconvenience. Sometimes, just a look can bring a strong man to tears. The look of hopelessness, of fear and abandonment, and hunger on their young faces compelled her to do something, anything to alleviate their pain.

Her brother ran behind her after every entrance was barricaded. Her sister was at the stove, alternately watching her and the stew that bubbled.

"Where are you going?", he asked in a hardened whisper.

Looking back quickly, yet avoiding their faces, she said, "To get us some food. Lock up behind me. And don't open it unless it's me." She knew how hard it sounded, and what it implied about Mother. But she wasn't here, being a mother. The door slowly came together with jamb. Nighttime was here.

Meeting with Jojas and eighteen others, they evaded the District Enforcers and was barely spotted by a roving flyer en route to their destination. "It wouldn't take long", someone said. It took them two hours. When the complaining began, it had to be reiterated that main roads and even side roads were being heavily watched. Just them being out here, getting caught, could get them either killed on the spot or beaten and detained. The complaining and bickering ceased.

Through thicket and bush they crept upon the Provincial Governor's home. They climbed the fence and broke the door down....

Her mind returned to the now. *There's no native life on this world,* she thought. *No birds, mammals, not even inse...*

"HEY! Watch it!", she screamed, after a long-legged Karuk wench bumped her, rammed her really. The blow almost knocked her over into the anemic grass. Her green eyes were emerald pits of fire. Her body tensed. She was ready for a fight. The girl was almost seven feet barefoot. Tahina stood a healthy five foot six.

In her guttural voice, she called Tahina a "Duriyan mud slut". Then she laughed. Haughtily, and extremely loud. The laughter of a show- off, or a bully. She despised both. Some other Karuk girls were coming over, barely intercepted by a crew of Duriyans. The numbers were even; all that was needed was a spark.

Without announcing themselves, from one of the four towers, C.O.'s were monitoring, a group getting ready for dispersal of the combatants. The order came down. "Don't intervene.... yet."

The Karuk swung first, just missing Tahina's nose. A gust of hostile breeze blew in her face. Just as bad as if she had spit in her face. Tahina clubbed her, knocking her back.

The giant struck back, a jab driving hard into her left side. Tahina hit her twice, grabbed her and side suplexed her into the dirt, where they rolled around, trading punches. A few Karuks suddenly rushed the Duriyans; the courtyard brawl exploded.

It was a fortunate thing that sexes were segregated. Many questioned the wisdom of a coed detention center, Quinn included. "Budget initiatives were strained", she was duly informed. If any males were around, it could've turned deadly. Not that the girls weren't vicious enough on their own.

Dirt was kicked up, dust flew, just a minor irritant to the electronic surveillance. Over telecommunicators, the order finally came "Dispersal team, go!! "

By the time Turlak and a squad of ten separated the warriors, Tahina had handfuls of locs in hand, blood trickling from the ends. Turlak had personally snatched her away, and she curled her bloodied (not hers) lips in violent disgust. A few of the girls had to be tasered and pushed away.

The girl Tahina fought was beaten to a pulp, cowering and stripped naked.

Being stripped naked was the worst humiliation that could happen in a place like this. Among her own, this girl could never live down the shame. She could only try to avenge herself in some way, to redeem herself in the eyes of her fellow Karuki prisoners.

As shackles were being placed on the combatants, some with force, Quinn had come to inspect the aftermath. She looked dainty, almost precious in her crisp, deep brown uni-suit. Resentment flooded the hearts of both prisoner and guard alike.

Tahina denied taking part in stripping her, but Turlak ("You fat, filthy, sexless, sack of sluck!", she screamed as she was led away) and Quinn refused to believe her, let alone allowing her to explain. It took two C.O.s and Turlak's ham of a forearm to restrain her. She was wrestled down to her knees, eyes all on her. Quinn ordered, in the hearing of all around, that she, Tahina, would be quarantined. Tahina alone would face the harshest punishment that was within Quinn's power to enforce.

She became the first guest in the Quiet (formerly Quarintine) Zone.

Led away, Tahina turned and spat. The volley splashed Quinn's right cheek. Turlak yanked her by the collar, almost breaking her neck. If Quinn could've gotten a hold of her, Tahina's blood would've stained the grass, her heart in Quinn's red, raged hand. The mask of death on Quinn's face sent shudders in those who gazed it. Tahina felt the hatred from behind, and she didn't care. It was mutual. Quinn, to her, was the face of everything wrong in the universe, wrong in what was her life. Her, and people of that ilk were an enemy to the oppressed. The pushing, the rough jostling, and the loud clanging of the solid steel slamming behind her had a become synonymous with that pampered, corporate whore whose living depended on the suffering of her and those here, those who would be coming, and who knows what else. Banging her fist hard on that grey brick wall, she daydreamed it was the face of Warden Ednisa Quinn.

Back in her office, she fumed. Having stalked off after the courtyard debacle was handled, she left the prison and came back. She was that angry. No one, absolutely no one had ever did anything like that, had humiliated her so basely. And she was not about to let this insult slide without retribution.

From that point on, Quinn carried a petty vendetta against the girl. Whatever that could be done, within her position of course, to injure or humiliate Tahina, she would do with the viciousness that befitted a corporate environment. From the snarkiest of comments, or having her singled out for any little mishap. But little, petty actions that wouldn't lead to being called before a review board. She would make her life, truly, a living hell.

But that would have to wait; she had to leave for Mournos. The meeting with the Directorship required her full mental focus. But when she returned, assuming she *still* would be running Asylon, she'd make that green- eyed bitch pay dearly...

After the first full day, she was beside herself with self- pity, self- loathing and a hatred for all things grey. It wasn't just the walls surrounding her, nor the solid, dirt soiled, drab suit she wore. It was the state of mind it represented. Inertia, unable to move. It wasn't just Hell. For her, it was also becoming Purgatory as well.

Pacing, she raged, banging the steel door, weeping bitterly. "I have no business being here!", she sobbed. She kept saying it over and over until she went to sleep.

The smell of food aroused her. It was a pungent, flavorless stench. Tahina smelled the blandness. She got up, quite hungry. She was willing to eat anything, even prison swill.

No utensils. *Clever on their part. Leave me nothing to slit my wrist or jugular with*, she thought ruefully. She ate hashed brown potatoes and smushed beef bacon with just cleaned fingers, then a half glass of water she gulped ferociously. Slightly belching, she washed herself up. She let the hot water almost singe her dark skin, partly as an act of self- punishment, partly because hot water was the one comfort allowed her. *They'd taken everything else, why not savor this, even if it burns?* she thought, feeling her oft braided hair slink limply along her back. She dried herself, dressed and brooded.

With nowhere to go, she did pushups, sit ups, ran in place; anything to keep herself from thinking too hard. Without no distractions, thinking was becoming her enemy. She had to laugh bitterly at that realization.

"You overthink everything", her mother told her more than once, as did Jojas, her teachers, neighbors, shopkeepers....

"I can't help being a smart person", she'd reply. "Nor can I help that you're not." The offended party would stare and walk away. She would half smile in small triumph. Her brain, her jewel, her most prized possession was, in this isolation, a bane. There was no greater torture than to make her wallow alone in misery. Nothing to do but linger, ruminate in limbo.

If I crash my head into the wall, hard enough, would it be enough to end this?

Suicide was a specter before her. Then she thought of her dead father, and sunlight touched her. A decent man, a smart man (save for dealing with her mother, but then, how else would she be here?) who died too young. Just eight when the accident happened, twins just turned one. Her first shattering experience ending, realizing fully as the urn was cast before the riverbed, a holographic image fading away into nothing, that "Pa-Pa" was never coming home again. Her mother's crying and cursing the heavens crystallized that reality for her. She now cried, not out of mimicking her mother, but because the loss was real for her.

After that, she hated riding subway cars until necessity forced her to confront her fears, to conquer her buried anger. The visage of a happy, albeit stern man smiling at his family played a large role in her achieving victory over the darkness within herself. As she navigated the waters of being a teenager, she remembered his words of love and counsel. She had no choice, really, since her mother had fallen into the trap of addiction. The neighbors and so-called elders were of little to no help at all. To the point of deification, her father's memory was, at times, brighter than the Duriyan sun itself. She drew on it now. She had to save herself from jumping into the pit of self murder.

Coming home from his job working on the Transit system's solar plasma distributor, his oldest child running towards him. Lifting her up and bringing her close, he kisses her lightly on the forehead. She often thought she saw golden flecks of the sun on the visor of his helmet (*how silly I was as a child!*, she mused).

His was a wide grin, wide as sunrise. She thought she could bask forever in that smile of his.

"We never give up", he told her once when she was dealing with a difficult trigonometry problem. "Look at it twice, three times if you need to. Consider everything before you, then go with the best conclusion."

"What if I'm wrong?", she asked shyly.

"Then you're wrong", he said compassionately, wanting to instill boldness in her but in a way that didn't frighten her. "Being wrong on something is just a part of life. Just like being right. Successful people are those who finally get it right after getting it wrong many, many times in the past." That encouraged her, and he left her to figure it out on her own.

There was nothing harsh about how he spoke, but he spoke in absolutes. Confident he could solve any problem in his way. And he made her confident, to see that she could do it, too. Reflecting on him, and how he approached life, she did something she thought she'd never do in this hellhole. She smiled.

Her father's words made her want to solve the problem facing her. His memory made her feel, briefly, ashamed that she wanted to kill herself. "The hardest road to travel is the one worth traveling, because it's the least crowded. And most rewarding in knowledge."

He told her that right before he passed, yet she heard it in her head as crystal clear as the day he spoke those words.

When she awoke the next morning, food was on the floor, already getting cold.

She ate, showered, dressed and began thinking.

She needed to get out. To escape.

She wanted to be free. She wanted to go home.

She wanted, more than anything imaginable, to make those who exiled her here and that witch Quinn suffer. Suffer, and roil in pain a hundred times greater than she had experienced over these past couple of months. She craved justice, yes. But even more, she had an appetite for vengeance. And she wanted to sate its rumbling pangs, lest it consume her.

How to solve the problem before her...

For an ominously labeled world, Mournos had an active nightlife.

The pedestrian tubes that shuttled workers from building to building were transformed into nexuses where amateur socialites and those just looking for a good time exited and entered. Helicabs flew in legion into a darkened horizon, though not outside the orange glow of the protective bio-support. Business affairs, hook ups, and grapevine gossipers congregated and meshed into an unexpected tapestry woven by both proximity and social bonding.

Warden Quinn was in her favorite restaurant on Mournos, *Jules and Leroi's Galaxy Barbeque*. It was unseemly that a place like this would be on Mournos, but what world didn't have its guilty pleasures? The food was as down home as down home could get: Beef ribs, Earth raised chicken, pot roast from Pleban Three, all cooked, grilled, fried, roasted and dipped in Jules ad Leroi's signature Barbeque sauces. Plus, Earth classics like candied yams, buffalo (?) wings and deserts like rice pudding and banana cake rounded out what turned out to be a varied, diverse, and strangely eclectic menu.

It was Mid-week, Hump day, and as usual, the evening crowds were sizable.

The circular tables that dotted the middle were packed and full, though many of the side booths were empty. The outside court was spacious, reserved for smokers only. Old time ceiling fans twirled in slow motion, creating a breeze that wasn't a disturbance to patrons, all the while spreading the aroma of the cuisine saturating the eating area to the outside, both front and back. An ancient trick, designed to attract and enthrall customers. It worked without fail.

Quinn fondly sat in her favorite booth, on the right side of the restaurant, where engraved plaques in the likenesses of the original founders and namesakes hung above (a six generational business), as if, from beyond, they were watching over their enduring legacy. This was probably the main thing Warden Quinn liked about this place: It's longevity. Each succeeding generation understood its importance and added its own imprint. "People learned to value the work of their ancestors", she muttered. Just then she felt a shadow beginning to loom over her. Based on how rapidly it descended on her, it's owner wasn't very subtle about their approach.

Naturally, she tensed. A faint glimmer of pale green danced on the bare spot of porcelain that food didn't touch.

As good natured as she could force herself to be, she gazed upwards into a smooth, pretty face, asking "Can I help you?" When recognition grabbed her, she winced inwardly.

An all too familiar face was looking down on her, and Quinn was extremely unhappy about it.

The woman wore, in multi tones, a metallic uni-suit (the new style of this decade, which was the new style two decades past), and a tiny green circle on her chest that read PRESS. Under which read in ghostly grey lettering GNN. Galactic News Network.

"I'm Jet Symmons, of the Galactic News Network", she began.

"I'm aware of who you are, Ms. Jet .... Symmons ".

An abrupt hush breezed through the restaurant, followed by a flurry of whispering.

"Is that...? "

"Oh my god, look at that tacky..."

"She's even more beautiful in person than ..."

Star reporter, investigative journalist, gadfly and professional pain in the ass (as quoted by many in political and business circles) had come to Mournos, like a plague of locusts bringing desolation in their wake. Ruthless, and forever looking for a story, this woman had a reputation as both a crusader and inquisitor. On the heels of her escape from the jaws of the Directorship, Quinn only wanted to eat her food and relax.

"Warden Quinn. Warden Ednisa Quinn, of the Asylon Correctional Facility, am I right?" She was amicable upon first contact, Quinn had to give her that. And she was strikingly beautiful, the very definition of a brown bomber. *Perhaps a former model like myself,* she thought with fleeting admiration.

"Would you be standing over me if you were wrong?", Quinn countered politely.

A short laugh, just as polite. Professionally polite. "No, I would not. Do you have a moment? I realize you're eating (meal looks delicious, by the way), however there are some questions that perhaps you'd like to shed light on? "

Quinn tried, really tried, to suppress her sudden nausea. As she did during most of Symmons' news streams, vlogcasts and daily coverage of interstellar events.

"What brings you to Mournos, Ms. Symmons?", she asked, growing exasperated as more shadows approached.

More whispers, now onlookers as three men made a bee line to Warden Quinn's booth.

A quick, cold hand grabbed Jet Symmons' right shoulder. She winced, feeling the icy touch through her garments. Turning, her mouth was wide open, as if she was about to speak.

The reporter couldn't get a word in, as two men, dressed in the silver and black of IREL security came to each shoulder, flanking Ms. Symmons. A ripple effect of murmuring and nervous stares made Quinn openly uneasy. Being the center of attention earlier was more than enough for one day.

"You've been warned once!", a harsh voice came from behind the men. The room fell to a deafening quiet, all eyes remained glued to the drama.

"The last I checked, Mr. Anwari, freedom of the press still exists", Jet said, facing him with obvious hostility. Security then abruptly grabbed the woman, jostling her forward.

"Who is he...?"

"Why are they treating her like ...? "

"I've seen him before. On a news stream. Is that the same....?"

"Make sure she makes it off world", Mr. Anwari said. "This time" was added with threatening emphasis.

Quinn, like everyone else watching the scene, was dumbfounded by the newswoman's rough handling. Being escorted out, Symmons turned.

"Human rights abuses are now a way of life, thanks to people like you", she hissed viciously, loud enough to everyone to hear. Disturbingly, Quinn felt the dig was aimed at her as well.

"Much like beauty, intergalactic justice is a subjective view", Anwari replied in a curt, dismissive manner. The reporter glared, but kept her dignity despite her better judgement. The cool wind and fresh aroma of down-home goodness followed her into the now grey and faded crimson evening.

"Dear patrons of this fine establishment, Anwari began in his best Head waiter impression, we humbly apologize for this evening's disturbance. Please continue to enjoy the fine cuisine here, compliments of Mr. Bevel."

His announcement caused a stir, then a gale of appreciative applause. Quinn stared, dumbfounded for the second time within five minutes. She hadn't long to keep that posture, as the attorney (with more power than anyone had ever realized beforehand) was now standing in the spot Symmons was evicted from. The eye contact was fleeting, just enough to glimpse this guy wasn't here for pleasantries.

"Nice save", Quinn replied, a bit impressed. She never met a lawyer with stones before, outside of a legal setting.

"Ironically enough, that's what I wanted to say to you. When I caught up with you, I meant." He smiled faintly, seemingly affable. But there was no warmth in his eyes, nor in the artificial praise he offered.

The clamor died down, and patrons resumed their gossip and office intrigues amongst the savory, tangy aroma of fruit infused barbeque sauces over a variety of well done to medium rare meats.

"Come again?", she asked, testing whether he was being facetious or not.

"Nice save, in the meeting", he said, taking the seat across from her. He didn't ask if someone else was sitting there, or if she minded yet another intrusion on her dinner, nor did he seem considerate enough to do so. It was a clear affront to her, but he didn't seem bothered by such things. The flashback to that afternoon was, yet again, another intrusion on her free time. He suddenly looked startled, perhaps divining her apparent dissatisfaction.

"Surely you don't mind conversation among colleagues, Warden?"

"We're hardly colleagues, Mr. Anwari ", she replied. Her tone was patient, even cordial. She hoped he'd pick up on the subtle hint (An abrupt hand to her mouth when she faked a cough) that his presence wasn't valued, nor wanted. She hoped in vain.

"I hope you don't hold hard feelings over this afternoon?", he asked, slightly amused by her attempt to run him off.

"What exactly are you referring to? Throwing that curveball of a question you asked?"

Chuckling, he took a quick stock of the place. *Hardly upscale*, he thought. It was a dining hall for those who work hard to earn a living. The decor was a quaint jamboree of wild colors (in actuality, its color scheme, in its latest incarnation, was solid earth tones with a splash of siesta red here and there), thorny, stained wooden furniture and the food itself. Not a venue he'd patronize, going by his reaction.

"Not to your liking?", she replied, picking up on his discomfort.

"I must say, I'm surprised you dine here", he answered, noting her sauce tipped fingers. The look he wore was one of judgement. She automatically resented him for the slight.

"You shouldn't be, as you don't know me." With a thin napkin she wiped away the smudges. "Try the beef stew ", she said curtly. Now it was her turn to get a rise out of him.

"For your edification, I'm an atheist", Anwari replied, with a smugness that was miles beyond arrogance. His manner was imperious, as if he were addressing one of his flunkies in his office. "However, I'll decline the invitation. You understand, a wise man eats wisely."

He was just off-putting, and she had to politely inform him in some way. On Mournos, corporate settings demanded a professional subterfuge when it came to doling out insults, or when voicing one's displeasure. Frankness was allowed only to Mr. Bevel and his peers, none of whom existed on Mournos.

"It *was* a pleasure, Mr. Anwari ", she said, eyes blazing. She moved the plate to her side, searching for the waitress. A few passersby, ex co-workers, waved and gave her a fleeting chorus of congratulations for her new position and success. She smiled, with a flash of nostalgia. The present, at this moment, was far less palatable. He returned the gesture, an obvious attempt to be conciliatory.

"No need for undue hostility, Warden. I merely came to speak with you." She noted his undertone remained relatively the same, despite the assurances of goodwill.

She had an idea about what, but she wanted to hear him say it.

"Does this afternoon concern you?", she asked him flatly. She knew there'd be doubters.

"Quite naturally ", he replied. Though he was looking directly at her, she could tell his eyes were moving around, rapidly taking in everyone and everything around him. *His situational awareness is phenomenal!,* she marveled. *Right up there with Turlak.* Which reminded her to get a status report as soon as she returned to her suite. More than fifteen billion miles away, but she was operating as if she were in her office.

"You believe my timetable is off, is that it?"

"Not so much off, as it is, well, unachievable". His last vestiges of cordiality vanished.

A sharp dressed, slick tongued Trexian mountain slug, she thought. From his prim, manicured nails to the swarthy arrogance that this cretin exuded, she finally decided she couldn't stand a minute more of this sleazoid bastard. A second later, the waitress heaved into view, and she summoned her over.

She again cleaned her fingers slowly, in silent contemplation.

"It's no reflection upon you, let me reassure you."

"So far, you've been anything but", she chided. She wasn't about to make a scene here, but this ... impromptu meeting had to end.

"Have you a psychologist on staff?"

"Mr. Anwari, if you've seen the reports you know the answer already. No, I don't. And frankly, why would we even need one?" IREL wasn't in the business of mental wellness. They were in the business of Trans-galactic Transport and Real Estate, and now in the suddenly lucrative endeavor of detaining and housing youthful offenders. As a start.

"Which speaks to my original point", he said.

"Which is?", she asked, well past weary of his presence.

"You'll find that when it comes to this "business" your parent company has decided to take on, on the fly answers fall flat in the face of logistics", Anwari said with a low growl. From the pocket of his deep brown and red uni-suit he handed her a miniature tablet.

"By the next meeting, a more thorough explanation as to how you've implemented these changes, in accord with current and future legal standings will be mandatory, Warden." His voice was now iron, authoritative when he had no right to be. Incensed, Quinn stood up.

"Mr. Anwari, or whatever it is. Know who you're speaking to. I'm not one of those paralegals you've become accustomed to bullying in a dingy law office. Ednisa Quinn works for IREL Unlimited, not you." She slid the tablet back. The waitress had come near, warily. Her face was uncertain. Instinctively, the smartly clad girl (in a crimson and maize uniform) sensed the negative vibes. Calmly, Mr. Anwari summoned the young lady over, took her tablet and with a thin, transparent cryptocoin disc, paid for the Warden's dinner and left the waitress excited with a hefty tip.

"You're a feisty one. Feisty and foolish. If you work for IREL, understand you work for me as well. In this capacity, this is a joint venture, between global governments, the GCW and your "employer". I am the official liaison on coordinating the co-operation and success of all three. Does that resolve your "issues?" Staring her down, he motioned with his eyes for her sit down again.

Before she could stutter a response, he continued. "Now Warden Quinn, your hard work is greatly appreciated and valued. Please don't misunderstand me. I'll take for granted that your job description has been delivered in part. That's something for you and the main office to resolve. My concerns, among others, is how the discipline is being administered currently. While it is appreciated there are difficulties in dealing with the (for lack of a better term) barely civilized, consider that they are, for the moment, still afforded rights. Rights that, if violated, would bring Trans galactic scrutiny down on this project. And end your current high paid, well regarded position. Snoopers like the insufferable, deluded Ms. Symmons would have no qualms about that, as it serves to feed their anti-corporate, anti-progressive agenda. We can't allow that, can we?"

Quinn said nothing, now sitting down, deadly silent. This was the culmination of two decades of working up the ranks. She thought of the long hours, the sacrifices, the emptiness that would be the only thing left to her if this came to an end. *Yes, he's manipulative, but he has the same interest as I do. Doesn't he?*

Weakly, she told Anwari "I'm listening... "

In her suite, there was a package that wasn't there when she left. Cautiously (she hated surprises), she opened it to find a lumenator. She'd heard about the latest advancements in lumenology and info-synthesis, but here she was holding the child of both disciplines of study in her hands.

Lumenology, being the science and study of illumination had come a long way since the ancient light bulb. Only in the last twelve decades had the discipline made serious headways in the consciousness of Man. Space travel and discovery, once it was realized, opened the pathway for utilizing the fullness of the luminary spectrum from different sources. Solar, lunar, starlight, whatever light could be concentrated and utilized, it became a practical reality. And Info-synthesis was a discipline of taking information processing technology (formerly solely in the realm of computer scientists) and making its tetrabits (TB), omnibits (OB), and GalactiBits (GAB) accessible to humans. More specifically, to the human touch. Concentrated information swirling in streams of ultra- ambient light, feeding the mind akin to how sunlight nourishes a plant. For the darker hued human being, it functioned much like melanin.

Excited, she raced through the instructions, getting the gist. And stepped on the extended platform, and said with a quivering, happy voice "Activate!".

It tickled, it bit. It surrounded her in hazy orange and golden light. She felt the raw tidbits of galactic trivia flowing through her; it was an infojunkie's ultimate high. Exhilarated, she almost forgot that the thing operated via brainwave, so even the most nonsensical facts and datum would filter through, if she didn't discipline her thoughts.

"Concentrate", she said to herself, loud enough for the device to pick up the command.

What scrolled through the twisting beams was statutes, ordinances and volumes of Trans galactic Law packaged in pure energy. She eventually found what she was looking for.

The Thirteenth Law.

The charter of the Galactic Community of Worlds was to have been the "Constitution" of the Human Diaspora. No matter what planet, moon or star station a person resided, everyone was expected to follow that set of primary laws and its appendages; national (planetary) laws only applied to whatever world one found himself, or herself residing.

Then, things happened.

Namely, the push further into what was now known as The Far worlds and the subsequent Independence Wars (which saw the sundering of the whole experiment in Trans galactic government), which lasted a hundred and twenty- three years (2452 A.D. - 2575 A.D.).

"No world national can be held in bondage except by prosecution for the pursuit of, and commission of acts of terrorism, sedition and or treason. All and any stripped of sovereign status can be subject to bondage based upon the revocation of national status. " LAW-13

By this definition, those held in Asylon, (and those who were to come to fill every cell in that place in short order. IREL would see to that.), were still subject to the legal systems of their respective worlds/ colonies. Which made Anwari's points of concern, in this respect at least, much clearer. But as she stepped off the platform, and infolight faded into ether, she was plagued by more daunting questions.

How she would proceed for the time being wasn't one of them. Obviously, she would walk the fine line between tough love and harsh discipline. With the likes of Jet Symmons lurking about... she stopped herself at the jamb of the bathroom. The scene in the restaurant replayed itself. What *does* she know, for her to seek her out in the manner she did? Was she privy to what had happened on the Titanus? Captain Aduk and his crew were paid handsomely for their silence, the bodies incinerated and that junker scrapped and smelted beyond recognition. The datalogs were stored in an IREL library somewhere on Pluto, she heard. Just what....

Anwari's smug face came into view. *Had she followed him? What did she learn? Obviously, they're not strangers. How long has she been hounding him?*

What do I know?, she said to herself, uncharacteristically uncertain. His presence was both exciting and overbearing. He upset her sense of things, and yet broadened her horizons of perception. Uneasiness began growing inside her. Her role wasn't what she had been told it was, and she had none to blame for this lack of knowledge but herself. Frustrated, she recalled that last bit of conversation:

"Mr. Bevel thinks highly of you", he told her in that booth at Jules and Leroi's. "I happen to think highly of your record. We think you're the right person for the job. But *are* you?"

She stared as he got up, and walked away, leaving her furious and speechless. Her anger faded at the sight of her new gift. But it didn't mean she forgot. Or would so readily forgive.

Before retiring, she turned on the holo-stream, which suddenly seemed archaic now, with the InfoLumina platform at her feet. "This is State of the Universe", with your host Baldwin Wright Hurston ...", a rotund, venerable Black man announced. Underneath, in dark red lettering, read "This is a rebroadcast... from earlier today..."

"My guests are "Mr. Anwar Anwari, of Galactic Trust... Professor Wilcok Danis, of ..."

Her eyes widened at the sight of him. It was him, alright. He was everywhere.

And she found that utterly frightening.

It was good to be out in the sunlight again, even if it was hidden behind the clouds of Hell.

Two weeks. By her count, she was kept in isolation for two weeks. Almost neglected, just about forgotten, except for meals and changes of clothing and the scant linens they supplied her. She survived it, and came out into the afternoon a stronger person, in body and mind.

What she came into, however, was a different situation. One she couldn't have fully anticipated.

When Tahina was released from the Quiet Zone, it was a week since the Sefu Trians arrived. She walked into to the girl's dorm, almost receiving a hero's welcome. The Duriyans had their side, the Karuki theirs. A single shower they shared; and girls were fed two hours after the boys. There was always tension, now running deeper than usual. Tension that she felt was thicker than a woolen blanket.

Two dozen or so Sefu Trian girls, with their tightly wound braids, large bulbous eyes, marny complexions caught her eye. They were sitting together, in a small corner of the dorm, taking up slithers of both sides. They were talking, carrying on in astute observation. Tahina noticed quickly that no one bothered them.

From behind she felt a hand on her shoulder. Tensing, she turned. When she saw Sali, she instantly relaxed. The two girls embraced, kissed each other on the cheek. Then they commenced walking.

"Who are they?", Tahina asked.

Sali told her "Sefu Trians. Don't let their soft looks fool you. They fight like hell. Sent a couple of girls to the infirmary. Neither one hasn't come back yet."

Wincing, Tahina thought about that shark toothed madman that posed as a Doctor. She felt bad for anyone, *anyone,* who had to endure a visit to "Dr. Butcher", as Dr. Wallim Reit was called. The girls walked into the area right before the cafeteria. Sali was a head taller than Tahina, and her junior by eleven months. They'd seen each other back home, but never really associated beyond several mutual acquaintances, Jojas being the main one. But Sali didn't give her the lukewarm greeting some of the others did. She was truly genuine in being happy to see her, in one piece no less.

On the steps, Sali briefed her on what had taken place in her absence. "Things have been getting quiet around here. The C. O's have been getting lax, and the new people haven't raised much of a fuss, except a few beatings here and there. Quinn and Turlak seem to favor them. "

"The Trians?", Tahina whispered, some derision carrying the question mark.

"More or less", Sali said. "I managed to get a message from the guys."

Tahina's eyes lit up. The answer to the problem seemed within her grasp. She didn't know how, she was just glad Sali had some communication. *They work hard to keep us separated,* she thought bitterly. *We're all we have, so far away from our home.*

"Soon", Sali whispered. Her brown eyes glinted with a knowing malice.

Tahina caught it, smiling herself. Under the right circumstances, Sali could go from sweet to vicious in a Duriyan minute. The mercurial nature they shared was one bonding point amongst many.

Sali was the closest person Tahina could call a friend on Asylon. That was before she met Jeth Akim.

Chapter Three

Amid the harshness of cosmic cold and neverending darkness, a hulking steel monolith slowed its speed.

"E.T.A to Asylon is now under two days away. Twenty hours, and thirty minutes exactly ", came over the aged intercom sstem. The static was thick, slurring each word. So another attempt was given, to no avail. Word of mouth, the go to method, had the Captain giving everyone, from staff to hired mercenary, the message personally.

"Keep our cargo on ice", the Captain of the junker ship said. "We don't want any problems like that last ship had."

When Jeth Akim felt his body move again, the S.S. Hardaway was at least 987,568 miles away from Asylon. His jaws began relaxing; the odor of sphincter, long suppressed, began fouling the holding bay. Like himself, another sixty Sefu Trians were emerging from their frozen state. Slowly, they were rejoining the world of the active living. And for them, that wasn't a good thing, by any stretch.

He remembered.

He remembered everything, from the near choking from the sulfuric clouds of laser fire to how hungry he was. Most of all, he recalled, with painful clarity, the last day on his home world. The death, the slaughter...her betrayal. Even now, even free (in body movement, such as it was) he found it brutal to even utter her name. Like the others, who were in various stages of grief and trauma, the horrid reality of being forcefully frozen and then removed from their home was bearing down with the impact of an asteroid colliding on a planet's surface. As a cadre of cobalt blue armor clad mercs entered the Holding Bay, brandishing their high- powered quick rifles and training them on the bereaving and bewildered Sefu Trians... Jeth's mind was stuck in perpetual replay. Reliving...

Home.

The last day he was home.

That morning, he hugged his younger sister. Rela was almost ten. A sliver of a girl, with rapid moving eyes and a mischief making smile.

"Take care of mama", he told her.

This alarmed the girl. Their mother was frail and ailing. And by no measure could a child take care of an adult, she thought.

"Jeth, what will you do?", the child demanded. Their mother was in her bed, roiling in pain. Her moans of suffering were awful to hear, unbearable to watch. It was all the more frustrating due to the deprivation of proper nourishment, which could be controlled by the hands of a caring government. But no such thing existed. No aid was to be found, nor, by this time, expected to come.

Over the circular hearth of their small apartment, a picture of their father, a soldier killed in action, hung lopsided. Faded earth tones cracked, and flaked the floorboards, near the corners of the emptied pantry.

To be heard over their mother's anguished squeal, she raised her voice "Where are you going? What are you...? "

"Shh!", he scolded. Then, quietly, he said "To the protest. To get us something to eat, to get Mother some form of relief." He spoke with a grimness she never heard in him before. It scared her, made her afraid for him. But even she knew how dire everyday life was becoming.

Rations had not come in a week. When they came last month, they were less than a month before. Yet the planet's ruler, Gen. Nazrym Hagit didn't seem to miss a meal, nor was he or that bloated sow he called a wife dressed in tatters. "Hogs living the life of hogs ", someone yelled furiously, whilst being dragged off by the police.

Given that Sefu Trius was more agriculturally adept than most Far worlds, that its populace was hungry was egregious, to say the least. Its communal system was intended to allow everyone to share in the harvest, and the resources it accrued. Yet, as the harvest grew more and more plentiful, the people found themselves with less and less. Hunger pains and poverty to show for their tireless efforts. Since Sefu Trius enjoyed an unusual tropical climate; it's growing seasons went all year (following their own calendar, four hundred sixty- nine days), and everyone worked hard and worked together. National pride and slogans of "Together" had long faded, dying in the grip of greedy, uncaring oligarchs. From the top, the cancer spread.

In Jeth's farming district, the community banded together. "What you don't have, I have" was a saying Jeth had grown up hearing, and seen put to practice. Until the last year or so, to the point where now virtually no one had a spare anything.

Many whispered their hatred for Hagit's regime, but they were slow to rebel based on his strongman's iron grip on the military, and the rumored SNITT agents among the population. The eyes and ears, whom no one could ever be certain their presence wasn't lurking around the corner, or drinking weak naju tea with you. People were disappearing, taken from markets, homes. Some went out for the day's assignment (as jobs were called) and never returned home. A thick cloak of fear was held tightly over Sefu Trius.

Yet a man can endure so much, especially when there are mouths to feed. His father's pension (little as it was), had run out, and though Jeth was a recent graduate of the Youth Brigade (all Sefu Trians were conscripted at age fifteen for a tour of duty of two years), he had little except experience to show for it. Wise, lanky, and yet deceptively strong, he spent his waking hours doing light mechanical repairs on farming equipment for spare change. He would arise at half past dawn, bird shower, go work until dusk and return, stomach growling. His face and clothes stained with perspiration and machine grease. He ate once a day; that was all he could afford with two other mouths to feed. As he slept on the thick shredded rug in the middle of the kitchen (his sister had shared the bedroom with their mother), he would dream of a loftier, fulfilling existence. He would dream of building spaceships; even as a child he was fascinated, enthralled really, with interspatial physics and cosmonautics. His father fed this obsession by supplying his young, inquisitive son with books on space flight, navigation manuals from his job assignments (often, as military hardware and technology is often updated by the Sefu Trian government, obsolete literature is put to the incinerator. As for the equipment, it found it's way to the recycler's plant, to be smelted or refurbished as parts for newer tech.), and what little the small local library carried. His mother sometimes worried, wishing for him to have more "Normal interests for a boy his age." His father countered by saying "Uli, let Jeth follow his passions. Try not to extinguish the flames within him."

His father was proven correct. Being homeschooled, Jeth found himself devouring books on ancient Earth airplanes and the evolution from the airplane to the shuttle and satellite stage of space exploration to the post national space race (when corporations and tech cartels began ramping up the push for exploration, a precursor to the Space Rush era) to when Earth was systemically evacuated after the Atomic Fall. Of course, he still got the rudiments of reading, writing and multiple levels of arithmetic. Often, his father was able to impart the wisdom and value of being a well- rounded learner. It stuck.

Unfortunately, dreams were sustenance for the mind, but not of the flesh. Reality had a cruel way of murdering dreams. Despite his best efforts, life was growing more and more unlivable.

Despite the rise of roamer gangs, Jeth steadfastly refused to join the waves of criminals antagonizing those who couldn't fend for themselves, or were too cowardly to focus their destructive efforts to attack the "real enemy ". But he did silently agree with one of their points: something had to be done.

Days before that fateful day at Trunza Square, he mulled over his options. There was to be a mass protest. Nothing violent, just people fed up and hungry. People past the limit with the iniquity, the inequality. The eroding of their freedom and dignity. In his mind, it was settled. He would go.

He hadn't discussed it, but his mother, Uli, knew. She sometimes knew what he would do or say before he did. Before her illness took hold, Uli was the most sought after woman in the district. Playful, always warm, she never had to look far for a helping hand. She didn't suffer for a loss of admirers. But she could never imagine herself being named anything other than Uli Akim. Even in sickness, there remained a regality, a brightness of the soul that refused to dim. If only the body could match the mind and soul.

The night before, as the stars brightened, she said to Jeth, " Do what you know is right, always." There was a poignancy, a haunting knowing in her words that he glimpsed, but was too frightened to decipher. But it didn't change his mind. It had to be done. And he would do so.

After hugging and speaking with his sister, he headed out into the uncertainty a new day held forth. The morning dew was still wet on the fauba leaves. Fretfully, he took one and chewed it, walking through the thicket outlining the dusty pathway. He traveled off the main road, avoiding the soldiers at any of the numerous checkpoints. He didn't bring his CD papers (Certification Documents) with him. He could be arrested just for a minor oversight like that. The soldiers, depending on their temperament or the day they were having, would stop a person for less. And if they were feeling generous, the detainee would be allowed to limp away. In great pain, but "free" to go.

Having evaded the bully squads, his confidence grew. He kept going, with thicket and hard bush, lightly rustling, being his primary protection. Sunlight, in slivers, were thin rays of hope.

He wondered how many would be there. If the gossip could be believed, hundreds, maybe thousands, made their way. And shouted, yelled, chanted their grievances before a formation of VLT tanks and green and silver camo clad soldiers poised to fire. To the amazement of many, the peace up held remarkably well. So far.

It was just becoming afternoon when he arrived at Trunza Square. How many miles, fields and riverbeds, he had to cross he didn't know. He didn't think to count. And hunger pained his steps, even though cool river water had parched his tongue. But he had made it. Hunger took a backseat to the sudden awe he felt. Thousands! Among thousands he had arrived to ask, no, demand what was a basic right! And with these thousands he would not be denied!

Looking upwards, the sun above Sefu Trius was clear, at its peak. A weeping began inside Jeth. It was without words. The most powerful attribute of the sun, the old folklore went, was justice. The sun shines its light on all....

The Trunza Square Massacre. No one would ever discover the exact minute it started.

An abrupt commotion cut through the chanting. Tussling, then shoving. Rocks were thrown. People yelling obscenities at the military and the oppression it stood for. The booming sound of shots being fired made the crowd panic. Chaos, deadly and now unfettered, began to take reign.

People were being gunned down mercilessly. Thin beams of laser fire found their unwilling targets, reducing people to charred flesh and bone. The victims screaming into oblivion, convulsing in a whirlwind of death as confusion spun about them. Emboldened, Hagit's soldiers began advancing, inch by murderous inch.

Human killers were horrible enough, but they soon paled next to the technological nightmare Hagit unleashed upon his dissenters.

Three of the tanks began to extend legs from the tracks. With terrifying, swift unsteadiness, they began rising in the air. The newest line, the creeper tank, or spider tank, began their deadly mission, picking off targets from above. Soldiers that were mounted on either the right side, or the left, began sniping their targets. As from below, so too from above. The monstrous vehicles towered just a little over twenty feet, casting a long blanket of shadowy terror over the scattering citizenry. Burning branches fell on some, embers bouncing from leaves, from limbs, adding another layer of atrocity.

Amid the ruthless fusillade Jeth scrambled as best he could. Screams pierced him, the wild jostling by people trying their damn best to get away unbalanced him. The obscene stench of singed flesh sickened him; had he a meal he would've retched it. He got knocked about. He saw a poor woman trampled upon. He was close enough to hear the lethal snap. The frozen horror in her wide, dead eyes chilled his being. A man, running ahead, was shot from above, pieces of him splattering onto lush thickets of bush. The furor had caused flocks of spotted moon crows, fowl native of Sefu Trius and the National Mascot, to flee in droves. Those that were collateral damage shrieked painfully as they crashed down on fleeing protestors. Their loud cawing almost drowned in the fury of the one- sided onslaught.

All around him, the Grim Reaper was collecting an abundant harvest.

A girl running beside him suddenly combusted. Flesh and bone burning, cinder and smoke almost strangling Jeth. But he kept running. In fact, he sped up his pace. To stop running would be fatal.

Tanks were firing ahead, keeping the already traumatized protestors beyond the edge. Platoons began rounding people up, throwing them to the walls of the plaza, walls that would be now and forever stained with soot and blood.

Some, mad and desperate, threw rocks, whatever they could at their attackers. Even severed body parts were slung the soldiers' way. Amid the carnage, a brave man, whilst burning alive dared to ask his murderers "Why are you murdering your own people?!! Whyy......?" The death scream drowned in the violent flames consuming him.

Jeth fled through the woods he came through. He didn't stop until exhaustion forced him. His hand propped on his knees, he breathed hard, taking in the billow blowing in the breeze. He coughed and spat out the smog, which reached upwards, harsh and thick.

For a moment, it looked as though the sun was blocked out. *Just as well,* he thought bitterly. He found a tree to support him; he felt himself carrying the weight of the universe on his gangly back. Slumped, with thin traces of burned blood on his clothes, and his back firmly against the thorny bark of an oyis tree, he began sobbing uncontrollably.

"How had life come to this?!", he asked himself, tears of anger travelling downwards without shame, nor mercy. A maelstrom of emotion overtook him, now that danger had passed for the moment. Hatred, sorrow, confusion, hatred. Hatred for what just transpired, what had been taking place for several years (when it became noticeable), and for those who were not only committing these horrors, but also their enablers. His neighbors, the whole damn population...himself.

This ... wasn't the Sefu Trius way of life he was taught about. This wasn't how they were supposed to live, let alone conduct themselves... A mockery of the "Ethics of The Sefu Trian". His wallowing allowed him to drop his guard. And she moved in, with efficient, deadly silence.

The nuzzle of a rifle poked his shoulder, bringing him back to his surroundings.

"Move, and I'll fire", a familiar voice said from behind. It was a feminine voice, though one bereft of warmth. Monotone, robotic. Jeth searched his memory for such a voice, and found no one he knew, or would know that could fit this bizarre feeling.

"Who...are you? Why do I think I know you?", he blurted out. Obviously, he wasn't thinking, but the surrealness of it all made him drunk with confusion. Confusion mixed with mortal fear. His life was face to face with The Reaper's scythe.

In a softer, tremulous voice she responded "Because you do. Now move!"

He stammered her name. " S-Sartha?" Recognition clashed with disbelief.

Sartha.

A friend from childhood. A friend who had become more. She was the same age, with bobbed black hair and sensual, seductive lips. Even on a good day she seemed to pout. Her body was well shaped, hard caramel in hue, and warm. Very warm. Jeth found that her mind was a tightly wound cabal of power wiring hanked together and hanging recklessly in the elements. Only the expert, or the well insulated should approach. With extreme wariness. Never a dull moment with this one.

But she was fun to be around. She was. Until he didn't see her anymore. He feared these thugs had taken her away. To his horror, they did, albeit in a way he never thought possible.

"How... Why are you here?", he managed to ask as he collected himself. He felt his anger rising, and he forced himself to hold it down. He didn't know what she would do. He didn't know her anymore.

"Why are you?", she countered, feeling defensive. "I 'm here trying to feed myself and my family."

"By murdering someone else's?! By helping Hagit kill and..."

The rifle butt crashed against his temple, making him stagger sideways.

"No one told you to be here... no body made you come", she said, looking past him, not at him. She avoided his eyes, not due to the hate they held, but because of the glowering shame in hers. In that moment, though he hated her just as much as he did Hagit, he felt a tiny shard of sympathy for what he was about to do.

He took that moment of inattention to run.

He sprinted, then jerked abruptly. He felt himself tense briefly, then slowly relax. He got drowsy, then restive. Then he stopped moving altogether. Yet he hadn't fallen down in the lush grass. He felt an abrupt chill envelope him. His mind, though, was alert and active. He wanted to yell, to scream indignities, to curse this devil whore he foolishly thought he could love. Did love, in his own way. And he thought she loved him, in her own bizarre, quirky way.

What did you do to me, Sartha? WHY??, he lamented within himself.

He was completely frozen. A human statue.

Thick boots crunched the springtime grass, and he smelled her perfumed scent. It was as pungent as sewage waste to him now.

"I was ordered to kill anyone fleeing the insurrection, she said coldly. You would've made number five."

Even in his new state of frozen animation, he felt his heart sink. Truly, she was dead to him.

She gave him a soft, quick peck on the cheek. "For old times. For what... could've been, had you not been such a damn fool! ", She angrily whispered to him as she began walking away, calling a superior for prisoner retrieval. A salty tear on his cheek lingered, then fell into the grass. Immobile, Jeth could only hear echoes of the slaughter rage on without mercy. A chorus of evil sang around him, and he was now frozen, helpless to shut out the abominable melody.

The past was shattered, its broken shards littered among the dead, lacerating those who survived, those who watched the massacre on vidscreens in homes, in the community pubs and meet centers. The present was the anguished shouting of the minions of Hagit, the beleaguered, hostile wailing of those who they punished with his tacit approval. The here and now was Trunza Square, the revered seat of government reduced to the safe house of a madman. The Trunza Square Gardens, reduced to a burning war zone, a dark horizon with no illumination, heavenly or otherwise.

Jeth heard more soldiers. From the rear of him. To the left and the right. He heard the sizzling sound more clearly. The crackling that the ice rifle made on contact with it's victim. He heard pleas, begging, callous laughter. For a moment, he swore he could hear Sartha among them, her high spirited, girlish fits of mirth no longer distinguishable from the brutish chortling, soulless snickering. Soon there were others like him, being lined up for "Pick-up and Transport".

Soon, hoarse rumbling echoed overhead. He recognized that sound; a rarity these days, but the air slashing noise of a Vertical Take Off Transport Vehicle was unmistakable to the trained ear. An XSX model, one that his father once travelled in. It wasn't a particularly huge craft, but too big for such a cramped space. The ship held a position almost twelve feet up. From its belly, the Soldier Lift descended.

It cast its long, oblong (not perfectly) shadow over captive and captor alike, a literal blanket of oppression. Abruptly, the lift came to a halt.

Four soldiers, clad in star white and navy blue, put him in a compactly designed cargo bay.

A space that could hold, under the best conditions, an armed platoon of fifty - five. However, comfort was far from the minds of those running this operation.

He was loaded with sixty-five other prisoners, plus ten guards. Everyone in "Freeze stasis", like himself, was young and able bodied.

One girl was frozen with her mouth agape, and she was a crouching statue. As she was being placed, a female guard made a mocking, lewd gesture, sticking the long rod of her iron truncheon in her mouth.

"How long will they stay like this?", another asked, adjusting the bandolier on his shoulder.

"Should hold until they reach Asylon. Freeze stasis can take anywhere from weeks, even months to thaw out", another said. Then added within Jeth's hearing, "if they live ".

Shaking his head, and with a dark hand probing the face of another prisoner being loaded aboard, the man said warily, "I can't imagine a punishment worse than this."

"Follow the news stream, they're coming my friend", the other replied.

"Objective complete. Prepare for ascent ", boomed throughout the vessel. Audio-com volume was on high, the announcing voice obnoxious, in a braying fashion. Rising, until its maximum level was reached, the XSX transport stopped, standing among the clouds.

Then, a jerking motion. Vertical lift offs shifting to horizontal flight patterns always began with turbulent movement, he remembered bitterly, reflecting on his time in the state's service.

From his position by the bay window, Jeth saw they were taking off. As the grey light of the planet's atmosphere became the pitch black and glitter of outer space, Jeth wept inside himself.

Sefu Trius transformed into a distant hazy colored marble.

Overhead an announcement:

"ETA to rendezvous: an hour, thirty-eight minutes. Repeat..."

Moon station Qualian Three was just below.

The place where his father was killed.

Numb memories of that day briefly replayed itself in his mind. The death announcement over the planet's radio stream. His mother telling him and his then toddler sister, through bitter tears, that their father was no longer with them. The state funeral, which Gen. Hagit attended. Back then, soldiers were celebrated, revered as heroes. His mother, with children flanking her and the other widows on the dais, was given an array of flowers, his pension papers, his national and a memorial plaque. The flag that still hung like a drape above his picture.

Deep hunter green (for the abundancy of fertile land) with a blue circle (for the planet) and four yellow stars at each pole, the flag of Sefu Trius was, until recently, a beacon of immense national pride. Sefu Trius was one of the first worlds to secede from the GCW, in turn helping to spark the Independence Wars.

He was being ripped away from that flag, that world, his family and the few he could call friend. Sefu Trius was lost to him. His soul was leaving him, he couldn't help thinking.

"Always do what you know is right."

Stars were scarce yet moving faster and faster. They were moving in hyperspeed. A speed, a ship of this caliber, size, and bulk was, theoretically, incapable of reaching. His mind turned on this mystery; anything to keep the overbearing grief at a brief distance.

As they grew nearer to the rendezvous point, the star craft sparkled in the green light of the systems' sun. A smooth, green orb One hundred and ninety- eight million miles from Sefu Trius. They were being taken into the "Mouth of the Far worlds".

Near Corsico Two, the first world of the Obadawu System (after Thelonius Obadawu, it's discoverer), an old relic of a star cruiser met them. The prisoners were transferred off world. Due to a mishap, three prisoners and a soldier were killed when a connector tube malfunction occurred, causing asphyxiation when the oxygen leaked into space. The frozen cold corpses were removed, cast off into space.

The repair job set everything back three hours.

The S.S. Ostraner reversed its course, beginning the journey to Asylon.

No one mentioned what had happened, nor was an official report ever taken. Four lives were lost. And not even as much as a moment of silence was given.

Warden Quinn had barely settled in when Turlak nearly burst into her office. He huffed; large nostrils flared when he was angry. Seemingly, that was to be most of the time. In his hand were six comm badges. A few of them were damaged beyond repair. Angrily, he slammed them down on her desk, giving her a moment to pause.

"I'm glad to see you as well, Turlak", she quipped, although not joking.

"Six in one week! Six!", he smoldered. Sometimes Quinn wondered what would happen if, rather when, he finally erupted. He slammed the badges hard onto the desk again.

Dismay turned into mild concern when he explained the circumstances. Two of the thin, pentagonal discs were cracked and battered, a third one fractured in half. Typical damage that came from being violently attacked.

The turnover rate was troubling; she had to constantly hire to offset those that quit. For the first time in her long managerial career she had a higher quit to fire ratio. It wasn't a great look, but she just couldn't divulge the reasoning, the true reasoning, behind the abrupt about face in policy. Not to Turlak, whom the guards (she only referred to their correct titles when dealing with them directly, through official communication, or through status reports) saw as their *real* leader. To them, she was just their aloof, pretty face employer who couldn't be deigned to "step into the trenches and handle the savages." Speaking of which, the Sefu Trians were due to arrive, and there was a backlog to slough through. Administrative matters played a part none of her underlings could be expected to understand. They didn't go to Mournos and stand before the judging eyes of the Directorship. Nor did they have to report to Mr. Bevel and Mr. Anwari, whose presence was becoming all the more overbearing, as far as she was concerned. "Line One" was reserved almost exclusively for him. And not a day, or every other day went by without him "consulting" her. Nor would they appreciate how hard she had worked to keep the lot of them in a job. But right now, she needed to coax Turlak to stick around and do his. Calmly, she looked at her beleaguered Chief of Guards, and asked evenly "Will you be number seven?"

He crooked his head in disbelief. Often, he thought she was in over her head. As a bean counter, she was excellent. As pampered bureaucrat, even better. As warden, an incredible lot to be desired. She was pandering, condescending. Was too lenient. She was letting these Farworlder mud rats run the place at first, damn near. Then she got a little backbone. But since that meeting at Home Office, she went back to really letting them shit and throw their feces around. Take the green-eyed devil in quarantine, for example. She should have buried her insolent ass underneath the damn facility.

"I'm strongly considering it", he said, just as matter of fact. One thing that Quinn knew she could count on, aside from his brusque mannerisms, was an unadulterated frankness that was equally irksome and admirable at the same time.

Looking outside, in the courtyard, the young men are hanging about. They kept to themselves (Turlak considered them gangs). One group on one side, the other opposite. Naturally, the outside tiers were lined with officers ready and poised. The girls were no different. In fact, their blatant viciousness made them far worse. Usually, he felt like a zookeeper. Only, the animals weren't allowed to be disciplined.

At her motion (she nodded her head at the chair in the corner), he pulled it up, sitting directly across from her. The chair was an old fashion secretary's chair, the one with wheels on the bottom that rolled the antique around. Ms. Roshin would often complain about the hard cushion, preferring the segue chair that could take one across a room in a matter of seconds.

"I like my office to feel official", Warden Quinn said more than once. It was her way of saying I like old style things and customs.

She pressed a button on her desk console. "Ms. Roshin, please bring some coffee."

"Yes", the secretary replied, the faint grumblings inaudible.

The coffee was brought in, and Quinn stirred in the creamer and brown sugar. *Some Earth customs needed to stay earth customs, with no deviation.*

"I take mine straight black", he said. He didn't hesitate to gulp his down.

Such an impatient lout, she thought. To her, coffee was a luxury to be savored.

After a few sips, she informed him that "You know I won't accept your resignation".

His reddened, cracked eyes widened. "The hell do you...?"

She cut him off. "What I just said. If it's a pay issue, say so."

"It isn't that", he said coldly.

"Problems on the home front, then?" She feigned a sympathetic smile.

"No", he said with an exaggerated o.

"Then what is it, then, my Chief of Guards?" A mocking smirk appeared. He hated that more than anything else about her. At times she could be aloof, almost a robot. A parrot of rules, regulations and trivial legalities. She seemed devoid of any original thinking, or a will that contradicted the dictates of "Home Office". Out of earshot, her cold demeanor was a constant source of derision. "Warden Frigid Pants" some called her. But somehow, Turlak found that more palatable. Keep her pampered ass away from the line of fire, where she'd likely be a detriment. Ice Queen mode, he didn't care about. At least she wasn't as condescending as she was being now.

"The truth, Warden?", he asked, deciding it was now or never.

"Yes", as she took another quick sip. Her cup wasn't even half empty. Slyly, she watched the clock on her console, calculating how much longer this would take.

"Your management style is trash", he told her, as evenly as he could.

"Trash...", she repeated contemplatively. "In what sense?"

He told her of the general malaise the officers were experiencing; how they were stifled, even arrested from meting out some "old fashioned discipline." Some that had already severed ties with Asylon complained about the blasé attitude of management, how the workers were held in such a minor regard, and how they didn't sign up to be "babysitters of hardened criminals".

"People will say what they say", she said with typical disregard for the formerly employed. "Now tell me, Chief, what's *your* trouble?"

"What many of these walking abortions need is a firm boot in the ass!", Turlak concluded.

"To my recollection, more than a few have experienced that", she returned. Though an effective intimidator, his methods were too brutal, she felt. For the moment.

"Some of the officers feel you coddle these fucking mud bastards", he said.

Mud bastard was a pejorative term for Far Worlders. She frowned on open displays of prejudice. Not just personally, but professionally as well. She had to terminate a Corrective Officer, a very fine one, for using such expletives at some of his charges.

"Just say *you* feel that way", she said, putting the cup down.

"I definitely feel that way, Ma'am. As do many of those under your "employ..."

That moment she received a communique from S.S Ostraner. ETA was within two hours.

"You'll handle that, I trust." She was asking to see if he'd be around that long.

He kept silent.

With the sand almost down the other end of the hourglass, she had to give him a little nibble on the bone.

"Turlak, besides my leadership style being, in your colorful description, trash, tell me just one time I've lied to you. Just one." Her pitch changed, from distant amusement to that of a confidante.

"I can't think of one", he admitted gruffly. He gave the devil her due.

"The recent changes came from Home Office, not me. I'm more than aware of the dissatisfaction. I can't but help to feel its aura. And people project that on me as much as possible. I understand. I accepted this when I took this assignment." She was doing her best to make it seem like she had empathy (somewhat, though not truly), and make herself into a martyr for their daily abuse (she was that anyway) while deflecting much of the change in policy on Home Office. Which really wasn't the case. The changes came from Anwari, of whom Turlak knew nothing about. And would know nothing about. She had to keep that tidbit of info away, lest she find herself being run around when it came to matters of authority. Home Office was a dense jungle of bureaucracy where a complaint would find itself easily lost. A complaint to Anwari's department would have a straight beeline to his ear, not to mention the press. The thought of Jet Symmons, or another nosy gadfly gave her shivers. Keeping time in the forefront, she needed to expedite things.

"Turlak, there are reasons why things are being run as they are. But within the next month (give or take), changes will be made as to how this prison is administered. ".

You'll be leaving? Thank the six suns, he thought.

She frowned, divining his disdain. " No, I'll not be going anywhere, much to your (and others) profound disappointment. But nevertheless, things will be changing."

He sat back, drank another cup as quickly as the first.

"And I need you here, because you'll help facilitate those changes."

"And just what are those changes? Why act so cryptic?", he spoke out of frustration. He liked everything to be simple and direct.

"Do you follow the news streams, on a regular basis at least?"

He nodded in the negative.

"You should ", she replied, slightly scolding him.

"Why should I?", he asked her, annoyed. He had a large distrust for "news". He took Twain's admonition regarding news as misinformation as a gospel fact.

"If you do, it'll help make understanding things much easier", she said. Without waiting for a rebuttal, she asked "Will you stay?"

Getting up, he told her "Another month, Warden. After that, if those "changes" don't come about, don't look for another face to face". The unsaid, yet understood threat dripped from his words.

She nodded, then asked, "Is that all?"

"Yes, for now", he said leaving out, not even looking back. He let the door slam.

Ignorant Brute, she thought carelessly.

She finished her coffee, and immediately typed on her desk keyboard Appstat (Application Status). Six spots to fill, maybe seven. An hour's work at best, on top of what already filled her plate. Wanting a brief diversion, she activated the news stream. An important announcement was expected to be made at this time. Pixels merged to form images, outside the Warrington Tower, the main building of GCW HQ where a throng of world leaders, business leaders (?) and the all too familiar face of Mr. Anwari, directly behind Mr. Bevel and his attendant, sat on a silver stage. Uneasiness ran through Warden Quinn. Concerned with his ubiquity; everywhere she turned, he was there. If unseen, still most certainly felt. Despite the bitter aftertaste of their introduction, she had to admit to a grudging admiration for a man that stood on the steps of the largest structure in human history, among the titans of the twenty-eighth century.

Who the hell are you truly, Anwar Anwari? What's the real story behind you? Why do you have so much power?

Loud commotion interrupted her; a fight had broken out between Duriyans and Karuks, again. Tear gas was thrown into the yard, and guards clad in gas masks were separating the combatants. The melee was over in less than ten minutes.

"Be it the boys or girls, all these Far worlders know is violence and strife", she said, unable to catch herself. Had Turlak heard that, he'd deride her as a hypocrite. And remind her of it every chance he got. But he didn't and she had to admit, facts were facts.

Now a third group would be added to the cauldron that was Asylon. She was again wondering if this stew of youthful rebellion and criminality would spill on her. Of course the risks, as well as the rewards were high. *But was it worth getting burned herself?*

The first two weeks was a tour of hell for Jeth Akim. That he and his brethren (as he referred to his fellow countrymen) were hardly conscious when they arrived was horroric in and of itself. Immediately they were accosted and shackled. After S.S Ostraner docked, they were being hurried through two chemically bleached, rust stained steel doors through a long, silver siding paneled corridor that seemed to stretch into forever. On either side, they were under the watchful (though helmeted) eye of a throng of corrective officers in all black uniforms. Their fire pulse rifles were trained on them. In between the armed goons, spots of rust and discolored corrosion peeked out from behind them, like a leper's wounds.

The corrosive stink added to the misery. Its putrid air caused many a person to retch; so foul and toxic a stench, a hapless young man began to convulse abruptly.

Two guards came forth, snatched the afflicted party, and unceremoniously slammed him into the wall, rendering him unconscious. With the Sefu Trians too disoriented, too shocked to react, they were chained one to another, to be herded into the prison like cattle.

"Where are we?!", a brazen soul asked, as the chained procession began. They were arranged one behind the other, regardless of gender. They were then forced to stretch out, hands touching the shoulders of the one in front.

"Shut the hell up!", was the brutal response.

Somewhere behind him, Jeth heard a girl sobbing loudly. Another boy cursed fate, yet another General Hagit.

"I said shut the hell up!", this time he could tell it was a woman talking. From the little he could glimpse, a very hard featured female. Because of her helmet, Jeth couldn't see her eyes. He wanted to see them because he wanted to see if she was just doing her job, or if she was truly an evil person.

"Always look a person in the eyes, Jeth", his father admonished him once. "That tells you the kind of person you're dealing with."

He thought of Sartha, that glance he gave. How she had turned her gaze away. The shame he churned in her. And the "humanity" of her exiling him to an unknown fate.

His heart waxed cold for her, but he could at least understand her motive at face value. Not so with the people here.

As they were only hours out of freeze stasis, many of the Sefu Trians were still off balance, physically. Motor skills and equilibrium came back slowly. Too slowly for some guards. A boy fell, bringing the procession to a halt. He was in the middle. A taser prod was thrust in his left, shocking him nearly unconscious. This slowed things up further. Eventually, he was removed and placed to the rear of the line, his limp, writhing body dragged by the small statured girl who, under stark terror, carried him like a sack of potatoes.

They were taken to a large circular room called Deposition. Under heavy guard, they were slowly unbonded, separated by sex, then forcibly stripped. A girl screamed, in abject horror at being suddenly naked in front of strangers, and especially boys. She was struck soundly and told "Quiet down!" All of them suffered the indignity of being exposed, genitalia fondled, made to be objects of derision and innuendo. *They are treating us worse than animals,* Jeth thought, resentful at this bout of humiliation.

Biometric scans were taken, as were a physical profile for the holo-stream. The data was to be uploaded into the prison's data stream, to be shared with the Home Office.

Humiliation would continue in the showers. They were made to shower together, as officers of both sexes laughed, spoke lewdly. Breasts and penises were again fondled and mocked. It seemed that the perverts were put on this detail, which was only partly true. These people were picked especially for this task; to break the spirit of the newcomers so that they'd prove more pliable than their predecessors. There was almost a riot with the Duriyans; their deposition had almost taken two days. They processed the Karuks on the ship. Warden Quinn and her staff had learned much in those first months.

Sexes were finally separated, the girls led to their dorm first. The solid grey jumpsuit felt stifling, Jeth felt as they were taken in the opposite direction. *No room for flexibility, nor comfort,* he thought. *They want us to be miserable, more than a soul can endure.* Thoughts of home and family plagued him, compounding his anguish. *What had become of his mother and sister, of Sefu Trius itself?*

A violent yank forward tore him away from his thoughts. They were now being forced out, being led elsewhere. The laser rifles trained on them quelled any thoughts of rebellion, or retaliation for this brutal welcome to Asylon. But, Sefu Trians have a long memory...

The pathway they were escorted through was another long tunnel, shielded in silver aluminex, more rusted than the first. Jeth would come to find that this tunnel had once been a waterway. Waterways were a long defunct process of ore processing, with its roots in another practice called hydraulic fracturing, or fracking. There were bends in metal roof, cracks in the wall, particularly around the rusted spots. That same toxic perfume that greeted them was everywhere, a lingering presence, as if to taunt him. *There is no escape.* Harsh nudging from the left side. "Keep up!", a harridan screamed impatiently.

Sharp, glinting stale sunlight marked the passing through from one corridor into a new one.

When they were brought into their dorm, a big building on the other side of the prison complex, Turlak was there to officially "greet" them.

Imposing, in a uniform tattered with rips, smudged with blood and grass stains, he stood before the iron double doors. His appearance sent a wave of ranging emotions within the Sefu Trians. After all they endured on their home world, and just now, how could this battered oaf compare?

"Many of you, he began sternly, don't know what to expect. Some might have a speck of an idea. I'm going to say it once. You've no idea what kind of a place you all have come to. Let me assure you, Trunza Square has got nothing on me, and my officers!", he barked snidely. This earned him the immediate hatred of the newcomers. However, there was no chorus of obscenities in response. Only a wave of soul piercing, indignant stares. But for one.

That last remark made a young man bold enough, foolish enough to curse him bitterly. Turlak simply walked through the crowd, up to the young man, and punched his lights out.

Stunned expressions about him made him smile perversely. He needed that outlet, especially since that brawl. He then strode back into place and broke down the rules.

1) "All officers are to be obeyed, quickly and without attitude or backtalk."

2) "All officials, officers, and general staff are to be called "Sir" or "Ma'am" at all times."

3) "Violence of any kind will not be tolerated. Punishment will be harsh and swift."

4) "There will be no fraternization with members of the opposite sex."

5) "All offenders will answer to me personally!"

After some moments, Turlak let it all sink in. "Are we clear?", he yelled.

A weak "Yes sir!" barely resounded.

"ARE WE CLEAR ?!"

"YES, SIR!", said the chorus. Save one.

The boy who was rendered unconscious was slowly coming to. The way his head snapped back when Turlak decked him was sickening. Jeth stood still, saying nothing, looking ahead. He would not be intimidated.

The end of those two weeks, Jeth had a long scar on his right torso, a deep bruise just under his left ear, and a stitched-up forearm. Three fights. One, a Duriyan punk he beat the life out of, just barely. Then the shower brawl with Karuks. And just hours ago, that incident in the library, of all places. And that girl. That Duriyan girl with deep green eyes.

Finding himself in the infirmary; the cuts were deep, but not life threatening. He turned his head to avoid the unforgiving glare of intense green light bearing down on him. This light was said to have some medicinal properties. It was a refined version of LED style lighting. Originally used to maximize the growth of domesticated remedies such as hicca roots and wild herbs such as Sadas Wort, it was shown to have healing properties the human body could benefit from. It was proven that this type of illumination, known in alternate circles as lumenopathic light, could heal skin by regenerating dead cells and increasing the healing time on punctures, cuts, and even burns (depending on the severity).

He turned on his side, the one not made into a pin cushion. He was now in a bed, not the brick hard gurney they brought him in on. His room was a solitary occupancy; only an armed officer was his company. In typical fashion, there was no expression of empathy to be seen on the solid onyx face that was staring over him into the lame grey and green color scheme. No picture, or décor on the walls, nor any place to hide clothing. Only a long, skinny pole, at arm's length, held his blood soaked prisoner's garb, draped over two of its three slender branches.

At room's entrance three shadows stood, in a whispering contest with other voices further away. One of whom he had a definite acquaintance with.

Staff nurses, two of them, clad in all white uniforms hurried by.

After consulting with Dr. Reit, Warden Quinn and Chief Turlak entered. Turlak wasn't exactly a welcome presence, but Jeth had never seen the Warden upclose. When he stopped squinting (the drugs made vision hazy), his eyes were deceiving him. He just couldn't believe a woman this beautiful could work in such a hellish place.

"Inmate 34421675 ST, or Jeth Akim", she read from a square, thin tablet folder.

He hesitated, then replied "Yes. Yes, Ma'am." He had enough of his wits about him to adhere to the protocol.

"Mr. Akim, she continued, are you able to talk?". *Obviously to the point*, Jeth cautiously observed. He nodded. She smiled grimly.

Turlak's grizzled face was much like his underling's, without even a scintilla of compassion. *Why am I foolish enough to expect such a thing like humanity from the likes of monstrosities like him?!*

A click, tiny and brief, sounded into his consciousness and faded out. She whispered a word. The screen flashed rapidly. And spoke feebly. She had activated the record feature.

"I need you to speak as loud as you're able. If, for any reason you need to stop or need to take a pill, please say so. Understood?"

"Yes, Ma'am", he said meekly.

There was a docility about him that pleased her. More like an appreciation for manners. That was something she could say about this latest group. They were far better at social interaction than the others, and were obviously given lessons in etiquette. Even irascible Turlak pointed that out. Albeit with his typical deep suspicion.

"Now begin relating what happened at Seventeen Thirty -Eight Hours, Universal Earth Standard Time."

Clearing his throat, and adjusting himself as best as he could, Jeth began, the traces of Sefu Trian dialect already muted by the verbio- scrambler:

"I was in the library, sitting at one of the small mezzanine desks, when two Karuks entered. I remembered one of them as one of the ones I'd beaten in the showers some days so ago. I felt him stare, his beady black eyes intent with malice. He had a fixed scowl on his face. His companion was also staring, nodding his head in agreement while the other whispered his dark intentions."

"I'd gone to the library, amazed there was such a place here. I wanted to use my time as best I could, so I was studying old flight accounts of travelers called astronauts. When I spied them watching me, I took to the stairwell and spiraled upwards. They followed me. The companion first, then the other. They split ways, while I watched them from a hidden corner. I hoped to avoid them, but the vengeful one caught me by the shoulder as I headed back down."

"I grabbed him, and lost balance. We tumbled, causing a commotion. The librarian on duty came over but stayed away. She called for a guard. I got the better of my first assailant, and pummeled him. From behind, his partner took me unaware, and stabbed me in the side." For a minute, he stopped. He took a pain reliever, and slowly swallowed it with lukewarm water. The taste was bitter, but its effects were surprisingly effective. His mind returned to the stabbing. The memory made him wince, but he withstood it.

"I was only able to give an elbow to the stomach when the girl with green eyes threw something, a heavy book at him. Turning, his yellow eyes fixed on her. I grabbed his testicles, yanking hard. He howled. She came over and kicked him in the stomach. Hard. He doubled over, and I kicked him off me."

"As he lay beside his friend, drooling, she helped me up, saying "You're hurt". Her accent wasn't thick, yet I could barely make out what she was saying. She was rather kind." For a brief nanosecond, Jeth thought he saw Warden Quinn roll her eyes in contempt.

"When the guards arrived, they separated all of us. The Karuks were hauled away to I know not where. The girl, though, they treated roughly. They cuffed her, berated her and led her away, her protests were loud. I told them she aided me, but they said "keep quiet".

"She's bad news. Stay away from her", one of the guards, a woman, said, as the gurney came.

"They gave me something to ease my pain. I fell asleep instantly. Then I woke up here."

At that, the recording stopped. There was a noticeable silence from both the Warden and Chief of Guards. Jeth wondered if Turlak would be true to his word this time. So far, the Sefu Trians beat back their attackers. And Duriyans and Karuks warred with one another. Yet, he never saw anyone ever punished beyond being yanked to the ground, or physically assaulted. He had only heard the whispers of how mean this guy was supposed to be.

They certainly were punishing that green- eyed girl. And she did something good.

"Thank you, Mr. Akim", Warden Quinn said finally. "Know that your attackers will be given the full measure of justice I can administer. "

Turlak raised his fuzzy eyebrows. Her words were flowery, almost sincere. Why would she treat this thing differently from the other hundred of times shit like this happened?

Jeth nodded. Perhaps, due to his state, he didn't understand her words. But he felt she was being upfront with him. At the very least, she made it seem like she gave half a damn.

"W-What of the girl?" he asked, his voice regaining strength. "S-She saved my life."

"The guard told you correctly. Keep away from her", the Warden said sharply. So curtly, that Jeth was taken aback. Her smile had vanished completely.

"You'll stay the night here, under guard and under supervision", she said as they exited. "Good night."

He sighed deeply, turning on his back to look at the ceiling. Dr. Reit popped his narrowed head in the entrance, saying something about a place called the "Quiet Zone". Extra coverage would be necessary, as there was a call-out. A groan. And Jeth found himself paying for this by being shackled to the bed. Ankles first, then wrists. Dr. Reit administered a sedative, talking in medical jargon as he did so. His teeth bore a sharp resemblance to the "Mecha Sharks" back home. And his demeanor was not that of a concerned physician. His mind turned again to the green- eyed girl who helped him. Exotic, with a pert nose, dark, smooth skin (shocking for a place like this!) and those glittering, green eyes! They were like jewels...He stopped himself, recalling both Sartha's betrayal and Warden Quinn's stern warning. True, he would regard her cautiously, but he already knew he would violate Quinn's admonition.

Tahina cursed herself. "Stupid! So slucking stupid!", she yelled in the confines of her cell.

She was sent back to the Quiet Zone, this time for a stay of sixty days. Maybe more, based on Quinn's mood.

Slumping down on the iron cot, she rued her involvement in what transpired. Not just because of what she did; but because of where it landed her. Again.

And she violated her own policy of non-interference. "Allow them to kill each other", she told Sali and some other girls when the Karuks did battle with the guards. "That's their battle, not ours." And aware to the fact that Duriyans had no allies in this hell hole, she was pleased to see their enemies weaken themselves. Their time was coming, and soon.

Which was what brought her to the library. Unlike most areas, the library was a place free of Warden Quinn's non fraternization policy. At least until this incident. And even though its two stories of tomes were monitored, there were ways of getting around it. Iajim proved that all too well.

She was there picking up a message he left for her in a volume of poetry. Something she loved, and he knew it. She should've just plucked the slip of paper from between the pages and left. But the quatrains penned by Solovius Wynt proved too intoxicating, and she found herself reading.

Almost an hour later, a rumbling from above. Shouts. The sound of fists beating onto flesh and cloth. Boots thudded and crashed against metal. The hard rumbling down the spiral. Angry words, then the frantic pace of another pair of boots clashing against the steps. Despite herself, she got up. The librarian screamed.

She saw the shiv enter the boy's side. He wasn't Duriyan. His skin marny, almost reddish brown for one thing. And his hair was sheared too close cropped for another. He was fending off two Karuks with a discipline many Duriyan males lacked, despite losing. She felt it, her hands holding that ten lb. tome. And she saw herself flinging it, and it crashed against that moplike skull before she realized fully what she had done. She tensed herself, already regretting thrusting herself into a violent situation she had nothing to do with.

The Karuk came for her, but his victim grabbed his jewels from behind, attempting to crush them to powder. Not being one to pass up a chance for petty violence, she rushed in, close enough to kick the sluckhead in his abdomen.

As they lay on the ground, moaning and wallowing in defeat, she helped the focus of their cowardly attack (Duriyans fought one on one) up to his feet.

He was wiry, although by no means light. And almost at the six-foot mark. His eyes were closed. A stream of tears fought its way down his left cheek.

"You're hurt", she said. He grunted, making a non-comprehending face. *Did they hit a vital area?* she thought. He murmured something. "T- Than..."

He wasn't given the opportunity to finish, as a squad of seven guards burst in, pushing her away. They grabbed the boy, who almost collapsed to the floor. Her hands forced behind her, she heard the familiar snap of cuffs ringing loudly in her ears yet again.

"I saved his life! What the hell are you...?", she protested earnestly. The Karuks were cuffed as well. C.O.s escorted them out with a heavy shove forward.

"Inmate 9102996 DU, a woman officer named Samuels said, why am I not surprised that you're involved in this?" A quick, silent wind from a hovering gurney breezed the room.

"Wait", the injured young man tried to say. "S- she aided me. She saved my life", he spoke weakly as they lifted him on.

"She's bad news. Stay away from her", Samuels said snidely.

Tahina wanted so badly to spit in her face, at least give her a vicious kick on the way out. She mumbled expletives as they lead her away. The boy. She never even learned his name. But at least he tried to speak up. At least *he* appreciated her help.

Not that it really mattered at this point.

There she was, back in the Quiet Zone, away from any line of communication. The timing couldn't be worse. She could only take solace that she wasn't strip searched; otherwise they would've found it. And ruined the whole thing. Iajim's scrawled message read *"WE"RE ALMOST READY."*

She crumpled up the tiny sheet, flushing it with her waste.

The whole thing would have to happen without her.

She knew Sali and the girls could manage without her. They'd have to. But she wanted to be there.

Soon, and finally, this slucking Hell would burn.

"Non- sovereigns In Exile", was the official term used by the Counselor General of the GCW. During a lengthy press conference, filled with legalese, hard to grasp semantics, and an uncharismatic delivery, the most powerful lawyer in the universe spelled out the meat of the "The Great Reunion."

"From this minute, this hour forward, let there be no longer be a separation of Inner Worlds and Far Worlds", he announced amid small, obligatory applause and the gaze of trillions on him.

"The Human Diaspora is once again, whole."

Among handclapping, there were murmurs of protests. Though not at Warrington Tower, nor within twenty miles of it. Anyone who was known to disagree was barred attendance. Travel had even been restricted to weekend status, whatever that meant.

"With our reembracing of each other, no matter where you were born, no matter the economic system or status you were born under, there can be no tolerance for those who would utilize terrorism to achieve their nefarious ends! What will come is a strict enforcement of the charter our forefathers drew together, and we discarded for but a time. And we now see our folly."

"We are stronger together, and with us all united, humanity can move into a new epoch of Progress."

He wasn't eloquent, nor even remotely interesting. Which was why Counselor General Owei was perfect for delivering, in hindsight for some, the most important speech that day. So many people tuned it out; so, they had absolutely no idea what lay in the winds.

His speech now mercifully over, reporters nearly climbed over themselves to start asking questions about the "future peace, security and prosperity" of humanity.

When pressed upon by a reporter about the Asylon Project, he said hurriedly, "The rights of the sovereign citizen are paramount. Those of Non-sovereign status is a matter best addressed in the Trans-Galactic Chamber of Justice, not in public discourse."

Anwari, seated on the second row behind the Counselor General, scanned the crowd. He was pleased by the looks of strained faces groping for understanding. Pleasure then turned to stark, silent horror as a familiar nemesis forced her way to the forefront.

A collective "Oh Shit!" whispered in silent chorus.

"But Counselor General, respectfully, aren't those currently held in places like Asylon considered to be as sovereign as anybody else?", Jet Symmons asked loudly enough for everyone to hear. Anwari grimaced with the growing awareness of a thorn pricking his side.

The brows of the Counselor General united in consternation. "Really, the matter is settled by a review of the charter. If you do that, your question is answered."

"So... that's a yes or no, Counselor General?"

A stifling hush came over the audience, which consisted of every available newsman and woman that could make the trip (many outlets weren't allowed access nor could they pay the rising costs of space travel). Those behind him, as Counselor General Owei stared directly in the face of the lone person fool enough to challenge him, gave no outward reaction. As if this insect buzzing around could sting.

Giving an out of place chuckle (designed to throw his opponent off), the lead tongued lawyer said only "The charter set forth is the guide to deal with all within the GCW. The Thirteenth Law is specific about these matters, as clear as the skies above. So be it an individual sovereign, non- sovereigns in exile, whatever may apply will be a matter of established law and the precedents that support it."

Just as Symmons was to offer a rebuttal, Counselor General Owei walked away, his haggard, leathery face sagging slightly. Perhaps the confrontation wearied him. Perhaps being a man of sixty- eight years was beginning to show its effects. Or perhaps the realization of the enormity of the gaffe he just committed was weighing down on him.

He took his seat, as another official, this time Undersecretary of the President took to the podium. His eyes staring out, deep in thought. Glints of sunlight were caught on image, causing a temporary over brightening of the Holographic stream.

At that point, Warden Quinn terminated the broadcast. There was nothing else to add. The Thirteenth Law would be applied, with a force many never thought was possible. How could they? They never knew the rule under a united humanity. She sat back, thinking about it. Soon, Asylons would be built in all corners of space. One system to control the whole of the Human sphere of life. She knew that last one was naive. Ever since humans came into existence, there were always a set of laws for the rich, the elite and a set for everyone else.

It was the selling of a bill of goods that, like all golden promises, was too good to be true. Would eventually prove to be too good to be true.

Even casual observers of inter galaxy affairs would know that. But the chaos in the Far worlds, a growing scourge of piracy had stoked the fears of many. The former Far worlds. The Independence Wars divided Humanity, creating in the aftermath a deep chasm of understanding between those close to Earth (the Inner Worlds, ruled under the single influence of the GCW), and the planets who broke away. There were fifteen worlds now being brought back into the fold of civilization once more. "Proper Civilization", was the preferred term.

An Inner worlder, she naturally viewed the situation with polite condescension. Polim Tef, a small exoplanet just three billion miles from the Milky Way. A child of the Boroughs (the populated areas were called that, in homage to the late, famed city of New York), she came of age during the decades long Recession Era. She worked tooth and nail from semi poverty to where she now stood, with an eye to the future: most prominently, the highest profile position in a burgeoning field. Job security and a guaranteed spot on the Directorship if Asylon proved successful. And a seven figure crypto-coin salary, plus a perfect credit portfolio as an added incentive. So, was the daily headaches, the stress coming from above and below, the vapid, disrespectful whispers worth it? Was being, in Turlak's vernacular, a "glorified zookeeper" worth it? In her mind, it was worth every bit of it. Asylon, Anwari, Home Office, if it got her where she ultimately wanted to be.

So, she kept the inmates in line, the guards well paid (failing that, compensated in other ways, like turning a blind eye to some "venting", provided their target wasn't seriously hurt or killed. Until Anwari made her clamp down on such practices, that is.) and Home Office satisfied. It became a balancing act she perfected.

During her monthly status conferences with the Board, no one asked about a High turnover rate, nor the abuse either the guards or their charges inflicted on each other. Certainly, no questions were asked about allocations for improvements and repairs. One person, she didn't know who, asked about that Karuk boy who committed suicide. She simply said "Measures are being taken to prevent a further occurrence of that nature."

No further questioning along those lines. The questions everyone had were:

"When will you be ready for more?"

"When will the first convicts be shipped out? We have contracts to fulfill. "

The first coincided with the latter. There was only room in Asylon for five hundred prisoners. A refurbished space could only hold so many. A little over three hundred were currently housed within Asylon's walls. And that was more than a handful. To bring in more would mean the place would have to lose close to half the populace currently there. Logistically, no less than forty prisoners per arrival would make the affair worthwhile.

Also, question number two was a matter of this: how many companies needed convict labor, and how many did they need to perform a needed task? And could those leased out be controlled? It wouldn't be profitable to send ten Duriyans and six Karuks to a mining world if they would rebel, try to kill those overseeing them and most certainly each other. No, it wouldn't do at all. The profit loss margin would be too great.

And Con-Leasing would be ground to a halt.

The whole effort to procure a cheap source of labor would have been for nothing.

Until now, it was illegal to do so. Until the "Great Reunion", those within Asylon's steel and brick walls had rights. They were held off world, but their home planets still had obligations to them that they had to maintain. Mostly, because the charter of GCW was not put into full effect. Until today. And most relevant, the Thirteenth Law. And as Owei spoke, it was beginning to redefine life for not just those under her charge, but the whole universe. Even she shuddered in grim realization.

At this point in time, what many didn't know, or would misconstrue for many years to come, was that the "Great Reunion" came at a great cost.

Rejoining the GCW meant the famines and food riots they sparked would be a memory; as would the dictators (General Hagit, by coincidence, had stepped down as "The voice of Sefu Trius" a week later. But the structure remained intact, save food distribution. The protests were successful in that minor regard, at least.) and the bumbling incompetents like President Ihus of Duriy and the corrupt leaders of the Karuks. GCW appointed Prime Magistrates would oversee managing the governance of these "troubled" worlds, and lifting others up to what many derisively labeled "The Human Standard". In short order, the Far Worlds lost their Independence.

So those held at Asylon were considered an "Exiled National", or "Non-Sovereign In Exile". Their respective worlds judged, tried, and renounced their sovereignty in absentia, and they were no longer citizens. And without the citizenship of a planet, they were left to the mercy of an unforgiving universe.

Warden Quinn received word from Anwari himself the moment it became official. It was a week or so after the "formalities", as he described it. Less than a minute later, she summoned Turlak to her office, keeping true to her word.

The moment Turlak had long savored finally arrived. But Warden Quinn was feeling a twinge of hesitation. Imagery of a pack of caged beasts being freed to terrorize sprang to mind. What she said, finally, was "Scare the living souls out of them, but don't kill anyone. They have to be useful".

He had a faint half smile. Lips that made a curved line. She wondered if Turlak had smiled a day in his life. Even when laughing (and his idea of releasing sadistic mirth was a boisterous bellow), he frowned.

Being ex- military (many planets retained a paramilitary force of some kind), he knew well the process of breaking the spirit of a recruit. They weren't recruits, not willingly, at least. But the same psychology applied, as did the methods involved. The work would be long, due to the time passed since the first arrivals came, but enjoyable.

"Operation Home Training" began with malicious earnest.

By week's end, Jeth Akim had witnessed more violence, more antagonism and sadism than he ever witnessed firsthand back home. Soldiers there treated the brutality as part of the job; a job they didn't care for, but needed to provide for a famished, bereft family. As he walked from cafeteria to courtyard, or from the courtyard back to his cell, always was there some incident, some clash about him. The cracking of an iron truncheon against a Karuk's back was a revolting sound. He thought they broke him in half.

He stood frozen, not knowing if he should help him, as he roiled about in pain, blood leaking from his mouth. A red stain began to form on the back of his jumpsuit. The blow had fractured something, causing a breakage in skin. Blood oozed into the faded grass.

"Hey, you, get moving!" the scowling face spit, over the crying howls of the kid now lying half unconscious. Too much in pain to move, too frightened to fade into blackness, lest it be permanently. The look they gave Jeth read *You're next!* He walked away, holding his injured side. Its pain had subsided in good measure since his release. What he just witnessed sickened him, causing new pain to rise within. He held it. He made it back to his cell, laying down on the slab of metal he had to call a bed. On a mattress as thin as the sheet that covered him. His bunkmate (he slept on the lower half) was out somewhere, probably stirring up more talk of "Uprising and rebelling". Despite the impracticality of his demands, Jeth more than not, found himself silently in agreement. The ill feeling carried him to sleep and when he awoke, still it was there.

Later that day, a fight had broken out between a Duriyan and a Karuk. Both young men were accosted by the emboldened guards who had tied them together. Hoisting them upwards to the ceiling of an empty room, five of them proceeded to beat the pair completely unconscious. They used them as human pinatas, bruising flesh and breaking bone mercilessly. Leaving them hanging for almost two hours, when they were finally retrieved their brown skins were battered and punctured, and dripping blood formed a large puddle on the concrete floor. They were laid up for a long stretch of time.

"Why doesn't Warden Quinn stop this?" Jeth bemoaned to a fellow countryman when he heard the chilling account.

"You put too much faith in devils ", the young man replied tersely, spitting on the dingy concrete floor for effect as he walked away. All around him, Jeth saw shades of his home world. Night had become day; he recalled Turlak's threats of reprisal, now regretting how lightly he took them to be. In the atmosphere fear permeated every step, any utterances. Corrective Officers were revealing their true nature, being the hired goons and thugs they were. Eating in the cafeteria, it was silent as a pin drop. Until one of the C.O.s started to provoke a fight with a group of Karuks. Wisely, they stalked off, leaving their trays of mush and black soda sitting on the table.

Some days later, in the middle of the courtyard, he was sitting on one of the hardwood tables, looking at the barbed shock wires that ran the whole of the roof. He mulled how far he could get before he was electrocuted, or cut to mincemeat when a loud howling turned him away.

His eyes widened. He thought it was a wild mirage. He was hoping it was, at the very least. His hopes were dashed, by an unspeakable humiliation.

From the side that snaked from the girl's dorm, a quintet of well-armed female guards were leading a procession. Flanked by four more on each side, twelve naked young women were made to walk exposed in public, hands clasped behind their heads, and kept from covering their forcefully displayed nudity. Some faces were stained with tears. Others blushed with unbridled humiliation. A few looked ahead stoically, but none could hide the shame being inflicted on them. The catcalls and yells of approval came mostly from the officers along the tower wall; most of the boys were either too stunned, or silently outraged at the naked procession to respond. Amid cries of embarrassment and blushing brown bodies, one of their tormentors yelled out "A pussy sale later tonight!" The scene ended as quickly as it began. The girls disappeared through a passage near the cafeteria, never to be seen again.

Warden Quinn exploded when it came to her attention. The guard who made the "sale" comment was fired immediately, and Turlak heard her use expletives in ways he never thought were possible. Calmly, he withstood the barrage and then said, "Whoa! Remember, you said I could, and I quote, "scare the living souls out of them, so long as they weren't killed." "You do remember, do you not?" He was smiling. She hated his twisted smile. It made him look uglier, more vicious than he was. It made her sick. But she was mostly mad at herself. She had finally given him free reign, and it would be foolish to put the leash back on for the second time.

"I only hope you never treated women like that during any of your tours of duty", she caustically replied.

"Only when necessary", he returned, just as bitter. Then replying "Warden, when it comes to justice, the law doesn't discriminate. So why do you? "

She shot him a stunned look. Did he dare accuse *her* of sexism?

"You have the audacity to label that stunt as justice?", she was as close to firing him as she'd ever been.

"You play favorites, Warden. The law works against us all, no matter the sex, planet of birth, even so-called class status. You'd be wise to recall that." He said it with a knowing she hadn't grasped. It cut at her sensibilities in a way she never suspected was possible. And immediately, she resented him even more for it. Dismissing himself, he left her to stew in anger. After the invoice for the twelve females was received, she took note of the hefty price paid upon delivery. She never called him back. Nor brought up the matter again.

For weeks after, the mood around Asylon was heavy and forbidding. Anger, grief and distress coated its steel and concrete walls like paint, casting long shadows in the corridors. Nearly everyone felt the sting of paranoia. *What would happen next? Who would be their next victims? And what could we do about it?*

The second phase of the Asylon Project had begun, quicker than anyone expected.

Twelve girls. Four Duriyan, four Sefu Trian, and lastly a quartet of Karuki. Humiliated, then they vanished. Next, ten boys were gone, picked out of a line up early one morning almost two weeks later. Spared the shame of being stripped, they were shackled one behind the other, led away to the Prison's docking center. Never to be seen or heard of again. Four Duriyans, four Karuks, and two from Sefu Trius.

This new development brought on a new despair. Twenty-two people had vanished without a trace. When one asked about their whereabouts, the typical response was "I never heard of inmate such and so." " Worry about yourself! " was for the more tactless.

The beatings, taserings, and the vanishings were making people angry. But more than that, they were becoming desperate. Two things that fuel chaos. Or forge unlikely alliances.

Chapter Five

Dr. Miles Silas sat at his desk, as he did for the whole month he was assigned to Asylon. As lead member of the Psych Ward (Warden Quinn wanted to make it seem as if he really had a staff), his job was to evaluate the prisoners they sent before him. He didn't peruse the landscape, nor asked any unnecessary questions. He simply evaluated, then gave Quinn his recommendations. Most subjects he evaluated never returned. Except this one. This was her second time here, and so far, it was just like the first. She sat directly opposite, saying nothing. The Rorschach test on the tablet transforming.

"Well, Miss Tahina, what do you see?"

She looked about the brightly lit office. Wall to wall wood cases were filled with books; books about general psychology, criminal psychology, psychology of sex, and other topics she considered of no value. Just like the man sitting across from her. His trophies, his awards, and his memorabilia (a sports addict of some sort) filled the walls in between the massive shelves and the top of his heavy oval glass desk.

A hoarder of useless junk, and thinks too highly of himself, the girl opined silently.

She was supposed to be looking at the tablet placed before her, black ink blobs morphing into God knew what. Impatient tapping of fingertip on the frosted glass edge was supposed to prompt a response. Defiant, she wouldn't give this overdressed sluck the satisfaction.

"Tahina, Warden Quinn would regard another session of you sitting here in brooding silence a wasted effort", Dr. Silas said, weary of her stubborn reticence. "And we both know how much she hates waste."

In response, Tahina turned her head away from him.

Looking down, shifting in the strait jacket that held her arms tightly bound. The slippers they let her wear were half off her feet. And her socks smelled. Her hair had grown wild, disheveled; she looked and felt as feral as Quinn described. Her clothes were smelly, dirty and slightly torn. And it appeared her feminine needs were being neglected.

More petty torment that Warden Quinn heaped upon her.

While Dr. Silas was here to only evaluate those brought before him, he found himself giving his assessment of Warden Quinn and her staff also. If grading were allowed, he would fail them miserably. This child alone... This alone would constitute a complaint of abuse. If only there was *someone*, some *agency* to send his grievances to.

Duties first, he admonished himself, pushing aside his misgivings for the present.

"Now, Tahina, what do you see?", the portly, nebbish man repeated, beads of sweat dripped from the jowls of his neck, into his lap. He took the tablet from her. And Tahina, after clearing her throat, informed him that he was a bloated, flatulant imbecile who was obsessed with past glories and rigged games. And she further said "Your delusions of intelligence far exceed your limited mental capabilities." Dr. Miles Silas had been a psychologist for nearly two decades. He never encountered a patient so verbose.

"You could've just called me stupid", he offered. It didn't surprise him that she would act like this. Having access to her files, he expected a more violent, nastier interaction. Almost two sessions in, Dr. Silas surmised that perhaps Quinn and her staff were a bit biased in their reporting.

"I did!", she returned, through gritted teeth. Her breath felt hot, unclean. They didn't supply her with toothpaste capsules, again. The filth on her made her so self-conscious, past the point of being ashamed. Her eyes went from the bland, plush beige carpeting and the bookcases that surrounded them back to Dr. Silas.

"After an essay, you most certainly did. But that's a start."

She leaned back, feeling her eyes roll.

"Tahina, he said in a friendly, soft voice, I'm not your enemy."

"You most certainly aren't a friend!", she shot back.

He held up the palms of his thick hands, in a gesture of hands up. "See me as you like, but I am here to help you. Whether you think so or not."

It took everything in her to neither curse him or spit on his treasures. *But how futile would that be?* she thought somberly.

"I'm sure, no, I'm positive you don't believe that", he said with frankness. He spoke the language of his patient, so that there was an understanding. He reserved the words of his profession for the journals and his peers.

"I'm absolutely positive I don't", she fired back, more restrained. It was pointless to be angry, she reasoned. It wouldn't get her out of this place.

"Miss Tahina... you have a surname, don't you?", he asked, feeling suddenly awkward, addressing her by only her first name. Her files made no indication of a surname. None of the Duriyans he interviewed had one. But she's the only one that made him address the matter.

"Where I'm from, people my age don't have them. We purchase them when we turn twenty - one."

"That's fascinating, he murmured. Such a unique custom." Here, he was revealing his cultural ignorance; He simply assumed that Far worlders still maintained any and all ancient Earth traditions, regardless of what they were.

"Because we don't ride the coattails of those who proceeded us?", she asked sharply. She was rebutting what she considered his air of condescension.

"No, it's just unusual", he said, making yet another palms up motion. He truly wasn't aware that such a custom existed. Thus, the knowledgeable Tahina took the opportunity to "educate" him.

The Rite of Name ritual was as old as the Founding of The Duriyan State itself. Those original settlers threw away the names they arrived with, thinking that a new environ had called for a new identification of self. Eventually, when adulthood came at twenty- one (a holdover from Earth), an individual could adopt a surname, or even change their first name. It was done in a small gathering of family and friends, an intimate ceremony.

Only now, Duriy was millions of miles away. A lifetime away, it seemed. And with no family, she could only hope to make friends. If only.

A friend was a treasure she could never acquire, much less keep. She'd always been a loner, an anti -social anomaly. She was too intelligent for those around her, so they shunned her. In retaliation, the air she cultivated kept people at bay, to tell herself she didn't need their company. To her shocking dismay, they heeded the unspoken message.

Then Jojas came in her life, and then his circle. Then the riots took it all away. Then, he departed in a hail of laser fire. Sali, from what she heard from the whispering guards, was gone. People were disappearing. Left and right, those she arrived with were vanishing. Being snatched away, or if the words from loose lips could be considered, shipped off somewhere to suffer much more dire fates.

"So, companies are renting them now?", a guard asked carelessly while the other broke Tahina's rest. They came to collect her for the first session with Dr. Silas

"That's what they say ", the other whispered, prodding Tahina awake with a nightstick. C.O.s could carry them around now, to add to the intimidation factor. It wasn't even a disciplinary infraction if they crashed it down on an unsuspecting inmate for "Batting practice".

Unbeknownst to both, Tahina was awake, listening to every word. They spoke of the girls humiliated and taken away. One of them matched Sali's description perfectly. Yet again, another friend, snatched cruelly away. That night in her cell, she sobbed herself to sleep.

By the time she crossed paths with Dr. Silas, Tahina had developed a skin of steel. And a heart to match. When she glared at a C.O., her green eyes reflected that icy ferocity. "The frigid eyes of a heartless bitch", one female officer mentioned to Turlak in passing.

Though he wouldn't say it to her, he found the girl's love of her home a segue way to a breakthrough. He decided to cautiously press on, lest she retreat into herself. Dr. Silas asked her questions about her home world, the culture she grew up in. She sensed his sincerity, and seeing she had nothing to lose, she began talking, and he found her to be extremely well informed. She spoke knowingly about her planet's history, how it was one of the most important shipbuilding planets in that part of the universe, and even today the Great Shipyards remained an inspiration of national pride. Though those days were long past. The great universities and the poets, from Dez Vulker to Benin Baz to Sharan Huj. The cultural festivals of Gurun Hasa (The Day of Arrival – The planet's founding) and the seven days feast of liberation (honoring those that died in the Independence Wars) were still venerated, though not celebrated due to the recent crises. She was encyclopedic, even relishing the chance to "educate" this fat oaf about her people.

"You realize, of course that Dez Vulker ranks far above Shakespeare, do you not?" He stared at her, thinking she was joking. But she was dead serious.

"Young lady, he stared in disbelief, Shakespeare has been renown for over millennia, this fellow..."

She cut him off with undue authority. It rankled him, but he kept his composure, allowing her to say: "Vulker's sonnets and long poems are far more memorable, far more vivid, both in description and poignancy. We know Shakespeare mostly for his plays, if, I may add, he truly wrote them." To add to her point, she nodded at the "Complete Works of Shakespeare" perched high above the shelf to the left of Silas. A well- worn tan hardback, with the spine cracked with stress and age.

Smugly, he remarked "Why I highly doubt you've even read Shakespeare", which indeed, he didn't. She was so incredibly well read. And what little information they were able to glean from Duriyan records (which, to their discredit, was horrifically lacking), showed she had incredible aptitude in many arenas.

"I've read Shakespeare, that very volume, eleven times. Hughes, Baraka, Heany, Dunbar, Dove, both Browning's, Pushkin. Shall I go on?" She faintly smiled, her familiar smugness returning to her.

He looked away for a second, then strangely, he smiled. He was truly impressed.

"Yes", he said, realizing his tone was warmer than he should've allowed.

Despite his iron clad professionalism, he found himself liking the girl.

"Giovanni, Sanchez, Hammon, even some of the obscure Sun Ra, guys like Holmes, Williams, Solomon..."

"I get it", he said, mocking exasperation. She certainly had a way of proving a point. "Is everyone on your world as well versed as you?" He asked because of the prevailing notion that many Far worlders were uneducated. The few he'd assessed neither confirmed nor contradicted the unfortunate stereotype.

"Few people are as well read as I am, no matter where they originate from", she declared arrogantly. He gave her an incredulous crook of the head. Now that he got her talking, he found himself wishing he could lower the flow of words from the spigot. She loved to talk. Or was it a case of having someone to vent to, being that she was kept in isolation, for so long and so often?

"Don't believe that we're all backwards and we're animals", she said with stinging reproach. "We did what we needed to do to survive."

"I make no judgements, Tahina." He said calmly.

"You don't have to. Others do it. I've glimpsed your media accounts." Which she did during her limited visits to the library. She was a frequent visitor. After some effort, she was given limited access to Quinn's new toy (less than five minutes). The initial experience frightened her, taking in so much information at one time. It was comparable to one stuffing their face, opposed to digesting and savoring every morsel of food. After a few more tries, she abandoned the affair altogether. That Quinn would even allow such a device, let alone her personal property, to be accessible in that manner made her feel a brief measure of respect towards her nemesis. Until the C.E.O.S (C.O.s or just guards) came to take her, strait-jacketed, back to her hellhole in the Quiet Zone.

So intelligent. If not for her acute sense of persecution, and penchant for making enemies of the wrong people, she could blossom, he thought, growing empathetic as their session continued.

After a brief respite, he returned the therapy session back towards her.

"Clearly, you see everyone as against you", he stated, noting the red bleating light that began to flash. They were coming to take her away. Suddenly, a cloud of sadness shadowed over him.

Inflecting all the frustration, fear and exasperation that welled up within, she replied "Well, aren't they?" The way she gestured, her arms, though imprisoned, made a shrugging motion to underscore her point. Watching the futility of it, Dr. Silas bit his lower lip in resignation. She *did* have a point.

Soon after the guards escorted her back to her cell, Miles Silas painfully realized he failed to ask more about her family life. Perhaps the oversight would be corrected at the next session. He needed to speak to the Warden about that, among other matters. *Things aren't right here*, he told himself. *Righteous indignation pushing aside a practiced, polished detachment?* Perhaps, but he needed to voice his concerns, he decided as he locked the office door.

When the door was opened, she was greeted with the fading aroma of warm food. A pile of linen and clothing sat in the middle of the iron frame they called a bed. Besides, a bowl containing toothpaste, soap, and generic feminine products slumped beside it. When they removed the strait jacket, and slammed the door shut, she rushed to clean the filth off her body. Beginning with her hair.

Running hot water through her thickened mane; cupping handfuls of soap over her scalp. Until she came to Asylon, she was always meticulous about her hair. "Little Miss Prissy Pris", friends, neighbors, even her own mother used to call her. It was a point of pride for her, to take time and care in how she presented herself. Pride and control over the one thing she did have full power over. Realizing she let them snatch that away from her, she decided to take it back, never allowing anyone to damage her pride again.

She smiled subversively, now concentrating on her body. Hot, splurging water felt good, even refreshing. *An unclean body was the beginning of a sullied soul*, she recalled from her youth. *Even the unfortunate shouldn't be too bad off to not keep themselves undirtied.*

Her own life proved that assertion a contradiction, if not a convenient untruth. *If being in hunger, or imprisonment captured the individual, just how important is a clean body in comparison to nourishment, or the gaining of one's freedom?*

Toweling off, dressing in clean, washed clothing that smelled surprisingly of lilacs and spring, she began eating. The food was the usual mush and lemon water, but it was good. As she devoured the meal, the realization came upon her that they were making her an animal. Slowly, yet surely. The treatment, the brutality both overt and subtle. Taking away her friends. The walls, the purgatory. After the last morsel, the last gulp, she flung the bowl across the room, it's spinning and low thud the only entertainment she was allowed.

Washing her hands, she forced herself on that pallet of iron and stiff spring. Making herself close her eyes, she thought bitterly about her mother, about the last time she saw her...

Her mother was talking to the District sentinels; she saw that clearly from her hiding place in the thicket behind what was the one floor, two-bedroom house she lived in. The gold and red emblazoned emblem on their sleeves read (she recalled things vividly) Shakur Province SDEA. They were tasked with rounding up the kids who raided, then razed the Prov. Governor's Palace and guest home, taking food and valuables on the way out. She was no thief, so she took only food.

Even so, they were looking for her. Righteousness and justice be damned. She knew to expect neither from them. Or understanding. It was only surprising it had taken them *this* long to catch up to her.

Her mother's head bobbing, nodding, like any other dujin head. *Like a damn big headed toy!* Even from afar, it was embarrassing.

While she couldn't make out what was spoken, she interpreted body language well. The pus thickened hand was held out to accept three bars of solid Gold (the planet's National currency, which most didn't have these days). And with nodded head, her mother let them in.

She woke up, the betrayal still vibrant in her thoughts. She pushed her past forcefully out of mind, deciding to focus on her pain filled today. The plan was in ruins, Sali, and perhaps Iajim by now were gone. She was still here, though for how much longer none could say. At that moment, a strange yet pleasant memory came to mind. Her parents had friends over, playing an ancient Earth game called, if she remembered correctly, poker. Yes. They had friends over, and in the smoke laden living room, they played hand after hand, her father paired with (she couldn't remember their names ... so long ago and forgettable were they) the man's wife, and her mother with the guy. Presumably a work buddy of her father. Her mother was beautiful then, a radiant and sheened obsidian skin that sparkled in the sunlight. The sundress she wore made her look celestial.

She was young, probably no older than five, as the twins weren't there yet. Walking about, talking just to get attention. Fumbling into the spacious (in the mind of a five- year old) room, with the giant slump sofas, sea blue overstuffed chairs, and spooky (again, a five- year old's perception) oak and taffir wood statues that evoked the blessings of the long departed, she incurred her mother's wrath and her father's rescue. He scooped her up and put her in his lap. She felt so secure there.

"The way you spoil her!", her mother admonished, throwing down the cards in disgust. The lady laughed, revealing a royal flush.

To the ire of the opposing team, her father said, between a guff of laughter, "See, there's an art to this."

"Which would be?", his friend asked, not the least bit suspicious.

"Been dealt a bad hand, he laughed, humor echoing in his daughter's young ears, bluff your way into a winning hand!" He drew the long face that he carried most of the game.

His resultant laughter, nor the advice never made sense to her, until now.

Jeth Akim was days into his work assignment detail. A new protocol that Warden Quinn implemented. A select group were given tasks around the prison. It was designed to reward the ones who seemed intent on reforming their lives. Or so she claimed. For meager pay, less than twenty young men and women were chosen to serve in the capacities of assistants, attendants, and custodians.

So Jeth became a custodian. His daily task was to go throughout the complex, collecting then incinerating the garbage. This undertaking took him, when he tried, no less than five hours, tops. Yet somehow, he always stretched it out to a full eight. He was supplied with a mobile hover compactor and collector, a scan badge, fiber steel work gloves, and a sickly, pale green uniform. That was always soiled after a day's work. He worked every day except for two. Those were days he could rest all day in his cell, or go do whatever he wanted. A speck of freedom traded for toil and soiled clothes and exposure to near fatal liquid fire. He thought it was a worthy trade, if it helped him reach his end goal.

So far, neither Warden Quinn nor Chief of Guards Turlak complained about his work. Perhaps because he did well enough, or that nobody else wanted it he couldn't tell. Nor did he care. It took him away from the dorms, and allowed him to explore the prison, its grounds and even sub-levels. And that was what he wanted to do anyway. It would give him the means to escape.

While cleaning, he learned the art of patience, and deception. Part of why Warden Quinn chose him for a work detail was her belief that he was a rather good but weak, docile kid in a bad situation. He looked submissive to authority, and was polite and soft spoken. Turlak, on the other hand, seemed distrustful of him, but he was that way with everybody. He didn't remark out of term, but he let him know, certainly, he was being watched.

Though much of his faith in Warden Quinn was eroded, he was careful not to show it. Even though it went against the honesty he was reared to believe in, this wasn't Sefu Trius. To his silent dismay, the home longed for wasn't just systems away. He found himself leaving the values he cherished behind, to be able to survive the new reality he found himself in. This realization gave him a melancholic aura that others, even fellow countrymen found intolerable. He isolated himself in hardened misery.

As he cleaned, he saw the new faces being brought from the Deposition. He saw the red shame lingering on the cheeks. The group was Karuks this week; the week before the Duriyans. No more of his countrymen had arrived, nor would they. The new, provincial government of Sefu Trius had declared a "Moratorium on Exiles".

A development that displeased Warden Quinn and her staff, because the few Sefu Trians left formed the core of her Work Detail Program, while both the Duriyans and Karuks were getting shipped off to work for companies like Brannc Terra-Mining and The Sayut

Terraformers League; cheap, hardy labor that pushed seasoned workers who demanded more pay and better conditions out of the workplace. And while the contracted labor brought money into the coffers of IREL for supplying the workers (who earned nothing but free food and shelter for free labor), the newly displaced developed a seething disdain for the indentured scabs who took away their livelihoods. Fights, even serious injuries on both sides were becoming commonplace.

The Sefu Trians made themselves into model prisoners; they kept and brokered uneasy peace among the other prisoners, especially new arrivals. Both Duriyans and Karuks alike despised them, but they hated the guards who terrorized them, now with a nearly unlimited impunity. Most of their original leaders were sold off, and those that remained were either too broken by injury, or weren't strong enough to command respect. Of the girls, The Sefu Trians came to dominate them, slowly but surely. Tahina was strong, but she was out of the picture, plus, she had the disadvantage of being disliked by many, even by those that knew her only by reputation. And the Karuks had no equivalent. The pecking order for the women ran: Sefu Trians, Duriyans and Karuks dead last. Sefu Trians lacked the numbers, but they had the fighting skill, cunning, and an understated viciousness that made the other groups back off, or just outright submit.

So, when Jeth went about his rounds, he weathered dirty looks, but no one threatened or did anything out of turn. If anything, there seemed to be a level of order among the population, however malignant, or even temporary. He went about performing his menial duties, disliked but unmolested.

Tahina found herself out of the Quiet Zone for at least ninety minutes daily, half the day on "Sunday". Why Standard Earth Time mattered, so far away from it's origin, she didn't know nor care.

But even out of the confines of her cell, she found herself isolated. She wasn't allowed to mingle within the general population, and she knew of no one that arrived with her that remained. In the library, where she became a fixture, she found herself poring through volumes; poetry, quantum physics and interspatial theory, anything to occupy her mind. But almost always, she came back to one overriding idea. *How do I get free of this Hell?*

"Dr Silas, Warden Quinn said as she sat down, the loud squeak indicating the chair's age, I'll hear no more of it!"

The Doctor was alternately enamored and flustered all in one moment.

"With due respect, Warden, this girl is the most brilliant mind I've come across since I arrived." There was firmness in his voice. When Dr. Silas believed something, he believed it with a resolution that only a divine act could waver. His assertion made Quinn furious, exasperated more so, but she was careful to control it. At first.

"Duly noted", returned Quinn, her distant words underscoring a point. That her authority could disregard counsel if she saw fit.

"You hire me for my expertise, then you ignore it?!", he was now incredulous, truly indignant and disgusted.

"I reserve my right, as head of this facility, to listen, evaluate and utilize whatever I deem necessary. All else can be dismissed." Here, there was no hesitancy. Just, unbridled arrogance. When Ednisa Quinn refused to be swayed, talking was pointless.

"She belongs in a university, studying..."

"No... she belongs where she is. I correct that, she deserves worse!", Quinn found herself yelling, and slamming her fist down on her desk, something she never had to do since she came here.

"You have something against this girl", he accused. His firmness morphed into open anger.

"I have something against the things she's done. I would think a man of your "expertise" would see past that charade she's pulled on you." She was now beyond anger. She was taking things personal, allowing her hatred for the girl to cancel out her professionalism.

Silas shook his head in disgust. His estimation of Quinn had fallen, fallen into the abyss. He excused himself. By week's end he offered his resignation. Not so graciously, Quinn accepted.

It was two years since all this had begun.

Warden Quinn sat by the bay window of her suite, overlooking the town that Asylon had built. It was merely less of a shell of a failed mining operation. Later, it was a ghost planet; a dilapidated waystation for weary pilots and crews that were looking for cheap swill, and needed a cheaper cot to rest for the night. Two years later, there were five (two more than necessary) towering apartment buildings, several restaurants and even the afterhours strip blocks away. The ship depot remained, but only a few rogue privateers used it. For all intents, this had become IREL territory.

This was something to be proud of, only she wasn't. She was feeling morose, more so today than yesterday, and worse than the day before. Languid, she slumped onto the flamingo pink chaise longue chair, drifting off to sleep. It was peaceful rest, peaceful then turbulent. Crashing waves of fatigue came down upon her, drowning and merciless. And she didn't care....

Jeth was making his rounds when he saw her. In the library, reading. Hair was in a thick, single braid. Eyes down (green, weren't they?), scanning the pages. He stiffened. He never expected to see her again. But there she was. And here he was, with stains of muck on his uniform. He strengthened his resolve and walked over.

It felt weird. Not because she was a Duriyan, nor because she was, despite being here, a strikingly beautiful girl. It was the specter of Sartha. Her betrayal cut him deeply, reducing his heart to fragments. He vowed never again to allow a female within close proximity to him. They were dangerous, treacherous. Yet this *(was it her, really?)* girl had helped him, saved his life. And was harassed and maltreated for her trouble. At least he could offer a proper "Thank You".

A whiff of foulness made her turn her head, face scrunched in dismay. He saw her scowl, and started to turn back. Too late. She spotted him.

"Is that you toxifying the air?", she spoke unceremoniously. A flicker of recollection came over her. "It's you", she said. The grit in her voice didn't vanish; if anything, it seemed to blossom into full blown hostility. Her expression softened mildly, though.

Her face was fuller than he remembered, and certainly she wasn't as pleasant. *Does she blame me for how they treated her?* he wondered.

"How's your side doing?"

"Fine...uh, fine", he stammered. Then not knowing what else to do, he approached.

She gave no indication that this displeased her. She thought her comments about the odor would've been enough of a hint.

"I want... wanted to say to you "Thank You", for before."

She looked at him, then back to her page. "You said that before". *Just go the sluck away, for Duriy's sake!*

"Everything happened so quickly, I thought I'd ... lost my manners..." Feeling foolish, it was incredible that she made him so nervous. *I never get nervous around them... Never!!*

Raising her head, she replied "You did. I appreciate your offering from the fountain of gratitude. But really, I want to get back to my reading". Instantly, she was stung with guilt. *Why did I have to say it like that?!*

Though slighted by her abrupt manner, it was understandable. "I'm Jeth Akim."He formed a half smile, a tiny crescent of flesh beneath his nose that she found slightly disarming. Awkwardly warm despite her curt behavior.

Now feeling unduly harsh, she obliged him. "My name is Tahina. I'm from Duriy."

"I'm from Sefu Trius", he said, a little bit more relaxed. "What are you reading?"

"A variety of subjects", she said, to keep it brief.

"Like what?", he persisted. By now, he was intensely curious, his own reservations be damned.

Thinking he wouldn't understand, let alone know, she told him anyway. *No necessity in lying,* she thought. She told him "Interspatial Relativity by Gulec Withim".

"I know of him", he said, much to her surprise. "He comes from my world." Now he gained her interest.

"Indeed, he does", she replied, now wondering how much of his theories he actually knew. "You work in sanitation, I see."

"...Yes, I'm the custodian", he said. He was stumbling and he knew it. She knew it too, and wasn't throwing him a line to save himself, it seemed.

"I don't blame you for what happened", she said. That removed the boulder from his shoulders. She saw he was relieved.

"How they treated you was horrible. I thought Warden Quinn would've done something about it."

Her burst of laughter was abrupt, bitter, even anguished. He was taken aback. And yet, totally enthralled. So much so, he didn't see the C.E.O.s coming to collect Tahina.

"You've much to learn about this place, Jeth Akim, if you think anything good of Warden Quinn." As she was getting up, he turned slightly to notice two officers were waiting, a restraining jacket in hand. Dour, hardened looks on their faces obscured any of the feminine radiance and warmth a female should have, he thought. Watching them put the strait jacket on Tahina made him feel sick, yet he couldn't turn away.

"See you around", she told him, her tone of bitterness echoing in his ears.

"Yes, I will", he said quietly, watching them lead her away. That menacing scowl from the officer to her left was meant as a warning to him. *Too late,* he thought, as he resumed his duties.

Coffee.

The aroma of fresh brewed coffee flew under Quinn's round tipped nose. Circling, tickling. Slowly, aggravating her to begrudged consciousness. Inhaling the inviting vapors for almost fifteen seconds, it wasn't long before she realized she was still at home, and she had unexpected company.

Rapidly she jerked herself to a sitting position. Hurriedly she put a golden silk housecoat over her pajamas and cautiously, nervously stalked out.

"Who's in here?! ", she foolishly screamed. *A robber isn't going to tell you he's robbing you, dummy!* she scolded herself. Hastily she scanned the kitchen and spacious living room. Eggs. Some variety of sausage. Toast. The smell of breakfast led outdoors.

On her patio, there was someone. The slider blinds were partially open. All she saw were hard heeled shoes, legs crossed, and a hand reaching for half a slice of toast.

"By the suns, who's there?!", she yelled out.

No response. Just the person eating. Looking closer, a second cup was waiting.

Nothing was disturbed. The automatic alarm was on. This was no thief. But still.

A Madolani machete (a deco replica of a weapon from Mado 10) in hand, she stalked outwards. Amused, Anwari laughed. Wiping away a dribble of coffee, he put down the news tablet.

"The hell?!", she exploded. " The arrogance of you! How dare..."

"Your coffee's getting cold", he replied, as if she said nothing. He fixed a plate for himself. Hers was empty; it was the Chinese porcelain set she acquired six months prior. *The one meant solely for decorative purposes. He had to know that. It was placed on a framing shelf!*

Home dressed and barefoot, her feelings of violation could only be worsened if she were naked. What was more, that he could this, to her, without apparently fearing an ember of retaliation. He came into her life as he pleased, and the resentment it stoked wasn't even a flicker of an afterthought.

Taking a bite into a piece of raisin bread toast, Anwari remarked casually "Lovely view". From this vantage, Quinn had seen the outstretching tepid grey skies touch down on a depleted, biologically stagnated world so many times, she now took the bland scenery for granted. IREL's arrival had done little to change that; sadly, it lent a putrid, morose quality to the atmosphere of the ruined planet. However, Quinn forced herself to nod her head affirmatively. He wiped the crumbs from his fingers with a pink napkin cloth. Then downed his cup. It was minutes before he saw her staring at him with a mix of indignation, awe, and lurking beneath the surface, fear.

"Are you going to eat? The food is getting cold, and I put considerable effort into it. Well, not much, I confess", he said, growing annoyed.

Reluctantly, she sat, drinking the coffee. Old school hazelnut, her favorite. She ate. A meal that was standard breakfast fare, but ...it tasted good.

"Don't bother to dress. Turlak knows you're not coming in today."

She nearly slammed the frail porcelain down in anger. "What gives you the bloody right to enter my home and rearrange things to your liking?! Moreover......"

He gestured, as if swatting away a fly. She interpreted it as him dismissing her petty concerns. As she was meant to.

"There's a visit from Home Office right at this moment. An ailing Warden Quinn present would only hinder matters, don't you think? "

She shrank with disbelief, then felt utterly mortified. "Ailing?!", she now responded incredulously. "How the hell am I ailing? I'm fine, perfectly fine!"

"Then explain why you didn't respond to no less than six communique requests for over the past twelve hours. Would you like to, with members of the IREL Board of Directorship present?"

Her fork dropped in between eggs and half eaten sausage. Her face was now flush, barren of both blood and feeling.

"T- That can't be", she muttered, abruptly uncertain. Within herself, she could concede to feeling drained of late, but never to him.

"It is, let me assure you", he continued, far less affable. "Thankfully, I contacted your Ms. Roshin, wonderful woman by the way. And gave her the script."

"Yes, she is wonderful", she said, now incredibly leery of Anwari. "Well, thank you, I think." Reaching over, he fondled a glass carafe filled with orange juice. Tidbits of fleshy pulp swirled about, as he shook it. Feeble sunlight refracted from between his fingers, making a grotesque shadow. Quinn drew from the disfigured apparition an odd notion of symbolism. It was an old wives' tale that someone's shadow, and the form it took, was a reflection of the real, flesh and blood person.

"Take care not to spill any of that. The tablecloth's expensive", she mentioned as he poured two glasses full. A subtle attempt to take charge, of some aspect in this unexpected, unholy interaction.

He laughed, began drinking his orange juice. The seriousness in her tone amused him. She sensed this, and promptly resented him even more. To him, she was merely a tool to achieve his ends. For her, he was an enigma. An enigma that kept paces ahead of everyone else, including Mr. Bevel himself. Most obviously the Directorship. And still, she hadn't a *single clue* as to what his responsibilities truly entailed.

Sliding her the tablet, he simply said "Congratulations".

She skimmed the headline of *Galaxy Finance,* which in old school bold print read: "New Planet sized Asylons to begin construction."

She had scarcely a minute before he recalled her attention. "Asylon is a success. The first two will be complete in two months. You should be overflowing with pride."

Pride. Yeah....

"However, the article......"

"It's only stating information recently approved for public consumption. You should know this by now." The glass he set had just a little swig of juice left. Hers was still half full. She really did feel tired. But she didn't want to return to bed.

She couldn't help but wonder what sparked this impromptu intrusion.

"Was it because of Silas?", she asked.

"Silas who?", he replied absently. He retrieved the tablet, cautiously deleting the article.

"Dr. Miles Silas?! The man you forced me to hire, and then he quit in a fit of righteous indignation!" Anwari saw she was mocking the man, and he suppressed a chortle in response.

"Now I recall him."

"Good."

"He's back to teaching on the University level", Anwari said, just as absently. "It takes so little with his type."

She said nothing to this. Oddly, relief and revulsion blended within her.

"His resignation raised an eyebrow or three, but that's not even a tertiary reason why this delegation is here."

"So why are you here? " She was weary. Of him. Of the Directorship. And even the part she was playing in all this. Where she should've been proud of the accomplishment, its weight was an albatross about her neck.

"To see what works and what doesn't, Warden Quinn. We're here to see how to perfect the incarceration and leasing processes as things move forward. "

The unspoken implication in his words, his callous tone gave her the sudden image of a younger version of herself trapped in quicksand, without a branch or helping hand within reach. Feeling uneasy, she excused herself and went back to bed. Though he seemed amicable at their parting, and to her great shock, cleaned everything and locked up, the eeriness he left behind had not only lingered, she found it had bloomed into paranoia. *Who are you, Anwari, and just what do you want? What do you want, or even need from me?!* Those questions dominated many hours of unrestful sleep.

It had been two weeks since he last saw her. That was how it felt at any rate. Time (if you could call it such) at Asylon had no meaning, or rather, there was no need for the concept of time. In the conventional sense anyway. Days, hours, and minutes had no place here. Only weeks, months and God forbid, years. That was how time was marked in this place. You counted only the sunrises and sunsets, keeping a somber tally.

Going by that, Jeth judged it was two weeks since last seeing Tahina. It occurred to him, more than once, that she might've been, in the words of a guard, "leased out".

Deducing the disappearance of others to that fate, his blood slowly boiled. When he cleaned the library, he stole a few moments, doing five minutes of research. He was looking to learn just how "convict leasing" affected the legal rights of the inmates here. And those that were coming. There were no books available on human leasing, and the Holo-stream was disabled by order of Warden Quinn.

As he continued with his now daily duties, he was learning the ins and outs of the prison, what areas allowed him access, what and where was off limits. He bided his time. He determined that they would not be leasing him. Not for the immediate future, at least.

The Quiet Zone was now filled. Twenty- five separate units that held the worse of the worse. Male or female, gender was no consideration. It was whispered the ones held in quarantine from the general populace were either such rotten apples they had to be removed, or traitors to their own, kept in protective custody from reprisal.

Jeth didn't bother himself with fruitless gossip. With the mini incinerator unit hovering nearby, he began the disgusting task of removing the waste unit containers to be cleaned for daily use. It was almost comical to him that so advanced a technology was applied to so ancient a task. Breathing heavily, he began with cell number one...

Coming to the last cell, he heard someone singing. After the swearing, and almost being stabbed in the hand, it was a most pleasant relief. It was also bizarre, that someone in this divinely forsaken place would be singing. And very well at that. An octave leaped over the torrent of shower water.

Enamored, and not thinking, he placed himself at the hole where the urinal box went between dusty grey brick and said, "You sound wonderful".

"Thank...." ,the other voice went dead. The water abruptly stopped.

Confused, he began to respond. Her blowback response was ferocious.

"Get the hell away, you slucking pervert! ", Tahina was shrill, obviously reaching for some cover. Instantly, he recognized her, and went straight to making amends.

"I'm sorry!", Jeth apologized profusely. "I'm sorry, I didn't see anything!"

"I don't care!!, I'll....", her voice came to an suden halt. Quietly, she asked in hesitation, "Jeth?"

Realizing the change in her tone of voice, he answered quickly. "Yes, I-It's me", he said, hoping to confirm his good will.

She swallowed, then replied "It's me, Tahina." He heard the animosity leave her. It was a strange thing to her that she couldn't stay angry at Jeth, despite not knowing this boy for (counting the times they encountered each other) less than a total half an hour.

"I didn't mean to... interrupt you", he began, then stopped abruptly. To keep saying the same thing made him sound disingenuous.

"You never do", she mumbled, almost carelessly. "It's fine. Really", she half lied.

"Your voice was angelic."

"Thank you", she replied. She even smiled grimly. No one praised her shower voice before. Except for her family, she let no one hear it.

He slid further down, now just under the hole. Though no visible cameras, nor hidden surveillance were (to his sketchy knowledge) monitoring this area, Turlak or one of the guards assigned to this section could walk in on him, or spy from a distance. After that close call earlier, he was doubly careful.

"On your rounds, again?", she asked, the towel covering her. She had crouched down at the brick shaped hole. The need for human contact (that wasn't oppressive) had outweighed any embarrassment she was feeling.

"As always."

His incinerator's motor began sputtering; it needed constant activity to function properly.

Just minutes more, he thought, knowing that it wasn't to be.

"I don't wish you to get in trouble", she said, somehow divining the time limits imposed. The last thing either of them needed was to be harassed by the overseers. She remembered well what that witch said to him.

He was about to speak, when she cut him off, "We should... meet again", she said. With noticeable uncertainty.

He wanted desperately to reassure her. But in this place, reassurance was next to non-existent. Yet, he didn't want part from her feeling hopeless.

"We will", he said as the urinal box slid back into place. Though saying it wouldn't make it so.

She sat still for a few minutes more. The water tricked from neck to back, from shoulder to floor. She looked about her; everything was still grey. Depressing, inert and dehumanizing. Life, that moved and had thoughts and vibrancy was held back, kept hostage. Everyone held here were placed in inertia; a societal purgatory. And she viewed this with a grim awareness that she was becoming numb to it. Everything around her was designed that way. To make her complacent to her own suppression.

They do this to crush us, she realized, almost despondent. But she kept her resolve.

Jeth from Sefu Trius wasn't like anyone she'd met. Whether that was good, bad, or worse she didn't know. But he was reaching. For something or somebody. She was too. Only he was open to receive, and she was wary to accept. When she had done so before, she found herself on the losing end. Either through death or removal. Even Dr. Silas. She enjoyed their last session, and was secretly crushed that he resigned. Not surprisingly, she had felt Quinn had everything to do with his dismissal. *Told her something she didn't want to hear.* Back to this Jeth Akim. Next time, she would allow herself the freedom to open herself. That was the one freedom they hadn't taken from her. Next time, it there was a next time to be.

Time.

Two years fully. Two years since the Asylon Project took root. Technically, longer than that, but why expend energy on technicalities? Though Ednisa lay in bed, for a third consecutive day, she was there from the start. It could be rightly said this was her baby. While she turned over, body aching and stomach roiling, she reflected on how it almost failed to come to pass.

The day Mr. Bevel called her to his office two years ago, she was the head of Transport Management for The Kemit Sida Colony, which interlocked between Mournos and a newly established route of travel through the Inner worlds path. She was there as a "problem solver". The head, the previous head, saw her head roll when the financial irregularities were unable to be reconciled with her monthly and quarterly reports for the past twelve fiscal cycles. The resultant twenty year stretch in a financial penal colony (upscale criminals were put in upscale detention colonies) and permanent "blackmark" through her name was enough to warn any would be thief against stealing from Heram Bevel.

"The problem with crooks is they can't stop", an acquaintance told Quinn. "You get away with it once, and then twice. After the third time, well, you think you're invincible, you're too good to get caught. That's when, BOOOM! the cuffs are on you!" It was funny, now, coming from him. That very thing happened to him less than a month later.

When she was told to report to Mr. Bevel directly, she didn't know what to think.

The double doors parted. And Ednisa Quinn never felt as nervous, as awestruck, almost certainly as afraid as she was feeling when she came face to face with Heram Bevel. The doting, grandfatherly image. That's what drew you in. Heram Bevel looked like that elderly man that gave out candy, or sage advice to the great grandchildren or to young passers-by.

Especially those who loved to drink in the fountain of wisdom. That was the first impression you got. It was a disarming, trust inducing impression. His rivals, and bitter ex-employees would warn you, though, that it was a web. The web that trapped you, the fly. And then came the spider stalking hungrily from the middle...

She heard the stories. Even skimmed an unauthorized bio stream (which to this day has been banned from public viewing). Keeping that in mind, she knew to be on alert. As if that would help.

Among ornate brass, bronzed, golden figurines and holo-sculpture, below multi -jeweled chandeliers that belonged more in a regal palace than an uber wealthy CEO's office, Bevel, flanked by two others, awaited her. The first was his personal nursing attendant, a woman probably eighty- five years his junior and twenty years hers. The second was a lawyer; the tepid brown and black suit and blood red leather briefcase was the giveaway. That and cold, iron balls for eyes that stared at her intently.

His nurse, with a measuring instrument in her soft, smoothly dark hands, smiled, then excused herself through a side door. Quinn guessed she wouldn't be far, knowing what she did about the old man's ever dilapidating health. Hell, everyone in IREL and half the universe knew about the peaks and valleys. Some even whispered it was an act, to keep people off guard and sympathetic. Whatever the actual truth, IREL, and the Human Diaspora by extension, would only be free of this man's avaricious hold when the Grim Reaper finally grabbed hold of what was his.

"I'll get to it", Bevel began, without ceremony. At present, we have a new undertaking on the horizon, and I need a bright, energetic girl to handle it." His brusqueness was legendary.

"Girl" made her stiffen.

"I talk plain when need be, so take no offense", he continued casually. To that his lawyer bent slightly, pushing a button on the right side on his giant oak desk. From its center the green image of a small exoplanet pixelated before her.

"Ever hear of Evir, Miss Quinn?", the old man said, barely managing to suppress a nasty cough. Quinn's eyes went from his wrinkled, pained face to the entrance his private nurse would no doubt be entering from at the next coughing fit.

"Vaguely, sir", she replied, making sure that the right amount of deference was audible.

"A former mining colony, that went bust around about a century ago, give or take," the attorney added. Words seemed to slither from between his gleaming white teeth.

"Ninety -eight point five years ago", Mr. Bevel interjected, visibly annoyed. The amateur historian in him was speaking. Every year, month, and minute had to be perfectly accurate. *The body may be failing, but the mind remains sharper than an assassin's sword,* Quinn observed, relishing the old man eviscerate this Plutonian mud snake. Flush, the lawyer humbly accepted the rebuke. Then he continued "It currently sits as a barren way station for the few ships that travel from the Inner worlds to the Far worlds."

She simply said, weakly nodding, "This is true". She could add nothing of interest. That section of the galaxy, called Hell's Gateway was what separated, besides a semblance of governmental order, the Inner and Far worlds. There were very few populated planets. And those that were, save Evir, were mostly dens of pirates and other unseemly persons of definite ill repute.

"We've acquired the rights to Evir", the attorney said. "The buildings that remain as well as the planet itself. "

Expressing marvel at first, she then felt foolish. IREL was rich beyond comprehension, as Mr. Bevel's great power attested. A saying which some people said with somber conviction was that "As IREL and the Bevels go, so too goes the universe".

"It will be the beginning of a decades long project in the works", Bevel interrupted yet again. "We've renamed it Asylon. And it will house a youth detention facility".

For a brief, ear shattering moment, she thought she misheard, or misunderstood what had just been said. The words were so surreal, she thought she heard him wrong. But she was way too scared to ask for clarification.

"Are you still with us, Ms. Quinn?" The question snapped her back to attention. She was afraid to admit she didn't understand, but she couldn't go forward with no idea what he was talking about. *Better to be shamed a little than chastised greatly,* went a proverb from her home world.

"Mr. Bevel, sir, I... I'm not following you, sir."

"The planet is perfect for such an undertaking. Inhabitable, isolated, and nondescript. Plans will be forwarded to you via an encrypted data stream. "

Her head was swirling. *Enough of this cryptic talk!* "Sir, I'm trying, but I really don't follow the direction of this meeting anymore!", she said, highly frustrated. Instantly, she regretted it. *There goes whatever opportunity he was offering me,* she was thinking ruefully.

Both men stared at each other, then laughed heartily. She vacillated between feelings of timid relief and loathing their condescension. "Ms. Quinn, Bevel sputtered out, how could I make it more obvious that I'm offering the Warden's position to you?" His faint, dark smile twisted into a grimace as he started coughing uncontrollably.

His lawyer, wide eyed, began to summon his personal nurse, but the old man stopped him. "Comes and goes", Bevel replied, wiping away a trail of spittle."Comes and goes…" , his attention back on Quinn as if the coughing fit never occurred.

"I know nothing of Penal systems, sir", she said, feeling stymied by her inability to keep both feet out of her mouth.

"Nothing months of paid training won't alleviate", the attorney said. For once, Quinn warmed up to his presence. She still didn't even know his name, nor did he offer it.

But what of national sovereignty? she thought.

Bevel shook his head in disapproval, which alarmed her. *Had I finally blown it?*

"When you should be asking questions, you still your tongue!" His scolding made her feel like she was less than a five- year old.

"What… of National Sovereignty Laws, sir?", she sheepishly asked. It felt dangerous to have this man angry at you. She heard the stories. Even the mild ones brought about a cold sweat.

"Things are in the wind, Miss Quinn. In the wind there is something we call change. I ask, here and now, will you be a part of that change?"

Every fiber of her being was screaming. Screaming loudly and clearly, *NO.*

"Yes, sir. Yes, I will", was what came from her mouth.

She rolled over, remembering paperwork, on tablets, that she had to read and re-read, then sign. And then there were the months, the hours of study at various planetary penal institutions. And the various lectures on teen and criminal psychology. And the building permits, the mass hiring, the contract privateers who smelled of lust and liquor, those unruly hellions, Turlak and that green-eyed bitch... etc. etc.

She rolled around once again, feeling both pain and triumph. *This is how it feels to have a heart attack*, she thought, as total darkness in mid-morning consumed her.

Amid the turmoil Quinn's sudden health crisis brought about, Jeth met Tahina two more times. Once very briefly in the library, the second in, of all places, the courtyard. She'd been granted an hour on the outside, and she was staring up at the stars. By chance, Jeth had started later than usual; an incident in the boy's dorm put the area on lockdown status. The second suicide since he arrived here. On Sefu Trius, suicide was condemned as "The way of the coward." But since coming here, he found many of his beliefs challenged, if not outright overturned. When he saw her, the glumness that was Asylon temporarily left him. She had smiled at him this time! Inviting, and with no one around, he went over to her.

Her guard was in the left tower, spreading more prison gossip, as he strode across the sickly lawn. Even nighttime couldn't obscure the decay in the atmosphere. Seeing him approach, she greeted him warmly. She had a brightening smile. She just didn't do it often, he thought, before remembering where they were. That she could find anything here to be happy about was miraculous.

He returned a smirk, taking a seat next to her.

"Surprised to see you here, free", he said. *He has a bad tendency to blurt out his thoughts before fully considering what to say,* she thought. *But still, he's the nicest guy I've met since being dragged to hell.*

She lifted her shackled hands from her lap, the light chains rattling a whisper.

He grimaced, feeling the foul taste of boot sole embracing his tongue.

"My minder's in that tower, spreading lies", she said. "Out a little late, are you not?" He remembered how engaging she was last time at the library. Uplifted, even.

She's so proper in speech, he thought. He found this both fascinating and slightly frustrating concurrently.

"An... incident slowed my day", he said. He told her what happened.

She frowned, realizing how much being in solitary had shielded her from the everyday brutal realities this place inflicted on others.

"Nobody hurt you, did they?" she asked. For the second time, she showed open concern. He found it flattering.

He laughed, mostly to appease her. "No, I'm left to myself most times."

Even though he was Sefu Trian, and they were by and large despised, there were no attacks, aside from two mornings past. Even then, it was aimed at one person, not all of them collectively. A one on one skirmish over nothing, in the grand scheme of things.

"But then I ask the same of you?"

"What's that, Jeth? "

"You're out rather late yourself?"

At that she smiled bitterly. " Part of my therapy ", she remarked, making quotation marks, for sarcastic emphasis.

"I... I don't understand."

"They let me come out for an hour daily now, to let me somewhat readjust to life outside The Quiet Zone." She looked up again, holding back a sigh of defeat.

"They intend to release you?", he spoke hastily, yet again. But he was intensely curious. Despite himself, despite Sartha and what she had done, he felt himself drawn to this strange, proper speaking girl from Duriy.

She again turned to him. Her green eyes, even in the darkness of evening, were distinct and radiant. And they were holding an unfathomable sadness.

"What's wrong?", he asked, dreading what would come.

Her voice broke as she said the words, " I... heard them whispering when they came for me this afternoon. They...intend to lease me out". She was speaking from afar, as if this was happening to someone else.

His mind, his heart stopped working for that moment. "When?", he heard himself ask in horror.

"Soon", she whispered meekly into the night. She was near crying.

He said nothing. He felt bereft of word, almost of feeling. Without insisting, or asking, he took her hands into his hands. And clutched them as hard, yet as gently as humanly possible.

Chapter Six

*The sun here is so bright, so relaxing... so natural....so...
everything....*

Life and vibrancy emanated from the sixth floor. It almost made her forget the drudgery of her penthouse that overlooked the desolation of Asylon. *Almost.* Not enough to not appreciate the irony.

In her bed at Saru Sypher Medical, Ednisa Quinn rested. She was feeling so much better, save exhaustion. Hasty surgery left a long scar on her right side. A permanent defacing on an otherwise smooth mural, she bemoaned silently when she gazed on it.

Minutes. Only minutes more, and I would have died.

When the med staff came, she was told later, she was slumped over, half on the floor, half between the royal blue bedsheets she soiled irreparably. How they got in her penthouse apartment, she didn't know, nor did she care, after she woke up. She felt the gloved hands check her pulse, her heart rate, the pushing open of her eyelids. The hands that lifted her, not so gently (she considered filing a report about this, once she was able), onto a hovering gurney. She didn't recall being injected with a stabilizing sedative and taken off world.

The first responders took her non- stop from Asylon to the nearest Medical outpost. Then once more stabilized, she went first class to Saru Sypher.

She remembered being sedated a third time; that was the last semi -conscious memory she had. It was weeks later. They'd induced an artificial comatosis, and under a healing- tube, fed her a variety of nutritional supplements via intravenous tubes. The process regulated her body functions and a moisture bath (since she was naked in the tube) was administered twice daily. The healing light slowly repaired the damage. What it could repair, rather.

When she was deemed well enough, soothing, soft earth tinged illumination and plush red cushion of the healer's capsule gave way to the sterile white walls and a comfortable gurney bed of the exclusive suite IREL's insurance package was providing. The day her doctor finally met her, Ednisa Quinn had just finished breakfast. Sitting in bed, in a semi pleasant inertia.

A handsome man in all white, looked to be her age if not less than five years her junior. Her mind went somewhere it shouldn't have, given where she found herself. *Dammit, I have needs!* She thought in rebellion. *It's been so long...* She stopped herself, taking notice of the grave expression this man was wearing. And then the wedding ring on his long fingered, left hand.

As it had taken him all this time to finally introduce himself, Quinn deduced *something's seriously wrong with me, despite my recovery.* He started to speak, then stopped short.

"Just give it to me, Doc", she said, with such flippancy that her physician was left somewhat stunned. Going by his brief change in facial expression, that is.

So, he told her.

"Gyddis' Disease", the Doctor said, soft and compassionate, yet still somewhat robotic. Like he was forcing himself to really care.

Her expression changed greatly. It became grim, very stone like.

The silence that followed was a courtesy, for her to sink in the reality of her condition. In her case, though, this harsh reality was a fear long entertained. She had seen the deteriorations of a granddad, both grandmas, and a great aunt at the brutal hands of this horrible malignancy. It was a disease first discovered on her home world, and became a lingering, cruel reminder that interstellar space travel and colonization brought about new challenges, new biological enemies.

"It runs in my family", she said hoarsely. "Usually it afflicts the elderly."

"Usually", the man said, adjusting the neuro- monitor on his right wrist. "But unfortunately, the young can be stricken as well." He kept it matter of fact, and she appreciated there was no false show of sympathy.

She knew what she could expect. More heart attack like symptoms. Gradual decay of motor reaction. Loss of vital senses, hearing and smell most prominently, and the jaundicing of her beautiful skin hue and the embrittlement of bone structure. Incurable, and the victims of its ravages lived no more than a decade in continual anguish. Her eyes turned to the sundrenched outside.

"Being so young, as you are, there are ways to alleviate your maladies", the doctor told her, now attempting to be lukewarm compassionate at least.

"Yet still condemned, as there's no cure", she replied tersely.

"Not just yet. But we have, for a lack of a better word, hope..." He offered at least a sliver of encouragement.

When she turned to him, her expression was full of bitterness and fury. He almost thought she blamed *him* for her affliction.

"Which I don't have, or even the luxury of enjoying!" she vented. "I have the damned disease!"

She turned herself away, head violently shaking as she broke down.

He said nothing. What could words do for her?

"Everything was going great... and now...", she couldn't finish the thought.

"Do you wish to be alone?", he asked softly, though hardly more concerned than before.

"Yes. Yes, God yes!", she said. She hadn't even turned back to see his shadow, which only lingered less than five seconds more.

Calling Jeth restless these days was an understatement. As of two days ago, his work detail was suspended. All details were. Acting Warden Turlak (until Home Office designated an emergency successor) had limited all prisoner movement for the time being. So, he sat brooding in his cell, or the courtyard, even in the library. It didn't matter where he went, or what he did, he wouldn't be able to see Tahina.

Who herself was on the razor's edge; hadn't Quinn's illness only postponed the inevitable? She'd be sent off to who knew where, to slave away doing God knows what. She wasn't even allowed the "freedom" she had a week ago. Such as it was. Turlak had everything and everyone on lockdown.

One night, before he retired, he witnessed something strange. In a cell near his, he saw an aberration: A Duriyan, a Karuk and Sefu Trian in a circle, whispering low. He glanced, then walked quickly away, to not draw attention. He saw the glint of murderous fury in the Karuk's eyes.

A storm was rising.

Scarcely a week later, the work details were resumed, with no further explanation.

This worried Jeth, because did it mean the leasing resumed as well? He realized how much he thought of Tahina. He found himself amazed at how little he knew of her, and how much that really didn't matter to him.

Though it should, as he second guessed himself. How long did he know Sartha? For that matter, how well he *thought* he knew her? A nagging bitterness stabbed at him. Yet, despite that, the face of that green eyed, smoothly dark sheened Duriyan girl with a sharp tongue and even sharper vocabulary he found extremely hard to dispel in his mind. Besides the most important thing…… freedom. He was consumed with being free.

Breaking free from this place, this existence. And he wanted her with him. She was, he realized, the only one he could consider a friend. An actual friendship in this abyss. Perhaps one that wasn't meant to be, yet it was. His own countrymen ignored him. There were no heated words, no baleful glances thrown his way. Yet, he felt the chasm, even when standing next to them. He didn't know if they thought him a traitor, or stool pigeon (if that was the right term). As he saw it, he was from them, but no longer of them. They left him alone. A young man isolated from the remnants of a world he deeply loved, but knew, almost instinctively, he'd never see again.

Afterwards, he went about his rounds, more carefully than before. Turlak was watching him; and now he had to show the guards his ID, something he never had to do before. He went about his duties as usual, though never lingering more than he had to. And certainly not bringing attention to himself.

Having even a limited access to restricted areas of the prison made him see just how much of it was put to functional use. Most of it was the old caverns from the foundry days. The smoothed plates of metal he recognized, turned, as he walked further, into molded, dusty, damp brick and chemical ravaged puddles of water. The hardened bleaching on the floor and bricked wall bottom left its permanent marks.

It was becoming apparent how much care was thrown into this prison. He walked ahead further.

The aroma of waste and slime water was strong. Ignoring it, he took the chance he'd be discovered and kept exploring. Prowling forward, he noted the non- existence of anything resembling cobwebs, or even mutated vermin. A testimony to man's never-ending capacity to eradicate life, he mused grimly. He remembered when his optimism went beyond the surface level. So long ago, so many lifetimes ago, it seemed...

Growing bolder, more defiant with each step, he pressed himself forward.

By chance, he came to yet another old auxiliary tunnel, far out of the view of surveillance, human or digital. Only two other places were out of the surveillance periphery: the library (since it was hardly used), and The Quiet Zone, which was amazing. But then, maybe not. He'd seen what guys looked like when they returned from a stay there.

He explored it for a while, cursing himself for not discovering its existence before. It was off the far beaten path, for sure. Dank, and smelled of waste and rusted terribly. It may have been a sewage pipe at one time. A sliver of light flashed over the rust flaked lesions of decay. Against better judgement, he ran ahead......

Evening. He stood in the twilight of day.

The creamy, grey light of evening was descending on Asylon, and he was watching it. *From the outside!!*

A tsunami of emotion crashed down on him, as did reality.

Half scared, half rupturing with abrupt joy, he kept going into the evening's light...

He stopped at the edge, to catch a breath of decent (for Asylon) air, and recover from the overpowering, foul stench.

Beneath him ran a polluted creek of water. Long dirtied, with weak, anemic flora dead, or slumping on either side, in sparse pockets. The grass on the other side fared no better. A grim reminder of human progress. But its dark lesson he would ponder later.

When he was *free, truly free,* he would all the time in the universe for questions like this. But for now, he'd have to bide his time. His instincts, that voice of reason that guided him were in unison. Leaving right now would be disastrous. For himself and the others who would follow.

Tahina came to mind. He would escape with her, provided she remained at Asylon long enough.

After forcing himself to head back, he began making the plans. If only time and circumstance were his allies....

Her bruises ached, but the swelling would start going down by tomorrow. On a cushioned slab called a gurney bed, Tahina rolled over to her good side, the one where they hadn't kicked her. Her cheek was deep red, her bottom lip swollen. The green healing light only made her pain slightly less bearable.

Ten. It took ten of them.

Ten girls jumped her, attacked her without provocation. There was a reason it happened all right, but nothing she did provoked it. A new queen bee displacing the old. It was just the nature of things. But what hurt more than the cuts and bruises, was the knowledge that other Duriyans had joined in, against one of their "own". She laughed bitterly; she had no people here. She was alone.

They cuffed her to the bed. Too pained to move, the only actions available left to her was thinking. And remembering.

Thinking about how they left her in the courtyard. Sitting alone, hands cuffed as always.

The late afternoon sun was tepid as usual; always there, never breaking through the clouds. Too weak to make itself known. Was it scared?

So much fear in people's hearts. So much to fear. Her mind went back to the day she was captured. She eluded the authorities for almost two weeks. Ten days. She knew that eventually, they would get her. And at first, fear and luck guided her steps. But she grew weary of being afraid, and hungry. She hadn't eaten for four, going on five days. In her haste, she failed to grab a portion for herself. Everything went to her family.

Oh, how I miss you all. Even you, Mother.

They found her at a community hangout. An "arcade", it was called. She was playing an antique video game, keeping herself occupied. She was doing well, when first, one officer, then another came from behind. She saw the images of their red and yellow camouflage growing on the game screen as they drew near.

Her time had come. And she wasn't afraid. Without a protest, nor skirmish, they led her outside into a waiting paramilitary truck that was hovering over the narrow street...

The danger of now brought her back from the land of bitter nostalgia.

First footsteps. Then a gang of shadows grew behind her.

"Hejimma?", a raspy voice croaked to her left. Certainly not the way a Duriyan would pronounce a name.

The insult let her know what was coming. The C.E.O who was minding her was nowhere to be found.

She began to stand, only to be forced down from behind.

Thin, small chains that bound her rattled, the only other noise to be heard in the static afternoon.

Quickly, her eyes were racing around; not a damn goon in sight. Not that they would help her anyway. But still...

Tahina tensed herself. She knew what was coming.

"Freina", said the main girl, directly to her left. "And you..." It began with a violent jerk of her collar backwards.

Her doubled fists slammed against the girl's stomach. Reaching, the hyenas went to work.

There was little she could do, restrained as she was. But Tahina kicked, clawed and even hit someone with the chain before everything went black. The kicks and punches kept coming well after unconsciousness.

When she came to, she was naked, bloodied and roiling in pain.

The worst thing to happen to a person here, aside sexual assault, was done to her. Only her chains were left to her.

Some of her "own people" were the main ones to do it.

As her body turned, so too did her mind. The wounds in her mind cut deeper than the bruises and bumps. For the majority of her stay there she kept wondering *Have I a friend anywhere in this desolate, God forsaken galaxy?!*

Infirmary nurses on duty told her later, "You're fortunate the clean-up boy found you. You might've bled out in the dirt."

Despite her intense pain, she forced a weak smile, then cried a little. Not due to the anguish, but of gratitude.

Her therapy began a week after her glum diagnosis. Nanobiotic therapy, whereby nanites would be introduced on the cellular level, to keep the disease at bay. At present, it was the best cure they could prescribe, and the most expensive. Her pension and her 5001- K plan would have to cover the balance, after the co-pay. Pre - existing conditions were frowned upon when administering medical care, so patients were penalized for them. She found herself somewhat fortunate to be in a higher income bracket than most.

She began a rigorous regimen of exercise therapy and underwent radical dietary changes. Doing this would lessen the pains she would still have to suffer. Any remedy was better than none, Quinn reasoned. When it came down to it, Ednisa Quinn was a very practical, realistic woman.

Meat was out, beans and protein supplements were in. She reduced her coffee intake, increased drinking tea and inhaling vapor water. Above all else, she needed to reduce her stress level, particularly right now. No mention of work, nor would any contact be allowed for a month. That, she could find agreeable, and treated it as a long deserved vacation.

And for that first month she received no visitors, nor received any calls wishing good health, or a speedy recovery. Admittedly, that bothered her a little bit. If nothing else, at least Home Office could have sent a missive of flowers, or a holo- card message. She expected nothing from Turlak, who was probably making a mess of things. Or the C.E.O's. On her return...

Which was up in the air. She didn't even know when or even if they'd cleared her for RETOW (return to work) status. She wasn't sure if she even wanted to return.

At times. True, there was a freedom she could barely describe, but she clearly felt, in not slaving for others. Despite the current stress brought upon her by her medical condition, she appreciated the peace and tranquility she was enjoying. However, peace, freedom and tranquility came at a cost she could hardly afford to pay. So, she had to eventually go back to work, whenever that would be.

So until that time came, she worked on stabilizing her health. and catching up with the universe. She had so much to get abreast on. Not to mention enjoy the wondrous atmosphere and landscape. This planet was called the "Hawaii of Outer Space", and while she could barely recall any historical facts, she did understand the allegory in terms of paradise. The trees were lush and abundant, as was the wildlife. There were no marks of human encroachment except the marble white buildings of the hospital, and the palatial estates that outlined the seashores. An expensive place to live, without a doubt. While coalescing, she pondered moving here after retiring. But, for now, she wanted to watch some news.

She had to go two floors down for the Data Stream. Thankfully, it was an upgraded version of the gift she received at Mournos. She missed not having it by her. She hated to share. And for some unseemly reason the Facility disallowed patients to have it in their quarters. And she had to wait at least fifteen minutes after the last user. She found that intolerable. The period passed, and she immersed herself, the tingling feeling of pure data flowing inside and around her. Its sensation, familiar and calming. *How I miss this!*

"The third week of The Sefu Trian Civil War has seen more than three thousand dead. GCW officials are calling for a unilateral intervention...."

"The protests against the recent deaths of thirteen inmates leased to terra mining companies have brought to light the dark side of Convict Leasing and Labor...."

"Another Petition for the removal of Corporate Influence in Interstellar politics has been making its way to..."

"Coming soon, the Era of A Unified Digital Currency..."

"The Asylon Project: A beacon to the New Dark Ages. A rare OP-Ed piece by Jet Symmons coming up next.... Note, this is a pre-...."

She stepped off the platform, turning the stream off in disgust. The transition from its smooth plated surface to the gritty face of the tile was unpalatable, and she cursed Symmons accordingly.

More hit pieces, more pablum, she thought. Then she activated the stream again.

"This situation has given us a glimmer of the erosion of human rights", spoke Intergalactic Law Professor Renak Dulhe of Khem University. "These young men, and women, these children, lost their lives for a few loads of Tridium Zinc ore. Does this punishment fit the crime; I ask?" His voice quivered, as he strained to contain the outrage that distorted his otherwise dark, handsome features.

"I believe you compare the proverbial apple and orange", rebutted Mrs. Ruth Jenis, an attorney for Brannc Terra-miners. "Do my clients do their best to ensure the safety of all who don their uniform and hard suits? Yes, they do. Brannc has a track record of over a century to reflect that. Also, a criminal investigation is being launched into the activities of certain labor unions...."

When the faces of the victims flashed before her, Quinn shut the stream off in an anxious huff. They were the faces of the kids she'd leased out to Brannc. She rushed out of there, almost running back to her room. She was struggling with herself. Suddenly, a blanket of guilt, fashioned by self- revulsion and shame covered her.

What have I been party to? She thought, as she pulled the sheets over her and wept.

Tahina looked better. Except a few scars, the cuts were tiny, and fading away. The bruises were vanishing as well. Only the memories...

Her muscles were still sore, though. No broken bones, not even a cracked rib. It was an attempt to humiliate her than to really hurt her. Physically. And they largely succeeded.

Those Duriyan girls, whom she' d never seen, seared her with intense hatred. She didn't know them, never had a cross word with any. Yet, they knew she was Duriyan, and they beat her. More than the others, it was they who kicked and punched the hardest. And referred to her with the name of a slucking traitor, as they beat her. *They called me a damn traitor!!*

"The wound that stabs most, come from the hands most near", opined Dez Vulker, her planet's most famous poet.

She was so bitter. She almost renounced all ties with her home planet. *Almost.* She rested, resentment smoldering even while she slept.

Abruptly, a noise invaded.

The removal of the urinal roused her from sleep. She still had to lay on the left side for a few days more, perhaps a week. "Shark Face" Dr. Reit refused to give her any painkillers. "What doesn't kill us makes us stronger", he said, hovering over her. Despite his unsavory reputation, she forced herself to agree. She didn't trust the bastard any further than she could kick him. In the height of her agony, that's precisely what she wanted to do.

"Tahina!", Jeth whispered. "Tahina, can you hear me?" His voice was hoarse. He waited, looking around anxiously. It took a few moments. Then, he heard the noise of hard plastic soles scrape the floor, and as she slumped down to the other end, softly groaning.

"Jeth?", she asked, nearly whispering herself.

"Yes, are you well? Are you doing...better?"

"I am... Thank you", she sounded like she was on the verge of crying. In fact, a tear or two welled up. From gratitude that she had a friend nearby, or from fatigue, she couldn't make up her mind. Maybe it was a bittersweet combination of both.

You did the same for me, he thought, growing apprehensive. He had to make this visit short. The work details were, all the sudden, being timed. He was fortunate his discovery happened a day before the change. Turlak would've gladly removed him.

"Did they... Did you get into trouble?", she asked. She wanted to know something. She wanted to confirm a suspicion.

"No", he said, matter of fact. "Turlak never mentioned anything about it." Behind, the portable waste liquefier hovered unevenly. Its power was near empty.

After a brief silence, Tahina replied "That's good". Oddly, she sounded distant. Then she asked him "Have you heard anything about Quinn? "

"Nothing's been said", he told her. Feeling nervous, he looked around. There weren't any guards lurking about. "Tahina, I've found us a way out of here", he whispered into the hole.

Another bout of silence. He looked around again. Then he asked her "Did you hear me?"

"The pain... broke my concentration. Plus, all this whispering... did you say what I *thought* I heard you say?"

Just briefly, Jeth wondered how badly they hurt her. She didn't sound like the headstrong, abrasive girl he had come to know.

Speaking slightly louder, he repeated it.

At first, she was incredulous, then let the disbelief die within her.

"How....? When....?", she was full of questions now. And he gave her the short version.

After nearly five minutes, he laid out a plan of escape.

She listened. For the first time since they came to be friends, she wasn't the primary voice speaking. He never thought a person could talk so much, and for such lengthy durations.

"When will ....?" she abruptly stopped, realizing her excitement threatened to overtake her sense of logic.

"When the chance arises", he said, in a way that signaled he had to end the clandestine meeting. He'd been there too long.

Before he could put the urinal box back in place, "Jeth."

Looking in, he saw her fingers in the hole. He only managed to touch them with the tips of his own. But it was enough.

Seven weeks later Ednisa received her first, and only visitor. She was just coming back from another session of physical rehab, when she was equally dismayed and pleasantly alarmed at the presence of Anwari in her room. On the dresser was a wide bouquet of Tilmarian Roses (rainbow hued flowers with multi petals, women went nuts over them) and the largest fruit and nut basket she'd seen in some time. She fondly recalled sending some out herself, during her brief stint as consolation manager in the HR department on Mournos. Genuinely, she was awed by the gesture, even though the messenger repulsed her.

"From Home Office, I send their regards, Warden."

" Thank you ", she said appreciatively. There was a holo-message on the left side of the basket. She'd look at it later. From the plush chair he sat in, Anwari reclined. He was near the window, glancing outwards. The sun was still over the horizon, its rays glinting off the steel pier over the ice clear ocean water.

"Most certainly a far cry from Asylon, isn't it?" In his voice, there was a discernible cloud of edginess. It made Quinn realize this visit was strictly business. And he had to know of the injunctions her doctors laid down. The order of non contact was extended a month. Why was he here, then, apparently in direct violation of those edicts?

"That it is", she returned. Seated on the edge of her bed, she could see he was hardly relaxed. Whatever was plaguing him, it made her feel perversely good about his discomfort.

He sat, saying nothing.

"Why are you here?", she asked, suddenly aloof.

Anwari turned his head. His unimpressive face held a look of cold amusement.

"You wound me, Warden", he said, his head shaking in mock dismay. "Why wouldn't I visit a treasured colleague in her time of need?"

Then she laughed, shaking her head in disbelief. "You... You are beyond the pale, you know that?!"

"Come now, Warden. After all this time, you still hold petty grudges?" He began smirking, his smug, lightly brown face becoming a mask of condescension. As always. Whatever bothered him, for the moment, he shoved it aside to antagonize her. And she couldn't take it.

"I'm holding far more than that!", she began to scream. A nurse, walking the halls, popped her head in, scanning for the disturbance.

"We're fine, ma'am", Anwari assured her. "She just has some venting to do. Being the pal that I am, I've allowed myself to be her punching bag." He gave a doleful look that earned him pity.

Though somewhat confused, the pretty brown face smiled at him, gave Quinn a quick glare of disapproval, and turned out again, vanishing back into the hallway.

"See what holding animosity does? ", he scolded her.

"I..I don't believe you!", she spit in revulsion. She wanted to chase that nurse down, slap some sense into her empty head. "What brings you here?"

His earlier amusement left him, like steam rising into the ether. For a few moments, he sat in concentrated silence. It, the ominous quiet, unnerved Quinn.

"You .... haven't answered my question. And why are you dressed down?" She had taken notice that he wasn't wearing the traditional lawyer's attire. What she was used to seeing him in. He was wearing a leisurely cream one-suit.

"Even a man as busy as I require some down time, Warden." His response was meant to be disarming, but it failed. There was something he wasn't saying, something that he was struggling with. Some goal that required her assistance.

Despite her prognosis, despite the fact his very shadow was causing her to stress, it came to her how much she missed *this*. It was perverted to her just how much she really *missed* the high levels of stress. A bizarre badge of honor it was. To be able to handle it, even thrive under such pressure.

"Yet you're here, with me, instead of skysurfing, or enjoying the waters of Neptune. Why am I so blessed?"

He shook his head. "Your sarcasm needs work." Then rising out of his seat, he went to the window. She watched him, a slipper half dangling from her foot.

"The kids sent to Brannc, she said, changing the subject, what work are they doing these days? What will be done for them?"

When he faced her, she saw he anticipated the question. Good attorneys always expect hard questions. They relish them, in fact.

"That will be a matter for law enforcement, I've been told."

"Nothing more?", she was dumbfounded that that was the end of it? Did not IREL bear responsibility in this? Didn't she? She felt she did.

"Nothing more", he said flatly. "The GCW is investigating the matter thoroughly. Our hands were washed clean after Brannc acquired them."

She could only stare at him.

"Isn't there.... anything human about you? You only see these kids as cheap labor, and nothing.... "

"Spare the sermonizing, Warden", he spit, sounding War-den out contemptuously. "It's unbecoming, and rather hypocritical, given *your* position. And you do recall the Asylon liability clause spelled out specifically on every contract agreed upon, do you not?"

Inwardly, she groaned. She knew, intellectually and legally, he was right. But she still wouldn't accept defeat.

"Answer or don't answer, it makes no difference. However, I didn't come for petty arguments."

Finally, she thought.

His demeanor fully changed. Less the affable nuisance she was used to, however grudgingly. He was all business now, without pretense nor offering graciousness.

As he began pacing the room, she noticed his gait had become more precise... his aura grew darker, dangerous. She suddenly found herself extemely uncomfortable.

"Have you looked into your RETOW status?"

"No, I have not", she admitted, feeling like a guilty child with a hand in a cookie jar. Then, looking straight past him, she inquired about Asylon.

"That's why I came. It's unfortunate, truly unfortunate."

Intense dread came over her, filling her. She wanted to change the subject, but she wanted to know what happened. And he was going to tell her, despite what she would've wanted. What she wanted simply didn't matter.

"Then, just give it to me, Anwari", she said, defeat in her voice. She liked receiving bad news immediately. Preferably with coffee.

When he sat down again, she found his pensive glare disturbing. Almost rueful, in a malignant sort of way.

"There's been a riot."

RIOT?!?

"A riot?", she whispered in disbelief. She thought she was hearing wrong, but her hearing was just fine (for now. In twenty years though, that would be the first sense to leave her, as Gyddis got progressively worse). Her eyes widened with incomprehensible horror.

"I was...... elsewhere when I received the news. The urgency sent me here to collect you. The damage was very extensive, and quite a few lives were lost. Sixty- nine inmates, eighteen officers. And.... Dr. Reit and a few of his staff."

"My GOD!? ", she couldn't help but start crying. She felt her world collapsing like a star before her eyes, its brightness in death blinding and drowning her simultaneously.

"Turlak...", Anwari began.

"Oh God! Not Turlak and Ms. Roshin!", she almost screamed. Of course, she couldn't, nor would her outburst be allowed to finish. Though slightly despising that brutish man, she'd never wish death on him. Her reliance on him was like no other. And Ms. Roshin! That bittersweet, grandmotherly crone who subtly despised her. She couldn't begin to imagine what ......had happened.

"I've yet to receive any official death lists", he said in strict confidence. He was right next to her, though he seemed so afar. "However, I got word your second in command survived, though only barely."

That offered a tiny shard of relief. But not enough. The stress monitor attached to her wrist was, as she side glanced it, slowly turning deep maroon. Despite that, she asked, "What else?"

For a moment he glanced at her. As if it really needed to be spelled out, his look appeared to say.

"Asylon is effectively, and permanently closed. Surviving inmates are, or should have been taken off world. By the time I, rather we return to my vessel, the reports should be available." He spoke rapidly, distracted. Almost like he was losing his breath.

"How many remain on the job?", she asked. She felt stupid, but she also felt she needed to know who was left. *Left for What??!!? It's gone... everything I spent two fucking years working to build is dust and ashes billowing in the skies of Asylon.*

"As you can foresee, many have opted to quit. They've been given just compensation. And those who elected to remain, they'll be shifted elsewhere and rewarded very handsomely. And, as you undoubtedly know, good, reliable help is hard to find and is a forever needed commodity." She had to smile grimly at the truism.

"It takes so much to build, yet so little to destroy", she replied softly.

"An observation noted repeatedly throughout humanity's history. Yet never is the lesson heeded. So many sacrifices...", he began before catching himself.

But she caught it. *You have tremendous stake in all this, more than you want to let on. But I also have a lot riding on this, whatever's left.*

"So, you're here, and not there because you need me", she said, the stress she had wanted desperately to avoid now overtaking her. She needed a pill, or better yet a drink.

"Do you truly need an answer?!", he replied sharply. Too sharp to betray any empathy. For her, at least.

"I suppose not", she answered, just as sharp, with a flicker of defiance. He said nothing as he rose again, going back to that beautiful view.

Real questions, the hard questions, she saw, would have to wait. Turning her head to the outside, the pearly white sands, ice clear waters and the beauty of a forever tropical planet couldn't take away the storm clouds in her soul.

"You'll be cleared to leave in less than forty- eight hours. Think hard about your statements to the press, to families of the deceased, and most importantly, what your statement before the Directorship will be." Abruptly, he walked out.

He left her wide mouthed, staring after him. For once, she saw the slump of defeat in his shoulders, and the long wished for celebration was nowhere in view. She found herself wondering what was the point in seeing him deflated while she was falling off a cliff....

It was everywhere. The top news story for almost two weeks running. Even after the "piranhas", as a beleaguered GCW official called the Intergalactic Press (experiencing a newfound obligation to report real news) sought sensationalism elsewhere, the most flagrant exposure of human rights abuses never truly left the collective consciousness of the diaspora, until an incident even more unspeakable, more unfathomable rocked humanity at its fragile core.

What became known as The Asylon Massacre, or more popularly the Asylon Prison Uprising began as a normal day. Inmates were run through their normal paces, with those overseeing them abusing their authority over them. Clouds blocked out the sun, and the day felt a usual 67 degrees Fahrenheit (going by Earth Standard Measures and Temperature). The prison courtyard was full of surly, combative young men, and the girl's dorm was unusually dormant. In the Quiet Zone where over two dozen languished, Tahina sat on her cot, waiting for Jeth to check on her. Suddenly, a deep feeling, maybe intuition, came fleetingly. It was strange, this portent that had overtook her. But she knew from prior experience not to leave this omen unheeded.

Out of desperation she worked to brace the door, to jam it from the inside. She tossed aside the mattress, began working on the steel frame. The cot was heavy, but she took it apart as best she could. *Jam the damn door!* From the overturned frame she pulled out her secret project, a handmade shiv. By that frame she crouched nervously.

Something's about to...

No one could say how it started, or just exactly where. All anyone knew was that when that first lick was passed, a cauldron that had been simmering for months spilled over. Asylon became a warzone. Soon, the carnage raged from the cafeteria, to the courtyard, then to the tiers and the dorms.

It was so simultaneous, the officers on shift found themselves off guard, overwhelmed and grievously outnumbered. By the time an alarm resounded through the prison, everyone was fighting for their lives, their colleague's lives or trying to fend off their attackers. Shivs or broken wood punctured bodies, glass shards slit throats and the rampaging teens beat their way slowly but surely all over Asylon.

The beat. The beat. The fists beating on the steel and concrete walls, amid the chaos, the death, was a war cry. More than a cry, it was a rhythm. A rhythm growing stronger with each guard felled, their screams an opera of justice and agony. A melody of revenge sang as their assailants moved with lethal coordination and precision.

While the boys maimed and killed their oppressors, the girls exacted a far more vicious, humiliating course of retaliation. Of the female officers caught in the hurricane, many were beaten, stripped and tortured before the end came for them. One nasty C.E.O., named Willus was especially sought after, and though brutalized (she even had half her face sliced off), two other female guards managed to pull the bleeding, shrieking, naked woman to safety.

They attacked with tactical precision, and an efficiency that comes with military training. That the Sefu Trians were leading the charge, with the other two groups acting out their long- held fantasies of retribution, was a bitter, brutal betrayal to the few guards that came to trust them.

Only Turlak would've appreciated the deceptive ruse, if not for the fact he was fighting for his very life.

Not Duriyan, not Karuki, nor Sefu Trian. They were a united army of angry young men and women. Looking to destroy those who, for months, injured them, humiliated countrymen and fellow prisoners. Shipping them off, even driving a few to suicide. This was seizing the moment, the hour, to strike back and get justice, bloody ruthless justice.

First, they took the cafeteria, then the dorms and courtyard. Some headed for Quinn's office. As others began breaching the towers, the bloody tide began turning. The kids had the numbers, but they didn't have the weapons.

After the initial shock, Turlak had given the order "No bloody mercy!!". Not that he needed to, but his confirmation emboldened the bloodied and embattled under his command.

A vicious barrage of laser fire came from the left side towers, raining down into the courtyard, after which they also flooded that area with tear and stun gasses. As clusters of officers began to regroup, they began to attack with an equally brutal efficiency, and the pushback was merciless.

These were no longer unruly, violent kids in their eyes. The enemy was a numerous, mindless mass of murderers coming to take their lives. Any moral qualms, any guilt was thrown aside in the face of pure survival.

"Keep it coming!", a lieutenant told his rag tag squad of five. Harrowing screams of the wounded and dying echoed the courtyard. Corpses twisted and fell, some without arms or legs, others charred beyond recognition.

The infirmary was raided. The Doctor had his throat slit by a group of Karuks, as supplies were hauled off. When it was pointed out that his knowledge could be useful to help the wounded, the one slicing his neck replied, "The wicked man won't help the righteous. Off with his head! "

"Bloodthirsty animals!", a Sefu Trian murmured under breath, thoroughly disgusted at the waste of knowledge. He then ransacked the remaining supplies, demanding the few hostages they had taken from the medical staff to start treating their wounded. Fearfully they had to step over the bodies of their fallen comrades, to save the lives of their would be murderers.

Cafeteria tables were overturned, a fire started in the mess hall. A torrent of laser blasts created small embers, that bounced and danced on steel and flesh, growing until full fires raged. Those trapped in the eating hall were smoked out and beaten savagely. A few were burned alive or later succumbed to smoke inhalation.

Turlak rallied his troops; he wasn't one to shy from violence. He saw combat, and he knew how to keep his people focused. Against the onslaught, he managed to withstand those moments of chaos and confusion that would've overwhelmed Quinn, if she were here. The image of her collapsed and crying on the floor, in a fetal position begging for mercy danced around in his consciousness, as rapid, blurred crimson light flashed in front of him. Another punk down, screaming in agony. Through his comm badge, he issued counsel.

From the communications tower, the SOS Signal was issued. Desperately, it was hoped someone in Home Office would send help, while people still lived to utilize it.

Turlak was thinking of Custer.

His pistol fired into the surging crowd, he winced, snarling contemptuously. The shiv that came from behind went somewhere.... somewhere vital, or close enough, he knew. With a quick reach around, he grabbed his attacker by her hair and shot her face to smoking ash. Enraged, a male called the dead girl's name, and kamikaze style lunged at the wounded burly man. The laser tore through him, slicing him in half. But three more rushed him from behind and began stabbing.

He let out a howling, monstrous laugh, which stunned his assailants. Shocked, but more so angered, they intensified their assault.

The big man took a while to fall, but fall he did...

Amid the death and madness, the power had been disabled. The whole prison became pitch black, save glints of flames and firelight.

The choking stench and soot of inferno thickened in the hallways and dorms. Screams of terror, cries for survival and curses of damnation echoed, an unholy chorus resounding through the halls and dorms of the burning Asylon Prison project.

This was a scene Jeth Akim knew all too well. In as many months, fire, death and conflict had made an indelible mark on his life. Worse than being scarred, he found, to his resigned horror, he was being shaped. Molded to withstand a lifetime of witnessing the worse humanity had to offer.

When everything kicked off, he was off doing his rounds. The violence was taking place in the main areas, the areas where everyone knew to congregate and wage war. He found himself in one of the sublevels, creeping quietly. For a time, flashbacks of Trunza Square held him in paralysis. Near fetal, on the verge of tears. But he started to remember himself, regaining his nerve. Now was the time. He began to trek through the madness en route to the Quiet Zone.

"Jeth!", he heard from behind.

The voice sounded familiar, almost friendly, but he took off. Remembering Sartha, he made sure to duck and dodge. He was less than a shadow in the fire's fading light. It was a guard, someone who knew him but was too preoccupied to chase after him.

The reinforcements had arrived, though far too little, and way too late for some. The few that did report, found themselves in a warzone. Almost immediately, they were attacked. But fresh, eager, and most importantly, berserk with anger, they were more than enough for their bloodied and weary attackers. Added fire power and superior military tactics proved to be the equalizer to the swarming, overwhelming numbers of the enemy.

Roughly almost an hour after the reinforcements arrived, The Asylon Massacre had run its bloody course. Its aftermath was just beginning, and none would come away unscathed.

Jeth took every route he could to evade the melee. He was truly blessed to have been given the lay of the land. He knew every inch of the prison. What areas to go to and where to avoid.

Even this far distant, he was disquieted by the abrupt ceasefire. It wasn't hard to guess who had won. His heart sank, but his feet kept moving. Another lesson Sartha taught him.

The darkness was complete, and eerie. Not to mention deadly. He moved in lurches, not with the usual brisk stride. A misstep could end with him being stabbed, or shot from behind.

He wondered, somewhat bitterly, why no one sought him out in the planning of this...maelstrom. Perhaps they felt him too close to the guards, and thus thought him a stoolie. Just the thought of such made him laugh bitterly in the blinding black. He reached in his left pouch pocket, getting the penlight in hand. Cautiously, he began to proceed down a level.

He would flick it on and off, ensuring he didn't attract any undue attention.

When he reached the Quiet Zone, he saw all the empty cells. Fear gripped him as he made his way to Tahina's cell. Against his best judgement, he flicked on the light.

Its feeble light illuminated the fruit of this wretched existence; in one cell, the body of an C.E.O. hung from the light fixture, uniform stained red, the blood long ceasing to drip. In another was the sprawled body of the Karuk who stabbed him months before. Any ill will Jeth had vanished, and he muttered a brief prayer for the deceased.

Sobered, yet unshaken, he made it to her cell.

Unexpectedly, and at the worst time possible, panic gripped him.

Is she still here? Is she still alive?! He thought wildly. *She must be!*

He calmed himself, taking the handle on the door.

He tested it. It held tight.

With urgency, he banged on her cell door. He struggled to remove the urinal, looking wildly about. Snatching it out of place, waste spilling on the floor, he yelled into the opening.

"Tahina!!"

It relieved him to hear sounds of movement inside. The door almost smashed into his face as she swung it open.

"JETH!!!", she hugged him as hard as she was able, her body heaving. He felt soft tears kiss his neck. He held her just as hard. "Come on, we need to leave!" He took her by the hand. But she stood still.

"W-What in the suns is happening!?", she said, hardly above a whisper. She was truly afraid, her green eyes wide, as she groped for understanding in the feeble light.

"War, he said grimly. There...was a war. We.... We need to go. Now."

He walked a step ahead, waiting for her to catch up.

"Who.... who won?", she asked, taking a stride behind him.

He replied, "No one." Then stood until she was by his side.

She was scared, he knew that. He was too. But this was it. Now.... or never.

He took her by the hand. A weak, thin finger of light guided them.

He led them through what remained of the chaos, stepping over the slumped and smoldering dead, while a mute chorus of rage and death still echoed around them.

Chapter Seven

The tall, green crystalline mug slid without effort down the long, uneven bar. Its recipient narrowly missed it.

"That's good Tumaryan Ale! Six Circos a bottle!", yelled Lubby, the barkeep, owner and proprietor of Lubby Lar's Tavern and Smokehouse, est. 2663 A.D. (he arranged to have it all squeezed on a flapping forest green awning that was dry rotting outside).

The space trucker just waved a gloved hand, stirred in the hard seat at the end, and drank. Deep green spirits filling his insides, beginning their enchantment.

Lubby's watering hole was the haunt of lone haulers coming through looking for booze and a place to crash from time to time. At best, no more than five souls at a time would set foot in the place. Until the officers came. Some nights, there was hardly an empty seat to be had. This past year was the best he experienced in eons.

Yet, he subtly despised the newcomers. It was something about them; their line of business had rubbed him the wrong way. Now the ruddy, round man with a permanent smile, or smirk, never turned away a paying customer, and he thrilled at the full houses and all his cherry wood chairs being filled. But he didn't have to like it.

As he was serving a customer, the double doors came alive.

"Geon, you old, red spotted hyena! How have ya been?!", the fat man exclaimed.

The man's name was Geoniphus Thu, a long-distance hauler who went from one side of the galaxy to the other. If the rate was reasonable, so was he.

"Went to Gellyn Three", he said wearily, taking a seat in the middle of the bar. His plaid checkered shirt had deep red stains on the sleeves, and his carbon wired cargo pants painted the same. The aroma of Fly whale blubber followed him, making heads turn. He turned his greying head, if someone wanted to address the issue, but everyone turned away. He was getting older, growing more irascible and quick tempered with time.

He didn't go about the universe looking for trouble, but when trouble reared its ugly face, he didn't go and hide.

"New Crowd, I see", he said with a dry rasp. Lubby clasped his extended right hand.

"Guards from the new youth prison, Lubby said nonchalantly. Well, new since you were here last. Now, about Gellyn Three? "

Fan blades began to rotor, dispelling the noxious aroma. A woman guard in the far right corner sighed in relief. Made a rude comment.

As it came within earshot, Geon announced to her and the room, "Darling, they say what you got down there smells way worse, like a plasma waste factory."

Either due to shock, or for lack of a quick comeback, the woman glared angrily and then went back to her drink.

Geon turned his attention to his snickering friend.

"Lemme tell you... I've been across this galaxy more times than I can count. My and my Baby have seen over billions upon billions of miles. Hundreds of light years. I've yet to see one reasonable, half bright, non- conniving Gellyn woman yet..."

His tale involved the transfer of the Gellyn damsel, her belongings, and over three metric tons of liquid blubber (she owns a cosmetic business) from Gellyn Three to New Star colony. The woman had nothing packed, organized or ready. So, he had to pack, then load everything, including the fat that he stored in five thirteen ft, cylindrical containment units. Then had to use Quantum Run, to make up for the travel time. Running behind schedule was bad enough. To make matters worse, the woman, for the extra services rendered, had a unique way of payment, rather than the money agreed upon. Geon, well past his limits in both patience and time, taught her a lesson she would never forget.

"All that fucking whale fat went flying and splashing down like a torrent of rain", Geon said, downing his brew. I can still hear her cursing me in that mumbling gibberish." He laughed maniacally. "Poor is the man who cannot, at times, laugh at his own misfortune", someone once philosophized.

Over Lubby's boisterous uproar, he said "That landing dock was a slip and slide the last I saw on the viewscreen. She had to clean up every bit of whale blubber."

Lubby, still laughing, asked him "Won't that hurt your business? A negative referral..."

"Dames like that don't give referrals, nor pass out Likeskype discs. Just users... Take what they want, and renege when it's time to pay. Well, I didn't get the money, but seeing her curse at the heavens while she flopped about in that pink and grey goop gave me what I needed for a long time-a good, hearty laugh."

Shaking his head, Lubby continued to laugh wildly. That was one thing about Geon. He didn't come through this part of the galaxy much, especially with the way business slowed down in recent years. But, when he did! Man, did he always have a story to tell!

One of the many hallmarks of a good, dear friend.

Geon had a seat on the opposite end of the bar, where the other patrons (the few that were there for the moment) would ignore him. His eyes were deep brown and exhausted. His hands were like gnarled leather. At sixty- three, the gaunt, greying figure was becoming a too familiar sight in the mirror. Not welcome, mind you. Just familiar.

"So, he asked, after fully downing his mug, how's business? "

"Good", Lubby said, sliding down another drink, this time Karukian Cider Beer. "Good, but not great."

Geon shot him a quizzical look. "Seems like the stormtroopers would be good patrons".

Lubby moved in closer, to confide something. "They are", he whispered. "I just don't like them."

He'd only been in the bar for just a little over ten minutes, yet Geon came to that same conclusion.

"My ship is at the Docking Centrix, drying out. Got a cot?"

Lubby laughed again, somehow deeper and harder than before. "Do I have a cot? I always have a cot!", he said jovially. Lubby had four to five empty rooms he rented out for a night. Small, little more than closet spaces with a sink and urinal.

Thirty circos a night. They weren't the best, with weak springs and torn sides, but they and the rooms were relatively clean. No one ever complained about bed bugs.

Pulling out a zero shaped, golden disc from a pants pocket, he put it in Lubby's wide left palm. "For the room, and the drinks." He took the bottle of Glens Dayle's scotch and went upstairs.

"Geon, what about your ship?"

Not bothering to turn his head, he replied with deep skepticism "The way that blubber stinks, nobody's going near my baby. Besides, I got the ignitor key!"

It was hours later.

A loud commotion brought Thu back to consciousness. Which he didn't appreciate, since he was having a nice dream, or given Glens Dayle's scotch's side effects, a great series of hallucinations.

Whatever he was experiencing, he was stumbling down the hard wood steps, shirt open, as the orange stair lights glistened on the white hairs of his chest. Purplish blobs, gold spots appeared before him. He put up his right hand to shield red cracked eyes.

Eyes and faces turned, suddenly glaring at him. He felt them, and he grew belligerent. There was a foul aroma in the air. The stink of something burning, or having been burned, assailed his still impeccable sense of smell.

"Tha hell...? Is something.... burning?", he began, still inebriated.

"You're imagining things. Geon, go back upstairs", Lubby said quickly, hurrying over to him.

"Why you sound worried?", Geon divined. The sullen quiet grabbed at him. Something was wrong. No one was speaking, but they didn't have to. Even half senseless, he could pick up the ill vibes.

"Just go back", his friend said, more insistently. The last thing he needed was a scene.

There were four officers in the tavern, staring at Geon. One of them on the verge of tears, another one had long passed that threshold of restraint. The rest stared soundlessly at the screen on the wall, as if in a morbid trance.

"What you...."

Lubby had all but tossed him up the stairs.

Those eight eyes went back from him to whatever was keeping them hostage emotionally. In all the years Geon had come through, it was rare that Lubby had that wall length holo-vision screen on longer than an hour at a time. He kept it going on all day on that terrible day.

In his sleep, Geon could hear the sounds of medic sirens singing nearby and above. In the air, the tremor of turbulence that signaled deep space, VTOL transport vehicles made sleep difficult.

Angry, he went to his door, and found it locked.

Disgruntled, he cursed at the doors and whoever else came to mind as he lay back down, and finally forced himself back to sleep.

"How much longer?!" Tahina whined.

"Shhh!... The sirens are still... they've stopped", Jeth said, sighing relief.

They were at the lip of the sewer tunnel. They had been there for hours, he estimated. They may stay there for hours more. That alone was a trying prospect to his nerves. But he had to deal with her also. Which was worse, because while he, at least could restrain himself, discipline himself, he had no such control over her. Not to the point where she couldn't mess things up.

He realized he was being unfair. Stepping over dead bodies, throwing up at the sight and stench of charred flesh and burned bone; of nearly getting caught would make anybody irritated and nervous. The aroma was toxic, and twice she almost vomited. Again.

Almost petulantly, she whispered, "Can we leave here now?"

He turned to her. "Give it a few more minutes. Please." He knew the smell was overpowering, but one wrong move could destroy everything.

Taking a chance, he craned his neck outwards. The skies were still bland grey, clouds of still billowing black smoke reaching, spreading into the horizon. In the air, the sound of a transporter rising into the heavens echoed, the wind generated by the takeoff blew dirt and debris around. Narrowly, he avoided being blinded by the dust cloud that flew into the tunnel pipe.

Bathed in the dirt, they both coughed. A few minutes after, Jeth went back to the tunnel's mouth.

What he was really checking for was if anyone, a guard, inmate or anyone else could see them, and what's more, identify them. Where they were standing, they could trust no one. But each other.

There were no lingering shadows, no loud noises nearby. No low voices or whispers. He turned to see her half hidden in the musky shadows. Her face was a half crescent, partly hidden by ill formed darkness. Sweat, or nervous tears streaked her left cheek. But her eyes were sparkling, the green of her irises nearly distracting. He noticed the strength in her eyes, the struggle to overcome her fear, her deep uncertainty.

Gently nudging her back, he crept slowly into the shadows. The light of evening was still dawning. And the chance was too great, they'd be caught if they moved right now. So, after much coaxing, he convinced her. They would wait a few more hours.

It was now a pitch black, dark night, and not a soul remained in the ruins of Asylon. The last of the medical transporters left the planet hours ago.

But, just to make sure, he went out fully, despite her look of protest.

After he was sure, he climbed onto the riverbank, and taking her hand, helped her up.

FREE!

"Turn your head", she whispered abruptly.

Not the words he expected from her. "Umm... I don't see..."

"I have to go!", she whispered, with her left foot tapping on the hardened dirt of the riverbank. It smushed the mud, making a deep imprint.

"Ohhh". he realized, feeling foolish. *Privacy in plain sight. How does THAT work?*

The unbuttoning was the fastest he'd ever heard. He heard her climb back down. A sigh of relief as she released the stream. Liquid thudding loudly on the packed, still damp mud.

"Keep your head turned", she said.

He shook his head impatiently. The anxiety was getting to him. *If we should get caught...*

While he was in mid thought, she was done.

Almost playfully she hooked her arm with his, and nearly yanked him forward.

"Hey!"

She held a grim smile, but there was nothing to laugh about.

On the faded grass of the riverbank, they could see faint traces of billowing smoke above the towers.

From its outside, Asylon looked just as dreary, as foreboding and oppressive it as did on the inside.

The Outside! They were free!

Taking a step into the night, they hugged and cried softly in each other's arms.

They were free of Asylon, and its daily horrors. It's physical traumas. What they experienced, what they saw and suffered, would remain within them for a lifetime.

But that was for another time, when they were off this wretched world. They needed to get as far from this ("Satan's playground", Tahina called it) horrid world as quick as possible.

"So, you have any ideas?" Jeth asked her. He was spent, physically and mentally.

Looking ahead at the small town, and full of Duriyan confidence, Tahina said, "It's simple. We'll just follow the light".

By the time Geon was fully awake, and mostly sober, nighttime had descended upon Asylon.

He never slept this hard on his ship. Geon's Baby wasn't built for comfort, in many respects. Besides, sleeping while careening in deep space, even on auto guide, was begging for disaster.

He splashed lukewarm water on his face and gargled one last swig of scotch. He still looked red eyed, even more than usual. How many times would he swear himself away from the temptation of the spirits, only to be seduced by their siren call, yet again?

His boots thudded on the loose plank boards, and he entered a crowded room with all eyes glued on the holo-screen. He craned his head, as two women officers scooted by, giving off strange looks.

"Wenches", he mumbled under breath.

"Still, no official word on the latest mining revolt on Belek Nine Outpost, but sources indicate...."

"This galaxy has gone mad!", Geon declared. Heads turned his way.

The volume went up twelve decibels in response.

"Breaking news... I repeat, Breaking news..."

The whole bar was graveyard silent. Lubby took Geon by the shoulder, gently sat him down at the other end of the bar. Where he kept a weapon, should he have to use it. *Lord knows I don't want to hurt anyone, especially on a night like this. But I won't allow any hell raising in my bar.*

For Geon, it was strange to see a packed house, but in the wake of the day's earlier events, there were so many people who wanted, needed really, to drown their sorrows away in drink. Or at least numb themselves temporarily to the horror they just suffered through. Behind the long counter, on a line of red wood shelves Lubby had nearly every scotch, rum, wine and beer from over thirty worlds. Kegs full of standard, old school Earth beer. For the first time in memory, a fourth of his impressive inventory was empty.

"The casualties are still unknown at this time. Neither Asylon nor IREL officials have made any statements to the press. GCW representatives have just made the following declaration: "We don't know, at this time, what started the riot, nor do we have all the facts to proclaim other than our deepest regret at the loss of life...."

Amid a furious chorus of booing and jeering the stream went abruptly offline.

Afterwards, there were no more protests, only somber quiet.

A group of five guards walked out, one scrawny young woman was being led out, with head in her hands, openly sobbing. Soot and tiny burn marks (laser fire often spit tiny sparks that singed the clothing of the one firing it) ruining her trousers.

Another officer walked to the bar, to pay the tab for the group.

"On the house", Lubby said.

"We lost good people today, a lot of good friends", the man replied sadly, nodding his thanks gratefully as he headed out the double doors.

"W-What happened?", Geon stammered, a little more lucid now. His head was slumping downwards. Headache throbbing hard, his stomach churning. A definite hangover.

"The gates of hell opened, and the demons flew out and snatched as many a soul as they could carry." Again, Lubby led his friend back upstairs, again fearful the scene might turn ugly.

"A winding landscape of confusion", she called it. "A labyrinth formed of concrete and shoddily erected structures."

The streets of Asylon were a maze. They twisted, contorted into a never-ending knot of poorly paved roads and crooked, curved back alleys that led back to step one. Behind a dark corner, Jeth and Tahina huddled in the shadows. They'd found a culvert behind a trash disposal. The generator next to it was an unexpected, but welcome source of warmth. Afterhours, the air was unusually chilly. The shelter it provided made up for the incredible stink. It reeked from weeks of filth sitting there, growing both in size and bacteria. Tahina feared something crawling on her until she remembered this place had no native, nor imported animal life. Save humans.

"What time do you think it is?" He asked. His understanding of time on this planet was never that advanced. And outside of Asylon's confines, he was truly lost in terms of hours and minutes.

She sighed slowly, hazarding a guess. "I'd assume past midnight, give or take an hour." She started to say something else, but she hesitated. Looking up past the lids of the disposal, into the darkness, she unsteadily spoke, her voice quivering.

"Jeth, if we do get caught...."

"We won't", he said confidently. More for himself than for her.

"Well, if we *do,* she continued, with annoyed persistence, I want to thank you anyway."

He shot her an derisive look.

"Thanks for the fleeting minutes of liberty we've, I've been able to enjoy." Even in the weak glare of dim lights, he could see no expression. But her words radiated with a morbid gratitude.

He didn't say anything to that. He didn't know what to say. He stepped out into the alley.

He scanned the skies of the afterhours. There were no detection beams nor the three men team of night snakes that stalked the cities of Sefu Trius on nights like this, hunting down dissidents. Here, they were so careless, so arrogant... so damn foolish. And that was a good thing, wasn't it?

He felt her grip. She was standing up, now beside him. She was a paradox. She made him feel both uncomfortable and capable in the same moment.

"What do you see?", she whispered, her hot breath made his neck hair stand up.

"No search parties", he said with cautious doubt. "I don't think they're looking for us."

"Not now", she added. "Not right now, but they will. They did on my... world."

He took notice of the distance inflected in her voice regarding her home planet.

"What happened?" he asked.

She told him briefly of the riots, the looting and the clashes with the Domestic Army. How she and many others were rounded up in the days and weeks afterward. He thought about how those eyes, green as emeralds, reflected in the moonlight, reflected the deep anger and sorrow her words didn't.

Abruptly, he asked, "Why are your eyes so green?"

His inquiry threw her off, and she laughed. Her laughter was brittle and clipped.

"It's due to genetics and slight alteration of DNA. Adjustment to a different biosphere", she added. In a way, she found it flattering.

"On my world your eyes would be considered the eyes of a Sultress", he said, almost warily. He didn't want to insult her. On his world, differing coloration in eye color was held in superstitious regards. The more exotic in color, the more malevolent in spirit was its possessor.

Again, she laughed.

"Are you equating me to a siren? The mythical one, I meant."

"No", he answered, a bit perturbed. *Does she think I'm an ignorant plows man?* "I'm only saying your eyes ...lure people in. It's not meant to insult you."

Taking it as a half- baked, good intentioned compliment, she said "May I return to telling my story?" He nodded, looking about for passersby. And others.

So, she continued. And told him about her mother, and her betrayal.

Jeth shook his head, disbelieving. That a mother would turn on her child. He had never seen addiction, nor how the need of a high trumped all else. Even offspring.

When she was finished, he half expected her to break down; at least stifle a sob. But, as her eyes peered down the black alleyway, she said, "Your turn."

He told her about his family, about how there used to be a sense of togetherness among his folk, and how people used to look after one another. Then came Hagit. Then Trunza Square. Then Sartha.

"I've forgiven her", he said sullenly. He knew how weak his words sounded.

"Have you?", asked Tahina, picking up on the lack of resolve his voice carried.

"Yes, he said, and I don't know if it's humanly possible, but I would hope you'll learn to know that you have to forgive your mother at some point."

"Never!", she said, almost yelling. "That's a thing you can't forgive!", her face now a mask of burning anger. This side of her had always lurked beneath the surface, he knew.

The look he gave her was an indication to quiet down.

"If I can forgive......", he began.

"It's not the same! She wasn't your blood", she pointed out.

"True enough, but all the same, it's not healthy."

"I'll handle my hurt in my own way, if you don't mind." Her tone made it clear this conversation was over.

That Duriyan stubbornness.

"Very well", he said, becoming abruptly impassive. "Any ideas how to get to the Docking Centrix?"

A docking centrix was an essential to interstellar travel, particularly to worlds where an orbital space station was an impracticality. It was, usually, a terminal where spacecraft arrived and departed in the planet's atmosphere. Some were simple platforms suspended at high altitudes by strict gravity controls. Others, like the moribund steel tree on Asylon, were tethered to the planet, in a far off, designated, secluded area from the majority of the populace. Normally, it was the largest man- made structure on a world. Until the full realization of the Star Stair.

She thought about it. Ships still came and went from Asylon, they both knew. In an alarmingly rash move, she stepped out of the alley, into the open street.

Beside himself, he wanted desperately to snatch her back into the darkness. "What in the suns are you doing?! You want us to get captured?!"

She turned, giving him a *Be quiet* glare. Stepping further into the low- lit streets, she exhaled freely. It was a soul soothing thing to do, after the hellish year she was having thus far. She could breathe.

Not a soul in view.

Jeth was now at her side, wanting to speak, or yell. But he simply stood, perhaps enjoying the elation that he could, without being coerced to move along. But he was worried.

Too cautious, she thought. Caution was like a cloak. Worn when necessary, and thrown on the side of the sofa when it wasn't. She stepped out further, drawing him onto the street.

They walked down a little further, ducking in and out of the narrow alleyways. She remarked how slim the streets were, in comparison to her home world.

"This place was probably never meant to be more than a miner's world", he told her.

A few blocks further, they came to a complete stop.

In the distance, to the far right of them the metallic monolith stood, supported by interlocking columns that twisted downwards. At several points, lights flashed and flared, stabbing through the midnight black. A barren, metal tree with few fruits, a testament to the planet's withered existence.

With that know it all smirk he'd come to know (much to his chagrin), she asked him, "How far do you think we need to walk?"

Sighing, he took the lead.

By the time Geon awakened, it was almost dawn. He slept hard and long. The satisfaction from a deep sleep, even on a bed like this, he had long forgotten. The last time he'd slept on a new one was before his divorce.

He thought of his ex -wife as little as possible; he could barely remember her face let alone her name sometimes. His daughter though, was another matter. Over the years since that bitter parting, he'd sent gifts, cards, even attended her graduation incognito. No response was ever reciprocated. So, he let her, and her son, be.

A man can reach out for so long, until he's tired of pulling back nothing.

His hangover had mostly vanished. *I'll be fine by the time I leave orbit*, he thought as he refreshed himself. Quick shower, light breakfast... he second guessed Lubby's cuisine. Back on the ship... *what do I have that's still edible, besides the leftovers?*

Vaguely, the confrontations with those prison guards came back to him, albeit through hazed memory. *Hopefully, Lubby didn't have to pull out his rifle on anyone. When that thing's in his hands, not even the ice- cold grip of death can pry it from him.* For a moment , he felt ashamed over his boorish behavior. Not the first time, because that scraggly wench had it coming. For him, the law of static applied: "Don't start none, won't be none". But that second encounter. The least he could do is apologize to Lubby.

With care he thudded back down the steps.

"Ah, back to the land of the living?", Lubby said. Lubby ran a twenty- two hour Operation, six days of the week. He was one of those types who just needed only two hours of sleep, and a hot pot of coffee to run smoothly.

"Had a dream, Geon began, that I was in a fight with a hundred eyed monster."

"Monsters eh?", Lubby said, the automatic dishwasher rinsing the suds off a dozen of dark colored mugs.

 His bar was nearly empty, except for a couple of hard looking traders going to Quolas, a planet that was two worlds ahead of Asylon. A world known for running underground black markets. Quolas was also a favored den of space pirates. The doors swung hard, closing behind the back of what appeared to be an out of place, ruggedly dressed female. In a flash, she was gone.

She was so fleeting, in fact, Geon didn't have the opportunity to push her out of mind.

Geon still had the feeling that something was terribly amiss.

Suppressing his trademark hearty laugh, Lubby said, somberly, "You really pissed off some of those guards. There was a riot yesterday."

"A riot?"

Lubby explained everything that transpired. Overhead, fan blades turned noisily, however, that didn't prevent Geon from hearing him. Nor from feeling even worse about his conduct.

"Sorry for how I acted", he said contritely, putting both palms on the liquid stained, hastily wiped down bar surface.

"Don't worry about it", Lubby assured him. "You didn't know. Besides, they dismissed you as a crazy drunk anyway. They were really hurting, though." Lubby's voice carried a quality of sadness. More so, it carried empathy.

Geon's head fell back in silent disbelief. Then it shook. "Just a matter of time", he said, disapprovingly. "You can't cage a man, and not make him an animal."

"So many kids were killed. Too damn many, and over a dozen of the officers. A bloody mess. The place is shut down, man." To be sure, Lubby was upset at the loss of life, but he couldn't help thinking about the lost revenue.

The traders drank quietly. They were lost in their own company. The foreboding nature of their garments, burnished and war worn, alone made a person keep clear of them. Also, the overt menace their aura radiated was the last omen necessary to ward away unwanted company.

Geon quick glanced them, then turned his attention back to Lubby.

"Way things are going, Geon opined, you'd think mankind forgot about what freedom is, what it means to a person. It's like, "We'll give you a bone, a meat scrap here and there, then yank that away from you. You know you'll need a GID soon just to travel in the expanse of "free space?"

"The hell is a GID?", asked the barkeep, perplexed. So much was changing it was extremely hard to keep track of it all. Almost every day, since this "Great Reunion" business, more laws were being passed, being announced.

"Galactic Identification Disc", Geon spoke indignantly. "All "citizens" will be by required to have it. It'll be five years mandatory without one."

Now understanding Geon's disgust, he whispered in mutual disdain, "Are you serious?"

"As a brain tumor. Five years in a penal institution or a multi-million credit fine, depending on whatever jurisdiction you're convicted in."

"Insane!", protested Lubby.

"I'll tell you something else, not only is the GCW going crazy with all this newfound power, but I believe this was...."

Double doors swung open, cutting off the flow of words.

Three officers from Asylon, two men and one woman entered. Normally, there wouldn't have been nothing out of the ordinary about them, just regular joes and joettes doing a shitty, thankless job. But at this moment, after the events of yesterday, their dark demeanor befitted the shock trooper that Geon referenced a day earlier. Lubby noted the steel black uniforms. Silver striping the sides of their legs. They didn't use that attire up there. At least he never seen any coming through his doors wearing that ominous design.

"Morning", the one in the forefront said gravely. "Sorry to intrude so abruptly." He was stone faced, yet he managed to be personable.

"Our condolences", Lubby offered for himself and his patrons. The nods from the others affirmed the same, however weak.

"Thanks", spoke the man, whose name plate bore the words Lieutenant Satille. He approached the bar, ignoring Geon. In his hand he held a square box. After a closer inspection, it was revealed to be a holographic projector. Without further pleasantries the Lieutenant began with urgency:

"We're looking for two young people. A young man and young woman. No need to alarm you, but we believe they may have come through this way."

The ensuing silence was not only tense, but fraught with a new undercurrent of hostility. For a few awkward moments, it appeared as though no one would speak, until Geon opened his mouth.

Good Lord, Lubby thought anxiously.

"Haven't seen anybody", Geon spoke tersely. Lubby wore a poker face. The lieutenant said nothing to that, but the woman glared angrily. The other man kept an eye on the two traders. There was no obvious reason. Just a precaution.

The square came alive, and the pixelated likenesses of Jeth Akim and Tahina shimmered above the device's center.

"The girl is seventeen, from Duriy, the male's from Sefu Trius, and nineteen years old. We don't believe they're armed, but they are considered dangerous all the same."

"Escaped, yesterday?", asked Lubby. He appeared to be scanning his memories, but no recollection came. He'd seen over a hundred or so faces in the past twenty-four hours. Neither face emanating from the projector jumped out at him.

"Affirmative, sir", the young man said.

"Sorry", Lubby said finally. "I don't recall them."

"Smart kids", quipped Geon. Which caused several stares, including from Lubby, being cast his way.

The other male officer turned his attention away from the traders to Geon; open, calculating hatred narrowing his eyes. Geon saw the silent threat and laughed inwardly. Their stare down ended when the lieutenant waved the others outside.

"If you do hear anything, call the office", he spoke solely to Lubby. He gave the barkeep a small hexagon. "This contains the pertinent info, as well as the reward info." To his credit, he kept his cool and professionalism in an obviously hostile environ.

Geon snorted in disgust. The young man simply brushed him off, thanked Lubby for his time, then left out with the others. Who, for their part, eyed Geon with scorn, even after the double doors closed after them.

"Was that necessary?", Lubby scolded.

"No, but it was amusing ", Geon scoffed. Authority types always bothered him. "The nerve of 'em!"

Its looks were deceiving.

"From the second level corridor, this ship doesn't seem as big", Jeth said.

They were exploring the starship they had managed to sneak onto. Its hanger bay was very large, exceptionally huge rather, and held numerous tools and moving equipment arrayed neatly on the makeshift shelving and on designated spaces along the cobalt hued steel walls. There were two entrances to the bay; they were now walking down a maze that was taking them into the propulsion chamber. Or so Jeth had hoped.

Tahina said nothing, instead taking note of every detail.

Faded glimmers of energy undercurrents were running weakly above, peeking through various openings, giving the otherwise dimly lit pathways illumination.

"At least the stench isn't as strong", Tahina complained. The stink of whale blubber lingered like vinegar.

"If that's the only complaint so far, I'll remind you this was your idea", he told her wearily. He was tired, very tired.

"Given our limited options, she said, it was better than waiting to get arrested. Or turned in. Those two guys were so creepy! And that ... whoever she was with them... it befuddles the mind."

He sighed, offering no counter.

It was miraculous that no one spotted them, even though everything had died down. Getting to the Docking Centrix was surprisingly uneventful. Even still, neither had let their guard down.

Finding a ship was now the hard part. One with a crew that would take them with no money, and by now, take in fugitives. Then, they had to go through inch by dilapidated inch of this aging fortress to find a way off Asylon. From the distance, the tiny town in the wasted background looked almost like a mirage.

"Could you imagine what this looked like when it was better utilized?", Jeth asked Tahina, betraying a sense of wonder.

"Given what we (rather I) know about the history of this hell portal, maybe little better than it does today."

"Such a know it all", he replied as they ascended. Immediately, Tahina thought of Dante's Hell. The circular plates they walked upon were kilometers wide (it was too dark to estimate an approximation) and the air was getting thinner. They had to find refuge fast, she thought (feeling extremely anxious obviously) before the dearth of quality oxygen and fatigue brought them down.

So many levels (nine total) that were just empty space, the tepid night air flowing in between gaping holes where ships could station for refueling, transferring of crew members from ship to ship and cargo in far more prosperous times. The metal tile that plated the floors were bent with neglect. Some spots rusted irreparably. Tahina had almost tripped more than once. That last time...

Those three people almost spotted them, crossing the platform. By luck, she'd seen that Geon's Baby was left wide open. Without hesitation, without even regard for what potential dangers could be on this ship, she led the way.

"What are you....?" He didn't finish, because she took him by the hand and hastily jerked him forward.

The more they explored, the more confusing it looked to Tahina.

Underneath, they could hear the sizzle of electric currents in protective tubing. It was running smoothly. More smoothly than a ship this old, seemingly, should be able to do.

"Wonder what type of engine system he, or she, has set up?", Jeth wondered loudly.

In some places, its inner walls looked warped. Forced, beaten metal sheets curved at the arches of the roof. Here and there, a strong yellowish glow lept through the openings.

"Let's hope it runs better than it appears", she said. It reminded her of the Titanus. That was not a good thing, on many levels.

The corridor they were canvassing suddenly forked. Left, Right. "I say let's go right", she said. Silence.

A right turn, then a left. Two rooms filled with junk, then a smaller one with an empty portal that led upwards. In the left corner, they could see ten large pyramids of solid steel, painted hunter green and mustard yellow lettering on one of the sides. A flash of recognition of what the chamber held caused him to grab her. He was so quick, so harsh, she glared at him disapprovingly.

"Don't touch anything", he warned her. Those are solar depth charges. If one is activated, it'll unleash enough force to blow this place apart."

How do you know?, came across her face.

"They trained us in using things like this", he said softly. "I was ex junior military, you know." He strained to keep annoyance out of his tone.

Right then, she wondered how far he could've gone in that direction.

"Rather foolish to put this sort of thing by the engines then, is it not?"

"We're nowhere close to the engines", he said, relishing the chagrin on her face. The feeling of proving her wrong for once was satisfying!

When Geon came aboard his ship, he sighed with deep relief.

Home!

He was only one of two ships at this depot of antiquity. A fossil of bygone days, when man's greed and ambition held considerable sway.

He found himself wondering if those days had returned. Or rather, did they ever truly go away.

Outside of Lubby, nobody who came to Evir (Now Asylon, though he never called it Asylon, nor changed the name in his computer data bank) had an impressive streak of success. Not the miners, and most certainly not the neo fascists formerly running a youth prison.

If only he could meet those fugitives. He'd gladly shake their hands.

He thought of Lubby, with a twinge of sadness. He didn't know the next time he'd see him again. Or ever. Neither one of them were spring chickens. The twilight years were often the most fickle. He determined silently, as he activated the closing sequence, to make a visit next year. Whether he had a reason to come this way or not.

As it was closing, he was content that the smell had past. Now he needed a job. Hauling and moving jobs were coming in few and far between. Very few had the money these days. And even worse, even less people were traveling across the universe. Most lived their entire lives on one planet. Never going past the sunrise, or sunset, of their native horizon.

How is that living?, he wondered, somewhat perturbed.

His boots clanked on the heavy steel of the stairwell that led to his cockpit.

The navigator's chair, a deep brown leather, with rips the size of his bushy forearms remained turned sideways. He always meant to throw the thing away. The console was a one- man affair, with half knobs and scroll keys protruding from the tarnished silver surface. Radar, destination tracking, and solar maps were on split screen, running on reserve.

Which reminded him. He needed to replace the solar batteries, which were close to overcharging again. For the fifth time in five years. True, Geon's Baby also ran on the plentiful ethosene and less on the very volatile cold fission. Of those other options, ethosene was getting very expensive, and cold fission was solely a last reserve option. Solar panel engines was by far more plentiful, and until the new tariffs took effect, as close to free as humanly possible, if you couldn't build your own. Charging systems were to rise another thirty five percent in cost.

They want to make it hard for the honest man to live, so they can put him in the grinder, he opined bitterly.

Just then, something above caught his eye.

He stared out, watching two starships descend into the atmosphere. Obviously, on the way to the prison. Dismissively, he shook his head.

He hadn't kept up with that business, except to piss off some people, Lubby excluded. He didn't like being rude, but really, he couldn't give a damn about those people.

While the big one loomed in the sky, its massive shadow blanketing the ground below, the other was much smaller, almost half the size of his own ship. Clearly, it was someone's personal space cruiser. A sleek cosmic vehicle, glassy black and, very obviously, a recent make that only the fattest of fat cats could afford.

In envy, Geon watched as the ant of a star craft zoomed towards the ruins, leaving no visible emissions trail to further poison the atmosphere.

After ten minutes, he put the ignitor key in (he kept it, partly in homage to pilots of old, and because this was one of the last designs to utilize one), and into the eternally grey horizon began his ascent.

"Two years ago, none of this existed", he said about the rooftops of the apartment complexes that now stood erect and making him climb 40,000 feet higher (due to intergalactic safety regulations) than he would've liked. His ship's design made piloting any lower very precarious. It wasn't a bulky design, just a clumsy one. Square in front, long and narrow in the middle, and a bulb like end in the rear. The first impression most often given was that of a metallic dragonfly, sans wings. "The aqua insect" became a derisive, very apt description that forever stuck (he hated it). The bulk of the vessel's rear was comprised of two vastly distinct, yet very integral components. The propulsion unit was sandwiched between two levels of magnetic pulsars, that had a peak capacity of tugging ships like those transports for distances of 95,000,000 kilometers. In fact, when Geon first got this ship, it was a subnuclear tugboat, on its last half million miles. With his technical knowledge (a former deep space propulsion engineer), money to burn, and a scorched earth policy (keeping his ex-wife from claiming a hefty alimony), he sunk his all into this vessel. Renaming it "Geon's Baby", he made a meager yet satisfying living for himself. A man, his ship, and the stars. What more could he want or need?

"Whoever he is, the man's a genius", Jeth said, impressed by the technical prowess.

Though far less impressed, Tahina had to admit this was, despite a hanging slab of flapping wall panel here, and a web of wiring hanging over there, a decently cobbled together operation. For a rigger upper, that is.

"It's all well and good that you're a fan, but have you given a thought as to how Mr. Thu will react to our intrusion here?"

Glaring, he told her acerbically, "I still can't believe you did that."

She simply shrugged.

"We needed to get some info, did we not?" She expressed herself with subtle aggravation. His tip toeing was frustrating as the Duriyan sun at Highpoint, when no amount of shade could protect you.

Recalling her snooping around in one of the surplus quarters they found as they began to start circling back. Again. Angrily, he told her, "Come on!" The look she gave him; her annoyance and mirth blended in a masque of impish amusement.

She was stubborn and determined to do what she wanted, when she wanted. Almost lacking discipline in both action *and* mouth. He nearly pulled her away, but not after she placed everything almost as she found it. After a brief, rest, they found finally found the engines a short while later.

Tersely, he told her, "Yes". He still fumed over that. Just the fact of violating someone's privacy bothered him. Because back home, privacy was as nonexistent as justice.

"His name's Geoniphus Thu", she reminded him. "Owner and proprietor of this vessel, Geon's Baby." He loathed the smug, triumphant note in her voice. Her arrogance was grating.

"Geon's Baby?!", he said, wincing in disbelief.

"Unimaginative, certainly, but..."

Abruptly, the ship was shaken by sudden turbulence.

She shut up when she realized they were skyborne. Silently, he was thankful.

Taking her by the forearm, he started looking for a place to hide behind the massive machinery.

"The hell....?!", she whispered. Yet follow him she did.

Inwardly, she had to laugh at the irony of the moment. They were *FREE*. And yet unable to savor the moment. *Is Jeth thinking about this as well?*

"We'll hide by the engines, he said hastily. It should take him a while to make his rounds. By then..."

Geon was well out of Asylon's orbit when he set a new heading. A job came up. Corryion. A job that would take him from that hulk of an outpost to Saturn 2.A. A college professor, changing jobs. Six hundred point nine Circos. Unless he changed the battery panels now, procrastination would turn nearly three weeks of travel to a month and a half. A system and a half away. Half a billion point forty- five thousand miles distance.

On one hand, Geon was happy for the call, because the work was needed. But on the other, this guy was taking his whole library, which consisted of crates upon crates of books. Oh yes, he loved to turn a page, so this would be tedious and not to mention heavy. 175 crates, going by the specs his holo- screen projected. *I'm getting way too old for this heavy lifting.*

"At least it's not a woman", he muttered, in bitter remembrance of the last job.

So, he zoomed forward, traveling on impulse, crawling towards System's end. The brilliant bulging, swirling of gas clouds, called a cosmic rainbow, was Aurora Boria. Not many of them existed. And of the few that did, they were gorgeous to gaze upon, but deadly to get within too close of a distance . Many a ship exploded on contact of the highly combustible fumes. A true case of deadly beauty.

Abruptly, he halted Geon's Baby. He needed to check the ship, and to evaluate what how much space he'd need to utilize and the equipment he'll need. And he needed to change those solar batteries. And there was a nagging feeling bothering him. A rare one, but he would investigate it anyways.

"Check the surveillance relays", he muttered before he left the bridge.

"Did we stop?", she whispered, suddenly nervous.

It took him less than a minute to answer.

"Yes, I think we did", Jeth rasped quietly, behind a hulking module that hummed with a mechanized harmony he never thought was possible.

She thought to look up, but her instincts, and his grip, forbade it. Resentfully, she snatched herself away. Jeth shot her a look of surprise.

One thing he needs to learn is I don't take well to being held down, she thought with unbridled viciousness. The flash of anger in her eyes made him, in turn, give her a hard glare.

Can I trust her, truly trust her? He found himself thinking for the first time. And at the wrong time, at that.

One thing they weren't lacking was a good hiding place.

The ship's engine was a monolith of complexity, a hydra of propulsion engineering that a limited few had attempted, let alone mastered. Jeth estimated that this chamber ran on at least the equivalent power of a trolley train back home. Spacious, expensive transportation. The mammoth ran wall to wall, with enough room for three people to service each section. Each a self- containing L from near ceiling to jutting out mid-way. Coppered. The coil wrap wiring hovered over the top of all three main chambers that controlled each energy source (solar, ethosene and lastly cold fission), protected by massive, multi layers of plastic steel shelling that kept the conducting material from disintegrating.

That alone was impressive.

Then, each fueling system was meticulously separated from the others. Cross mixing fuels, especially cold fission, was akin to adding water and cesium. Somehow, Geon Thu made it work. His three headed hydra seemed fully functional. It was a series of varying propulsion theories weaved into virtual fact.

He pivoted hard on the metallic surface, making a point to be heard.

Tahina suddenly ducked behind the solar section, yanking on Jeth's right sleeve.

"He's close!", she whispered frantically.

Loud footsteps panged the hard steel paneled floor. From the sound he was coming toward them. Both fugitives kept deathly still, so not to betray themselves.

Hard footsteps paused again, then crunched on steel. From the shadows Jeth could make out the silhouetted figure as that of an older man. Fleetingly, he pondered the thought that the pair of them could overtake him. And just as immediately, a flush of shame overcame him. No matter his recent circumstances, nothing could justify harming an elder.

Out of view, Geon went to the opposite side of the Solar engine, and began fiddling with a safety release valve. Wearing gloves formed of steel fibering and padded leather made the task awkward.

Time to flush these two fools out the hard way.

He began replacing a solar energy distributor dish.

"Shit!", Geon rasped, the thing nearly burned through the gloves he was wearing. If handled the wrong way, he could burn his hands into permanent disuse.

Absently, he threw it in a circular trough, then went for another. They needed to cool off for at least six hours. Subsequently, a rush of water sizzled loudly as the room was cloaked in a soup thick, immediate fog. Its billowing thickness made Jeth gag, loudly and uncontrollably.

"He might hear you!", Tahina said, losing herself as anxiety tightened its hold on her.

"No, Geon said, yanking her up, I do hear you!" She had staggered back, gasping. Way too stunned to act, she only managed to eke out an awkward "Ummm ... Hi."

His chair screeched loudly on the steel surface. It was unnerving, and Geon meant it to be that way. Both kids were sitting on makeshift wire crates. He stared down, and she glared ice hard at him. He sat slowly, like a man who had all the time in the universe. Between the boy or the girl, he was waiting to see who'd break first.

His aging, yellowed eyes went from him to her, her to him. He was used to stare downs, epic battles of will. And he was not in the habit of losing them.

Somehow, their presence made his cargo bay look smaller, the corridors of his hallways less cavernous. They made him feel his world wasn't that large anymore. The feeling was making him conscious of being alone. And he didn't like it.

"How long have you been aboard my ship?", he snapped at them.

Neither spoke. So, after a few more minutes, he said, dryly, "Asylon's not that far from here. It's nothing to turn around. I'd start pleading my case, if I were either of you."

Jeth kept his silence, his cool. But Tahina had had enough.

"What does it matter, if you intend to turn us in?!", she raged, green eyes flaring her hatred at him. Not surprisingly, Geon turned to Jeth.

"She's going to get you sent back there", he told him sternly. The boy raised his eyes to his. He saw his sense of reason, his sense of loyalty towards her. *Obviously, he's the sensible one.*

Jeth squeezed her arm gently. "Where she goes, I go", Jeth said softly. Tahina smiled at him faintly. She stopped looking at the old man, realizing the futility in a staring contest. But she wasn't about to concede an inch.

Geon decided to try another route.

"You're both fugitives", he began, pausing for a rebuttal, a denial or an explanation. He knew they could only tell the truth.

"We're all aware of that ", she stated bitterly. Jeth shot her a look.

Geon looked at her, then continued. "You don't belong here", the old man said.

"Well, we're here!", she spit defiantly. Jeth finally turned his head, telling her "By the suns, will you please fall silent?!" This had been the angriest she'd ever seen him. And to have it directed at her, of all people, made her still her tongue reluctantly. Momentarily.

"You're Duriyan, all right. Arrogant and... " he shook his head. "Enough of this, you kids can't stay here. "

Turning from Tahina to this man, Jeth had to salvage this. This was their only chance.

"Do you know what they did to us on Asylon?! People like us?", Jeth exclaimed, fiery and passionate. He spoke with a furious indignation that an outsider like Geon could only slightly fathom. But the pain, the horror in his words made him want to empathize with him. With the both of them.

"I heard about the riot", Geon said tersely. I don't know the particulars..."

"Then allow us to enlighten you", Tahina snidely offered.

"Shut the hell up!", Geon exploded. He said with force, force that made her quiet down, the hostility between them growing steadily. He began to rise, to monitor the ship's status.

Seeing this, Jeth again quickly interceded.

"Tahina, please!", he pleaded. Then to Geon, he said, "We…. had no other option. They were killing us. We were lucky to escape, with our lives. So much murder... too many people dead." Jeth stopped himself, and Tahina gave a soothing caress of the left forearm. Geon studied her momentarily. Despite her hostility, her haughtiness, Geon glimpsed the damage being in a place like Asylon had inflicted on her.

Neither of them would ever be the same. Nevermore to be children, but hardly suited for the difficulties in a new era of rushed adulthood.

Geon had again taken his seat in front them, this time sitting directly in front of them.

There was another bout of tense silence. Jeth recovered himself, and Tahina struggled with her emotions, keeping them in check.

Geon reclined back, as he did when he got comfortable. Finally, he told them to "Tell me your stories."

Cautiously, Jeth sighed relief. Tahina, glaring past him, parted lips, but no words came forth. The whole experience still felt surreal, otherworldly. Rather, it was as though she was outside of herself, watching it happen to her. A spectator in her own, months long degradation.

"You first, green eyes, and keep it civil", Geon warned.

So, she spoke. And as she did, she couldn't help herself as the tears welled, and then fell to her chest. A tender grasp of the hand from Jeth made her feel a little better. Just a little.

He listened, thinking about the guards that came through Lubby's doors, and about the recent turmoil with the terra-miners. He listened with rekindled fury when Jeth gave his tale of life behind the walls of Asylon.

While they talked, he took full measure of the prison garments. Soot stained, smudged with mud and waste. He noted the lingering nicks on her cheek that the gang beating had left her. He reflected, again, on the mental scars that would inflict them for the rest of their days. If they allowed it. He came to a decision. But they had to understand the gravity of the consequences all of them faced.

"You know, both of you, that they're looking for you", Geon reminded them gravely.

"We... we didn't mean to impose ourselves on you", Jeth said lowly. Tahina gave him a fleeting glance of disgust. But she knew he was right.

"What's done is done", Geon said hurriedly. Clearly, they could see what he was thinking. So, they thought. Not waiting for Jeth, Tahina spoke up.

"So, what will you do?", she demanded of Geon. She hated him, but she was well past fearful. She was terrified. She knew Jeth well enough to know he wouldn't attack an old man. She might be vicious enough, even fast enough, but she didn't know anything about piloting a starship. Plus, being fugitives, adding assault or murder to their list of charges just... *wasn't intelligent.*

Geon rubbed his eyes slowly, ignoring her. "Sending you back won't be in my best interest. You staying here (eying Tahina) *really* wouldn't be in my best interest." His inflection seemed to offer a compromise of some sort.

For the third time, an *awkward* silence filled Geon's cargo bay.

Jeth started to look around. He saw all the manual equipment. The hover dollies and stringy cords that were wrapped in long, blue bundles. *How many jobs did this man, this one man, work on his own?*, Jeth wondered. *What if he needed help?*

Taking a chance, Jeth asked, "What if we work for you?"

Tahina, stunned, shot him a look that said, *What the hell are you saying?! Have you lost your puny mind?!!*

Geon scoffed.

"Listen, we'll work for passage to the nearest space station or colony. Anywhere .... That can or will give us refuge."

Geon shook his head, whether in disbelief or grim amusement neither of them could tell. Tahina didn't like this proposition, yet she knew better than to speak. Like it or hate it, this was the best option. *Maybe the only option, for now.*

Geon closed his eyes, seemingly in meditation. He developed the habit of shutting his eyes when deep in thought. "Keeping out distraction", he once told his daughter, when the parent – child bond existed once upon a time.

They didn't know what to think. Abruptly, he opened them, now focusing squarely on Jeth.

"Kid... Jeth, is it?"

"Yes sir", he answered tepidly.

"Are you aware what's been going on since you've been locked up?"

"No, I'm not." A familiar dread grew inside him, gnawing at him. He didn't want to imagine what was happening on Sefu Trius. To his mother and sister. Even... Sartha.

"And what about you, Ms. smarty pants?"

She nodded in the negative. She knew how remote returning to Duriy had become. They were on the run. That reality had fought its way to the forefront of her mind. Still, she was trying her best to fight it. To hold on to a shard of hope.

He got up, looking at them equally. They looked at one another, then nervously at him.

"It's a different universe than the one you *thought* you knew ", he began. "I think we can work something out."

If either felt a surge of joy, neither had expressed it. But Geon could sense the cautious optimism in them. As much as he was loathe to admit it, even a smidgen within himself. That a long standing, long held shield of loneliness could be laid down. But in degrees.

"You both have some catching up to do", he said. Reluctantly, he told them to follow as he entered the cockpit.

"Where....?", Tahina asked.

"Shut up, sit down." He pointed towards the empty navigator's seat and the edge of the iron steps.

"You went in first?", he asked of Tahina.

"Yes.... sir", she said, hesitantly. She didn't like this man.

Just behind the navigator's seat there was a blank, diamond screen that was four panels that made into one. The holographic television was a reconfigured information receiver controlled by a blueberry pi device hidden behind the point where all four joined.

Geon told them how to work the device, the instant recall feature especially.

"Particularly, you both need to know about the Thirteenth Law", he warned. "And all the implications that applies to the both of you. And me."

"That will take hours", Jeth protested.

"We've got time", Geon said morosely, setting the course to Corryion. It was almost a day later until Geon's Baby left Asylon's system.

Chapter Eight

Warden Ednisa Quinn stood still in the middle of it all. Still and in silent bereavement.

Her office. Her career. Her life. What remained of it all.

She stood in the ruins, doing everything possible to hold herself together. To not collapse down on what was and bawl her soul away.

Shards of glass, splintered wood and strewn about, ripped pages littered the floor. Charred consoles still spat out feeble trails of sparks. The Neo Persian carpeting, she had laid down before her absence, was reduced to largely charred heaps that taunted her.

Blood, charred and by now dried, stained the fractured jamb.

Halfway into the smoldered ruination, Warden Quinn stepped over the overturned bookshelves that were smashed to splinter, the remains of rare books that were beyond salvageable. The banker's chair that she loved so much was hurled out the gaping hole that was the bay window. Its broken frame littered the erstwhile battlefield, the wheels upturned. Her desk, that commanded so much of this space, was now just another pile of debri in the wasteland.

As were all her awards, her plaques.... everything she worked for.

A physical mirror of what was going on within her. Life became a living, endless fiery abyss.

Yet, she couldn't help but count her good fortune that she wasn't present when this maelstrom took place.

Ms. Roshin, hospitalized and traumatized beyond words, quit. She was so frantic, so incoherent, it was a kindness to file the resignation letter herself. The Doctor and some of his staff were butchered mercilessly.

Those bloodthirsty animals! Revulsion surged through her when she heard about it. She restrained herself, taking it all in.

Then, there was Turlak. His condition was upgraded from life threatening to serious. The man took twenty stab wounds, including one to the left kidney. She couldn't help but marvel at his toughness, and the strength and durability of pliable body armor. She would make sure to see him after his next round of surgeries.

Medi-porters arrived before she and Anwari did. As did the Class One, militarized Star Dirges that currently housed the surviving prisoners. Anwari and herself took his personal vehicle (or so he claimed), a Galaxian class Star Bolt that went far beyond the recommended FTL (Faster Than Light) travel speeds. The reason he went as "slow as he did" (he eschewed trans-warp speeds) was because of her "wellbeing."

Another transport arrived just ahead of them, to evacuate the staff that remained. The Asylon Project ended in little over two years of existence.

When this was finished, she would go to clear out her penthouse. The transporter wouldn't leave without her. Only the buildings would be left, both apartment buildings and the ruined prison. To what fate, she didn't have time to ponder on.

Her own future was a still billowing, rising cloud of smog particles entering the ether.

Just where in the hell was he?

Once, twice she looked about for that damned Anwari. He had taken off somewhere. An unsettling, familiar conflict arose in her yet again; she clearly despised him, yet right now she *needed* his presence, his overbearing authority. His haughty confidence. She was so far out of her league, and needed someone to hold her hand through this. Unfortunately, it was *him*.

She spoke at length to the Officer on Duty, and then she walked about the wreckage. She took her time, to take it all in.

First, the courtyard. The hardest step first.

The courtyard, after it was all over, was used to hold the dead. Dark green for the guards, weak yellow for inmates. The Doctor was covered in traditional white. Bodies were the last to be taken aboard the Medi-ports, the morgue being overfilled. Several of the most critically wounded from both sides died on board, raising the death count.

Again, she counted her good fortune not to have seen such a grisly sight.

Smoke, though less obnoxious, still lingered here and there. Soot blackened both brick and smelted metal. A few embers played, flickering about. Hard, stale, polluted water added to the nausea that was gripping her. The cafeteria was hollowed out, the gaseous aroma making her vomit. Quickening her pace, she toured the towers, the piers, the dorms. Finally, the Quiet Zone. Only the stress pills she had taken before arrival kept her moderately sane.

And this was only the *start,* she starkly realized. Again.

There would be weeks of nonstop press conferences, of public demonstrations. Already, a moratorium was placed on the next phase of the Asylon Project. Not to mention...

The Directorship.

She had to face that board, and most of all, old man Bevel. *How in the suns will I be able to explain this?,* she pondered in mild frenzy (a testament to the strength of the pills).

At this moment, having a degenerative, incurable disease paled to this hellish predicament.

The job went off, minus a glitch or two.

Geon's Baby was gaining altitude in Corryion's atmosphere when turbulence rocked and throttled the ship sideways.

"Hold on to something!", Geon warned. "Up here it gets rocky!"

The client, a harried, wooly haired man named Edward Tulle, hung for dear life in the navigator's seat. His multitude of books rocked in the cargo bay, but the stasis field was holding.

Tahina had barely enough time to grab the pot of mush. "Jeth, give me..."

As he got to her, the oatmeal splashed on him, on the floor and both she and it went flying across the small kitchen.

"Aungh!", she exclaimed. The wave of turbulence settled, then died down. But not in time to save dinner. She wiped the slop off disgustedly. Jeth was holding on to a thin, hand sized wall rail.

"I'll get the mop", he said.

She wiped her forehead, getting oatmeal in her hair, adding to an already frustrating day.

Three weeks aboard, and life had become somewhat settled. Geon and the teens had a long, heart to ear talk (meaning he talked, they listened). They'd stay on, but they would work for him. Until a better solution came along, either of them returning home was simply not in the cards.

In addition to their fugitive status, other factors were at play.

To Jeth's deep dismay, Sefu Trius was engaged in a bloody civil war. He had to fight back tears, thinking about his sister and mother. And he felt in some way responsible. For days, his mood was low and sullen, saying little and keeping to himself.

Which left Tahina, who by now gave up all illusions about returning home, to work closely with Geon. At first, she just wanted to avoid him as best she could, not really engaging him at all. But that wasn't realistic. She was stuck, and without a buffer. Her Duriyan resilience (a trait ingrained since birth, and universally respected) kicked in, and she played the hand life dealt her as best she could.

After comforting Jeth as able as she could, she went about the domestic duties that were delegated to her.

Cleaning, doing inventories, secretarial and general administration, and tending to the tiny hydroponics garden he maintained on the lowest level of the starcraft. And naturally, she took over the culinary chores.

In the process, she came to see that many of her assumptions about him were just that.

He wasn't a mean man. Just a man who lived life on his terms. He did what he wanted, as he wanted. The last thing he wanted was to have two teenagers, fugitives at that, under his care.

She could appreciate the ramifications if they were caught or discovered. She knew all too well the authorities would stop at nothing to find their whereabouts, hauling them in, heavily chained and humiliated.

But that was on Duriy. A different place and time that, for her, was as distant as Asylon was to Earth.

No, she didn't like it, but as her father told her on numerous occasions, "There are things in life you won't like, but you have to understand why it's that way".

Grudgingly, she understood the truism about not going home again. Now, she had to struggle to make life work on a rigged up, jambalaya of a space trawler.

All these things to deal with, but at least she could celebrate that she was free. A freedom that kept her and Jeth in the shadows, always looking over their shoulders, but they could move about within reason. There were no more correctional officers, detainment officers, or snitches lurking about. No more Quiet Zones or beatings. And for the moment, she could let her hair down, figuratively speaking. She could be herself. And, to her uneasy surprise, she was finding that person wasn't the self that was dragged kicking and screaming off Duriy, nor the "Green eyed devil" from Asylon. Those experiences had shaped her, molded her into a person she didn't readily recognize, but knew to be her just the same.

"I wonder if Jeth ponders on this?", she said once, looking into the cracked mirror Geon lent out to her.

And as for him, she found that, for the most part, she really liked the old man. Still, they clashed for weeks, off and on. Nothing major, nothing to get her kicked off his ship. She did something, he'd correct her on the right (his) way of doing it. Then they'd bicker for a few minutes. Then it was back to normal.

On the way to Corryion, they were passing an asteroid belt very similar to the one the Karuks inhabited. She had finished cleaning up, and about to head to her personal quarters (both she and Jeth had their own quarters. Two cleaned out junk closets. She also had a makeshift shower after that incident when Jeth walked in on her. The language that day!) The obstacle course of glinting rocks, varying in size caught her eye, and lured her to the bridge.

Brief flashes of refracted starlight bounced off the metallics in the stones; the allure of their cosmic glitter was indeed intoxicating.

Geon glimpsed her peering face in the polish of the dashboard.

"Sit next to me", he said, turning the navigator's chair.

It reminded her of something in the junk bin behind a thrift store not far from her former home (she had to remind herself of that. Duriy being in the past). The arms ripped, the seat smashed in, a sunken hole in the upholstery, the foot crest out of joint and crooked. Yet, even in this state of disrepair and plain ickiness, something about it screamed comfortability.

She hesitated, smiled, and then sat. It *was* comfortable! He slowed his ship down to a speed so slow that she could take in the celestial beauty. The gesture made her open up, more than she had done previously. They spent the rest of the trip talking, venting, and talking some more. Jeth overheard the civility of their conversation, half smiling. Then he turned in for the day, wiping a trail of pulse modulator grease on his pants leg.

A world whose beauty was criminally underrated.

Corryion had skies of deep blue. In the middle of afternoon, with the sun fully blazing down, its horizon was a milky azure that stretched out infinitely. The Blue Marble, it was called. A planet that rotated around a dwarf sun (in comparison to the one that brightened the Milky Way) an approximate One hundred and seventy- nine days, three hours, and forty- four seconds. It was a planet with more peaks than valleys, its mountain ranges dominating the landscape. Where there weren't rocks and the deep, mist strewn valleys, there were thin stretches of plains that produced checkered maize. A chief agricultural staple that could only be found on Corryion.

Geon's Baby was docked at the Moiraca Bay loading terminal. Carved out of the Mountain range that looked over a clean, very blue translucent sea, Edward Tulle awaited them at a storage facility. One hundred fifty crates of books, datum disc files and hologrammics equipment to be loaded aboard. The teens looked at each other, then at Geon. His look indicated that he had every intention of holding them to their word. Suppressed sighs, and then the job began.

When it was over, Tahina struggled to remember a time when she worked that hard. Geon was inwardly pleased with how well everything went on this job. The kids worked well and efficient, and they made things go faster. A misstep here and there, but nothing the untrained eye could catch. Nothing that earned either one a verbal scolding. A six hours load up done in almost half the time. And the esteemed Professor of Quantum Cybernetics Theory didn't question their presence.

They had readied themselves for any questioning, barring any inquiries about Identification Discs.

"Lisea", Tahina told him when he asked her name.

"Maurice", said Jeth.

"My adopted children", Geon told him in polite haste. Professor Tulle didn't press any further with that line of query. Though he did speak, at length, about current events and the places he visited.

Their prison garb was dyed blue, to pass off as work clothes. Geon and Jeth would do the loading and hauling, and they used Tahina to pack the cargo bay. By fortunate circumstance, there were no people other than Tulle and the storage management at the facility. No one seemingly cared about two teens working on an interstellar vessel. But still, a risk is a risk. And this was pushing their collective luck.

After this, they needed to get fake galactic identification.

It was regretful that neither could truly take in the wondrous beauty outstretched before them; reddish and auburn mountains overlooking the blue ice colored (so it appeared to Tahina) ocean. Sunlight fingered the waters in thin, slim beams.

"Like a Neo Bearden work of art", Geon said to them all in near whisper.

As Professor Tulle boarded, he turned, giving a last, long wistful look. Such rare displays of natural beauty must be savored for as long as possible, burned in both memory and heart. Giving Mankind's fickleness, it could be gone tomorrow.

Soaring off into the blue, they ran into the turbulence that Corryion's heavenly pulchritude disguised so well.

The stasis field kept everything in his now full cargo bay in place. Thankfully.

Escaping turbulence, they ascended into orbit. Corriyon's tiny moon, named Ibidar, hung a distant right.

Over a shoddy intercom system, Geon announced "Head's up, everyone. We're about to do a Quantum Run."

His client held himself nervously. He hadn't travelled among the stars in over a decade and was seriously out of touch with its rigors.

"You'll want to take off your glasses, Professor. This kind of ride gets bumpy."

A Quantum Run would cover half the distance in a short amount of time. They'd reach their destination two days, maybe three, earlier. But it was turbulent. And if the pilot wasn't competent or experienced enough to maneuver through the rapid shifts in space and time, it was lethal.

Quantum Run had its origins in a short-lived technology fad named Mass dispersion and reforming. Or Teleportation, as the popular culture of the time referred to it. A fantastic idea best left to the funny books. It took Man billions upon billions of EarthCoin (then the primary currency of that era of galactic expansion), the loss of lives and subsequent litigation to realize its folly. There was to be no shortcut to the further development of FTL technology.

Almost by accident, a propulsion designs expert named Dannis Creed found that while mass forms of matter couldn't be dispersed and then subsequently reassembled for deep space travel, it could be sprinted across the vast expanse for brief periods of time. Thus, Creed's law made this method of exploration and, afterwards, commerce a viable reality, though he himself "ended his own life" in a poorhouse on Io's skid row colony.

The galaxy around them became a kaleidoscopic lens, shades of lime green, deep oranges and flares of maroon melded and blended with the eternal darkness around them. Stars disappeared, completely drowned in the waves of light. Only to reemerge even brighter. To sit through it was feeling every molecule rattle. One felt giddy, nervous, exultant and cursed, all at once and then serene the minute after. If a one could imagine an out of body experience, literally sitting right next to your own body, crying, weeping, screaming with complete abandon. To feel the ultimate rush. No psychedelic, no mind-altering drug or device compared.

When the run was finished, Geon slowed the ship to impulse, its slowest speed. A long stretch of crab nebula nearby gave them cause for a little sight- seeing. The ship crept by, Professor Tulle captivated by celestial marvel.

Is there any doubt God is the supreme of artists?, the man of science pondered.

Tahina found herself over the sinkhole retching. Sweaty hands gripped beaten, burnished steel, salty tears wet cheeks and collar. She was a ramble of bad nerves, breathing harshly.

From behind, Jeth took her by the waist. Pouring a cup of hot water, he gave it to her. Her hands trembled slightly. After ensuring she wouldn't drop it, he took her to the makeshift room she now slept in. He lay her down on the pallet, resting by the door until she fell asleep.

Weeks later, it still burned the shit out of her. Staring out of the port window of her temporary lodging, gazing at the infinity that surrounded her, she just couldn't, she refused to let this latest calamity rest. Ignoring the warnings about stress levels, she allowed herself to fume. Her mind kept replaying that revelation, which failed to make it into the lengthy, tortuous report she was forced to make:

"You've checked everywhere, Lieutenant Anos?"

"Y-yes, Ma'am", the sheepish wisp of a woman replied.

"You're supremely sure about this?", Quinn reiterated, wanting to be absolutely certain about this possibility.

"We've followed procedure to the letter. There's no doubt about this", Lt. Anos replied.

Behind a silver and black desk in a broom closet of an office, Warden Quinn eyed the Acting Chief of Guards coldly, desperately missing Turlak. The woman opposite winced as she stood statue still.

Anos was small, middle aged, with a soft voice and mild, grating demeanor. She looked like Quinn could be her mother, rather than a contemporary. She was intelligent, enough, for Turlak to put his trust in her. So there was that. And there was also the fact that she was good with the officers. Those that were left, rather.

But these attributes paled before the disaster before them. Daily, Quinn found herself immersed in some new difficulties, adding to the fires around her. Asylon was completely shut down. The inmates were being scattered by the four winds. And the companies competing for their labor enacted a moratorium. The whole thing came to an abrupt, grinding halt.

Threatened by grieving families (whose demands for their loved one's pensions were dubious because they were hardly a year into the job. The attorneys balked, but IREL did pay, negative publicity outweighing pride), in hourly contact with the Home Office, and Anwari lurked about. Off and on. Why he kept disappearing, and reappearing like a ghost, she still didn't know.

With the full course on her plate, she couldn't spare a moment to care.

When all the DNA samples, the biometric scans and physical data was compiled, analyzed, and brought before her, she reached the inescapable conclusion that two inmates had escaped.

I really, really needed this. Thank you, Providence, for this ever-increasing boon!

Lieutenant Anos looked every bit like one of the condemned.

"Thank you, Lieutenant Anos", Quinn replied peevishly.

Quickly, she nodded, and Anos scurried out of there.

She felt like she was sitting on a stone. Cheap steel and plastic chair! At this moment she saw how uncomfortable this dump was; *just to be able to recline and think!*

She had escapees on her hands.

Two inmates had escaped. Amidst the fury of death and destruction, she'd lost two of them. Jeth Akim and Tahina. She sat there, fuming. Trying to decide which of the two she hated more.

Almost from the first that green eyed wench had been a bane, a vicious thorn in her side. No doubt she corrupted that simpleton...

A feeling of betrayal nudged at her. She'd been too kind, and thus, foolish to place any trust in the Sefu Trians. Jeth most of all.

An overwhelming desire to exact retribution on the pair of them nearly overcame her.

But first, the important thing.

She had to keep this under wraps.

Speaking of which, since she hadn't seen Anwari, she began to worry. *What if...?* She recalled Lieutenant Anos back to her office.

"Yes, ma'am?", Anos asked, strangely more confident, less deferential than before.

She was sitting upright, almost fiddling with the console knobs. "Who else, besides me, knows about this turn of events?"

"And me?", Anwari came in from the hallway, moving past Lieutenant Anos.

Quinn's expression changed. The sudden rush of panic turned her face into a mask of anguish.

"Tell her, again, what you told me", he said to the Lieutenant. Quinn noticed how emboldened his presence made her (disliking him even more), and saw how her underlings responded better to his authority than hers. It annoyed her that she could never enjoy this level of fealty.

Anos recounted a few officers going to town, into the bars and whatever businesses were open at the time. They even checked the apartments. Anwari listened intently. Both women couldn't help but stare at him. Anos in marvel. Quinn with deepening dread.

After she finished, Anwari made his way over to Quinn.

Turning halfway, Anwari said " Thank You, Lieutenant. You're dismissed."

Deeply relieved, once more, the woman speedily walked away.

"No reprisals are to come her way", Anwari said lowly, implying a threat. Dread was suddenly overcome by fierce indignation.

"Oh, don't you dare....", she began.

"Silence!", he demanded, bereft of his customary smug genteel that marked all their previous encounters. She rose, fully enraged, and ready to strike him.

"Know that your career's teetering on the line, and this will plunge you into oblivion."

"Do you truly think I give a...."

"Yes, because you're looking at the big picture", Anwari cut her off. "Not only a chance at the Directorship. But your pension, denied if you were cast out like a leper. Where would you go? How would you live? And who'll take a chance on so colossal a failure?" His eyes mocked her, more so than usual. And she couldn't turn away. The snake was coiling it's meal, applying the fatal pressure. "Without a generous source of income, Gyddis' disease will be a terrible battle to fight; you wouldn't make it to sixty."

She sighed, shoulders slumped in defeat.

Although, even in defeat, the urge to sock him one was tremendous, almost irresistible.

"But we needn't go down that route", he said abruptly. So fast, she thought him to be mad.

He's not mad, just .... so cold and calculating in ways I never fathomed could exist, she thought ruefully.

"Are you thinking, he asked, what the hell am I getting at?"

In quiet fury, she answered him. "The hell I am. Just who are you, Anwari? What is it that you expect to achieve through all this? Why do you need me? Really, just lay all the damn cards on the table!" Months of frustration and confusion poured out of her. She felt drained. But the release was cathartic.

Regarding her, the man finally laughed. "So proud you are! Proud and foolish. For the last question, I've no need of you at all. Factually speaking, when Mr. Bevel spoke of candidates, I brought your name to *his* attention. And for the first, I am everything you know me as, and more. For the second.... I leave that to your wild imaginings."

His withering response left her shell shocked, and justifiably deflated.

"I'm already pursuing our two escapees. The leads we've been able to obtain are few, but rather reliable."

"How...? ", was all she could muster. However, she didn't hide her relief at this revelation.

"For now, consider it better that you don't know. In the wrong hands, knowledge is a dangerous thing."

Again, anger flashed through her like lighting; coming and going in an instant. For some reason, she felt his statement was more than a cryptic insult.

"For now, keep worrying about the press, and your response to the Directorship", he counseled, walking out. He left her pondering how much everything was slipping out of her hands. And worse, if she ever had it in the first place.

Speaking of places, it was truly disturbing to find her penthouse suite had been violated. Thieves, or a thief, broke in and copied some information off several flash discs she used as a back -up. She was perturbed that someone would do so much for so tiny a gain. There was nothing on them but quarterly figures a lay person couldn't begin to understand...

By the time Tahina was up and able, Geon's Baby had passed the thin blue rock rings of Saturn 2.A, which were babies compared to the original. A quarter of the span, but still, the fragments glinted in the distant sunlight. The planet's dense atmosphere would make for another rough ride.

Her body and space travel were arguing, and she wasn't getting the better of it.

Hikka root tea that Geon's guest provided had settled her stomach, and cleared away most of the migraine headache. Creed's curse was a common aftermath of the Quantum Run. Disorientation, headaches and upset stomach and pains that ran its course within a span of a week, sometimes up to two weeks.

She lay down, the smell of Mali candle flowing through the room. Mali, an aromatic native to her home system and from where Professor Tulle had just left. She found it so remarkable how home remedies were just as effective in the deepness of the cosmos as they were on Duriy, or where the planet bound had full access. She began to appreciate the traditions of home a lot more.

Home.

She missed Duriy. During these bouts of homesickness, she missed the dreams she had, and the possibilities of who she was, who she wanted to be. The riots changed all that; being exiled off world changed all that. She would forever be living on the fringe. Not a full member of society, that is. Not as Tahina of Duriy. She was finding that acceptance of the now was harder than she imagined.

Life as a fugitive was proving to be another shackle about her being. Only more insidious, because she'd never escape its iron grip.

Turning in dismay, she almost slumped onto the floor, only to turn again. Face down, she began to dream. Bad dreams.

Asylon and its horrors persisted in haunting her. Once, Jeth had to shake her from the grip of a nightmare; This was especially vivid. Warden Quinn and a man she had never seen before in her life were standing over her, torturing her. Imprisoned in a cylindrical tank, banging to get out. Filled to its brim with green liquid, thick as slime, fluid as water. They were laughing at her, mockingly pointing at some poor girl who entered the darkened chamber (even dimly lit, Tahina could surmise it was medical in nature), wearing a maid's uniform, and a gold bracelet, adorning her ankle, that flashed green light.

A controller, of a sort, she realized. She banged and kicked, screaming inaudibly.

The girl in the maid's uniform was summoned to come hither. Her feet bare, eyes were devoid of personality, meaning, even life. When Tahina recognized her, she screamed, absent a voice. She saw...herself.

Still sleeping, she screamed.

Jeth. He awoke her.

Rousing her, she blubbered what little she remembered. He stood at the entrance, a faint radiance sprinkling his face. He looked like an angel emerging from deep darkness. The oil smell on his hands disturbed the flow of the tyfirr spice candle she had lit.

"You don't suffer... premonitions, do you?", he asked. Though the faded light covered most of him, she saw the concern on his face.

"No... that's unreal", she said tersely. "Just silly superstition."

"Then just chalk it up to a rather graphic nightmare", he replied softly. As he turned to leave, she called him back.

"Can you... sit for a while?" In the time he had known her, she never sounded so sheepish, so... afraid. A gang beating couldn't illicit the fear he was now observing. He wondered, silently, what was it that had her so rattled.

Nodding, he did so.

And they talked for almost two hours. They talked about everything. The universe, the events and happenings on their respective worlds, politics. Everything except Asylon.

Jeth had been a darling to her during this time, bringing her meals and ginger water. Geon had checked on her when he was able. Even the good Professor popped his shiny bulb of a head in, to ask if she was feeling better. She was greatly touched by the outpouring she was receiving. It made her feel special, even loved.

She couldn't remember the last time she felt that way. But she warmly remembered the last person who did make her feel loved and cared for. Her dad. His memory made her turbulent rest turn blissful. Her fears began to melt away like snow, after meeting sunshine.

Here they were....

Quolas was truly a den of thieves, a nest of vipers. One of the biggest, and most reviled cesspools in the galaxy, it was the last planet before Big Red, the giant sun of this system. Also called Hell's Gate, as traveling past Big Red led into the Far worlds. No person of good repute would be caught under the conical, sun stained biodome.

But he himself was not necessarily well reputed. Nor was he afraid of pirates, swindlers and traffickers of Dujin. Those things bore him no consequence. He'd seen the foul underbelly that made humans human a long time ago. In moments of deep self reflection, it almost disturbed him just how much he was at home within it.

Looking at the device on his wrist, it took the appearance of a standard Rolex. In reality, it was neuro- reader, a new model of biometrical GPS. Like a fingerprint, everyone has a distinct neurological imprint. And here, he found who he was looking for.

Piculo was a tavern on one of the side streets that marked the planet's only city, Furon. A phantom world with a populace less than fifty thousand. Populated with broken lives, dashed dreams, and those desperate to evade the ever expanding, tightening leash of trans- galactic law.

Forever humid, from the sun burned soil to the hot plate pavements to the tin rooftops that smoldered and burned without fail. If Hell was really a real place, then this would qualify.

Boiling remains of alley cats, and some unfortunates lay near the entrance. He stepped over corpse and carcass. The doors swung wide open as he scanned the room. A few heads turned, analyzing the crispness of his pressed military attire, wondering where his weapon was hidden. Unsatisfied, the denizens of this quarter of Hell resumed their card games and downing diluted, brown colored swill.

Two men sat at the far corner table, wearing deep brown poncho shirts over rugged and slightly torn deep brown trousers drinking to themselves. A jukebox warbled from the right side of the room.

Three men and a dingy, hard faced woman were at the bar whispering. The middle table had a card game going on. The man to the left, back to the long, chipped, granite topped bar was cheating.

Someone will kill him soon, the newcomer thought.

His crud stained boots made a bee line to where the traders sat; in the immediate corner, a dusty man and woman snuggled. She giggled, as he licked her reddened left ear lustfully.

Without invitation, he took an aged chair from another table. He sat as he placed himself directly across from the traders. They stared, neither pair of crusty lips opening in protest.

A waitress walked over, her rugged looking feet squeaking loudly on the splinter laced floorboards. Her tray, made of burnished copper, held two empty, dirty glasses.

"House special", he snapped at her, not even looking at the craggy face. Bloodshot eyes shone at him with contempt. "And another round for these two. In clean glasses, if you're able."

Wordlessly, the woman skulked away.

"You're brave to come here", said the one on the right. His upper left arm was hideously scarred, the forearm of which was wrapped in silver coil wire. His voice had a deep, irreparable rasp.

And the other on the left nodded. A quick, surveying glance about the room.

A swarm of horn flies buzzed outdoors, noisily enjoying the feast of dead carcass.

"How fast of a shot are you?", he asked them both. He sat, with both arms under the table, holding a .57 caliber laser revolver in his left hand. It seemed he was almost *daring* either of them to take a shot.

The man to the right said, "As fast as you looked around for trouble, that's how fast my Tor pistol is ready to blast." He spoke in such a way that it was fact rather than boasting.

The drinks came hastily. "Your tip's already in the registry", he told her, still not looking up. She snorted her chagrin, stalking off. His attention returned to the purpose of being here. The immediate purpose.

"Some days ago, you were on Evir, at a bar." He stopped, knowing that many here would never call Asylon by other than its original name. Seeing the instant reaction (eyes blinked wide, in sudden disbelief), he knew that they knew he had the right men.

The one on the left, who wore a snake like scar running from the right temple to the left chin, said "What's your trouble, then, if that be true?"

A little better educated than the other, he deduced. "A young man came in with this, now revealing the small box projector in his hand. Looking for a young man and woman."

"Aye", Leftie responded, noncommittal.

He smiled faintly. His hunt was growing. The lead was getting hot.

"Now tell me, were there any others in the bar that morning? And of that woman who arrived with you, what became of her?"

Chapter Nine

There was a universe of difference between them, she thought ruefully.

Surviving the onslaught of angry families, and then a public tribunal known as a press conference, Warden Quinn now had to steel herself for the greatest trial of all: The Directorship.

In the most literal sense of the phrase, all eyes were on her. And she was more than aware that daggers, swords and machetes were pointed in her direction. Looking for blood. A scapegoat.

Of that last fact she was painfully aware. And readied herself for the onslaught.

She was determined to go down fighting; she wouldn't be anyone's fall guy.

When she entered the building, she was at least fifteen minutes early. A lot of changes were taking place on Mournos. A more automated workforce, with service, maintenance and administrative droids overseeing the more, mundane day to day operations. A robot greeter met her as she was coming through the crystalline portal, the dry monotone putting her ill at ease. Feigning a smile, she pressed on.

Many of the familiar faces she'd seen over time were gone. She went to Mournos right after the press conference. Four days before this meeting. She arrived late yesterday, just settling into yet another temporary suite. For the first in many years, she felt the sting of being a transient, roaming place to place without a destination in view. It pained her all the more, as she thought herself far above and removed from that lifestyle of desperation.

But there were other pains to endure.

She was grieved to hear that Gus had passed away; his heart warming smile and easy going demeanor would be sorely missed. At a time like this, a genteel presence would be most a welcome salve.

When she came to the security desk, she was told to wait in the lobby.

An older black female, in a newly issued gold and navy uniform, glared up at her, annoyed. A hand tablet babbling celebrity gossip was overturned. Overhead, a security drone hovered by, recording every interaction. Its cyclopean eye focused on Quinn's exasperated face, and the patent laziness of building security.

"I have business before the Directorship", she said somewhat haughtily.

"You'll have to wait", the security officer responded without care. "Those are the orders, Miss."

Orders Quinn found very unusual, to say the least. She gaped her mouth at the surly, sharpness of tone, but she complied.

She could only wait, briefcase by her feet, while sitting in the lobby. The same diamond glass plated floor lobby that not less than nine months ago she strode through with unfettered confidence.

After ten minutes, she pulled out her own tablet, to catch a quick review of the latest news briefings.

"This is GNN. News you can rely upon. With guest host…"

"Jet Symmons remains on forced hiatus after the debacle at Warrington Tower…."

"What can we learn from the Asylon tragedy, coming up…"

"Should the Thirteenth Law be repealed. That's the topic of today's…." Quickly she turned it off, unable to stomach any of the drivel. She elected to suffer this indignity in silence.

It was almost forty-nine minutes later, when she was finally summoned. *Humiliating beyond words!,* she thought as the elevator arrived at ground zero. Any ill will she bore disappeared. She put on her best poker face. Her best chance at survival. Slim though her chances might be.

The bell rung once upon arrival. *The Death Knell,* she thought morbidly. *No need to stave off the inevitable. Let's get it over and done with.* She stepped off and entered King Bevel's Court.

Instantly, she noted how dimmed the room was. Their faces were draped in shadow. *The feasting hall of demons,* she thought fleetingly.

She could feel the accusations, a silent consensus that she failed IREL, and Mr. Bevel, most horribly. She felt that judgement had already been rendered.

There was to be no introduction, nor any formal greeting given, nor was there any traces of emotion as she took to the podium. She tasted the tension. Her head was on the chopping block.

Most disturbingly, there was no Anwari in sight. She knew then and there she had no allies, no advocates.

She'd better make the best plea for clemency that she could muster.

Before she could speak, technology spoke.

Without a word, recycled news streams from weeks past appeared before her.

"At this time, no word has been ......"

"Dozens of inmates have been reported dead...."

"The death of dozens of inmates at Asylon have sparked a new wave of......"

"IREL stocks have plummeted......"

"Thearman's is the latest interstellar mining firm to rescind its labor contract with the shipping and transfer titan, stating...."

Transmissions terminated abruptly. The lights came on fully.

"No one here can be as deeply angered, or as letdown than I, Ms. Quinn", Bevel spoke in a weak, hoarse voice. Coughing fiercely, a face or three turned from her, out of concern for him. His face was reddened, much more jaundice and sallow than the last time she saw him. But his eyes! His irises had the focus of a laser, burning black amid the sea of red that was, under normal circumstances, a sea of white and distilled yellow.

That same twinkle of life was still there, just greatly diminished. It occurred to her, fully, that the stress of this debacle would take its toll on his always fragile health. At that moment, a brief but deep empathy came over her.

When he was better composed, he continued. "I realize that, in fairness to all involved, the current state of things does not fall on you entirely."

While some nearby him murmured, Quinn inwardly sighed relief. But she'd been around long enough to know not to let her protective shielding lower, even a notch.

With great difficulty, Mr. Bevel continued. "However, Ms. Quinn, a majority of this catastrophe *does* fall in *your lap!* This...", he pointed with unbridled rage, he turned deep red, stopping.

As confusion played on the faces gazing the geezer, Quinn's own heartbeat skipped. *This is it. I'm done for, and not even a chance to defend myself.*

What happened next only she could call a miracle.

The old man abruptly jerked, then sputtered. Spittle ejected onto his clothes, blood began to trickle from the twisted mouth corners. He began to convulse, causing a mass panic.

"Call his nurse!", cried a fraught woman."

"Call the medic team! His pulse is weak! ", said another, grabbing the stricken man's wrist.

A smallish man in grey pinstripes pushed the summoner's button on his hoverchair over and over. His face, flustered and frantic, was swatted by the old man when he reached up.

They're smothering him!, Quinn thought in frozen horror. *They're killing him by trying to help!*

Even with that realization, Quinn stood perfectly *still.* In the chaos, she stepped out of view. *Perhaps a private call to the Med Staff would improve my chances...*

By the time the Medic Squad arrived, they had to fight through a half dozen frenzied and useless people. The other half sat either paralyzed, wept from a safe distance, or began plotting their role in the next regime.

"Not good", a man in an all clean, all white unisuit said, the stethomometer beating erratically. "The newest transplant isn't taking." He had to yell instructions over the frenzy and chaos.

Minutes later, Heram Bevel was taken from his court directly to the closest medical facility. Everyone in the room, in the connector tubes, even in the apartments, watched anxiously. The yellow, flashing streak was the only bright speck in the red, darkened skies of Mournos.

Meeting Adjourned. For now, Ednisa Quinn's fate was in limbo. That was good enough for her. It would have to be.

For the first time since he was taken from Sefu Trius, he was feeling life fully return to him.

Jeth stood over the massive engine, looking over its complex yet simply organized layout. He had studied it since he came aboard. Propulsion mechanics was a thing to put his passion in, his energy and mind power in. From the first, there was no doubt that Geon would let him work on this multiplex of conduits, hydraulics, cables, transfer chambers and split wiring. It helped that he had tons of experience at being handy, as his mother would say teasingly. "The Handy Angel", she called him.

In between jobs, which were becoming much more plentiful according to Geon, he would watch the news streams. Specifically segments on Sefu Trius. The civil war had reached its fifteenth week. All the bloodshed, the destruction...he felt responsible for, despite the assurances from both Tahina and Geon.

"The first contingent of GCW troops are hovering above the atmosphere of Sefu Trius..."

He cut the thing off, sulking the rest of the day.

"Have we traded one set of tyrants for another?", He wondered aloud, removing a layer of solar paneling. He barely restrained the passion to hurl the pieces across the room. However, he stopped himself.

"Always do what you think is right." Those were the last words his mother spoke to him. Searching further into the valley of memory, those very words, or some variation were the words of his father. He stopped working. Not to brood, but to meditate.

He thought about his life then, and what was life for him now. Billions of kilometers away from a world he knew he'd never lay a physical eye on again, nor walk the streets of his early years. But that didn't mean he had to leave Sefu Trius completely behind. Or compromise the principles he learned. Skulking about was no longer an option. Life dealt him blows he had withstood. He survived the worst. The pain was still there, perhaps it would be with him forever. But he resolved to endure.

"Now, I strive for the best, to be the best", he spoke through clenched teeth, turning his head as he replaced one group of solar panels for another. He decided to "rejoin the world of the living", in Tahina's words.

When he came for dinner, and decided to sit down with Geon and herself, Tahina was pleased, both through her elated facial expressions and her non-stop array of platitudes. Geon, between bites, stared at the lad, as if to say, *Traded your peace and quiet to endure this. A fool you are.*

I agree.

"As you get used to working on this mechanized boobytrap of mine, make sure you get an understanding of not just how this behemoth works, but *why* it works this way."

Understanding.

How did this work? What made this function? Why was coil warp wired facing the right opposed to the left side? Why was the cold fission chamber so awkward to service? Why was the ethosene tank (a dual chamber tank that went two levels, the only part of this engine to have such a design) only kept at three quarters full?

How did he manage to not blow himself up?

Tahina kept herself busy elsewhere, and for that he was glad. She disliked coming down here. "Too mechanical ", she said once. Which threw him, because he knew she understood the basic principles. She could understand most of everything, except how to keep quiet.

She always talked. It was something he noticed at Asylon; but he chalked it up to being isolated so often; the ear of another was a luxury. Now it was a nuisance. And she was so pedantic. "Did you know that ...? " was her favorite opening phrase. Not "Good Morn" or "How are you today? ", like a normal person. At times, whilst in conversation, he found himself thinking, *is she capable of keeping all these tidbits of information to herself, and just hold a normal conversation? As in, letting someone else talk?*

Also, she was becoming too clingy. As if being alone would...

He shook the thought away, as he was searching through the tool cabinet.

Recalibrating a molecular screwdriver, he knew he was being too harsh. *She's such a lovely girl,* he thought. Shapely, highly intelligent, with a rather brusque temper. She was doing better in that regard, certainly not as combative as she was that first night aboard. Especially since Geon gave her unlimited access to his, as it turned out vast library. If she didn't have any duties (mostly domestic in nature, such things as the cooking, administrative stuff for the moving/hauling or light machine maintenance), she could be there for hours. Or watching the news streams, catching up on the doings and happenings on her own home world. And complaining about the direction life was going. She'd also badger him about reading more, improving himself. Her way. Her effort was appreciated, but it was grating as hell. He was down here, working on engines, making a little money with Geon. He was on the lam, but that was the main downside to his life. Making himself accept "it is what it is" for pretty much everything in life. And excepting those bad spots, life was good. As good as things could get. He realized she was not only lonely, but she needed an outlet to express herself. Reading and soaking up current events weren't enough. He ached for a way to tell her, without it blowing up into a big fight.

Another job came and went, then another. Work had been coming in more regular this month. Geon was satisfied, but not happy. The word of mouth was spreading. So was the danger. The kids, helpful as they were, were hot. And though no word was flashed through the data stream, or through the news cycles, there had be someone out there, hunting for them. *Some days, he told himself, it was only a matter of time.*

"Well, what should we do, then?!", Tahina asked, looking down into a half finished bowl of Duriyan vegetable and fruit stew.

They were sitting around the triangular table he used during a time, long ago, when he used to have card games aboard his ship.

Such a long, long time ago, he thought, as he told them they weren't allowed to leave the ship. Once again.

"We play it smart", Geon said, gauging the reactions from both. Neither were happy.

"This is almost Asylon all over again", Jeth grumbled. But he knew better. The current reality was near unbearable, yet the wisest path they could walk for the moment.

One of them brought up the new GID laws. Geon mulled the prospect over ever since they "showed up".

"Guys, the risk is too great. GID is read biometrically. It's a database that contains every single human being in the GCW registry. Over trillions of people, and each one recorded. Let that sink in."

"Oh, that can be maneuvered around!" , she countered. "People do it all the time! On Duriy, we could fake bio-scanning easily!"

He looked at her. An argument had started.

"First consideration, Tah, Geon began his counterargument (almost always starting with Tah), is that this isn't, with due respect, a singular technologically stagnant world we're speaking of. The GCW database is the most comprehensive, and most improved upon information gathering system humanity has ever seen. And, *it's expanding.* Every three months it undergoes a routine upgrading. Every planetary census, every birth and death, is factored in. And the addition of the Far worlds only allows for improving an already finely tuned and operating data gathering and population management system."

Silence.

She rolled her eyes in anger, as she did when, in argument, there was a point she couldn't contest. Jeth sighed. He knew she wouldn't accept defeat. Yet.

"As for your second comment, people have tried, and failed miserably to circumvent that system. I can't recall anyone who succeeded."

"Come now, Geon, she said, you really expect them to admit that someone can, and has beaten their precious human tracking system? We just haven't met them yet. I'm certain the pirates that bandy about, robbing and looting, have "beat" the system."

He shrugged. *She never gives up. More of her Duriyan pride.* "No, Tah, I don't expect them to do any such thing like that. But people talk. And as they talk, others listen ", he said, a subtle hint being thrown her way.

She went silent as Geon continued to lay out why going down this course of action was best. Jeth seemed to be listening intently, in silent agreement as always. Tahina found herself drifting in and out of attention, wandering into the ether of her mind. *From one cage to another! What's the point of being among the stars if you aren't allowed freedom?,* she thought bitterly.

In his death, Heram Bevel was as circumspect as in life; just a fraction of an millisecond on all the news streams. The Home Office was closed in his honor. Family was present. The entire Directorship was there; and very few others, such as business friends and enemies. A few heads of state. From the balcony of her suite, Ednisa Quinn overlooked the ceremony.

A lowly employee such as herself, won't have made it past the well-wisher's gate. Which appeared rather thin, looking from her vantage point.

So many feared him, so few loved him. If not for the politics of position, how many of those on the Directorship would be in attendance?

No official word yet. On the cause of death, or more importantly (to her), her status.

The man lived a quarter century longer than he should have, she thought resentfully. Gyddis' disease would take her by eighty, if she wasn't careful.

And she'd hadn't heard from, or seen that insufferable Anwari.

Relief and anxiety knotted, as she was thinking about him.

Suddenly, the bell buzzer to her suite rang, loud and urgently.

"Have I summoned the devil, by conjuring his visage?", she said half mockingly as she went to the door.

It was room service. She was relieved. Somewhat disappointed, but relieved.

It was just breakfast. Eggs, croissants, a fruit platter and coffee. And a pink card at the end of the round tray.

She thanked room service, and the tray hovered to the patio. She plucked up the card, curiously opened it to find the following message neatly scribbled:

"The Exidus Building on 495th and Curtis Lane. 5:00 p.m., EST. Anwari."

He never failed to surprise her, nor shed a light upon himself. He was cloak and dagger personified.

Pedicured feet on the table's spiraling cylindrical base, she ate slowly, gazing into the early Mournos day. For a fraction of a moment, this world had come to a standstill. Tomorrow it would roar to life with vengeance. Heram Bevel wouldn't have wanted it any different.

The Exidus building was one of the oldest buildings on Mournos; the last of the original mortar and brick titans that arose within the first half century of settlement. The old- style letterings were rustic and quaint, recalling the haberdasheries of centuries and worlds past. "Norrie's Deli " was now more a museum than eatery. But the brown leather seats, the ancient lunch counter, and the primitive music box wasn't just for nostalgia. It was a barometer of no matter how much things changed, people would always revere the past.

4:59 p.m., Earth Standard Time. Her left hand held on to the brass knob, almost not wanting to enter. Getting the better of herself, she turned it and walked inside.

When she saw Anwari in a corner booth, motioning to her with a wave, she felt a morbid warmth that made her both uncomfortable and strangely affable at once.

"Never knew you liked the things of old", she said flatly, sitting directly across from him.

"They have their uses", he returned dully. He slid her a menu.

The place had hardly five people in it, not including the cook and waitress.

"I didn't see you at the funeral", she said in a low conversational tone.

"I was there", said Anwari, just above a whisper. "And I saw... well, you're here."

A chill ran through her. Yet the air was set on a comfortable eighty- five degrees.

"I'm not that hungry", she said, when the waitress, in a dapper blue and red apron over pale blue dress came for their orders. "Just blueberry lemonade."

Turning to Anwari, he said "Special # 6".

The thin brown woman smiled and went.

She waited for him to initiate conversation. It was by now a ritual. After an awkward silence, it was she who broke tradition.

"Where have you been the past two weeks? I expected you at the...meeting with the Directorship." Here, she was betraying an expectation that he would be there, to defend her, though Bevel's unexpected demise negated any assistance necessary. But still.

"I don't see why; I was disposed elsewhere", he returned nonchalantly.

Her eyes narrowed.

"As for your job, I wouldn't worry, if I were you. The Directorship is in upheaval, and will be for some time. IREL's plan will go through."

"You act very strangely Anwari", she spoke with deep suspicion. "The place is falling apart at the seams." she fell silent as her lemonade and ice water with lime and lemon slices came to them.

"Thank you", both said in a unison that took her by surprise.

"Most viewing from the outside see things that way, as do people who only consider their personal... situations. When you see things in expanse, the troubles before you are but minor nicks in the fabric." The tell- tale, know it all smirk had arrived.

"Are you are making an effort at being philosophical?"

"It's me saying there are bigger shrimp on the barbie right now. By the time you come up for review again, the demand for a prison system of Asylon's magnitude will be greater than before. You needn't worry ..."

"Special # 6", the waitress interrupted.

"My thanks!", Anwari said cheerfully.

Quinn looked at the cuisine derisively. Roasted beef and side potatoes drowned in rich brown gravy. Sautee vegetables and curried rice filled out the rest of the oval porcelain. *How I wish I could still eat like this, instead of polyfibered cardboard.* The breakfast she took in hours ago was a cheat, barely falling under the prescribed diet she'd been ordered to follow.

His eyes were closed, as if silently saying a prayer.

"You were saying?", she asked, shifting in the cushioned seat. Comfortable, but a little stiff. She needed to take a pill soon.

His closed eyes open, then he took a few careful bites. "You should keep a clean nose, a low profile. Much like your archnemesis and her friend."

"Have you found them yet?", she nearly spat out, with too much force. Instinctively she looked about, to see that the waitress was watching her as if she were crazy.

He ate a little bit more, enjoying her stew. She realized this, growing even more incensed. His presence instantly raised her blood pressure and stress levels.

"I suppose you won't tell me anything?", she asked. Her entire countenance had changed. Dark and vindictive.

"Those children have a lot of power over you", he counseled. "As it stands, I know some things about their whereabouts." He looked about the room. A few more people walked in, some others were walking in the halls. A young woman especially caught his eye.

"Well?", she was now impatient, livid.

"Just let it be. For the moment", he said, suddenly cautious. Picking up the change in vibes, Quinn too fell silent.

With a side glance, Anwari scanned the hallway as he finished eating. The young woman was gone. Not a big thing, as people come and go through Exidus daily. Still, there was an ember of realization.

At the top of the tower, the door to the women's restroom opened. A young lady garbed in a shimmering aqua silver uni-suit came through, her fro'd out hairstyle fluttering under the flowing air condtioner. A deep blue purse hugged her side. The nearest stall was open. She slammed the polished, metal door shut.

She fiddled with an earpiece, then she reached into her purse, and fingered a green diamond shaped listening device. It played back. Slightly garbled, nothing of true value.

Jet Symmons silently cursed. All this effort for... She caught something. She played it back.

Whitening out the static (she had to utilize rather quaint espionage techniques, since this assignment was completely unauthorized), she picked up some key words and phrases:

"Whereabouts".

"Archnemesis".

"Those children have a lot of power over you".

"Have you found them yet?"

Hearing the door open made her shove down the handle.

The flushing drowned out the sound increase.

She left the Exidus building hurriedly. There was a story brewing. She had only just time enough to jump on the shuttle back to her hotel.

From a distance, in the late afternoon of Mournos, wary, angry, hateful eyes were trailing her.

Chapter Ten

Eighteen. Today, Tahina was now eighteen. It wasn't the milestone of old (under Duriyan law she'd be an adult in three more years), but it was still her born day. Woke, showered, and put on that frilly lime dress she'd been wearing of late. The one Geon got for her from the Salvage shop. It went to her ankles and canvas tennis did the rest. While she resented him picking out her clothes (as she couldn't leave the ship, and he certainly didn't know the first thing about how a female shopped for clothes), she winced at some of his choices. But this one, she liked.

Hers was the small room on the other side that led away from the engines. And those damnable depth charges. She wouldn't sleep anywhere near anything that could explode. Her tiny closet (imagine comparing a finger to an arm in terms of space) held the few articles of clothing and shoes she owned. Some camisoles, two pairs of jeans. What remained of her ruined prison jumpsuit (a morbid reminder that kept a practical use), and a few pairs of shoes. Rummaging through the second- hand clothing barrels produced a few treasures; if only she could've done it herself.

As she was fixing her hair, she ruminated on her clothing; not because it was secondhand, nor even that one of her jeans were ripped at the knees and the leftside. It was that she had multilayered garments. The brilliant, light refracting attire females wore on the news streams, and on the "Fashionistas" show (mass marketing didn't go away, it evolved with the times) were, as she was painfully aware, signs of status and affluence. Fabrics like denim, cotton, and even linen (depending on what planet you were from) were the garb of the poor and perennially destitute. She frowned, the thought of being forever sentenced to a life arrayed in the dress of a "societal untouchable", or SU (as they called it on Duriy) was not only discomforting, but depressing, given the limit of options before her.

Moodily, she looked at herself in the cracked half mirror. She was pleased with her looks. At least she could feel good about that. Her lot in life kept a glimmer of contentment at bay. She chafed at being cooped up and confined. What was more, that this was the best option, no, the only option made her demeanor grim, her spirit morose and laden with resentment. Sometimes, she just hated to get up out of bed.

Though she was careful to keep this bottled up feeling to herself, especially around a client of Geon's, both he and Jeth noticed the lethargy in her spirit. And not even the money Geon gave (though it wasn't much, after fuel and repairs were factored in), nor spending half a day reading could raise her spirits. She rebuffed efforts to talk about it, going the whole day sometimes in a fog of misery.

"She'll come around when she's ready. Don't force it", Geon counseled Jeth after several attempts. She wanted to be left alone, so let her be.

What is the purpose of having freedom, if you're not allowed to celebrate it?

She thought on this for days, then as she was turning away from the glass shard, it came to her: In times like these, who are the *truly liberated?*

The Galactic Identification Disc was now in effect. This was more of the laws that were designed to make Interstellar governance more efficient, more responsive to the needs of the people. The disc was a biometric marker, holding the unique characteristics of all the billions upon billions of human beings who lived under the GCW. But as Geon opined: "There is no such animal as efficient bureaucracy."

She shuddered to think of the waves of protest on her home world over this, and the basic capitulation of the planet's leaders to rejoin the GCW. A betrayal of everything that flag, the squadron of five grey star cruisers prominent in the royal blue background, stood for.

Every life lost in the battle of Gauma, where two thousand Duriyans were slaughtered by Trans-Galactic Troops (at that time the standing army of the GCW was known as the Trans- Galaxia, or Pax Galaxia. After the Independence Wars, it was disbanded, in favor of planetary jurisdiction. Only in the past decade, circa 2707, was a modified intergalactic military force reestablished). Their ultimate sacrifice, and inspiring a planet's rallying cry ("Remember Gauma!") was now a sacrifice in futility. Almost daily she followed the news streams, for signs of planetary insurrection. Not one to be seen, nor heard. She would terminate the stream in obvious disgust. *Had the whole planet become spineless and weak willed since her exile? Had Dujin taken over the minds of all the adults, making them as docile and dumb as her mother? Were the sacrifices made by herself, by Jojas, Iajim and the others like Sali nothing except spittle in the wind?! What in the hells had happened to her home planet's spirit of defiance? The tradition of rebellion against tyranny?*

Some days, she envied that Jeth's people were in rebellion. Though she'd never tell him. He would only be appalled, and he was morally uptight as it was. Thinking of her friend brought a strange cloud of melancholy. Neither had really spoken, to each other, for a few days now. It was two months, almost three, since they escaped.

The long reach of Asylon had eluded them. For now. And sometimes, it was almost like a nightmare, all that had taken place. But scars seen and unseen told her differently. The fact that Duriy was now a place forever away told her differently. The fact that today, she would be alone, with relative strangers, told her different. She took her time getting to that makeshift domain called a kitchen. It wasn't hers, but she made it her own anyway. Jeth had the engines, and the general ship maintenance to keep him busy. *More like non-thinking,* she thought. But whatever demons haunted his dreams, he found a way to mute them, to keep them at bay.

Cooking didn't grant her any such luxury, nor did handling the minute administration duties for so tiny an operation, nor even reading. There was something inside her, a voice that plagued her, aching for release. If only she knew how to appease it!

Making her way into the kitchen, the little cupcake with a lit half candle on the table caught her by surprise. Her countenance brightened by leaps and bounds. *He remembered!*

Jet Symmons peered out the window. It was afternoon, and the sun was exceptionally bright. The skies of Sau Saku were a seasonably, very romantic sky blue.

Yet the crashing, wavy waters and finely ground sands on the shoreline went virtually untouched. Hardly a soul could be seen in the hotels, or parasailing. Another resort world that became a failed ghost planet. It had been like this for the better part of a decade.

"What good is beauty if no one sees it?", she mused behind bamboo stalks halved, fashioned into curtains. She grimly laughed at herself with the irony of her thoughts. She herself didn't come to the middle of the galaxy for surf, sun, and satisfaction. She was here to hide.

"On sabbatical", she told the starstruck woman at the lobby desk. "Forced Sabbatical", she added with elegant bitterness. Though that barely registered. She couldn't get around being an intergalactic celebrity. Trillions had seen her face. That was the only card in her favor. But ultimately, that wasn't enough, she knew. She was going against some extremely dangerous forces. Forces that operated in the shadows, in the underworld that made the universe run. Since Mournos, she felt eyes watching, stalking her every move.

She sat on the bed, replaying the bits of information she gleaned from that conversation on the day of Bevel's funeral. His people were too involved with the intrigues of corporate empire to notice her slipping into their midst, however thinly veiled she was.

"Damned GID!", she muttered. The pieces were coming slowly together.

"Hiatus?!"

When it was announced, very publicly, that the Jet Symmons Hour was going on hiatus, immediately, Jet herself was the very last to hear about it. It went without saying that she was beyond furious. She exploded.

For all the graciousness, all the gentility she could demonstrate, Jet Symmons was known to have a volcanic temper when she was crossed, or humiliated in any form or fashion. The incident on Mournos, with that shyster slime Anwari, was an exception. But she made sure to place him in her mental database. His time would come.

After a terse, accusing look, she calmed herself.

"This isn't for the reasons you think", her boss began, then fell silent. "We just need you to cool your... jets, as the saying goes." His attempt at humor fell flat.

Fuming, Jet squirmed in the plush chair opposite. The Journalistic Integrity Award on his desk gleamed with irony. The thought of smashing it to the floor raced through her mind, as he explained the reasoning behind gagging her.

"You'll still get paid as if you were actually working", he explained.

"Except I won't be!" she exclaimed. With the universe bursting at the seams, there was a wealth of stories that needed reporting. Taking her and putting her on the shelf deprived GNN viewers of those stories, those voices that were going unheard. And there was no one who could deliver those voices and stories more capably than her.

Knowing her frustration, Baldwin Wright Hurston (B.W., to close friends and favorite employees, such as Jet) relented a little. What he then told her that was she could pursue news stories the old-fashioned way, the way that "Brought you to the doorsteps of GNN."

She forced herself to smile. *Falling backwards to move forward,* she thought. She needed to get a story, a big, giant story that would bust open a dam of questions. The kind of news story that gets everyone in the universe talking. She realized that, after her anger finally subsided, this was a chance to get that story. And who knew better than she how to get that kind of news to the masses?

No one could ever stop Jet Symmons from doing anything.

And since she wasn't on their time, nor their dime, she was relatively free to do as she pleased. They weren't about to let her go; an award winning, hard hitting investigative journalist was a rarity these days. One so easy on the eyes with a slightly abrasive, sometime flirtatious (when called for) style? An endangered species. She took the challenge, and began the course of events that led her to Sau Saku.

First, she made it to Asylon, a day after the uprising (as uprising made it sound more befitting), she canvased the town. Not Asylon Prison itself, since it was closed off. The remaining officers went about in abject uncertainty. Looks of molten anger on some faces were downright chilling. Their jobs, as they knew them, were gone. Colleagues were maimed and killed. Families needed to be fed. For a time, as she sat in Lubby's bar, soaking in the dire atmosphere, she wondered did people give so much as an afterthought to the plight of everyone's suffering, not just the nominal victims. Despite whatever personal biases she held, she was professional and kept a general empathy for people, even when she was completely against you.

Even she could take but so much, before exiting the bar, looking for answers. Lurking about in plain sight, her mind went back to her arrival and what she learned so far....

That those traders were willing to take her was miraculous. That she didn't need to defend herself (a small laser pistol in her belt) was even more divine fortune. As it just so happened, they just wanted extra pay and weren't very concerned with her at all.

"Don't need any complications, sweets", the talkative one said dryly. "We just go where the money is. Or takes us."

Their ship was, in comparison to the luxury vessels and hyper warp star cruisers she'd become accustomed to, extremely tiny. Organized chaos, and the tools of an unseemly trade made the space uncomfortable. But she would make due.

Lubby's Smokehouse and Tavern was half filled the morning she walked in.

Incognito (she thought it amazing what a difference cheap make-up, slummed down clothing made when it came to disguises), she drank cheap, weak ice bourbon.

Around her, people were talking.

So, as she drank, she listened.

"They tell you anything...?"

"Naw, man. Quinn doesn't know shit. And that lawyer...."

"Brown guy? Indian Dude?"

"They're not called that anymore, but yeah..."

"Guy gives me the creeps, but yeah, he told me..."

"Yeah? Well, he seems like he's over her anyway. One step ahead... "

Over clanking glasses and bad mouthing, one of them gave a description that fit a person she knew all too well.

Now, it became crystal clear that Anwari wasn't just a lawyer.

So, as she listened and drank the swill Lubby's hole in the wall offered, she realized several things:

A series of atrocities had taken place well before this incident, which climaxed in this tragic loss of life.

If Asylon, or anything like it were duplicated, it would lead to a revival of systemic mass abuse and disregard of human rights. It would be a reversion to life in the nineteenth or twentieth centuries.

The human diaspora, though momentarily disgusted, would toss this out of it's memory. Humans had a dangerous penchant for failing to heed the lethal lessons of history.

There was nothing, or no one here that could give me the full story on what the Hells happened here, she thought pensively.

Prowling the streets of Asylon, she made a fateful decision.

She decided to trail Anwari, or Quinn, if she could find either one. Despite the harsh assessment of her underlings, Quinn had to know something. Or at least lead her to Anwari, given their now obvious close relationship.

Finding where she lived, she broke into her penthouse suite. In times past, shame would've come over Jet. For so long, she thought she had evolved from such tactics in gathering the truth. But, in times like this, truth was a rarer commodity than privacy.

After a meticulous search, and nearly tripping a sensor alarm, she found some information discs she could copy. What they contained was only a tiny patch of a larger tapestry. She crept as she came in, unsatisfied that so huge an effort rewarded her with so miniscule a pay-off. She had to keep tracking Quinn.

Unbeknownst to the embattled Warden, she now had a second shadow.

From Asylon to the Press Conferences to Mournos. From what little she could gather, Quinn was due to give an accounting of the events of the uprising.

On route to that hellish world, there were a pair of ex C.E.O.s talking in the ship's lounge. They were wearing faded green and hunter green uni-suits, provided by ship's security. They were talking wistfully about Asylon. Quietly, she slipped next to them, a table away, recording.

"You think they'll fire the old ax?", one of them asked the other, his gaze lost in the dark reflection he cast in the tall mug's metal skin.

"Maybe. But I don't see how, seeing as she wasn't there when it all went down."

"Georgie, get real, man. You know they need a scapegoat."

From the bay portal window, another transport ship stood still, gleaming brightly.

For a minute, Jet stared off in confusion, wondering what was going on.

"That ship is a straight shot to Mournos, the other man said. Quinn's getting on, and anyone else that's going...."

Jet flew out the door with that last bit of info, so fast she seemed a blur to the inebriated or inattentive.

By the skin of her pearly whites, she managed to get onto the same star cruiser that was taking Quinn.

Not an easy feat by any means, but a plausible false identity and a wide swath of money did wonders.

She lost track of her for a few days, but being who she was, she expected to see her at the funeral. By chance, she caught her going into the Exidus Building.

By further good fortune, she was able to get snippets of her conversation with him.

By furious digging, she came to know that his public files (all citizenry files were kept in the Publica Datus) were available. It was such an obvious first step, she almost kicked herself for not going that route. *You got used to having assistants do the grunt work for you, girl,* she scolded herself. Her fingers, bony and feminine, typed in "Anwar Anwari" on the smart screen of a palm sized computer.

Birth name. Home Planet. Vital Statistics. Lineage, and Social

Identifaction number (S.I.N), all basic information. Yet she found it was consdered:

Classified Materials.

How is a citizen of the GCW filed under Classified Materials?

She made several other attempts; utilizing the Cross-Referencing apps as well as any law journals, any past broadcasts Anwari should've been featured on, given his relatively high status. Each attempt met with failure.

Prior to leaving Mournos, she suspected she was being trailed.

I saw him. Did he see me? If so, did he recognize me?

The intuition she'd come to depend upon screamed *yes!* and she switched destinations at the final moment, giving the Travel Department a conniption fit.

So, Sau Saku, with its gorgeous climate, scarcity of tourists, and sun- soaked shores, gave her a refuge to reflect and regroup.

In the brightest of day, how could dark clouds lurk?, she was thinking, anxiously walking down one of the bamboo reed and copper lined piers constructed simply for vanity purposes. The burgeoning sunset was a welcome distraction. So welcoming, Jet let her guard down for a moment. *A moment is all it takes.*

They learned about the greatest terrorist attack in modern history by almost getting themselves captured.

"Ease up on the controls!", Geon cautioned her. "Don't be so quick to press down. Treat those controls like you would a babe."

Giving him a startled look, she quipped, "Do you realize how primitive you sound at this moment?"

"Girl, you're smart enough to understand me!", he fired back. "Just remember what I said."

And she did, to the best of her ability. She was in her third day of learning to fly a starship. And so far, everything from the first day was blurred with everything so far from today; It was maddening to remember everything exactly. Which control did what, recalling which console not to touch at a certain point and time. Not getting distracted by the holo-streams or looking in the wrong direction.

Then there were the stars. So sparse, so damn many. Usually, she looked away, making it all the more breathtaking that way. But sitting in the pilot's seat, staring forward for hours on end, she felt like she'd lose her mind if she had to do this on a regular basis.

Geon studied her, as both the ship and the navigator seat, rocked. She was going way too fast. Going too fast in outer space had fatal consequences, in more ways than he could bother to count.

Everything was coming in too fast!

In her mind, that is. More than once he scolded her to "Slow up that brain of yours, and listen."

She grimaced, telling herself to clear her mind. Star to the left seemed too close. Veering right way too early. A wormhole would, out of nowhere, suddenly appear. She'd accidentally go into a Quantum Run, and retch all over the cockpit, causing a massive short that would...

"Space is infinite, Geon counseled, time is not".

She sighed nervously, and then steadied the starship. After a few moments, Geon's Baby was moving smoothly again.

"Not bad, but not great". He made sure to praise her effort, while doling out harsh, honest criticism. She glared at him, red and yellow lights bearing down, sheening her forehead and thickly braided hair.

"I'm not gonna lie to you, Tah", he gruffly replied. "You'll need hours of practice, and I'll make sure you get it."

She really hated the sound of that.

"Why isn't Jeth up here, he doesn't know how to fly!", she protested. Her hands froze over the controls.

"Touch the red shift rod", he said evenly. "And yes, he does. He grasps the basics, and unlike you, he's had applied experience."

Like he had a say in the matter, she thought, resentful of how her current situation mirrored his involuntary conscription. She was slowing the ship down, almost to an impulse velocity. The stars seemed to run past them.

"Then he's the one you *NEED* up here, not I!", she said.

His wizened brows furrowed, then joined. The eyes were dead on her. As he spoke, measuredly and without compassion, he said, bluntly, "As long as you're aboard this ship, you'll be the second pilot on board. There is no further discussion. Now, shift back to normal, and maneuver ahead. Straight, this time."

She grumbled, but with no way out, she did as she was told. *So much for being free among the stars,* she whined inwardly.

When Jet came to, the first thing to grab her was how dark her suite was. But something wasn't right. The darkness was formless, oppressive. Nighttime on Sau Saku was in mere shades, an almost see through, heavenly transparency.

There was an abrupt stench, dank, foul, just as constrictive. This was not the smell of a seashore. Nor that of an empty, idyllic resort planet.

This wasn't Sau Saku.

Immediately, she knew. Something was wrong, *with her.*

Her memory was disjointed, hazed, a collage of half pixelated images. Her usual rapid pace of mind was stunted and lethargic. Thoughts, vivid and crystal clear, were reduced to shards and blurred. She couldn't concentrate, or even speak. Her tongue felt heavy, made of lead. And words. Words. Words came easy to her. Since an infant, she'd always had a gift for verbal expression. Her mouth, slowly, painfully parted burdened lips. It hurt to move them. It hurt to think. The horror she felt when no sound escaped.

Her terror grew when, incrementally, she realized was unable to move.

Her body was as sluggish as her mind; her hearing, at least, was rather sharp though not as usual. As if whoever did this to her wanted her to be able to hear. Hear them torment her, ridicule her and her unfortunate predicament.

From a distance (though she knew not exactly where), the sound of footsteps on a hollowed, polished steel floor echoed.

In degrees, a glowering green, then dark red light blanketed her, dispelling the cloak of dark surroundings that concealed her. She still couldn't see perfectly, but she could glimpse a sliver. Enough to make out that she was being held prisoner.

The quick sounds of a door sliding open, then closing.

Her eyes strained, to catch a shadow of her captors. Futility. A useless exercise that only served to aggravate her roiling misery. Inaudibly, she moaned, blood stained spit leaked from mouth to chin to the roughened cloth that held her arms bound to body.

"How is her progress?", the voice asked from the shadows of a concealed observation room. More precisely, at the door's jamb.

"The short answer, or do you prefer the full details, Colonel?", a raspy voice returned, as the woman it belonged to sat at a monitoring console. X-ray scans of the human brain hung over her left, while she sat before the screen that held detailed readouts of her latest subject.

"I'll take the full report at another time. With so much going on, in so many places at one time, just give me the basics." Then, as if expecting pity, he said, "The burdens of one man in service to so many."

There was a momentary pause, as if she was going to speak to that. But she gave him what was asked for.

"The syathin- 9 is taking effect. But the dosage administered was rather... excessive, sir", she returned. Her response was measured with respect, but she couldn't help but voice her minor disapproval.

"Doctor, he said, slightly amused, I'm proving a point."

She turned to face him.

"I....I don't follow, sir ", the woman said, face sheened with the tints of deep colored pixilation's from the screen. Mid-forties, if not early fifties. Rotund face, but that was the only portly aspect of her. Keen, intelligent, and cruel. *Excellent choice to head this project,* he thought cheerfully. Though he was careful not to expose that.

"This is a teachable moment ", her superior told her, an air of smugness on his half visible features. "An example of why you keep your dog on a leash. Has he been notified?"

Sigh.

"Yes, sir. I've been informed that Mr. Hurston's on his way to collect her." Comforted by anonymity, her superior fully entered the room to stand over her.

"As you're aware, this is far and away from the "Hejimma" line of maid-girls you and your colleague, your late colleague, Dr. Reit, have labored so hard to develop. And how is she working out? Mine has been experiencing difficulties, as of late."

"Hejimma is working fine", the woman said, slightly annoyed. "You probably have to increase the dosage, to make her more docile." The inflection suggested that she wanted to return to what was before her, not that it was any less unscrupulous.

"The end results of this "treatment"....... He paused, to allow her to enunciate.

"Will be the same as if Ms. Symmons had experienced a legitimate stroke."

"Very good. Very, very good. I will miss the cat and mouse, but she was getting too close. We've staked so much, come too far... ", a wistful sigh.

"She's... She'll be less than a shadow of what she was."

"Regret?"

".. No, sir!" she said hurriedly. "I'm as invested as you are, and with less protection, if you'll allow me to add. I'm just speaking the facts of the matter."

To this he chuckled lightly. Which caused her to grow slightly offended, though she took great, great care to conceal it.

"Only this once. Concentrate on gathering the facts at hand. Everything with her has been... taken care of, I trust?" She wanted to sigh again, in open exasperation this time. She didn't understand why he asked questions he knew the answers to.

"Everything's been confiscated, and is being destroyed, if it hasn't already been. Those kids she's referring to...

"What...kids ?" His annoyance underscored those two words in a sneer.

"The ones..."

His abrupt, dismissive wave of hand cut her off.

"A minor inconvenience. However, an unexpected boon that will pay great dividends in the not so immediate future. Rest assured, we'll bring that part of the game to its climax, when the timing and responsive legislation is in place."

Another sigh. "Yes, Colonel." The Doctor overseeing Jet Symmons' mutilation returned to her work, her dark face hazed in light and dark thoughts. Another shot of pain surged through Jet, and her soul screamed.

They almost missed them.

On radar, they read as two massive blips, mere kilometers away.

At first, Geon thought them derelicts. Decrepit monuments to simpler, more honest times.

Thinking to test Tahina's maneuvering skills, to have her race alongside the wall of the behemoth to the right. He made her come in closer, closer....

The hailing signal came just in the nick of time.

Near panicking, he ordered her to "Grab Jeth and hide!!"

Did he have time?

Only just enough time to get them hidden, and to switch on the anti- sensory shields.

They would detect human life on board only if he responded, or if they chose to board.

What was coming fast towards him was anything but derelict. Far from decrepit, he observed, as newness of form and make made itself horribly apparent.

These two vessels were of a new series; a GCW controlled fleet of mobile space stations entitled "The Whale." Designated for interstellar policing and rapid military interventions. Eight times the size of a normal class of trans- galactic star bruiser. Sub-orbital docking stations were in construction to fully service and maintain them. Bulky, massive yet startlingly efficient and fast , the elongated hull even curved at its rear, as to recall an actual resemblance to its Earthborn namesake.

Geon's Baby was but an ant to these behemoths. A baby ant.

Wracking his brains on this new threat, Geon only now remembered the very brief news bit on the "newest weapon in the arsenal of order and justice".

There were to be Five for every solar system, every sphere of the Human Diaspora. Each carrying, he recalled now, a standing army of five thousand or more armed soldiers, detention officers (the term guard was now considered obsolete) and a rigid command structure for each department.

Loudly, he cursed himself for not being more attentive; he put himself and those kids in this most unholy of predicaments.

Too late now to turn back, and far too risky to make the attempt to outrun it. He could only play this out, hoping for a barely favorable outcome.

The hailing signal returned, louder, more persistent.

No other options were available. Grudgingly, he cursed as he yielded to respond.

"Vessel Designated 0003457689360.... comply to request or be boarded."

The demand was repeated twice more, then suddenly, "Hold your horses already! A man has got to use the john, you know!"

Subsequent, long silence was more irritable than awkward.

Then, the voice, ice cold and thinly metallic, returned.

"Vessel 0003457689360, this is the last ...."

"Dammit, I comply!", he yelled, hating what came out of his mouth and himself for saying it. But there was nothing he could do.

He was given stern instructions to enter the behemoth to his incoming left.

Veering left, he saw its massive hangar bay. Just like looking into the inside of a terminal style space station. Over thirty of these things were now patrolling the galaxy. Yet, Geon didn't find himself feeling any safer.

"Reduce speed to low impulse", came through, from their communications to his. "Very slowly."

He acquiesced.

At the bottom of the hull, a circular entrance port revealed itself, as layers of blue and deep grey steel parted. Around the mouth there were rings of protrusions circling, row after row of metallic teeth that threatened even the sturdiest of heart. Deep orange light radiated within, its illumination menacing Geon further.

"Jonah", he said aloud, as he entered.

"Proceed to these co-ordinates ..."

The assault was immediate; orange and yellow warning lights ran from stem to stern, blinking and agitating him to shut out the illumination completely. That likely would've aroused instant suspicion, so he had to bear it. The dense concentration was meant to disorient. A dangerous game to play in so confined an area.

Behind the light were steel-glass walls on either side of him. Seemingly thin, rather transparent, this glass could survive a ship crashing into it. In between squints, he saw movement of tiny shadows in the distance. Platoons of men and women in ranks. He barely made out their sky- blue uniforms with newly issued long range hyper fire rifles strapped to their backsides.

How did they manage to get these things up and running so damn fast? He found himself wondering, in between feeling awe and violent disgust.

Tracker drones swarmed Geon's Baby from above. They moved so stealthily, they didn't register on his radar; nor did the pesky machines trigger his extremely sensitive sensor alarm. This revelation was extremely unnerving.

"Vessel 0003457689360, report to docking station 19.", a mechanical voice bellowed.

He sighed faintly. Going further, his conviction sealed that the universe had taken a definitively sharp turn for the worse. He again thought of the kids, now hiding in that tiny coffin of a compartment between the lower half of the engine and the lower magnetic pulsator. A panic room, one of many he'd installed on board, in case of pirates. But would it be enough? Could he get them out before the set time limitation on the oxygen expired?

All he could do for them, and himself was to get through this hellish situation as fast as he was able. Deflated, he pressed on.

Forging ahead two kilometers more, docking station 19 heaved into ominous view.

Cautiously, he steered into its mandible grip. The clicking sound was like mild thunder.

He anchored Geon's Baby perfectly. He saw clearly behind the walls now. There were tiers above tiers of activity. As he was anchoring, he saw a small group of young men and women being led away in chains. They were three tiers above. A spherical taser drone spurring them to hurry their movement. Though hobbled, they kept a good pace. Seeing them recalled Jeth telling him about how the Sefu Trians were herded into Asylon. It gave the old man an epiphany on human degradation, about its ability to infect, to spread itself wide and far.

Geon's Baby began rising. Then, a trembling halt.

"Vessel 0003457689360, prepare to be boarded."

Dread . Dread became a hardened pit in his stomach. One that he couldn't allow to overcome him. Two other people were depending on him to pull them through this. Abruptly, the movement stopped. The warning lights, that had stilled as he progressed on this journey into the steel bowels of humanity's new hell, returned with relentless, unnecessary vengeance. As Geon began to rise out of his seat, he felt his age in a way he never felt previously. By the time he rose fully, he almost swore to himself he aged another five years.

Putting on his poker face, he went to greet the phalanx of thugs coming to.... do whatever they were empowered to do.

His cargo bay door opened, the slow hiss layering his already high anxiety level.

The soul of the universe is dying.

Almost immediately, he was taken roughly to the side . The gloved hands were rough, the gloves themselves felt like steel wool, making thin abrasions on his open skin. They lightly pushed him. Palms to the wall, made to stand indignantly, as a squad of seven accosted his vessel.

First, the storm troopers.

Three males, then three females. The uniforms were hard gold and hunter green camo. Their faces were half covered (from crown to nostril) with bio-scanner attachments at the tip of horn- rimmed helmets that took bio-readings and sought out nano-threats.

For God's sake I hope that shield is enough, Geon thought, burying his face in the wall so as not to betray his expression.

The last of them came aboard. *Someone in authority,* Geon intuited. The caution, the lack of participation was a dead giveaway.

A slight man, with a twitchy left eye, and dark, long face by the name of Captain Luucas Braw, commanded the search party. Dour and unforgiving , he spit out orders in a rapid staccato. The kind of commanding officer that, if caught out of uniform, his subordinates would gladly give him a good and satisfying pummeling.

"Harin. Juyes. Begin sweep! Jurbes, Numes, search the cockpit, halls and personal quarters! Geoffs and Kolm, remain here!" Without a single verbal acknowledgement, they did as commanded.

Geon took inventory of the invaders. Not a one of them, excepting Braw, was over thirty. They stepped and moved with robotic fluidity; no questioning glances nor any flickers of empathy could he glimpse in them. The scuffling around of hard toed boot bitterly echoed into the halls past his cargo bay. Their superior inspected the moving equipment, running a tan gloved index finger over one of the anti-gravity lifts he kept in a disorganized corner. Turning, he gave Geon a distinct look of contempt when he lifted his finger, revealing a deep, dark smudge of caked up oil.

After a few minutes, Braw began his interrogation. His questions were perfunctory, not penetrating. That could wait. He sent Geoffs and Kolm off ship, for something or another Geon couldn't overhear what.

"Can I sit down?", Geon protested. He did his best to stay calm. *No need to be ornery, or antagonizing. Or draw this out longer than I have to. The kids.*

"No", Captain Braw said flatly. He loved his position, and clearly loved to abuse it. The whole time Geon had his eyes to the wall of his cargo bay, his hands numbed by the contact. He heard, but he was kept inhibited from looking. Footsteps again. This time animated and swift. Those two officers returned to flank Geon on both sides. If this was an intimidation tactic, it really wasn't working.

The man to the right of him spun him around. He was now face to face with Captain Braw. Who began repeating his questions, this time for his audience, then for an upcoming mandatory recording that was required of all interrogations, no matter how sudden or informal.

"Name."

"Geoniphus Thu."

"World of Birth, or Colonial outpost."

"Trikkah Septum."

"Age."

"Sixty - three years old."

"Name of star ship, registry number, and how many years in your possession...."

By the time Braw was nearly finished, the sweep of the cockpit, his personal quarters and the main level of the ship were completed.

"All secure Captain", Jurbes rasped.

"Flight logs secured and check out?"

"Clean, sir. Not a parsec near Polim Tef."

Polim Tef? Geon wondered.

"Good, Jurbes", said Braw, abruptly noncommittal. When Nums emerged from Geon's personal quarters, he confirmed the same.

Braw bore a grimace of incomplete satisfaction. His sadism had to be satisfied.

Nodding his head, Nums, Jurbes, Geoffs and Kolm led Geon off his ship. Neither cuffed, nor restrained. He had that much, at least, to be grateful about. The floor was a smooth, polished steel, with the tinges of warning light bouncing about, giving rise to spots in his line of vision. A tier above, he could spy a brief scuffle, the image of a young (presumably) woman being knocked across the face with the butt of a rifle. The thud against the transparent wall muted against the malevolent humming of energy flowing to and fro.

"To processing room Ninety- eight", Braw said coldly, looking around.

They gave him no chance to protest, or even offer at least an anxious glance of despair. They just whisked him away, a tired leaf swept away by the swift, abrupt breeze.

A panic box, Geon told them. It was truly that. An elongated, brief space that was designed to hold a maximum of twelve hours of oxygen for one person.

Two people cutting that time was bad enough. Two people hastily packed into it, like an emergency ration of sardines was catastrophe.

"Stop moving!", she complained angrily.

"Stop talking!", he countered, as upset and uncomfortable as she was.

Fingers of light seeped through the air holes, adding even more to their mutual discomfort. Petulantly, her heel rammed hard into his lower calf. Biting his lip, he grimaced.

"Such a child" he whispered, just loud enough for her to barely hear him. Just then, they heard it.

The clanging grew louder. The metal soles scraped the surface.

"Go right. I'll take the left", they overheard.

Footsteps clanged for paces more, then stopped directly over them.

She sucked in her breath, her lips. *I will not exhale... I will not exhale......*

Jeth slowed his breathing, using techniques he learned at home. Ironically, he was more at peace, in this moment, than any other time in his life. His life was shades of blue, of royal purple and yellow. He saw everyone he knew, every place he'd been, everything he did...in a sublime multi- hazing tapestry of light that was turning and shifting...

"This is some set up this guy has!", praised Harin, visibly impressed with the master mechanical puzzle Geon had put together.

"Eh", Juyes replied, far less than impressed.

"Philistine."

Jeth and Tahina heard them stalking about, taking everything apart with their eyes.

"How long are they going to hold this guy?", Juyes asked impatiently, wanting nothing more than to get back to her station. There was a seat at a pinochle game waiting for her.

"You and your stupid game", Harin said, disgruntled. He'd lost fifty Etherins at the last game he played. To her. A broken half smile appeared on her face, the part that was visible.

"Reminds me, when are you paying up the rest?", she asked, standing sentinel, while he was looking the multi systems over. None of what she was standing among held any interest for her. "Too mechanical in this place", she said, just within earshot of both Jeth and Tahina. The latter, despite herself, smirked ironically. *A woman thing,* Jeth thought derisively.

"Next pay", he said absently. He saw an emergency ladder mounted on the wall, and began ascending. *That's what you said last payday,* she thought.

Divining, Harin yelled down as he climbed, "Having problems with Arnae and the kids." She shook her head, glancing incredulously.

"So, what is this guy supposed to be, that we're wasting our time here?"

He made his way up, now standing on the next level.

The pathway Harin walked along was narrow, and led to a sub room where the magnetic pulsators could be controlled manually.

"According to DataGrid, just an old hauler and junk trader. Does small transfer jobs from time to time." He then disappeared.

"A nobody then", she said carelessly.

He came out the room, sated. She repeated the scorn laced appraisal.

"Well, now even the nobodies need to be checked out", Harin said, descending. His boots thudded hard on metal rung. " You know about the attack...by now, right?"

"Who hasn't heard?!", Juyes yelled, suddenly animated. "Damn shame, those fucking Far worlders..."

"They haven't confirmed it was actually Far Worlders", Harin spoke correctively.

"Then, protesters for them, I meant to say", she corrected herself, as they held still for a few minutes, then trekked back through back the corridors, for yet another sweep. "You have marches and protests to whine about human rights, then you blow shit up?! Shit's insane..."

They stopped at the arching jamb, near Tahina's room.

"Harin to Braw, Harin to Braw."

"What are your findings?", Braw spoke through a thick haze of static.

"All clear, sir. Making a recommendation for an extraction squad."

Words were garbled, drowned in static. Then "For?", managed to break through.

"There's a cold fission chamber that's intricately connected to the engine systems. It needs removal."

Exasperated, Braw ordered him to "Proceed immediately".

Juyes gave him a quizzical look.

"A cold fission bomb was used in the attack", said Harin, suddenly low and sullen.

"There're nutjobs out there" , returned Juyes as they walked ahead, hard footsteps echoing in the dimly lit pathways.

When she thought they were far away, she exhaled every particle of air she could spare.

"Jeth... are you okay?"

Silence. This sent her into a quick panic.

"Jeth?!" Her right hand doubled, hit hard into his back.

"Oww!", he said through a wince. This was the spot he was stabbed. He grew a little incensed, then calmed himself.

"Why didn't you answer?", she whispered furiously. *I thought you were dead fool! And... I had helped kill you.*

Not knowing how else to describe the experience, he said only "I was in thought."

She said nothing to that. "Did you hear what they said?"

"Vaguely."

She repeated the little she picked up.

He said nothing at first, then only "Makes our problems seem quite small, in the scheme of things, doesn't it?"

As with most of what Geon had seen thus far, the interrogation room they ferried him into kept the pristine newness of a vessel on its maiden voyage. Smooth, metal mirrors on all sides of him. Virtual screens, far more advanced than any he'd encountered to date, lined the top ends of the walls, barely touching the ceiling. He was taunted by non-stop imagery of destruction. The many voices commenting ran together into an almost unintelligible gibberish that only highlighted the madness he couldn't shut out.

He was sitting at the opposite side of a long, black metal table that curved into smile. He thought, grimly of the mockery when Capt. Braw entered the room, with two others in similar uniform on each side of him.

A heavy-set male, a dour, sour faced female. Their dark faces stared into his dark face with a glaring contempt. For Geon's part, it was completely mutual.

There were three chairs opposite, one directly, the others on each end. Braw took one end, sourpuss on the other. The big man took the middle; Beyond the meticulously arranged regalia, Geon saw the distinctive purple and green stripes of an interplanetary veteran, more specifically the pendant of a man wounded in service. He then noticed that, in his movement, his left arm dangled lifeless.

"Mr. Thu, he began with ceremony, we have some questions to ask you. Foremost, what are you doing hauling around a cold fission chamber, and what involvement do you have with everything above you?"

Light, finally.

When she came to, Jet Symmons was in a bed. The light burned sun bright, and she wearily turned away from its blinding glare. She saw she could see out of a circular bay window. Clear waves crashed down on the rock and red stained coral in the distance. She winced in agony, head throbbing. The whole of her cried in immense pain.

"Take it easy, Jet", a familiar voice counseled her. It took a long while for her to try to recollect. Something was very wrong. Really wrong. It never took her this long to gather her bearings. Nor was it ever this painful to rise from the realm of unconsciousness. Frowning, she could feel the heaviness of her lips, her facial muscles. The left side of her head was wrapped in adhesive bands.

She felt his eyes, felt them guiding her, delicately, in his direction.

She looked at the face of her boss, and the immaculate, sterile surroundings of a hospital. Pristine, clinical. And with no memory of how she got here. Painfully, she turned away, this time to the door. And saw her. Lurking at the door jamb, was a slim, brown, rotund faced woman, holding a stethio-pad in slim brown fingers.

Without knowing why, Jet felt herself shudder as she came closer. Mr. Hurston, sitting near, stared intently at her. Almost protectively.

"Try not to speak Ms. Symmons", the woman said. You suffered a major injury. Nod if you understand me so far."

She was nearly unintelligible, Jet struggling to grasp the gist. Her mind was sludge, her thoughts slurred. Mr. Hurston bent,whispered softly in her right ear. It was then that she nodded slowly, mournfully. Her boss, her friend looked at his star reporter gravely. Almost as if he was guilty of doing her harm.

"You suffered severe neurological damage; massive damage to your vocal cords and cerebral cortex. Not to mention a near paralysis of your right side. You've just suffered, and barely survived a massive stroke.

Faintly, an ember of lucidity stung her.

In recognition, Jet nodded, then began heaving. Flowing tears streamed down the distorted ruins of her beautiful face.

As Hurston took her by the hand, she clutched the sleeve of his jacket, shamelessly, tremulously weeping now.

He looked from Symmons to the doctor, who looked at the moving scene with seeming dispassion. But he grew infuriated as he glimpsed cruel amusement in her eyes.

You've ruined her! You brutes destroyed my star reporter!

Returning a vicious smile, Hurston caught it, and squeezed Symmons' hand harder, much more protectively. The message was sent, and sheepishly, he received it:

We wanted to do worse, far worse. But this is a favor to you. You were careless, and this is the price you settled for.

Twelve hours.

After twelve hours, Geon was finally allowed to leave. Stalking away from the Interrogation room, drenched in sweat, withered and humiliated. From station nineteen to his own ship , the walk seemed an eternity. No escort, not to mention a weak, disingenuous "Our sincere apologies for holding you." He was merely shooed away, an immediate afterthought. Obviously, there were bigger fish to fry. Only glimpses of nonchalance trailed him. His ship. Drawing near, he thought of how important it was to him, and how this experience had suddenly made it useless in the same thought. There was no telling what happened to his ship. But at least they didn't get them...

The kids! Thinking they may have suffocated gave urgency to his stride. It was his fault all this happened. He should've been more observant, more alert. Never reckoning on a situation like this in a universe turning increasingly fascistic by the minute; his error may yet prove fatal. His pace quickened.

He said nothing, passing a squad of five goons going the opposite way. To them, he was just some an old derelict hauler, a dusty old fart in mismatched (since two- piece outfits were the mark of poor people) clothes, who smelled of coil warp oil and weak bourbon. A cosmic hobo. He ignored their coldly amused looks, the little too audible snickers as he passed. They were automatons covered in flesh, far worse than those he saw on Asylon; the ones here were totally bereft of a conscience, of empathy. Of a soul.

They're murdering the soul, the very heart of humanity itself.

Geon's Baby. His ship was nearing him.

He had to play this cool. Not even give them yet another reason to stop him.

He hastily closed shut the cargo bay. He slumped in the seat, and began maneuvering his ship out of the belly of the whale. It took almost all his remaining restraint to guide it steadily. He already knew they heavily damaged his vessel. It wasn't moving as it should, the.. He couldn't worry now. The lights assaulted him, strained his vision.

Images of Tahina and Jeth suffocated teased him, tormented him almost to distraction. His sole consolation was a belated recognition of clenched metal teeth drawing closer.

Its iron mouth noisily opened to allow him egress. Geon's Baby limped away into the dark expanse.

When he was away, far enough to avoid detection, he slowly came to a full stop. His craft wobbled, which it had never done. Indignant, he fled to the panic box, relieving himself on the way.

He breathed deeply when he was halfway there. He gathered himself. Then breathed out in anguish, "Jeth! Tah!"

Behind, a smooth hand jerked his elbow.

Spasmatic, he whirled around, his tightened fists balled (for a split attosecond, he thought they left someone behind), he was half angered, half relieved to see Tahina standing behind him. He exhaled hard, almost not noticing the pistol in her hand. *His pistol.*

She was looking at him, almost as though he were a stranger.

"Girl, are you *insane?!* ", he asked her wildly.

"Insane times we live in", she sullenly returned. Then, in the dimmed light, she whispered, "We thought.... they hurt you. Even, ...killed you."

He didn't meet her intent stare, suddenly dwelling on how he must be appearing to her. He said, reservedly, "They hurt me all right. Just not in the ways you see. " A moment of silent understanding .

"Jeth is...?"

She nodded forward.

"Gathering the remains of what they left behind. Making sense of it. They gutted the whole thing nearly."

He knew, better than either of them. They hauled the core of the cold fission chamber before him. In a sensational manner each oscillator core, grid chip panel and hyper warp channeling core that sealed it from exposure and contaminating the other energies he relied upon was categorized, and inventoried. In front of him, they flaunted the destruction of over two decades of sweat, hours, and hard, thought straining labor.

"Jeth said they left us with less than low impulse. They did damage to the other sections as well. " She was relating to him what he already surmised. But something she wanted to ask, she couldn't bring herself to do it .

"They found your clothes", he said flatly. "Both yours and Jeth's."

"However, they didn't find us", she said, a little confused.

"I told them my kids went off to the universities. That I keep the clothing around for memories. He grumped about that a bit. How long were you both in that hole?"

They were walking to what was left of his engine room. She explained how, after the first squad left, they fled to another part of the ship. To another hiding box.

"My pistol...how did you....?" He fell disturbingly silent. The ramifications if *something DID happen*. He was already fraught with anger and anxiety as it was.

"I recalled where you keep it hidden", she said, matter of fact. "I took it when we stole away, the second time." She felt foolish that she had to clarify, but she felt the need to make the distinction. By the time they were at the jamb of the entrance, He asked her, in earshot of Jeth, "What have you heard about Polim Tef?"

"By now, who hasn't heard?"

Those fuckers attacked my HOME!!

She spent the whole day crying. News streams wouldn't stop talking about it, except for sparse, grim tidbits about the cruel twist of fate that befell Jet Symmons, or financial ups and downs.

"Who cares about that overbearing, overrated hack!", Quinn, in a deep rage, screamed, uncontrollably, thrashing about on the platform, causing energy distortions.

Grieving, she stepped off, deactivating the machine. Dejectedly, she slumped hard on the high lounge sofa in her "temporary (nearly three months now)" suite. Rage, grief, more rage and grief, and then, an uneasy rest.

THEY ATTACKED MY HOME WORLD!!!!

Polim Tef was her home, despite never returning for anything , even funerals. She never saw the urban renewal, nor the eviction of the poor into more rural, though less fertile areas of the wide swath of countryside. And certainly, while donating somewhat generously to her alma mater, she never once answered a communique concerning being a commencement orator. But her home was attacked. And like all her fellow countrymen and women, her blood boiled with unfathomable fury. *THOSE MAD DOGS ATTACKED THE WHOLE OF CIVILIZATION, NOT JUST POLIM TEF !!!*

Two coordinated assaults using part cold fission, part nano nuclear bombs (For simplicity, it was reported as *solely* cold fission. The average terrorist, extremist or radical had far easier access to cold fission materials than nano nuclear technology. A fact that was hammered home ruthlessly in the first forty- eight hours of coverage).

The first happened at Akebulan University. A service shuttle , holding some five hundred students, staffers and regular passengers, was hijacked by campus radicals, who then used the vessel as a projectile.

Screams of horror, pleadings for reason from the terrified, doomed students and faculty did nothing to dissuade their soon to be murderers. "FOR ASYLON! STRIKE AGAINST TRYANNY!!", their death cry had managed to be recorded and sent viral by before detonation.

There was no time to react.

A massive explosion roared, quaking the immediate area, blinding, horrifying the unwilling spectators.

Fourteen buildings were evaporating, as were the people within their walls, and in the immediate proximity. Steam stood in place of stone, steel, glass, bone and flesh.

Government officials and response teams were scrambling to make sense of everything, to mobilize a search and rescue. To enact lockdown protocols, to bring the guilty to whatever severe justice Polim Tef, and the GCW could muster.

Then, the second bomb struck. This time, the Government's Citadel was the victim, in the heart of its downtown district. Thousands reduced to instant cinder.

Blue steam reached the ether, overtaking the cloudy afternoon skies, billowing, blinding, and choking. Those that were out of range were stung with its toxic radiation, and the life altering experience of having survived such a dastardly strike against life, against order and reason.

The only consolation lay in the fact that since the campus was on Spring Recess, many students and staff weren't present.

A campus capable of holding well over two hundred thousand a given semester, destroyed beyond salvation. The seat of planetary government, the bustling downtown district that supplemented it, reduced to a steaming crater, and the resulting release of toxic gases that rendered the planet uninhabitable.

Seven hundred thousand died. The majority in the attacks, but others perished days, weeks, months and years later from radioactive poisoning. The attack on the "Harvard of the Cosmos" left a deep scarring on the future of academia. If the greats seats of learning couldn't be protected, then where was the security?

The backlash to this tragedy came swiftly, and with blinding fury.

As the Counselor General came from Polim Tef, it was highly speculated this was an attack on him personally.

The New Democratic Society, a radical political group, claimed responsibility for the assaults, resulting in a massive shockwave surging through the collegiate system in the aftermath. There were thousands, if not hundreds of thousands, of college and university students in that very organization. And others like it. One of the tenets of the college radicals and protestors was the revoking of the Thirteenth Law. And the abolition of the neo-slavery its re-emergence had established. The Asylon uprising was a focal point of mass galvanization. The Young Protestors movement was gaining in support, in members, rapidly picking up steam.

Then, Polim Tef happened.

Most of the news cycle (thirty- six hours) after this ghastly declaration were spent roundly denouncing the group, the students, and there were almost as many counter denunciations and denials. Many chapter heads vehemently denied "Any knowledge and participation in the heinous attacks and we revile those who acted in the name of our organization." In the wake of the worst terrorist attack in the history of humanity (in recent times, certainly), such statements rang hollow and decidedly false.

Before the Governance Council, with a traumatized galaxy watching, looking for a shred of security, the Counselor General tearfully, passionately vowed to "Bring to blindingly swift and harsh justice the terrorists, enablers, and those who support, either through deeds or word, returning the barbarity of bygone eras to the Humanity of 2718."

Within the first forty- eight hours, thousands, on various worlds, were arrested.

Ordinances allowing for free interplanetary travel were suspended .

Various heads of planetary governments took the opportunity to denounce vociferously the "subversive elements that threaten common decency and the order of civilization."

Several worlds began passing laws severely curtailing interplanetary immigration. Schools of higher learning were adopting draconian measures for acceptance. And attendance. Millions of students were expelled summarily, the work of the past several years wiped away. Political activism on campuses was outlawed.

In the eyes of world leaders and those they subjugated, the Thirteenth Law had become THE LAW.

Under the Thirteenth law ,whose once narrow definitions were vastly expanding, those placed under arrest were now detained indefinitely, and their sovereignty status removed. Just a mere inkling of conspiracy was cause enough to stop an individual, check both their G.I.D. and the newly revamped S.I.N. . Travelling without one or either would land a person in one of the newly established detention outposts or one of the whales.

Protestors were now side eyed with deep suspicion.

Public opinion was now for a strict, penal system. A system that punished, yet somehow avoided the justice of a fair trial, presumed innocence and the notion that association didn't equate guilt.

As the dead were mourned, and the (nominally) guilty were rounded up, few were brave enough to buck the force of the tidal wave, and publicly denounce wholesale incarceration and the detaining of those who had no actual involvement, nor those who had, when their public records were held to scrutiny, no history nor incidents of "extremist radicalism".

And very few spoke to injustice, because they were scared that they'd be persecuted next. Soon enough, some were. Having "contrary views" became not just a social crime, but a legal offense whose exact penalty, beyond a depleted credit, negative S.I.N. score, and general banishment to the "Abyss inhabited by the Untouchables", had yet to be defined in clarity.

A net of fear had been cast about the Human Diaspora. And was tightening its insidious grip daily. Though Outer Space expanded for miles incalculable, there was, almost literally, no place to run.

Not too long after that run in with the law, Geon hobbled his ship to a waystation just above Currev, the second to last world before entering The Milky Way. Currev, itself was left uninhabited, due to its high concentration of poisonous gases. "Venus' little sister", it was called. Just a million miles above orbit, what began life as an obscure observatory for a now defunct gas extracting company evolved into a popular pit stop for long distance interstellar craft, or planetary tradership with crew looking for R and R. It was often called Trexegon, for it's unusual design, and it had a hold capacity of two million plus people. Detached docking stations hovered eerily close. Tiny specks of lights flittered, as people were going to and fro in shuttlecrafts. "False Star" (shortened from False Star Space Station) became its most popular designation, due to the intensity of illumination it and its various addendums generated.

The immensity of False Star was a source of awe to any who glimpsed it for the first time. There were literally hundreds of vessels, from giants to dwarfs holding in both the slanting docks, or the long, cylindrical limbs that stretched out east and west, or the collection of piers that looked like a permanent welding operation gone wrong. To date, it remained, still, the largest docking station and depot in the known universe.

Though rarely excited, Geon called both Tahina and Jeth to come see it as its immensity drew near.

From the cockpit, the teens marveled at the vast construction.

"How much steel you think went into building this?", Jeth asked with widened eyes, obviously impressed.

"The average estimate is twenty- nine point twenty- four quadrillion metric tons", Tahina answered.

"I was being rhetorical", Jeth responded, eyes rolling.

"Then, you should have specified beforehand", she replied curtly.

"Knock it off ", said Geon, annoyed with the pair of them.

Resembling portable power grids, the dock stations were recently added appendixes. A descendant of the earlier space elevator, that were still in use on the few worlds that could afford the expense and headache of managing one. Here, docking stations more than made up for the massive cost of operation.

Circling, Geon eventually found an opening at False Star itself.

After a rough docking sequence, they soon found themselves among a wide ocean of people. A slow moving mass, moving slower than the stars outside. Sighs, humming, pouting and other signs of impatience (save cursing, oddly enough), accompanied Geon and his charges as they navigated the hordes. Finally, the horizontal escalator.

Outside, shuttle crafts gleamed brilliantly, taking people to and fro, as solar powered vertical escalators on all levels (seventy-seven exactly) ferried the landbound from points A to B. Each side of the escalator was braced by iron ore gating, which, at certain points revealed openings allowing people to get off, and on. Hyper lifts less than fifteen paces away, were filled to the capacity taking people in ascent or descent throughout the man made juggernaut.

Way above them, far beyond the traffic and hard steel that towered for thousands of miles, sparkling stars faintly touched, then bounced sadly off multi layered, re-enforced steel glass that kept the oxygen inside as some quietly marveled at an apex of human ingenuity.

And that was just the entry *into* the outpost proper.

Metallic tiled streets were filled with busy people, many being service technicians or other blue class (formerly called blue collar) professional types who maintained places like False Star. Brown and blue uni-suits were ubiquitous. Many others were stars men in the uniform of their respective starships, with the insignia of the respective worlds and companies that sent them.

So many shades of brown and beige faces, Tahina thought, suddenly clutching Jeth by the forearm.

He blushed with wary attraction. Dismissing it, and her, he fixed his stone like gaze on all and everything around him, taking it all in. Amazement, disdain, curiosity and indifference all competed to solidify his initial impression of all this. How, if Asylon and everything associated with it, and men like Hagit, could represent the worst the race had to offer, and a place like this, and men like Geon and his father, Tahina's father (based on how glowingly she talks of him) represent the best, then why did the abyss of Humanity constantly hold the upper hand?

Places like False Star, a gleaming nova bright in the cosmos, were becoming those increasingly rare segue ways where all types of people crossed paths. The professional sailor, the workman, the slum bum, and far worse congregated here, whether invisible to the other's existence or no.

As they managed themselves onto another moving walkway, Jeth grimaced. He didn't like crowds. Too many bad memories. Trunza Square was months ago. In all actuality, that tragic day was coming upon a nine month anniversary. But it never left the forefront of his thinking. Tahina once said, out of earshot (so she thought) "It's almost like his life ended on that day, and he keeps reliving it, from morning rise to night fall." Of course, after a heated argument (of which there was many of late), Jeth considered her observation. And refocused on life in the here and now. And of late, he was doing better.

Turning to Tahina, Geon half grinned. "Makes you feel good, doesn't it?"

She didn't openly respond. The look of triumph on her face was enough. For over the full three months they were onboard, after almost (for her) a year of being confined to Asylon, it was enough to be acknowledged as being right. In anything. By Geon Thu, no less.

Danger lurked, but how great it felt to walk freely, and among so many people !

"Rather risky, isn't it?", Jeth inquired cautiously . People were walking close, bustling and hurried. Some curious stares came their way, sure, but mostly all were going about their own business.

People who wore more than one suit of multifiber, wasn't a cause of scrutiny. Poor people were everywhere on False Star .

"Everything's risky these days", Geon said over the noise of the crowd. "Some risks are better taken than others."

"So, we're going to do it? ", she asked, now openly beaming with triumph.

Geon side glanced her. "For a smart girl, you really like asking the obvious, don't you?"

"Just because you finally said ..."

"You want to do this, or not?!". That was the closest Geon would bring himself to admit that she was right on this occasion.

"I'll take that", she said, in smug revelry. At her side, Jeth shook his head.

Even if either teenager had heard the name, no words could adequately describe this, an artificial world all its own, with its own laws and logic, an internal rhythm that only the longstanding tenant truly grasped.

Lining its streets were retail kiosks, storefront eateries, cyber tattooing parlors, tech servicing cubicles and littered here and there, upscale boutiques with the newest fads.

Tahina found herself enamored by one of these economic sirens. She saw a one piece Uni-suit of swirling blues that, if that price were within range, she'd be glad to possess it.

"Don't get any ideas, Geon warned, we won't be here long."

"I'd rather be on board working on the engines", grumbled Jeth.

She whirled, thinking he was mad. She saw his frustration, and relented. She gave a kindly squeeze of forearm. He smiled at the gesture, saying nothing. His morose reticence irked her beyond what was humane. Angrily, she let go of his forearm. He frowned.

It was a long stretch; after a time, everyone and everything began to look the same, to feel non-distinct. Before either could protest (he subliminally picked up on the growing boredom in their body language), Geon informed them "We're getting close."

Overhead, dense, bright holographic red lettering hung over, saying "THIS WAY TO OLDTOWN."

"What in all the worlds is an Old Town?", Jeth asked, leery.

"You'll see", was Geon's cryptic reply. Tahina said nothing, taking silent note.

Continuing, the streets became less and less crowded. The walkways thinned out on both sides. They traveled past the info grid panels that sometimes works, the flickering holo-streams that blinked in and out, and finally the cobalt walls that, upon a close inspection had lesions of rust plaguing the upper half of the arched roof.

"Here we are", Geon said, getting off at section 32.

"This took forever", Tahina complained.

"This is the Old Town?", Jeth asked stupidly.

Turning, Geon said with portent, "Yes".

They quickly looked at each other, and then at him...

The entry wasn't anything grand, nor even remotely kept up. A dingy, time worn cavern that linked one part of False Star to the other. *They've seen the good part, now for the bad. Though I know they've been exposed to far worse. May Providence be kind to their souls.* Geon led them into a different shadow and light....

Overhead, news streams played on diamond shaped holo-tronics, ancestors of the very system on Geon's Baby. News and sports. Not even news, but more bits on the entertainment world. Jeth had taken notice how, more and more frequently, news cycles were pushing the frivolous, the asinine to the forefront of the public consciousness. Before coming here, he remarked about it at the Table.

"Bread and circuses", Geon said, downing the last of the Duriyan squash and bean soup Tahina had made.

"Come again?". Jeth was unfamiliar with the term.

"Naturally", Tahina chimed in, in her encylopedic way. "The term gives reference to the history of Ancient Rome, one of the largest empires seen in the history of Ancient Earth. It serves as an allegory to the strategy of mass distraction employed by various governments since to supply a never-ending array of diversions to keep the populace from focusing on the more important matters of...."

By the time she finished her lengthy dissertation, he was halfway out the room.

Before them, around them, and above them was the ruins of the original False Star, a subspace science station designed to make money siphoning the gaseous elements from Currev. Ghosts of a distant past spoke in tarnished, rusting panel plating , in now gutted and left to posterity extractor tubes, long neglected and robbed of the precious elements (specifically AU) that made the hulking containers function. A sacrifice to both profit and modernity. Rows of metallic flames lined the entrance. On further scrutiny Tahina saw that it was clear steel glass, with whatever energy source they used would flow through, simulating an actual flame.

"Quaint", she commented, nearly passing through them until she saw the cobwebs. Visions of creepy crawlers pouncing on her made her avoid them, unexpectedly giving both Geon and Jeth a mild chuckle. She glared, dismayed they would find humor in her paranoid phobia.

Moving on, there was nothing left, really, for the imagination, except a ceremonial plaque that cracked, halved beyond readability.

"Look alive and be alert, Geon warned, this is unholy land we're treading upon."

"Really, now?!", Tahina blurted, obviously apprehensive. Recalling the long stretches of no man's lands back home. Barren areas that served as a hub for dujin heads. She trembled when her mother left out the front door, returning some days later, eyes dull and glassed over, with one less tooth. Fresh, long, thin scars on her arms and legs, though, reddened and blistered, always stuck with her. It repulsed her, frightened her. Slowly, it began to solidify her contempt for her mother.

"So how does coming here help us to achieve our ends?", she asked, to refrain from dwelling too much on the past.

"By visiting an old friend", Geon answered tersely. "Follow me."

In the distance somewhere, the Counselor General could be heard through shoddy audio, lethargically bleating something or other about "Intergalactic Justice for the victims of Polim Tef, intergalactic justice for us all." Glitches in the ancient system caused the tinny voice to abruptly terminate. The further they went, among the stripped down husks of hover trucks that used to hold the container tubes, the flooring was corroded, tarnished by long time exposure. *What could make metal crack and burnish like this? There are no signs of a fire,* Jeth wondered.

They crossed over the inlaid transporter tracks, which was contorted out of usefulness in some areas. Not too far off, a group of obelisks, octagonal in shape, rose and slumped unevenly in the background. On this side, the station's gravitational field in some parts was very thin, Geon warned them.

"What kind of friend would you have here?", Tahina asked him.

"The type that can get us things off radar, like your GID", Geon retorted, near snapping at her. Since their incident with the whales, he was edgy. Low spirited, holding them somewhat at a distance. Tahina, wondering when he'd finally explode, slid away.

Abruptly turning, he said to her, " Sorry for that ". She nodded at him warily, lips drawn in. They kept walking, almost being pulled into a sudden gravity vortex. "Like going through a field of land mines", the old man groused.

Not meters from the obelisks lay another, more decrepit grouping of buildings; Five in all, interconnected both in structure, in malignant aura. Coming to a pentagonal shaped entry point. Scarred into the beaten metal read "**OLDTOWN**".

"We're here, at last", said Geon. There was a level of intensity in his tone that was sudden, like a red alert.

"So... here's the universally infamous Old Town?!", said the girl incredulously.

"It's what the sign says, genius", replied the boy.

"Shut up the both of you, and come on", said the man. He took the reins, and stepped into the tin lined corridor. They began walking into a maze of iniquity. A lair conceived by a latent , hidden genius. Of societies within society. For Jeth and Tahina, this was the formal introduction to the underbelly of the Human Diaspora. A harrowing journey into the reality as far as how people chose to live their lives.

Turning the first corner, a sharp left down another. Decay, disrepute and disregard became worse as they walked the faint, neon lit (first hard orange, then purple, then choking blue) pathways, humming lights sizzling at one point far ahead, spitting sparks that jumped about and died on the dingy, chrome alloyed floor. Briefly Tahina went back to the ship that brought her to Asylon.

The lost battle, the dead ...the snapping neck.

She was shaken back to reality. Jeth took the rear, on guard against anyone coming from behind. His look was as grave as she'd ever seen him, and that made her very uncomfortable. Something she never felt from him before.

It was winding down, this last passageway, its walls blood smeared, almost like scenes of art in a twisted sense.

When the light died finally, they were greeted to another full eye's view of structural degradation.

Steel pavement rusted in degrees. Storefronts were now husks of buildings, abandoned to inactivity and neglect. In some places up high and on a wall to the right of them, lay a chaotic pattern of multi-colored scribbling, mostly profanities. Written advertisements for girls Lisa and Maris Ada and the good times they offered. Above, red and maroon, subbing for solar brilliance, offered a devilish substitute.

For the first time in almost hours, they encountered other people.

The question now was what kind of people.

The few that straggled about, were lost in the fog and despair of their own worlds. Air, from vents, breezed and blew about any debris scattered about. Though artificial, its breath was unseasonably (for a station with climate control) cold and harsh.

A pair of derelicts staggered in the wind, obviously inebriated. A man, far in the background, hunched over a battered metal drum barrel, cursing the sudden loss of his heat. The sudden cool made Tahina fold her arms over breasts, almost stepping on Geon's heels. This place had the very look and definite feel of the worst urban obliteration she'd ever witnessed. A woman, this time, was huddling herself in a clump of ragged cloth, sleeping in a culvert, crying to be heard. Shadows speaking, weeping, and most shockingly, laughing.

Soon they came to another block; the skeletal remains of power silos.

"Where in Blue Hades are we now? ", the girl whispered. Jeth was near, his eyes wandering, taking everything in. Even for his now wizened eyes, this place was unsettling.

"One of the biggest black markets in this half of the galaxy", Geon said grimly. "Maybe the universe."

"A dubious claim, I imagine", Jeth said. Geon almost turned, expecting Tahina to make such a statement.

"Only to those who haven't seen it."

"Well, where... ?"

"Under your very feet.", Geon said baldly.

"Why is such a place here?", Jeth couldn't help but ask. The silos around them, cobalt steel plated and windowless, forbade and reeked of depravity. If peered at closely enough, a person could see some distorted image of themselves. One especially leaned sideways like a drunkard. The foundation was rusted, flaking beyond repair.

"It brings good business", Geon said flatly, as he headed toward it. Tahina and Jeth eyed him suspiciously, then followed. He went to another building, sharply turning a hard right. And kept walking.

"Does it remind you of home, Tah?", Jeth whispered. To his recollection, Sefu Trius didn't have the problems with failing infrastructure that other Far worlds had. He found it disturbing that there was at least a sliver of good that Hagit could be credited for.

Side eying him, she responded tersely, "Some aspects, yes. Not all of us are fortunate to grow up in a farming commune."

He said defensively, "I didn't mean it offensively..."

"Regardless, it *was* offensive."

"Knock it...off", Geon said, his patience wearing thin from their constant sniping. Lately they started behaving like unruly children. The whole Polim Tef situation, and that encounter with the "law" was more than enough to make a person jittery, act other than their normal selves. But it was getting ridiculous.

Jonah.

The parable of Jonah played over and over in his mind. The prophet trapped in the belly of the whale, the ginormous beast. Allegory had become reality for him...Which was one of the primary reasons he came here.

"We're here", he announced.

They were at the last silo, better maintained than the others. Geon half circled to its right, to, of all things, a simple code lock door. Was a code lock door. Only the ripped off face that hung by a rusted screw remained.

It, the door, looked to have been slapped on, as an afterthought. The broken jamb fractured haphazardly. Its handle was still intact, though, as Geon, with Jeth's help, had to wrest it open.

Stark desolation was shoved aside for a cavalcade of lights and the kinetic energy of illicit affairs. Geon was sure to keep them close; the place they entered was a bar room, filled with some of the familiar brown and blue suits, and many others. There was a woman, ragged, and without shame, picking and eating the yellowed scabs on her diseased legs in a corner. Some others sat at the end of a long, cracked in the middle, granite bar, nodding their lives away. Tobacco smoke flowed from tables where some of the suits and a couple of ladies, obviously good time girls, were enjoying a game of cards.

A fight almost broke out between two women over some guy named "Rufus".

"We're going downstairs", Geon said pointedly to Jeth's unasked questioning.

Tahina felt the stares coming from the bar. And from the tables. She tensed. Slightly, in response, Geon raised his plaid shirt slightly. The handle of his quick pistol stood out between left hip and widening waistline. Some heads turned quickly away. A few, their heads moving at a sloth's pace, contemplating whether their lust was worth the raw, excruciating pain laser fire could inflict.

"Young people, especially runaways, fetch a nice price in places like this."

Jeth gaped his mouth , saying nothing.

Tahina looked behind and then at the hyper lift they were about to enter, wondering how many suffered that very fate. Daily, monthly, yearly. For the first time she started to seriously contemplate the darker side of being free. Liberty had its vices as it had its virtues.

It was an old school model, yet another holdover from the original outpost. Geon banged hard on the red rectangular button to summon it. One had to wonder what the designers, if they could be brought back to the land of the living, would make of what their creation had become. *Would they be appalled, or grimly amazed?* Tahina wondered.

Garbled, a faint ding announced arrival. Weakly, its rust speckled doors parted. It was crowded. The people, most of them, began filing out. Some gave curious stares. The stink of hard liquor and filthy sex failed to go with them. The light in the roof, which was missing a few panels (exposing the cobweb and dust covered wiring) ebbed and dimmed, almost blacking out.

There were only six levels indicated on the wall panel, including the basement. In the sputtering intercom, Geon repeated three times "Basement!"

A man, slumping over on the bannister, warbled weakly, "The basement is... What a basement does... My life is there...just because." His once bright tan overalls were stained, reeking of a mix of ethosene and Plutonian scotch. His glass eye moved comically as he nodded his balding, scarred head to an unspoken song.

Undisturbed, the would - be poet crooned slowly, and off key. Tahina kept herself at the filth stained metal doors, as they began their descent. Making sure to not actually touch them, of course. And to give herself enough space between her and the wino. A sense of pity briefly came over her. She had seen this so many times. And still had no understanding as to how someone could think that a substance like drugs or alcohol could be an escape. That kernel of empathy crumbled when her mother came to mind. *I can't forgive her. I just can't....*

Aching, their transportation rumbled as it moved, pained from who knows how many years of abuse. Jeth thought they might get stuck. Tahina winced at the leering glass eye watching her. The wino cocked his head, as he pulled out the miniature for another swig. Then he regaled them with another hit.

"Black beauty, black beauty... she was a ... green eyed, black...be..." his head lurched down as he began snoring, crumpled in the corner. She suppressed a smile at the drunk man's awkwardly rendered compliment.

It continued to shake downwards.

Finally, they made it to the basement. Doors creaked their way open. For both teens, it was like re-entering the Pit of Hell.

"Let's go", Geon said tensely. "Eyes open and be ready for anything." Jeth and Tahina exchanged a glance. *As if he needed to tell us that!*

The final leg of their journey began down a long, dank, crooked hallway where the malodor of wasted lives and depravity continued.

This part of Old Town was called the sub ruins; the place of dregs and the hopelessly destitute. In groups of twos, threes and fives, gangs of people huddled together at various points down the disquieting, low lit corridor; engaging in games of chance (craps), soliciting favors (of all kinds), slumped over in stupor, or backs to the walls . A young man, hypodermic puncturing his blistered, pus ridden arm, had grown cold as he lay folded in front of a sliding, bronze colored door that was numbered Suite 125 (Suite was more recently added). His eyes were fixed in his head, permanently in mid roll. Only from the small sliver of ice blue could someone tell he had blue eyes.

For a good minute, Tahina stood, staring. Either out of impatience, or growing revulsion of everything surrounding him, Jeth nudged her forward.

"I've never seen an albinoid before", she said carelessly. Someone heard, looked at her quizzically.

"He's... He wasn't an albino", Jeth corrected, placing a protective distance between her and the offended party. "And you're not missing anything." And to keep her moving, he added, "I'll tell you later."

What struck out to her was how pale he was. Revulsed as she was, she couldn't look away so easily as Jeth . She never saw someone of that hue before. Living or dead.

He couldn't have been no older than Jeth.

Going further, Jeth couldn't take it anymore.

"I... never thought people lived like this, on purpose", Jeth spoke out, openly disgusted.

"For thousands of years, people have", Geon said, his face expressionless. "For millennia after we're gone, they'll continue to live this way."

Tahina turned herself away. This was too much like home. Only difference was that the moral and physical decay was stronger, cloistered. The carpet was blood stained, waste stained, ripped and torn past any point of repair. Beads of its rotted fabric were everywhere, and for some reason the image of seedlings came to her mind.

"Why?", Jeth, asked, though not desiring an answer. Bad things were what others inflicted on you, or you hurting them. He never imagined about the evil people perpetually do to themselves.

Even in Asylon... he remembered before they escaped, just before the uprising, the suicides. It was almost one a week. The most grotesque image was of the girl who took some loose barbed wire and hung herself. The wound was obscene, almost decapitating her.

Even now, the image made him want to hurl up his lunch. And even though a fellow Sefu Trian took his own life, he couldn't fault him. He considered that one of the many sins of places like Asylon, not the cowardly act he was taught suicide is supposed to be. *Isn't all of this around us suicide, in one form or another?*, he pondered morbidly.

"Because they can, and because they wish to", Tahina blurted out. Impatiently, she almost moved past Geon, who grabbed her right arm gently. And shoved her back behind him not so gingerly. Jeth barely formed a smirk.

Another group of five huddled near an open incinerator shaft, its putrid burning smell permeating the immediate area. Faded and beaten leather showed its age in the smoldering firelight. A quintet of three men and two women, seemingly in their late twenties. Jeth caught a glimpse of the curiosity in their eyes, the muted fury. Fury at what exactly he couldn't decipher. *Just so long as they keep their distance.*

"Turn your head, or keep it down", he cautioned. "We're almost there."

Without warning, a door less than five paces ahead flew open, and a naked, drugged up banshee flew out, cowering and screaming. Everything, everyone in the hallway came to a halt.

Instantly, Geon drew his pistol. The kids lurched back. The wall and floor people nearby, that were lucid enough, staggered away in a hurry, rancorous whispering trailing them.

The naked woman was near fetal, holding up a trembling, bloodied arm, in obvious surrender. Smooth and brown, the smudges on her, the widened, red lined, cracked corneas, and the etched horror reminded Tahina of scenes she had to watch all too often back home. She stood behind Geon, torn violently between memory and getting involved.

Another woman came from out the room, bigger than two men put together, looking two times meaner. Face curled in a snarl, the cut on the cheek leaking, blood flowing out mercilessly. Red stained her neck and a tattered half shirt. There was the weapon of attack, a bloodied meat cleaver in her manlike hand, blood spitting down on soiled, wiry carpet.

Geon fired two shots. One pierced the wall behind the fear struck naked girl, the second sliced the cleaver's handle, just above her would be murderer's thumb. Blood tarnished blade thumped hard on the floor.

Stunned, her antagonist promptly fled back inside the room, slamming the door. The girl was lucid enough to run further up the hallway, turning the left corner. The shadows swallowed her whole.

"Fugih is a hell of a drug", Geon whispered aloud.

"Obviously", Jeth replied with unusual sarcasm.

"What narcotic isn't?", Tahina groused. This was common to her by now. By far, she was more worlds weary than Jeth. There were times she envied the farm boy's naivete, then others when she pitied him. Like now.

The whole episode made him shake his head in contempt. Once, he thought Hagit was the worst thing humanity exemplified. But Asylon proved him wrong. Now the "free" universe where people "Lived lives free of despair and oppression", was showing itself as depraved and undignified as the Far worlds supposedly were. On the news streams, he could hear, behind the flowery and tongue twisting words Tahina loves so much, the arrogance, the condescension. Particularly in the ones who claimed to "Speak for those who had not the wherewithal to speak for themselves." People were laying around in their own waste, lives wasting away. *What a deception!* An outer shell of magnificence hid a rotted and diseased core, the true heart of it all. Suite 147. This time he didn't announce it.

He banged furiously on the door. What happened next was almost magical. In the door's middle , a circle appeared, like an illusion. Or some form of high- tech surveillance equipment that was outlawed. Or hidden in plain sight. Just the type of technology Geon was looking for.

"Code?" , a fembotic voice asked demurely, almost seductively.

Geon scrunched his face, laboring to remember. "Seven damned numbers. Now I got it...777....7777."

"Passage... allowed." The door slid open, an aroma of fragrance and burned Yammum root flooded the hallway. It was strong, yet not overpowering. And strangely welcoming. Whether it was inviting them to solace or impending danger, they were about to discover a new thread in the tapestry of mankind.

First scent, then they were assailed, yet again, by another cavalcade of multi- hued illumination. The brilliance wasn't blinding, nor an irritant. It was merely unexpected.

Speaking with a wonder no one knew he had, Jeth said, above a clattering of noise, "Look at how high up we are!"

They were on the top deck of what was a gutted out Etrimean Tanker. Hull consisting of the hardest steel and Thaladium alloyed metals of its day. Electricity was running through the place through braids of coil wire that hid behind the hard paneling, flowing through wall to wall, ceiling to floor. The skylight, under which they were standing, turned a concentrated yellow, mimicking the sun, while climate control was set at an estimable seventy degrees of heat.

"The floor's heated as well, as is the walls, Geon explained, to keep the place habitable." They went down a level.

"What's that?", Jeth asked over continuous, furious chatter going on around them. Very large pockets of crowds. On this level alone, there had to be at least, some hundreds of makeshift stalls.

"By itself, this relic would be below subzero temperatures", Tahina explained. "Given how long this type of ship has been decommissioned, most likely it was only a hull when they... found it, I suppose. Environmental stabilization is the proper terminology." Then, as they weaved through the crowders and the hagglers, she commented, "This is a bargainer's bazaar, in essence?"

Geon pulled her close, when an abrupt laser blast thundered.

Collectively, an "Oooo!!" waved through the excited crowd, then died out just as immediately. Evidently a common occurrence, Tahina surmised.

People were agitated, tensions were thick like the steel walls that seemed to vanish behind the furious hustle of activity. One suits, while not exactly a rarity, were mostly replaced by the multi clothed. Crews of young men and eight females huddled in the front of a cyber imprinting stall. Tahina winced when blue liquid metal sizzled on the arm of one of the males, his teeth clenched. Liquid morphed and played until a cybernetic tattoo, that of fang bearing dragon, formed completely. What struck her more was his age. He looked a full two years younger than herself. So did the girl who engaged her in a mini stare down.

"When we get to our destination, try not to talk so much. You'll annoy her." Geon obviously meant her.

Her?

A heated shouting match turned into a full- blown brawl. Geon hurried them through a short cut through one of the vendor stalls. They made it past the rowdies and got on the hyper lift. The cylindrical door closed on another loud argument between long distance merchant sailors working for rival companies.

"Level Five", he spoke into the voice commander.

A second later the door reopened. Another layer of this hidden realm revealed itself.

Level Five was less crowded, but more bizarre. Luminescent neon blue and grey encompassed the walls, making it look eternally twilight, and atmospheric controls were set to resemble a rainy, spring day. That no actual rain was capable of falling made it all the more surreal. Moisture was thick, omnipresent. A crackling of thunder roared briefly. A white and dirty beige awning over a retro tech store flapped as gusts of faux breeze passed through.

It really did feel like a rainy, spring day.

There a lot of gadget stands, Tahina noted, with little interest. One kiosk, five stands ahead of them held the latest wave of virtual tech and robotics. The kind that produced artificial flesh and wire facsimile women, and holograms. Strangely, this caught her eye, especially noting how Jeth was looking one of the models over. For a minute, she felt repulsed by its existence. The type of thing that would never be seen in the hands of regular Duriyans, like her.

Here, technology was up for grabs, provided if one could afford the prices, or steal what they wanted. She had a feeling that thieves were dealt with very harshly, if the not too well concealed butt of a laser pistol that retro tech vendor had on him was any indication.

One vendor was hawking decryption routers, which came and went out of date decades ago. Yet, they looked no more than a year old. And he had a sizable crowd, waiting to install them in Hack drive systems that proliferated black markets such as this.

A technological wonderworld hidden, in plain sight from the mass of civilization and a growing authoritarianism. Grimy and disgusting as it looked, places like Old Town were fast becoming the final embers of freedom.

"They barter a lot in here?", Jeth asked.

To that Geon laughed dryly . "Barter's a dirty word around here, kid. Gold, Silver, Cryptocoin and Quantum stardrives only."

Perturbed, Jeth thought in dismay *Was the art of trading good for good lost to all? Except on my home world?* Two men could trade a bag of beans for a half bag of rice, and both would be content. Then wretched Hagit came and snatched it away. But out here, people were so selfish, so self- absorbed. Home world values clashed against a tidal wave of corruption, and once again he feared he was fighting a losing battle, within himself.

A group of three sailors, wearing deep green unisuits, walked past them, giving Tahina a curious eye. Young women, especially attractive ones, were a rarity in this part of False Star. She glanced back at the tall one with the smooth, dark skin, smiling in return. Instantly, Jeth impeded her view, not too gently nudging his "little sister" forward.

"That was rude!" , she whispered in anger.

"You were being foolish", he countered.

"Both of you are foolish", Geon scolded them both. He was growing impatient with the petty bickering. This was the part of parenthood he didn't get to, but was now getting a crash course in presently. Dealing with teenagers.

Just ahead, a half booth away, an unexpected show took place.

To the awe of a small crowd to the left, a quartet of four drone globes rose above the red lettering on the side awning, began whirling in a dervish spin. This impressed onlookers, who clapped in appreciation. The drones then started to morph into varying shapes.

"Cryptocoin. Precious metals especially are good!", spoke the jovial man at the center of it all." While his attire wasn't too flashy, his demeanor was that of an intergalactic P.T. Barnum.

"Take all four home today for..."

Geon swerved hard left to avoid the sidewalk show. The owner gave them a half glance, denoting displeasure. In his line of work, a non-customer was a missed opportunity that rarely came again.

His squad of drones, in their seductive swirl, began a light show. The crowd roared with delight at their dizzying, spectrum blending display, blues meshing hard with red, jade greens kissed blood oranges in a blending of visual beauty.

Somewhere nearby, an unexpected sight. A gaggle of silver birds, native to a mineral rich world called Pluma, took flight, squawking loudly. Near perfect silver feathers gleaming in the light.

Halfway, they came to a stop. The clamor behind them had died down. The pier above, someone whistled a cat call. Feeling the attention, Tahina blushed. Had she turned, she would've been shocked to see that her admirer was a female.

They were in front of a storefront. Not many were in this part of False Star. The large circle window, grime streaked and brown spotted, was tinted a solid black. On its door, which hung halfway crooked , read in faded red letters "RETINA'S". Just above, water dripped slowly from the air distributor. Hard plastic gills fluttered evenly. The face of the machine was battered, ready to fall to the iron pavement.

From his pocket, Geon pulled a black rectangle. A tiny monolith responder. Pressing down on the screen, it abruptly flashed yellow.

"She's in", Geon rasped . The teens looked at each other again, not knowing what to expect. They only knew they could trust Geoniphus Thu. He rang the entrance bell, which croaked slow and painfully.

Tahina fidgeted in the high back chair, disliking the texture. It was azure, stout and incredibly soiled. Just the thought of her skin making contact made her furrow her brows in revulsion. She would burn this shirt, and these jeans when she got back. Shame. Her favorite outfit.

"Nervous , dearie?", a voice behind the silver partition asked her.

"No Ma'am", she replied, overly polite. *I'm more disgusted than anything else.*

This place is a wreck, she observed with contempt. Spirit bottles were strewn about, as were layers of linens, lumped in piles, matted and soiled. Braided bio scanner wiring and an intricately woven web of lighting cords running along the walls and touching the ceiling. Overcooked, rotted cabbage made her nauseous. Geon and Jeth had left out, to get needed equipment and lunar tech to build a new third option engine. *They might take hours,* she grumbled inwardly.

The bulky figure of Sam Quill stepped from behind the partition. A strongly built woman of fifty-seven, her toes just hung over the Birkenstock sandals that scraped the floor.

"You gotta keep still for the reader to get you right ", she said as if speaking to a child, agitating Tahina even more. Her stained fingers wiped the flax linen shorts, just above the racing cougar tattoo on her thigh. Her face, cream like, freckle dotted, frowned deeply.

The girl winced, swallowing her disgust. She sat back, a spring or two, creaking softly. There was a damp spot now on her shirt. For sure, she was tossing this outfit in the incinerator.

"Better", Quill whispered, as if in contemplation. Her portly shadow lingered as she returned behind the partition. The sheet of silver came alive, glowering, faintly blinding her. But she barely kept her hands from obscuring her face.

"It's best not to cover your eyes, sweetie", Quill warned her gently. The thin slab of siliconium shielding jostled as she moved behind it.

Easy for you to say, Tahina thought bitterly. *And WHY does she drone on with this "sweetie" business? She doesn't know me, for sluck's sake!*

Biometric scanning didn't take long, on paper. It depended largely on the skill of the technician and the equipment in utilization. Sam Quill didn't take all day, but she was a dedicated perfectionist, a trait she shared with Geon. For Tahina, it only made things tedious and aggravating. Every vital statistic would be taken and coded. Only her name, planet of origin, family history and age (no, she liked her age) would be changed.

Thick, shimmering waves of light washed over her, concentrated beams, making her ticklish. Though not in a way she found pleasing. She felt a sense of violation. And she wondered if this woman knew what she was doing, before disregarding her doubts. If Geon had faith in her, so should she. Yet still.

It was hard to believe what he told her. "Kids, in his normal drawl, Sam is the finest identity craftswoman in two solar systems. She'll make you totally new people..."

Halfway through his spiel, her attention turned to her gross surroundings. A threadbare front with a shoddy desk, with two weak looking fold up chairs, and a ratty, torn blue sofa that looked older than both her and Jeth combined. There were panels of sheet metal, either hanging limp on a nail, or completely missing from the wall. A large circular waste pail was overfilled with white, food stained containers made (she learned later) from an ancient substance from Earth, Styrofoam.

Only the outstretched hand, that recalled a block of ham, brought her back to the current moment. Again, she straightened up, to let the machine do its job.

What burned her most was that she was left here, alone, with a stranger. While the guys were away, looking into some new parts and anti-detection tech, she was here, wallowing in the grime and filth. She felt left behind, like she was missing out.

"Are we finished?", asked Tahina after what seemed a half hour at least.

"Just about dearie."

Up to this point she'd kept Geon's commandment about overtalking. She knew it wore on people's nerves, which was partly her reason for doing it so often. She savored the attention, good or negative. But right now, she needed to vent. She'd deal with the consequences later.

"How long have you lived... here?", she asked, somewhat hesitant.

"Too long, sweetie. Far too long and way past my scheduled time", was the cheerful reply. Which left the teenager befuddled. *What does it take to get this woman upset? She never seems to go without a smile.*

Continuing her crusade against better judgement, Tahina asked questions. To her host's dismay, she was becoming animated when she did so. By nature, Tahina was expressive, an extrovert. When her tongue moved, so did her hands, her head, and she stirred quite a bit.

Finally, tired of both the questions and the questioner's erratic demeanor, Quill came from behind the partition, telling her to "Hush!" in the sweetest way possible. *Guess I discovered her angry button,* Tahina thought, feeling perversely triumphant.

Later, Geon laughed, shaking his head. "I'll get on her about that later", he said.

"Don't. I'm sure she means nothing by it. But have you ever thought about her studying in class, attending a school somewhere?"

He furrowed his brows as he sat on the sofa, whose cushions wheezed. From a high wall cabinet Quill pulled out a dusty bottle of liquor. Pouring its contents into two very large, spherical glasses.

"Honestly, no. I've only had them aboard for over three, make it four months now."

"Have you taken them to Marvie's, Geon?", she asked her longtime friend over glasses of Uranian Rum and Merlot.

"No! They're way too young for a place like that", he said, lounging on her time worn sofa. "Even if they think they aren't."

"Hell, I was too young at twenty-five", Sam said, openly laughing.

"You were *that* old when we met?", Geon asked, now counting the years.

"Anyway, she said (exaggerating the way), this isn't about me, this is about them."

"Too young and it's still too hot. Maybe in ... never ."

"So...Quartey?" She was fishing around for confirmation.

"Still want to go there, right? Consider it payment for services rendered."

"It's near Festival time, isn't it? I could set up shop there virtually anonymous."

"Completely anonymous", he assured her between sips. "For now."

"Quartey isn't Duriy, or Sefu Trius, or the Proxima Expanse", she told him.

"Not yet, but it'll get there, before long. They're sure to beef up the security over One thousand-fold after what happened on Polim Tef."

"I still don't buy the "official" story", she whispered, her cheery face now becoming a mask, grim and sober. She leaned down and scratched a red sore on her left calf. Another tattoo that she just got. Still in the itching phase.

"Nobody with a functioning brain buys it. Unfortunately, stupid people are far more plentiful than smart people. Always has been, it seems. Sheep willing to trade their sovereignty for the illusion of a security blanket."

Sam Quill looked at her friend, listened to the bitterness that undergirded his words. She saw the stress in the lines of his face, the sleepless nights and long, long days. At first, she thought it was due to the extra mouths he'd taken on. Then, as she listened, she saw it wasn't them, it was this new order, the naked fascism being imposed without mercy. But she asked anyway.

"Have things gotten *that* bad out there?" Being stationary, she could only see, feel and hear so much.

"It's worse, worse than anybody thought it'd be", he said. He told her about his recent run in with those whales. After he finished, she thought it was she who'd been accosted and humiliated.

"Just thank your stars they didn't find those kids of yours", Quill replied, feeling both anger and extreme sympathy at his harassment.

"Oh, I am. The interior anti- sensor system does a good job against biometric scanners." Then he stopped, began to swish what was left of his drink. Contemplating, he raised the question within him once more. *Why weren't they looking for a pair of runaways from Asylon?*

"A relief, most definitely", she said wistfully, downing another gulp. She drank like a fish and cooked like a gourmet. ... he let his mind stop there. He was still friends with this woman for three decades for a reason.

"Around False Star, I see the neighborhood's changing."

She scoffed. "It's getting harder and harder to keep even a footstep ahead. They're getting new surveillance set up, especially on the space docks. The station will get a new security force; I don't plan on being here when they finalize the arrangements." And she added, in a confidential voice, "I've seen stories about neurological trackers being *placed into human beings!*"

"That was tried centuries ago, and it failed then!", he said derisively.

"Well, you know how humans learn. We don't."

"Hear, hear", he drawled, over another glass. Then another. He was semi drunk when he rose. She, too, stood up.

Looking past him, to ensure they were alone, Sam asked him pointedly, "Have you heard the rumors? Or considered the prospect, at least?"

"Rumors of what?", he asked, intrigued. Sam didn't engage in rumors.

"When you and the boy were out and about?", she spoke cryptically.

"I... heard some things", he admitted. "Talked to some people." He wondered just what she knew. And how much.

"We can talk about it further when I come on board. Thin walls."

To himself Geon grinned. *She knows way more than she's telling. Nice to see that some things do stay the same.*

"Well, now that it's settled, when will you be ready to pack?"

Giggling, she told him impishly, " We haven't settled on anything." The heartiness of this woman was accentuated by her physical appearance. A stereotypical mama bear. Warmhearted and generous, so long as you didn't try to take advantage.

"You want to relocate to Quartey, right? Just get your stuff and come on!"

Giggling became a full- on laugh. "My bag's been packed for the last ten years!"

In a mere matter of hours, a new universe had presented itself. More a wormhole, but neither Jeth Akim nor Tahina would split hairs on the matter.

False Star, for them both, became Free Star. The shackles of the past were cut, existentially. Its shadow would remain, but just as that. They were walking openly in clouded sunshine.

Geon let them go exploring. It would be good to see how they handled their new found, sought after freedom. Sam told them where to get something to eat. Something good, Tahina hoped. The hyper lift took them to level three. When the silver doors slid apart, they walked into an all- out attack of the spices and charcoal smoke. Chargrilling was a staple method of cooking for many worlds. Mere differences lay in the spice pallets and varying qualities of meat.

Jeth and Tahina found themselves fighting against the throngs of people that overcrowded the area. Some stood in between stalls, eating. Morsels of charred meat drenched in mayonnaise, French dressing (many a person puzzled at the reference) dropped onto the meshed layering that draped the metal pavement. Lingering flashes of red light permeated the background, making a scene reminiscent of a Geores Futuristico neo abstract (an infamous artist/painter/ sculptor from the earliest period of Duriyan history).

Looking around for what seemed the best choice, they (mostly Tahina) settled on a small sized eatery called Faruk's, where food was cooked outside underneath a blue tent whose time hardened plastic coverings overlapped the other haphazardly. There was one solid iron bench, painted a now chipping black, with space left. As they sat, a young man standing on the side, wearing a white smock over black shirt and cream pants shuffled over, smiling, and gave them each a menu tablet. In the back somewhere, the sizzling of fish being dropped into cooking grease temporarily drowned out the steady conversation going on around them. People talking about average things, like the results of the late game, or bragging on sexual conquest (or lying about such, rather. Even an inexperienced one as Tahina knew such lies when she overheard them), not politics, nor governmental oppression. A nice diversion in thought was a good thing, she decided.

"Have ever you had fried fish with fries?", she asked him, laboring over an oft used menu tablet. Two of the buttons were missing, the left side permanently smudged in deep brown grease. She was careful to avoid it.

"Honestly, I never knew such a thing existed", he replied absently. His demeanor hadn't changed since he got the fake G.I.D. and S.I.N. And it annoyed her.

"What is your world's cuisine?", she asked, hoping to spark a conversation. To spark some life into him. She had grown increasingly frustrated with his anti- social demeanor. She missed the Jeth she met in Asylon; goofy, sweet and deceptively cunning. She was hoping, with this new situation, he'd make a comeback.

He took his time answering, prompting a look of exasperation. All around them, people were, in varying degrees, finding *some* joy, something to place hope in. She wanted desperately, after so long, to do the same. She wished Jeth could bring himself to do the same. Take interest in something other than machine parts and equilibrium stabilizers .

"Hunger, despair and desperation ", he finally answered. She groaned. His reaction read bewilderment. "I don't know what you mean to know", he said, throwing out an answer.

"After all this time, you *should* know what I mean!", she answered furiously. Flustered, she looked over the menu.

"It's, it's nothing. I'll try it." His answer was rushed. Obviously, he was preoccupied. It irritated her that he wasn't as open to her like he used to be, didn't seem to concern himself with her well-being like he did previously.

"I... didn't order...yet ", she replied through barely visible, clenched teeth.

"Ohhh", he said, feeling even more lost. He was staring away, avoiding her glare.

"I was just making conversation. Forget I ever..." The waiter hovered over, breaking her sentence.

"I'll take your orders now, sir and ma'am." Nice, mannerable and attentive. Tahina found herself wondering where he was from. *He's in his early twenties. He must be. Poised and self- confident, despite the menial employment.*

"Your orders?", he repeated gently. Miffed, Tahina told him:

"Two orders of fried fish with fries", she spoke hastily. Jeth made no motion to contradict her.

"Any juice? Tea? Black water?"

"Coffee", said Jeth, who looked around the moving throngs of people. And those sitting. Eating, playing tonk or spades or chess. That one guy over on the far right of him had a nice holographic set.

He thought of home. And the old man with the one good arm he used to play chess with. How he lost its use he never found out, but the man could move queen or a rook with a quickness that bordered on cheat- he experienced a hard rap on the left arm.

"I'm talking to you!", came from across the table.

"Sorry! I..I didn't hear you say..."

"Of course not ! You're ....elsewhere! Again!" Now she was extremely irate.If there was one thing to be wary of, the old timers used to say, it was an angry woman from the Far worlds. *Particularly a Duriyan female.*

Feeling bad, he stammered "I'm sorry, Tah. It's just... well..."

She crossed her arms, not daring to put them on a table that was cleaned half assed. She looked at him very intently. "Well?"

"What? What do you want me to say?" He began feeling defensive, even indignant. He had no idea as to what offense he committed (this time), or what he could say to get her either away from him or salve whatever was fueling her latest outburst. *She's so mercurial. And melodramatic. And pardon the swear words (On Sefu Trius, the use of profanities was the mark of the spiritually illiterate. "Foul People use foul words", the saying went), but she's so fucking annoying!!*

She had had enough.

"How you feel, you fool!", she blurted out. Her arms uncrossed, on the tables. And she promptly removed them. "What are you feeling about this?! We're finally free!" She moved her head not just to indicate the place where they found themselves physically, but the fact that they were now free of their pasts. What she really wanted to know was how he felt about *life today.* The life they could live now, if they chose. She wanted to know what were his plans, his dreams, now that he could have something to dream about. Yes, the galaxy had taken a hard, rapid turn to fascism. But as of now, he didn't have to live the life of an outlaw. She sure as sluck wasn't, if she could help it. Which was the driving point of her angst. She wanted to know if, should she leave Geon, would he be coming with her?

He looked bewildered. She read the confusion on his face. She gazed left, at the nearby couple deeply entrenched in a kiss. Filthy as they appeared, they enjoyed each other's company. She envied them. She thought fleetingly about Jojas. *That damned fool!* Irritating. And so lovely, in his own, disruptive way. So different.... so...dead.

It suddenly came to her how she had little to no closure on the chapter of Jojas. Since him...there was no one else. And Jeth...

Their drinks arrived .

"I mean, there's nothing to think about. You're my best friend."

She sipped her drink a little. "And you are mine."

Two men were walking behind him, dressed in oil stained silver one suits. Older guys, though not Geon old. One had deep smudges of grease on his face, on the other man's face no one could tell. Their conversation was swift.

"You hear they claim that wasn't no fission bomb."

"Man, come on with the conspiracy bullshit...."

Jeth turned from them to her, and he could see, finally, what she was asking of him. And, how best to break it to her.

"I..I can't imagine you not being in my life. But I know it will be." Eyes met, then turned.

From a place within that she couldn't discern, a loud, screeching halt echoed in her brain. Her ears rang with disbelief.

"Come again?" She was floored he would say this. She knew the possibility was there. But, to hear it....

"Asylon brought us together, he said, but... isn't it time we faced the fact that we're destined for different paths?" His words were slow, almost sounding rehearsed, if she didn't know him better.

She turned her head away in distress.

" You're too intelligent not to see that", he answered calmly.

She fumed. Inside, she felt herself beginning to cry. She stopped herself. Using everything she had, she restrained herself, the tidal wave of emotion rising inside her.

"We're too different. Really, what do we have in common, Tah?"

"We have Asylon. We're alone in a crazy, changing universe." As strange as it seemed to her, she was nearly pleading with him. This was not customary for her; pride and haughtiness kept her from making a spectacle (in her mind) of herself. Yet the idea of them going their separate ways... frightened her on levels that she, in her mere eighteen years of life, could only have begun to guess existed.

"Is that, he asked, looking into his drink, really enough for you?" For emphasis, he tapped on the copper colored, brass disc. "Where I am, I want to be. Can you really say that about *yourself*?"

Punches to her soul. This... she never imagined this would be happening. Not like this.

"What I'm saying", Jeth stopped as the food was coming into view. The charred tips and edges of the fish hardly looked appetizing. "What I'm saying is that you have the chance for the life you always wanted. All those dreams, everything you yearned to be... go be that person, live that life. Forget Geon and his ship." Hesitatingly, he added, "Forget me."

Inside her, something snapped. She was no longer mad at him, nor anyone else. She wasn't even mad at herself for initiating this. Like it or not, she had her answer. She could only accept the ugly, inalienable truth of her life: People will come, and they will eventually go, no matter if she wanted them desperately to linger.

For what seemed like forever the food before them sat untouched, ice melting in the drinks. Realizing how foolish they were beginning to look, they began dining.

Finally, she spoke.

"I..I really don't know what to say ", she said, quiet as she could be.

Between bites of fish and fries, Jeth replied somberly, "Since we've met, that's the first time I've heard you say such a thing."

Chapter Twelve

She was back!

And despite everything that transpired over the past half year, she could honestly say she never enjoyed working as much as she did now. Right now. After her health reality check. After Asylon burning. After Polim Tef, she needed a vacation.

It felt good to be active again, to be immersed with the troubles of maintaining an ever expanding bureaucracy. Through the metallic, gleaming halls, everyone from prisoner to detainment officer noted how much Warden Quinn openly enjoyed being back on the job.

The hallways of The Globe, a new youth detention center in the Far worlds, were still new. And being new, they gleamed spotlessly and were smooth and polished. Its novelty hadn't worn away after a week. The Globe, a literal prison planet. The first of fifty such mobile prisons, they told her at her reinstatement hearing.

"Great Uncle Heram spoke highly of you", Herod Bevel, IREL's new ruler, said. "Things got out of hand, but in fairness, you were not present for that. We believe you can get things back on schedule."

Despite the assuring words, the vote to reinstate her was a slim margin, with the young Herod himself being the tie breaker. And though he was young, he had three things to his advantage starting out: He had a tremendous business pedigree, running start-up businesses he created for fun. He was shrewd and manipulative, and he was a Bevel. That last thing made others, even those decades older, highly deferential. And that was all the difference that mattered.

"We trust that your policies towards this project will be in accord with the political reality we currently find ourselves immersed in", he subtly warned her.

To that, she betrayed a faint, grim smirk.

If there were lingering concerns about her previous liberalism towards the felons whose lives she would hold under lock and key, and lease to others, she let Herod Bevel know that was in the past. Her experiences at Asylon, and most definitely Polim Tef hardened her views on "the scourge of criminality in the hearts of men and women". Hardened her heart and resolve towards interplanetary discipline. Polim Tef made her a fanatical believer. As it did with many in the galaxy. Globes, Whales, the GCW unified justice force, GID, and search on suspicion (S.O.S) policies that were being implemented not only on Duriy and its sister planet Vekraas, but especially on the grief-stricken refugee colonies that held the survivors of Polim Tef (FAR more accepted there) were merely the tip of the glacier. Almost every day it appeared the news streams announced new measures, new addendums to THE LAW. And she welcomed all of it.

"Mr. Bevel, I not only appreciate the reality of where this universe is headed, but I want you, and the whole of the directorship to know not only do I firmly support it, I will do everything within my power to assist the maintaining of law and order." After a thunderous applause, she was then asked, "If reinstated as Warden Prime, who or what would you require to make your efforts successful?"

Verdia.

When entering the Far worlds (which, as of a month now, they were officially formerly known, but many still kept the term alive, if only for discriminatory reasons), the third planet from the rippling surface of a massive spot pocked sun was the Green Planet. Its atmosphere, vegetation, and even its titanic oceans were in varying shades of emerald.

Green = Life.

The irony was delicious to Quinn, hilariously so. A man so committed to death living on a planet overabundant with the force of life.

"Not on my horizon", he told her, laughing, body rocking in the gurney chair . He was improving, rapidly, but still required help moving around, especially in tight quarters. His mobility machine was bulky and awkward, and he resembled a cyborg more than a gravely, almost fatally, injured man. "I think my days as a Prison Chief are done."

However, Quinn wasn't. If he knew anything about this woman at all, it was that she stopped at nothing to get what she wanted. Or who she needed to make her operation run fluidly. She kept talking, and he kept listening.

They were sitting on his spacious front porch. The deep green and lime horizon, for her, was breathtaking, and unsettling at the same time. Homestead life suited Turlak, though she never imagined him a farmer. His crops were just beginning to mature.

His hovering wheelchair against her chair, an airondack style made of solid wood, he told her again about the riot (they refused to call it anything else) and the weeks that lead up to it. This time, as he wasn't hopped up on pain soothing drugs, he was more lucid.

"Understand that girl and that boy ran off", he said. Corners of his heavy lips twitching in mock triumph. She caught it, and sighed, nodding acknowledgement.

"You were right", she said, admitting her errors. "In more ways than one."

He heard iron in her voice. *Finally*, he thought to himself. She's cured of that pompous, liberal ineffectiveness.

Swirling, disjointed bright green clouds swirled above, becoming thicker.

Reaching in her valise, she pulled out a protocol tablet. He asked, "Is all that necessary for me to return to duty?" He only wanted her to admit that she was wrong. About anything.

Smiling faintly, she put it back. In the jade twilight of afternoon, they enjoyed the view amid his bleating cattle and then a sudden downpour that passed through, her small VTK Cruiser getting drenched. A limited few had one these days. IREL sanctioned its use.

"I always wanted to ask you, as rain tapered to a light drizzle, if you hate Far worlders so much, why choose to live here?" Verdia was two planets away from Sefu Trius and a full system away from Duriy. Of all the worlds that comprised the renamed "Astro sectors Twelve and Thirteen", respectively, Verdia had the smallest population.

"The cost of living here is cheap", he answered in such a way to make her laugh. "The land's workable, and hardly a person can be seen within ten kilometers of me. Those Far worlder scum can't afford to live here, much less fly over planet. To that she had to laugh, but within she realized just far she'd come, or rather fallen into the abyss of prejudice that made doing her job easier (to justify to herself).

After a few minutes of light banter (which neither had previously enjoyed with the other), Quinn finally asked him, "When would you like to start?"

"After dinner. I'll give it a look through", he said, turning a gaze into his living room. The circle clock on the wall read 7:15 p.m. EST (Earth Standard Time).

She realized she hadn't eaten, but the smirk on Turlak's face let her know an extra place was being set.

Wearing a smile as wide as the horizon, she asked "What are we having?"

With Turlak now on board, her job was a lot smoother. Not easier, because her workload was increased ten- fold. Travelling to each prison world as they became operational, setting up the systems, vetting the personnel, and putting her experience to an institutional model that would be duplicated over and over. Having a Turlak on each of the Globes, with GCW oversight (which was lacking last time), made her apprehensions about the constant travelling a passing anxiety. She was, initially, very concerned he wouldn't get Directorship approval, but he was unanimously approved. While she made it by the skin of her pearly whites. That stung her greatly. But she had buried it; his presence and experience far outweighed any hard feelings she felt.

At the time of her reinstatement , there were over ten Globes waiting to be cleared for operational status. Within the next two years, there would be another twenty. The inmate holding capacity was ten thousand. The capacity of D.O.G.S. (Detainment Officers and Guard Squadrons) tapered off at four thousand. There were hundreds of thousands of applicants, and with the tide of public opinion turned, the prisoner leasing program was quietly revived. The Trans- Galactic penal industry had finally arrived, and she stood at the forefront. A chair on the Directorship was all but assured now.

At moments when she was at her busiest, she almost forgot she had a degenerative, terminal illness.

The treatments she was taking, so long as she took them regularly, kept the pain at bay. Through uncounted hours of physical and mental therapy, she strengthened herself to make the most of her time and stop pitying herself. *Even on borrowed time, there is much to live for* became her private affirmation. Eventually, even that dark spot dissipated in the bright aura that enveloped her these days.

Yet there remained one scratch on the mirror, one thing that clouded her perfect reflection. No matter the euphoria, the exaltation of her recent triumphs, one question nagged her, a silent taunt.

Where in the damn universe are they?

Sometimes, while stalking the halls of her primary residence (Globes held dorms for those assigned to each one; charged with bringing Asylon, the parts that worked, to each one allowed her to have quarters on each one), she would ask that question. At times privately, at others vocally. Sometimes she would ask it so loud it caused her subordinates to stare at her from afar. One fool openly laughed. She was put on trash detail three weeks straight. Those two criminals getting away, being out of her grip gnawed at her without let up. Besides her pride, the backlash against her, should this ever come to light, would finish her completely. This was a pain that, while most unbearable, was a cross that she willingly had to bear, alternatives considering. This was the first and main reason she perpetually tortured herself asking that. And the second reason...

Anwari.

It was now three months since she'd last seen him. And every time, except the last, Anwari's appearance in her life was a harbinger of calamity. Exaggeration, of course, but he didn't do her any favors.

Except get her the job in the first damned place. She still debated if she believed that. But there was one thing she knew with glum certainty. Anwari would cross paths, at some point, with her once again.

Just a week after Polim Tef, he was making the streaming circuit, bellowing harder than ever about "law, order, and security." This time, there was no parrying with professors, activists or bleeding hearts. No sane person, or anyone appearing to be of sound mind, could oppose his iron clad arguments. Besides, to do so ran the risk of "seditionist speech". And suffering the attending consequences.

Going through the hallways from her spacious, marble tiled and polished chrome colored office, she pondered on this mystery man. How long had she tried to delve into his shadowy background? An attorney for Galactic Law? That panned out. But where he came from, his schooling, and family life was "inaccessible due to clerical mishap."

Still undeterred, she peeked into his record at the GCW Justice (a renaming of what was now, arguably, the most powerful division in the Intergalactic government) Dept. Only to run into the proverbial brick wall. Though she expected pertinent information to be classified, she couldn't even get past his name.

"ACCESS TO THIS FILE DENIED", the screen read in blood red lettering, over the pixelated black background.

"It makes no damn sense!", she exclaimed after another go at peeking into the "Anwari Mystery" as she came to call it. She was still at a disadvantage when it came to him. Making her resent him all the more. Except, the few times when he gave her cause to be grateful.

However else she perceived him as a person, he was true to his word. No one found out. Anos, and the few that knew were persuaded to keep silent. Their reward for their reticence was abundant, and they were well promoted. Anos, in fact , was the Chief of Guards on Globe 3. Her mentor Turlak taught her well. In fact, he beamed like a proud father when she told him about the promotion.

And, she couldn't take away how often he looked after her, which made his overbearing, sinister being tolerable. *But, that damned question!*

Whatever his reasons, Anwari still hadn't delivered on the one thing that mattered to her most at this point and time. She wanted them. She wanted the heads of Jeth Akim and Tahina on a platter.

Despite hating him as she did, she fully expected for him to live up to his word. To what came as an immense surprise to her, she felt profoundly disappointed when it became apparent he failed her.

It had been a long one. A week's travel from Globe One to Globe Five had culminated into a full day's worth of conference calls, personal appeals from inmates (she typically denied them. Bitterness over Jeth's betrayal of her kindness made her cold hearted, a more unforgiving administrator), plus settling disputes between some subordinates and those looking to lease a cheap source of labor.

Not only was business back, it was booming. In record breaking numbers, paid employees were becoming an endangered species. The demand was too great, the concern for such frivolous spending on things such as decent pay, benefits, health and life insurance, and basic dignity was now non-existent. But there were other changes, which caused the occasional headache. Companies that were interested in prison labor now had to pick up their designated numbers on location. A dispute between a couple of DOGS and a privateer had turned to fisticuffs.

"Mr. Brenf, be advised, behavior of that sort will not be tolerated here! Consider yourself fortunate that you're not the one being hauled off in chains!", she warned the deeply reddened in the face Seymour Brenf, of Brenf and Sons, Tridium, LLC ."

"Warden Quinn, he thundered, I'll have your head for this! Mind who you're speaking to!" Seymour Brenf was a domineering man, a man that was unaccustomed to the likes of Ednisa Quinn.

"Mr. Brenf, I know very well who I'm talking to, and I'll leave you *with* this: Your company is merely one of thousands whom I have on contract. Yours can be vaporized into ether, and others can receive your portion. And they pay way, way more lucratively. So, losing you would be a matter of addition by subtraction!"

His gaping mouth, his beet red face abruptly turned black. She laughed long and heartily afterwards, trying to recall the last time she'd spoken to some blowhard jackass in that brusque, obliterating manner, and won. The picture of that buffoon being put in his pitiful place carried her in high spirits throughout the rest of the day.

By the end of yet another fifteen- hour day, she was dog tired. She didn't know where the expression originated exactly, but she liked it. Informal, yet it captured her fatigue perfectly. Today she leased a hundred and seventy - five convicts. Just at this one individual site alone. The numbers for the others had yet to arrive. On a good day, she could average well over five hundred. A daily amount topped over three hundred. There was no shortage of inmates these days, plus the assets to liabilities ratio of using them was beginning to mark the final days of hired labor.

And being the intelligent woman she is, she saw it for exactly what it was.

It was the dawning of a new slavery system. Asylon being the prototype. A prototype her DNA was imprinted on. In a minor fashion, of course (she was still humble enough to recognize her role as employee and servant of IREL). But it was there, nonetheless.

It was there.

Occasionally, on the news streams, activists still managed to find a forum. Though diminished greatly in the eyes of the public, and far fewer in number (and courage) than before Polim Tef, they still pointed to abuses in the terraforming and shipbuilding industries, the rise in hate crimes against leased laborers (especially those from planets formerly labeled as the Far Worlds), harsh working environments, the increasing stripping away of liberties, and perhaps the dirtiest secret among the GCW elites, maid girls.

It was a fact that people had died, had been abused in those aforementioned industries, but the latter was a bald-faced lie, Quinn concluded.

It was also a fact that life in the Human Diaspora had taken a harsher, harder, authoritarian turn. And Asylon was by no means a small part of that ongoing transformation. No one who possessed a scintilla of intellectual honesty could deny that.

She realized those harsh truths at times. She also realized she had an ocean of blood on her hands. But the rewards were just too great to turn away from. And after her home world was blown into inhabitability, her fleeting compassion and conscientiousness also dissolved into the ether. All those that were hauled about in chains and electroshocked into submission, thrown into the mineral mines and terraforming schemes, and worse, deserved their fate.

The news stream was the normative talking points; unrest spreading in the former Far Worlds yet again. This time Duriy. A police state that had been engulfing that wretched world since the riots was tightening its grip. A group of unarmed young men were attacked by soldier police, killing three. The main building of the University had been set on fire as a result.

"Barbarians!", she voiced carelessly, as she stepped off the platform, out of the stream. She since acquired three more of the Info Synthesis pads, installing one on her personal vehicle, her main quarters and her office.

The scene in her old office with that damn fool Silas made her laugh.

She read his reports on her; the girl was intellectually gifted. Suffers anxiety, abandonment issues and a persecution complex (she distilled that from the psycho jargon).

A bloody sociopath is what she is. Like all of them.

Almost by instinct, she got back on, reactivating the pad.

"A series of daring raids by pirates on mining colonies have resulted in the escape of..."

" The IREL stock raised another five points on the Tran-stellar Stock Exchange..."

"The specter of Intergalactic Piracy rears its head yet again...."

"In confirmation of the endless swirl of rumors and speculation, the Secretary of Finance of the GCW announced the finalization of one standard currency..."

"Reporting from the cease fire accord on Sefu Trius, this is Tris Buvi reporting for GNN..."

The new girl that replaced Jet Symmons. Smooth, browner, her clothing style more understated, and less *in your face* than her idiot predecessor, of whom it was said that she'll never speak a word again. *Thankfully,* Quinn thought. Of course, rumors abounded, but came to nothing. Just another star that burned out way too soon.

Two hours into a blissful rest, she was abruptly disturbed by a call from, of all places, Docking Center Nine.

"Warden... warden...", the caller was timid, uncertain.

Heaving indignantly, she banged down on the communication console on her nightstand.

"Yes! Can I help you?", The resulting feedback distorted the line of communications for a moment.

"Ma'am?"

"Can I bloody well help you?", Quinn repeated, cranky as hell.

"Ma'am, there's a Colonel... Harudamapati that needs to see you. Urgent."

Ill-formed familiarity attacked her. But she was too tired to recollect names and faces.

"At this time of night? That's ridiculous! Tell him to wait..."

"Matters of an urgent nature require I speak to you, now!", his all too familiar voice booming through the intercom.

Quinn, now up and wide awake, could hardly believe it. *Anwari*, she was thinking in delirium. *What in hell is HE doing here? And under ANOTHER name?!*

Silence seemed an eternity until the youthful voice found itself.

"Ma'am, are you there?", the responder asked, with growing anxiety.

"Yes, inform... the Colonel I'll be with him momentarily."

"He says he's pleased , and he eagerly awaits your presence. "

The line of communication died abruptly .

Hurriedly, she showered and dressed. And cursed him over a thousand times. *That son of a bitch! What game is he playing now? And what's with the colonel act?*

Her train of thought came to a screeching halt.

What if this isn't an act?

What if he's revealing his true self? If so, why the hell now?

Questions. Always questions with him.

As she snapped on the cufflinks of her all black warden's uniform, Quinn resolved to finally get some answers.

Docking Center Nine was a good twenty-nine minutes from her quarters. In heels, it was thirty- eight. When she arrived, his star craft's entry portal was open. Its style was nothing she'd seen prior. Sleek, crackling with energy, it was an alien technology completely unfamiliar to her. From the opening, peering inside, she saw people, young men and women, in all black with silver stripes down the side of their pant legs moving here and about, with an efficiency she found both equally impressive and disquieting.

Militarily efficient, yet she couldn't place from where exactly. *Notches above what she had under employ.*

"Where's the colonel?", she asked, feeling envious. *All this effort and he doesn't have the decency to...*

"He went back on board, awaiting you ma'am", the young woman responded. Slightly heavy girl, with cherry red hair, reminding Quinn of a chocolate sundae. Her cheerful heft belied her timidity.

Of course! Always on HIS terms, the stinking bastard!

"He's really nice" , the young lady, named Officer Ruygers replied sheepishly.

"I'm sure he is", Quinn replied dryly. Shaking her head at the power of youthful lust, she walked gingerly into the ship's entrance.

She found herself stepping into another world...

Definitely nothing she'd ever seen before, and she had traveled on countless vessels. Its paneling was alive with red energy and pulses that ran from section to section. Standard bulky consoles that protruded outwards, consuming space and power were conspicuously absent. And then the crew. She took a better, lengthy look at them. There seemed to be no one under thirty-five aboard. Capable, strapping young men. Able, striding young women. Many of those faces that looked so much like hers at that age. There wasn't a smile, even a frivolous smirk, to be found among them.

After GID verification (she almost left the stupid thing), she was told to "Follow me, Warden", by a young woman whose steps were brisk and dutiful. She complied, quietly marveling the smooth black steel walls that reflected better than glass. She was tempted to engage the young lady, whose braided hair rustled only slightly with each step, with a question or two. They stopped at a hyper-lift. It went virtually unnoticed until the young officer stopped in front of it. Like magic, it revealed its features.

Placing an open palm on the side panel, a red glow briefly flashed on palm, and a new passageway opened rapidly.

The young woman then told her, "You may enter, Warden Quinn."

Realizing that this young lady , so professional and frustratingly stoic, wasn't going with her, gave her a bout of sudden distress. Her pretty, blank face disappeared behind a wall of solid, obsidian smooth black.

Clearly, this is for my eyes only.

When the door reopened, she was staring face to face with Colonel Harudamapati.

His uniform looked tight, but it was just snug. There was little that separated his from the girl she had just left save for the seven brass bars on both shoulders, and an insignia featuring worlds interlocked in a cluster on his right chest. It stood out, proud and arrogant.

Harudamapati, Anwari, Mitch for all I know. Who in the suns are you, really ?

"Warden Ednisa Quinn, A pleasure once more", he said, with his typical smugness. Yet he was conspicuously less warm. Even for him.

She felt she could take no more.

"The hell it is!", she snapped. "What's the meaning of waking me up at this ungodly hour? And this... Colonel business?"

"Your new surroundings do you justice", he responded calmly, ignoring the outburst. I hear they've upgraded your responsibilities, as well as your salary."

"You should know", she retorted snidely. "But enough about me. Why are you here?"

He scoffed.

"I can't even congratulate an old friend on her newfound success?", he asked sarcastically, turning to a port window. The stars they were among were sparse and distant, but still, they sparkled more radiant than diamonds.

"I've a busy schedule, so if this is all..."

Whirling, he told her "Come with me." There was no banter in his voice, nor any of the mirthful condescension she'd come to loathe. He may as well have said, "Shut the hell up."

Infuriated, and yet intrigued, she followed him out.

The path led down another hallway then to another hyper lift. All the while, she took note of what she saw. Solar paneling above lit the halls and the hyper lift. Everything was uber hi-tech, impossible and spartan. She wondered, suddenly, how fast this ship could go at its maximum speed.

Meanwhile, Harudamapati, or Anwari, moved as brisk as his subordinates. Truly, he was a completely different person. She corrected that thought immediately. *I never knew him at all.*

Another floor. A sharp left turn. Then a series of obvious rooms. He took them to the last one to the right. There was a young woman posted outside the door.

"Asleep still?", Harudamapati asked.

"Aye, sir", the young officer responded sharply, not giving Quinn a direct look. Quinn regarded her presence with mute curiosity.

"Proceed", he said crisply, as his palm pressed on the wall plate.

It opened, with Quinn going in first.

"I had to be sure before I summoned you", he said, now being somewhat chummy. Again, for him.

Harsh green light radiated from the stasis capsule.

Quinn's eyes widened. Seeing was truly believing.

"She ... she put up a hell of a fight", said Harudamapati with a rare, shocking admiration.

This night was truly one of surprises.

They were standing above an imprisoned Tahina. In stasis, nude and sleeping.

An air mask over her face allowed her to breathe normally in the liquid amber solution.

Quinn shook her head with vindication. Her eyes afire with sadistic visions of things to come.

"I imagine she did", Quinn said softly. Indescribable satisfaction ran through her veins. Malicious thoughts beginning to form. Almost playfully, Harudamapati nudged her.

"A really funny story ......"

Tahina's last weeks aboard Geon's Baby was relatively uneventful. It was an amazing feat, considering the tension between her and everyone else. She had to take over the piloting, while Geon and Jeth were working around the clock to get the new engine fully functional. Consequently, Sam took over the cooking duties, and she was decidedly better. Everyone, including Tahina, thought so. She brought them their meals, bonded with Jeth while she was stuck in the purgatory of the cockpit. Occasionally, Geon would check on her, chide her (he didn't ride her too hard, as he didn't want to rattle her confidence), keep her focused. She flew as slow as circumstances allowed. Even that proved to be a bane; any awe and wonder she used to feel about flying freely through space was replaced by dread and boredom. As she secretly feared would happen.

Once it was repaired, and the star ship was back to normal, things didn't go back to normal. For the rest of her stay, Sam continued to cook for them, do many of the things she used to do. Hating this, and the fact that Geon was essentially regulating her to pilot duty, made her resentful of the older woman's presence. She felt she was shunted aside. As a result, she spoke less, and withdrew more. She felt herself becoming a ghost.

She and Jeth barely spoke since they took off for Quartey. That conversation was eye opening. The most brutal shocks to the system turn out that way. If he wanted to be an oil and grease jockey, to piddle around on jerry-rigged machines, so be it. He was right about one thing, no matter how crudely he expressed it: She was meant for better things than this. However, she was scared to take the first step.

While doing some defensive maneuvering on the way to Quartey, they were cutting it close to a nearby asteroid field. On the fly, Geon decided to have her navigate through the field. She protested at first, then quickly conceded. There was no talking him out of this. So, she did it. Midway through, Geon started some small talk.

"Know how the Karuki got started?"

"No, I don't", she answered. She hadn't thought about a Karuk since Asylon. Now that she was, she remembered how much she hated them. Time made her forget, but it didn't make her forgive their barbarism.

"They were independent ore miners and traders at first. Space nomads, since their inception as a loosely connected people . Eventually, they built intricate, self -sustaining, life supporting settlements among the Delany Belt (the original name)." Then, like it was out of the blue, he asked her, "Have you given any serious thought about your future?"

"In terms of what?", she asked him warily.

She passed the first round of rocks, only to encounter another.

A belt of mid- sized asteroids lay before them. He advised her on the best way to get through them. Reluctant, she accepted the advice. Not because she didn't trust him, specifically. She was finding it increasingly hard to trust anyone.

They cleared the asteroid belt, then he made her switch to intermediate power.

"In terms of what you want to do, he said, holding back a sigh. Now that you got that, what's really keeping you here?" His eyes were on the GID necklace that dangled loosely about her neck. She gripped on the controls, smoldering.

"Have you approached Jeth with that same question?", she questioned, eyes narrowing.

"I'm not talking about him, I'm talking to you", Geon retorted. "For the record, so that you don't think that I'm being biased, yes, I did. And you'll have to ask him if you want to know what he said."

She was avoiding him, and she knew he had to know that. She was reserved and reticent when he was present, and more and more he busied himself with the engine system Geon had to reconstruct after that run-in. He was content, too content to bother with her. He had found his purpose in his new life; she was still groping for hers.

"Are you asking me to leave?", she said.

"No. I'm asking you to think about your life. You've been on board going on nearly five months, and I gotta admit, you panned out very well. I didn't think you would, but you did. That said, let's be honest. This life isn't for you. The stress of deep space travel doesn't agree with you, and though you've gotten better with the attitude, you're still not the happiest camper in the bunch."

"Under the circumstances, she began defensively, I'd like to think I perform up to your rather lofty expectations." Eyes widened, she was indignant. Her left fingers began fidgeting impulsively. She was getting heated. Geon, by now, knew the signs well.

"Calm down, Tah. I'm not attacking you."

"It certainly sounds that way."

"Only because there's something in the way, something you don't want to acknowledge. Or admit to yourself. And when there are things you hide from yourself, you do things that eventually hurt you. You get what I'm saying?"

Her anger wanted desperately to leap out of her, but she tightened the leash.

"Your life is yours again. Make the most of it, is what I'm saying. If you want to stay, fine. If not, that's fine as well. I'm not asking you to do anything you don't want to do. Especially for somebody else. That's all. Think about it."

And she did. The rest of that time before they entered Quartey's orbit, she spent her time in her room, reading. Reading, and thinking. From reading and thinking, she began to write. There were some ancient writing tools Geon had stuffed somewhere. She recalled them, and retrieved some pens, a tablet and thin sheets of paper. He let her have them. She had to remember the art of cursive. Ancient writing had always fascinated her, but it was so long ago. After a few tries, she figured she had the hang of it. And she wrote :

So near are you

but so far you remain

The horizon on the twilight

Shall I see you again ?

She read it over, and over. There was something missing. She tried again.

So close to my heart

Yet the distance you keep

makes me weep cross the expanse of deep

space .

The hurt you've brought me

Was the one gift I never thought of

you.

So, as the horizon, where sun bids farewell,

I walk, alone, in the twilight

To wonder... what could've been.

She liked it much better. Liked it so much she cried a little. It really felt like a Dez Vulker poem. In shape, in pain. In the rawness of feeling. The ability to make you, the poor soul reading his love-stricken rants and down in life observations, feel the experience. To feel and cry, laugh, or grit your teeth. Vulker was the master of evoking that passion, that feeling in his works. A quality she admired greatly, and wanted to emulate in her own works.

At that point, *her* calling had come to greet her.

And she wrote some more.

From the fractured mirror the shards

of respect lay strewn about,

dusted among the splinters and long dried

film of waste that was our lives.

The dujin cloud rose, filling the room with

the smoke of crushed dreams and maternal

neglect.

From whence you come...

Spurn those who neglect the younglings

whilst they ride the bulleteer nonstop to

obliviated bliss.

This one she titled "Mother, I hate thee".

She spent the night and part of the next day writing, until the ink ran dry. Frustrated, she threw it away and slept. Slept hard, and ideas and words and thoughts turned wheels in her hyperactive mind. Why had she not done this earlier? Unconsciously turning words in sentences, and those sentences became quatrains. Before she knew it, she had written a small book in her head.

To her great dismay, when she woke, she'd forgotten half of it. The scream she let out that day!

After her chores, she spent the rest of her day, remembering, and writing what she remembered. And if it wasn't exactly what she recalled, she improvised. This time, she was using the old solar tablet. Geon had so much useless stuff; the guy was a packrat. *How much money could he raise selling some of this?*, she wondered. It then surprised her just how little it mattered. And it was even more surprising that, in that instance of clarity, her decision had come, and she almost didn't even recognize it.

She was leaving.

There was no heartrending, overwrought melodrama like in many of the novels she used to read back home. Nor was it as simple as a shrug of shoulders and uttering a heartless "Sluck it, I'm out (that fool Jojas used to say that all the time)". Her bout of melancholy had come, lingered briefly and went. It was done. Now, after this latest set of poems, she'd tell Geon her decision. But first, she wanted to rest. Suddenly, she felt drained of all her energy. Hours later, an indiscreet buzzing woke her up.

"For Duriy's sake, Mama", she whined, half awake, let me sle…"

"Tahina, report to the bridge", interrupted her last word.

"Sluck! ", she cursed faintly, remembering herself and her surroundings. Absently, she walked into the hallway.

Dragging her feet, she chanced to run into Jeth. He saw her, smiled faintly. He smelled of engine grease and solar collector residue. His stock, trade and life had become Geon's engine systems. He hardly left it alone, going so far as to set up a cot in the corner.

She returned a weak smile of her own. *Could they leave things, each other as friends?*

Turning to go back to what he loved, she knew what the answer was. And she resented herself, and him, for not seeing it sooner.

They were going in opposite directions, almost a month into their escape from Asylon. For a moment, resentment turned to anger. With herself, because she failed to realize it. The futility of expecting, wanting more from a person than they wanted from themselves. She thought back on how hard she pushed her mother to get her mind right, lecturing Jojas on the importance of bettering himself in all aspects, not just the financial end. And, how she must've frayed that farm boy's nerves. Anger changed into subtle, belated guilt.

By the time she started to call his name, Jeth was already out of earshot.

"Tahina...", came over the intercom. This time, it was Sam. *How that woman annoys me!*

"I'm coming, I'm coming!", she said, almost stamping her bare feet. Oddly, the floor didn't feel as artic as she imagined it would. Maybe the currents of energy running underneath the steel panels had something to do with it.

"What do you...", she began , over Sam's wide shoulders.

"Come and look" , Geon said. "And where are your shoes?!"

"Didn't have time to put them on", the girl replied nonchalantly.

She peered over Sam, gasping subtly.

It was breathtaking, a visage she never imagined possible. From its two moons to the hastily constructed space docks that, twelve in number, encircled the medium sized world. Entrapping the misty brown and sparkling black marble in a sphere of energy, trail emissions and traffic. Amid the techno-kinetic frenzy, solar beam flares of all colors and shapes burst and exploded in the cosmos. A harmless light show welcoming all to the biggest, the greatest celebration in human history. The intergalactic Mardi Gras.

So much was taking place at one time, Geon brought his ship to a near screeching halt. The slightest miscalculation could get them, and some careless idiot piloting a freighter, space dock to planet shuttle, or sub space transporter, killed. While in cosmic limbo, Geon decided to give his newly installed pulse wave radar a try. The nose of Geon's Baby began glaring in deep green light, slightly sheening the view.

Tahina stood quiet as Sam asked Geon, "What in the blazes are you doing?"

"Giving this new toy of mine a try."

"Silly, they won't have those big ass whales off world. They tripled the police and army forces, plus they have some GCW battalions on loan. Not to mention the fact that the natives will violently end anybody who interrupts their party."

The two continued to playfully bicker, reminding Tahina of how she and Jeth *used* to be. She wondered if they could patch things up before she left. Just as she was getting seated in that train of thought, they began moving. After another thirty minutes of deft maneuvering, they began descent.

Entry into Quartey's atmosphere was free of turbulence and the rapid, high winds they'd become accustomed to elsewhere. The sky was a faded biege and clear. Even, at now a hundred thousand and five feet (and descending), travelling flocks of birds were faintly visible to her bare, naked eyes. On the magnifier, Tahina could see, in ice crystal clarity, the dark brown and white spot speckled plumage. That is, when a sky sled or oval shaped tourist transporter didn't obscure the view.

Mount Zafir, the highest mountain peak on the planet, was covered with a thin, glassy track of ice and snow.

Now flying over the mainland of Quartey, a single pangea that stretched some twenty million squares miles the planet over. The waters were clear black; the main ingredient of black soda was the water of Quartey. Quartey was one of the second tier planets; not a first- rate world, but certainly not a basket case as the erstwhile labeled Far worlds were considered to be. It had a surprisingly mid-sized population of no more than a billion point three people.

A virtual desert on land, only a sparse smattering of trees in the northern most hemisphere lent the planet a patch of arbor. Port Alim, the world's only city, (after the planet's discoverer, founding father Alim Abu Bakr), was one of few working examples in the galaxy of an ecumenopolis, and it was barely functional. Quartey had been a technologically stagnant hub for decades now, its glory days long past. However, tourists came to the "Party Planet" for two main reasons :

The first being the Army of Green Men, that lined the southern shores like sentinels in wait. Solid, enormous jade heads stood a staggering seventeen feet tall, with clearly negroid features, causing many to speculate about date, origin, and creators. Forensics dated the monoliths beyond *fifty thousand years* prior to the planet's discovery. The proof of men from another planet created quite the controversy. Others less academically minded denounced the whole thing as a "fraud of the lowest caliber". Those were the polite ones.

"Who's gonna believe in space niggers?", opined one Cecil Roofe, a leading figure in the history of interstellar anthropology. His stupid, inappropriate usage of racial ephitets cost him his decades long and distinctly colorful career.

Wherever one stood on the matter, there was no denying that the chiseled heads were truly breathtaking, and most definitely hand carved. The attention to detail, meticulous and pain staking had to have taken hours upon hours. Even from this distance, the line of tourists snaked around. Deep space shore men, wealthy touristas and scatterbrained revelers made up the bulk of off world visitors.

The second reason? Obviously, The Festival of Quartey. The planet's yearly celebration of its founding was a mass exercise in national pride, intergalactic comraderies and unabashed hedonism in a single day. From midnight to midnight, the entire world became a galactic party central. And made the planet's leaders, the organizers and establishment owners extraordinarily wealthy people. It was the only day that all workers, save military, planetary police, and employees of the various businesses were mandated to take off. The carnival atmosphere, parades, and throngs of bodily painted nude dancers performing in the streets, and grilled oxen and yellow cow whose garlic and ginger flavored stench billowed into the heavens as giddily drunk and horny partiers roamed the smoothly paved streets of Port Alim with abandon.

When they finally reached the docking station at Port Alim, Geon had to fly around three times. The area being packed as it was, plus they needed to find a tier that allowed for solar battery maintenance. They repaired his battery processor, but he needed to take this opportunity to recharge his vessel properly.

The Docking Centrix of Quartey (DCQ as the natives called it) was like a giant, iron tree in the peak of summer, in all its leafy glory.

Whose branches extended far and wide, well into the crisp, clear biege heavens, full of healthy, ubiquitous leaves. If only for a day.

Finally, Geon found the desired space in the midsection . The crackling blue light signal read "For Solar Thrust Powered Star Vessels Only". He nestled in the narrow confines with ease. It took him a few minutes to decompress. Shadow danced and morphed, shading Geon's Baby. He allowed Sam to get her things, while he sat in the relative silence. Between repowering his engine, and getting Sam settled in her new base of operations, there was Tahina to deal with. He knew it was time. The way she looked at him, silent but faintly grim, during the whole flight to Port Alim let him know. There were very few people in this wide universe that he could just look at, and see what was on their mind. Tahina was one of them. Whether she accepted it or not.

"When you're ready, just see me", he said, barely looking over his shoulder. He had to get a minute's shut eye. Quietly, she went off, looking back once. *He knows, and he knows that I know. Amazing how that works,* she thought as she went to her quarters to pack.

Later, she was sitting in the cargo bay, peering down into the frenzied madness below. From her vantage point, the people looked like lively specks in a rhythmic convulsion. Dots in multicolor overcrowding the pavements, the roads and bridges. And just as filled were the terraces and rooftops. Yellers, screamers, fools, revelers and fireworks all assaulted her hearing. On one roof she thought she could make out an orgy of five. The planet was alive with frivolity; as a horde of small craft and some as big as Geon's Baby streaked the skyways, their emissions becoming a rainbow.

A celebration. A yearly offering to the Gods of hedonism and carnal abandon, she thought.

She was frightened a bit by the worldwide catharsis, but found herself more intrigued than anything else. Duriy had Founder's Day, but that was a somber, dignified day. Being on Quartey at this time you were sucked in, enveloped in the energy and spirit around you, even if you stood afar off. She realized for the first time how much of a prude she was. *I'm no prude, rather I'm particularly conservative,* she corrected herself. Minus the mercurial flashes of anger and violence (which only happened under provocation or desperation), and her admitted know it all ness, she was relatively a moral person.

Though she was prone to impulse (a rare character flaw she willingly owned up to), she didn't go too far.

Even from this view, looking down, she could see glinting sparks from metal beaded necklaces that swung and swayed from the necks of the happy, the nude, the drunken and the frenzied patriotic. It provoked a sense of envy in her that she hadn't felt that way about her own world for some time now. Since that beating, that stripping back on Asylon....

She shook her head in protest, as if thinking the action would rid her of those unpleasant memories. It didn't, so she allowed herself to be swept away by the currents of her new environment, however reluctant a participant she was.

From someplace close, yet afar, the banging of conga drum caught her ear and the sultry melody of a sax solo followed. Against her will, she found her head bobbing side to side, and the rest of her rocking rhythmically to its call. There was a loudspeaker somewhere, because the pulsation was lucid, and soon she found herself standing, swaying her hips in sync with the music. She danced, as she would in rare, private moments back home. When her father was living, he often called her "Ailey, the Dancing Star". After he passed, she stopped for a long time, only in secluded moments did she let the rhythm of inspiration guide her soul, prodding a response in movement.

She was moving and swaying, turning and twisting to its will as if she never stopped. And as she performed, she was completely unaware of spectators watching her from afar.

The first was Jeth who was taking a break from the engine he loved so much. He spied her, and so as not to embarrass her, he observed her from the shadows. He awed at her fluidity, but more than that, he was enthralled by the joy on her face, and how it emanated from every step, every turn. He slid back, holding back silent tears. It confirmed to him, more than ever, that he was right about telling her to leave. Sartha had hurt him. But she had saved him in more ways than one; she helped him to heal. Though not in the way she imagined. In return, he hurt her. He had to. Not because he wanted to; but because he didn't want to hold her back.

Love is something you never hold back, it is something you let go of, the saying went. He cared about her. He cared that she wasn't happy as a prisoner. Not here, absolutely not on Asylon. The free star bird that could never be contained, that flew in the wild, rough, windy skies of his home world. It's deep black and smoky grey plume streaking unmistakably in the heavens. Unabashed and untamed. This was Tahina. In mid spin, Tahina stopped, suddenly feeling eyes upon her.

"Jeth?", she called. No response. No one was there.

"What's the use?", she said aloud, a cloud of funk suddenly coming over her. Her recital to herself finished, she sat down. In the corner, where her small rucksack was sitting. Geon would be back soon, she hoped. The sooner she left, the better.

From a high-rise apartment, some fifteen meters away, a heavy man in a jet black uni-suit with silver striping was watching . Since the Polim Tef attack, security was tightened to the nth degree. And his presence, and of those dressed like him, was assumed to be extra security.

His hyper optic binoculars, which could view distances a good fifteen point seventy- two meters away, was scanning the piers of the Docking Centrix, when someone of high interest caught his eye.

That girl's face, he thought, *looked familiar.* He was just close enough to capture a good image. And so he did.

Discreetly, he walked away. Into the next room of the apartment, which, though sparsely furnished, served as a monitoring terminal.

He put the hyper optic binoculars to the side. The imager was activated, and the face of Tahina was pixelated to form a tiny image.

"Magnify times one seventy- five", his husky voice demanded.

Her face grew to a quarter wall size, enough to begin a thorough comparative analysis. When he was certain of her identity, he brought it to his superior's attention.

"Are you sure it's her, Agent Hom? You know the Colonel has taken a special interest in *this* fugitive", the female sitting at the surveillance console said, doubtfully. Yet barely withholding an undercurrent of spite.

Mockingly, Agent Hom responded, jowls moving. "If *anyone* should remember her face, it should be *you,* Lieutenant Royst." And

Royst glared viciously, but took the slight on the chin. She'd pay him back later. She would.

"If it isn't, I hope you're prepared to face the Colonel's wrath", she warned. Her mind flashed back to the Titanus, level seven. Being held hostage, almost killed, made her quit law enforcement. Worse, made her question herself and her resolve. Then Harudamapati, himself, came calling. And after a lengthy persuasion session, she became a field agent for the intelligence agency known by a very selected few, Galactipol.

She was haunted very much by those events, but Lieutenant Jalice Royst was a survivor. She endured the bad memories to view the face. That face in her memory did, indeed, match Hom's crude hologram, and that of the one circulated on Asylon.

"Agent Hom, Royst said, a thin smile creasing her long face, you just earned yourself a free steak dinner every Friday for the next five years."

The skies were a sweet, milky light brown and weak grey.

Dawn over Quartey was remarkably beautiful. Below, another story. The streets were overfilled with litter; half- filled kegs, emptied liquor trucks (whose hoses were splayed around in all directions) and heaps of drunkards still laying about unconscious, or leaning against building walls, slumped over in transports in mass stupor. Hills of trash was neatly piled for easy collection and firecracker ash blew in the pre morning breeze. As the sun kept rising, Tahina was carefully walking the streets of the unknown. She was scared, but fully confident. She'd be alright.

She and Geon had a long, long talk. Then he gave her the longest hug she ever received. She didn't want to let him go, nor let her life aboard this ridiculously named starship slip away. Yet, she knew it was time.

"I was hoping you'd stay, but you already had your mind made up", he told her.

"I just ask that... you two take care of each other", she said, holding back tears.

She was doing her best to keep from bawling her eyes out.

"I'll be fine, and so will Jeth", he said, wondering if they reconciled for a moment. *The best loves never do*, he realized the moment after. "But you take care of yourself."

After he hugged her, and wiping away some tears of his own, he handed her a tiny box.

"Gifts?", she asked, surprised.

"Consider it insurance", he said. "The first is seventy-five credits of Crypto coin on this credit disc, the second is a light projector you can use as a weapon (if need be), and the last is a Tran-stellar communications signal, just in case."

".. I... I don't know what to say", she began crying.

"Just say you'll be in touch." He embraced her, let her cry on his shoulder. A strong twinge of regret flowed through him. Tahina was like a daughter to him. While he was saddened their time together, though not without turbulence, was so brief, he knew this was the right thing, the best thing for her. Most importantly, she knew.

The bay door closing behind her, she thought she saw the old man cry a little.

Maybe her own tears had blurred her vision.

Within hours, Geon's Baby was soaring into Quartey's atmosphere, retreating back into the deep, never ending cosmic expanse. That first day, she would spend hours wondering which emissions trail belonged to them. Now landbound, she marveled how little she gazed out into the stars, enthralled in wonder, while amongst them. Now, she could only recall somewhat ruefully...

She stopped herself. "I don't know the future, I can only walk into it", she said to herself.

The old Duriyan proverb provided moral and homespun comfort. She would need to remind herself every now and then. Morning mists swirled, hot and thin. The similarities to her home world were astonishing.

She walked around and around for hours. Avoiding the drunks, ignoring the barely coherent cat calls. Taking it all in...

The city was so big, so spread out, so metallic. Mortar and brick buildings seemed so hard to come by. A ray of sunshine could nearly blind a person, she thought, as a morning glare made her turn her head in the nick of time. Many people were stumbling about. She stepped over one, was cursed out unintelligibly by another, and searched about for food and lodging for the next half hour.

This big city here was nothing like the city districts on Duriy. For one, This place could fit districts twelve through twenty in its metropolitan area. And the people here, even inebriated, seemed nicer. Except for that one sluckhead. Even so, she kept her valuables tightly close and on her person. Except her weapon, which she held tightly in her left palm.

This will be a day. I'll have to play this slow and smart.

By the time mid-day had settled in, she found food and a job. The first was at a diner called Shel's, not too far from the Docking station. She heard Geon mention it to Sam while they were arriving. She was eating a flat cake special (super thin pancakes. Five per serving), when a gangly harried man in a green tunic and sickly blue pants came in.

Shel's was a standard trope on every world or outpost. A dank, seedy dive where a person could get some cheap eats and drink. She'd seen places like this back home, and there was even one on False Star. The aura of the joint had a melancholy feel to it. Oddly, despite being a foreigner, she didn't feel out of place here.

She was sitting at the counter, which was shaped strangely. Rather than a straight standard, it was light blue and wavy, recalling an ocean, specifically Earth's once blue waters. Each break in the waves was for a sitting customer.

"Mert", called the man behind the odd counter, "what's your trouble this morning?" The cook doubled as server this morning. His help no doubt sprawled over her sofa, in the midst of a massive hangover. But he was a man capable of multitasking, despite the frail appearance. He was beating off flour when Mert began to speak.

"Ahh, Orrin, Orrin, Mert said, half in jest, half despondent, I'm in a dandy of a pickle."

He took the stool two seats from Tahina, who could feel his eyes probing her. Slowly the cup of mint and lime tea came down on the milky white saucer.

"Can I help you?!", she asked, the rising octave inflecting her indignation.

"Come again, young madam?", asked Mert, astounded, who began moving himself away in his seat.

"I'd appreciate your eyes staying in front of you, not on my..."

"Take it easy! Everyone, take it easy!", Orrin cut in. His eyes went from her to Mert. He diffused the situation, in no mood for any arguments this morning. He was having trouble fighting a migraine as it was. When she first walked in his diner, Orrin Shel instantly realized this girl wasn't someone that should be taken lightly. No matter where she came from.

Then he said, after they quieted, "How's the food?"

She gave him the thumbs up sign. The universal hand sign of approval.

"Now Mert. What's your trouble? The one you *walked* in the door with?"

Pervy Mert must be a regular here, Tahina thought.

The place was barely alive. No more than ten people in the place. After yesterday, she guessed that could be expected. The blue glass diamonds glared in the sunlight above; he had a windowed dome that sat in the middle of the roof. And the sound, when someone spoke loud enough, echoed through the place. The sturdy appearance was a façade to hide the paper- thin walls.

"I'm looking for people, Mert said with a slight whine, to give Moniquu Bay a good cleaning."

"Ha, good luck with that!", Orrin laughed. "That'll take you to next year!"

Mert seemed genuinely troubled, or slightly inebriated himself. "Well, the work has to be done, and I'm paying well enough", Mert spoke out loud. He had a pompous, hollow ringing voice, which bounced around the room.

"How many people do you need?", Tahina found herself asking. A slight grin forming. "And how much do you pay?"

Both men, deep brown and with protruding foreheads (it seemed to her), looked at this brazen young woman.

"Young lady, Mert began, mildly hostile, do you have the temerity to ask for a job?!" He stared at her in disbelief.

She sipped her tea, turning to Mert. "Sir, I'm not asking for anything. That would be you. Are you looking for help, or not?" Her eyes were questioning and fierce.

Orrin, hiding a chuckle, said, "She's got a point, Mert. Finding people this time of day, after the festival, is like finding a fish on Earth." Conceding, he turned to Tahina and asked her age .

"Old enough", she spoke caustically, yet demurely enough for him to use her. Geon's money wouldn't last forever, and she needed steady income. At least a good start.

After considerable consternation, Mert reluctantly hired her on the spot. Fingering the GID that clung to her neck, she paid for her meal and followed him out into the Quarteyan mid- day.

He explained what the job was in detail, how they were to go about doing it, and his (it seemed to her) high expectations about getting everything done in one day.

In conversation, she told him where she was from. It surprised him, but not greatly. There were always people coming to Quartey from other parts of the galaxy. Enough for natives to grumble about "losing jobs". He asked her why she had come to this world, and she replied tersely, "For a change."

He didn't press the point; he already saw she had a quick temper. And he needed the help. A cloud of mystery hung over her, as that necklace clung to her neck and torso. He changed his line of questioning, to keep his mind on the right track.

"Ever do this type of work on Duriy? ", he asked as they came to a halt. They were now past nine blocks from the diner. *Maybe I'm wrong about the size of this city*, Tahina thought. They came to his skiff runner, that was docked on the southern pier of Moniquu Bay. It was large, and as they walked up, and onto the bow, she saw why. The bottom half was converted into a waste processor/incinerator. It looked a good twenty- eight feet in length, the nose of which was dulled and rust freckled, both front and hull. The bottom was slimed with algae and black sludge. It looked and smelled disgusting. The skimmer legs were completely subsumed in filth. Front and back of hull stilted by golden chrome skim skis that could support fifty tons. Tahina wondered how long he owned this thing, and had he ever bothered to clean it. It reeked of water scum.

While she was overlooking the Bay, taking it in and reconsidering her fondness of Black water soda, Mert went into the tiny cabin that doubled as both his office and bridge. She began to chafe under the full fury of the Quarteyan sun, thinking about Geon and Jeth. Just absent for mere hours, she missed both terribly. At some point, she would look Sam up. Geon had advised her to do so, but she was still rather leery of her. More like disgusted by that slovenly woman.

It was almost two hours later until the other help arrived. Two young guys, and a girl. All from Quartey. As they came aboard, Mert greeted them warmly, shaking hands with the boys, smiling sternly at the girl. Their manner of dress was threadbare, obviously overused. For this kind of work, it was acceptable. They eyed Tahina with mute curiosity. Her clothes, though used, were better kept. But her manner and exotic eyes piqued interest. She was mature, sullen and to a man, deadly serious. The girl watched her nervously, even after Mert gave brief introductions. Five minutes after the others boarded, he explained their duties, and the workday began.

The skiff runner was to go all over Moniquu Bay, collecting all the trash and accumulated waste from The Festival. The Bay was , supposedly, a contained reservoir, where people jogged around, played water sports and made out on the piers under the cover of evening (some while they sailed, causing the occasional fatality). Tahina's task was to man the hose that suctioned up the reminders of yesterday's festivities from the Bay. It was an enormous black snake that weighed over a hundred lbs. without water flowing through it. Mert wanted to give her another assignment, but she insisted, "I can handle this." The others looked at her, noncommittal. After the engine roared, the hose came alive. The skiff runner began moving, almost too rapidly for her to brace herself.

Water reeked and the hose now weighed an extra two hundred plus lbs. More, it seemed to her. She had a time guiding the thing as they skittered the water's surface . Twice, she almost dropped the damned water snake. It was getting slippery. The waste, muck and the trash kept coming. She hated this with a passion. But she found solace in the fact that this wasn't the worst part of the job. That was below deck, at the liquefier.

The liquefier was manned by the girl, named Merkaa. She looked to be a pup, the youngest of the group, but she had the build of a woman nearing twenty and eight. Quiet, she was too quiet, Tahina thought, catching the girl glancing at her. Probably sneaky as well. Tahina felt better about locking up her bag in that safe closet Mert allowed her to use. The task of condensing what could be salvaged (and thus sellable, another side business for Mert) went to the sturdily built youngster named Thuum. A laughing livewire, he seemed to revel in everything. And rarely took anything seriously. Little did Tahina suspect that the nineteen year- old was a Merit Scholar working his way through his planet's University system and the Tradesman Guild as an apprentice. Bionanotechnology was a growing, lucrative field, and he held aspirations of running his own research firm. The last guy Nizur, held the other end of the heavy hose down into the opening. He kept away from Tahina, and maybe that was just as well. Long, lanky and reserved, the similarities to Jeth made her leery of him. She'd never find out that he belonged to a pro Quarteyan nationalist group, who hated the recent chain of events, and wanted Quartey to be a separatist entity. And they despised the foreigners that were "invading our home and stealing our bread."

The debate, or argument would've been epic, had it come to pass. For all involved, it was fortunate it didn't.

Mert ran the ship. It turned out he was a private contractor, whose sole contract with the Quarteyan government was this one assignment. Slightly neurotic, he showed everyone what to do, and never told you again. "It was as simple as basic calculus", he'd say. Only once did he look out his cabin to see if there were any problems. Then nobody saw him again until lunch break.

While the others went walking around, Tahina sat on the deck, her rucksack nearby. Her pad was out.

The golden light danced among the

ruins of celebration and, from

above walks in the aftermath

of perdition a strange soul whose sole

reason is the way of the wanderer.

In so distant a land, in so weird waters

swim the possibilities of things yet to be

seen, and of words still hidden behind the cloak of

revelation.

This morning....

She thought about its flow, it's cadence when she read it in her mind. She shifted the glass screen, to keep the afternoon glare from ruining her eyes. She wondered how hot a Quartey afternoon could truly get.

From the other side of the deck, Mert walked over in tattered sole flip flops. His toes were knobs, almost curled. She thought about the shoes he had on hours before. He walked like he was really discomforted in some way. Now she knew why.

His woolen, lumpy calves looked comical, though Tahina didn't laugh. She half glanced at him. Taking in the alien culture and all it beheld for her would take some doing, she again realized.

"You're not with the others?", he asked curiously. Not many teenagers hung aboard in all his years of cleaning the bay. All twenty of them.

" I don't know them", she said evenly. "And I'm not looking for friends, yet."

"You might want to, given you're from another world. Someone to show you around would come just in handy." He was half smiling, half frowning. He was friendlier than he'd previously been, but given that they only knew each other for mere hours, certainly that didn't count for much. The implication, or perceived implication, made her cringe inwardly.

"I do better on my own", she said, staring past him. Steel stalactites touched the skies, tower vanes pricked the bright hazy, creamy biege. Streaks of exhaust fumes were fading into the distance as the last of the visiting ships were leaving the planet.

"Such a proud one you are", Mert said crisply. He stared at her momentarily before finally deciding he didn't like her. And she knew it and didn't care. And what's more, that she didn't like him either.

When the work was finished, he gave her the day's pay. Exactly what it should've been. *At least he's not a cheat,* she thought, inwardly relieved. She was prepared to give him the riot act.

After she thanked him, he said "Quartey isn't a bad place, if you take it slow and keep your wits about you." His tone was conciliatory, leaving open the possibility of him offering her future employment. She worked out well. Better than most of the others, actually.

Almost over shoulder, she replied "I intend to do exactly that."

That night, she found a half room not far from Moniquu Bay. Rather, it was the place that Mert, being more gracious than she deserved, told her about. She felt somewhat like an ass that she was so abrasive. *In the morning, I should find him and apologize.* Her tendency to push people away was working overtime, she realized. To the point where it was working to her detriment.

A bed, a stand, and a half closet. She shared the bathroom and the rest of the room with a girl named Minna, who looked every bit of the addict she was. The large, brown, piercing eyes followed her everywhere, Tahina thought, as if waiting for a person to let their guard down. Her head was the biggest part of her. And if she lost any further weight, she'd be a walking twig.

She scratched the inflammations on her arms and legs, even the gross scab that ran across her abdomen. Just looking at her made Tahina flinch in disgust.

Her halter shirt was a soiled cream, her ripped pants a deep brown that hid the dirt of alleyways and tree bark inadequately. Her toenails were chipped, brittle, near the point of discoloration. Her hair was, however, fairly maintained. A morsel of pride remained with her, at least.

For what seemed like infinity, the girls kept to their sides of the room, neither speaking. Then, Minna slowly rose from her bed. Tahina at first ignored her.

Nervously, she walked over, extended a blistered, scarred hand.

As menacingly as possible, she told Minna, "If anything of mine turns up missing, I'll kick your ass into the next lifetime."

Amazed, but more importantly, frightened, the other girl shrank back to her side of the room. She curled herself on the weak wooden chair in the corner, the one with the yellow paint flaking off. Then she began sobbing uncontrollably.

Tahina opened her mouth, then turned away in shame. "Look... I..I didn't mean ...." she stopped herself, knowing full well she did.

She kept on crying, completely uncaring about losing her dignity. She lost that a while ago, when her addiction became her lord and master. Tahina crossed over, sat on the girl's bed. Steeling herself, she put a hand on an uncovered shoulder, saying three times, "I'm very sorry. I'm so very deeply sorry."

After the third time, Minna recovered herself enough to ask, "Why do you say the same damn thing over again?" More out of curiosity than indignation. Despite her harshness, this foreigner with emerald eyes and a fiery disposition equally intrigued and repelled Minna.

"On my world, when you wrong someone, you admit to them your error three times. If accepted, wonderful. If not...," she let herself trail off, letting the girl come to her own conclusions.

"I'm not after your stuff!", Minna said defensively. "Everybody wants to accuse. Accuse me and point at me, when I didn't do anything!" She turned to face Tahina, then turned away. She was a liar, for sure. Her addiction, sating it, obeying its commands, was her first and main priority.

"Do they apologize when they're wrong?", Tahina asked her. Minna nodded her head in the negative slowly, deliberately.

"I'm not everybody", Tahina told her softly. *Great job. You've managed to alienate two potential friends in one day.*

Meekly, she smiled. Tahina began to get up. The left hand touched the side of her jeans.

"I accept your apology."

"Thank you", Tahina replied, surprising her with her sincerity.

"Where are you from?"

"A place that doesn't exist any longer", Tahina said wistfully. She left it at that. Minna watched her as she went into the bathroom. An ancient knob was turned. A rickety shower head came alive. Water at first spit, then spurted in force. Undressed, Tahina stepped in, subsumed by the torrent.

Minna, stared intently at the rucksack, the wheels in her mind turning at what wonders it held. But she forced herself to stay put. Despite the beck and call of addiction, despite its hold on her, she didn't budge. The first glimmer of compassion she'd seen in so long began to slowly dispel the cloud of shame and disgrace that hung over her. And she liked feeling a glimpse of sunshine above her.

Tahina's body relaxed under the hot water. This world had much to teach her, and perhaps she could teach it. She laughed at that grandiose thought. The first day, the proverb went, was always the hardest. Yet she felt she succeeded with flying colors.

That sad girl needed help, she thought. She'd seen drugs, what it did to people. Her mother. She didn't, rather, she couldn't help her; maybe she could help Minna. That is, if she wanted it. She left the rucksack out there as a test. Nothing of value was in there. Just clothing. Which she needed to change anyway. *Let her come to me,* she reasoned. She thought then of Duriy. Then Geon. And Jeth. Why did all the people that mattered, that would come to matter, leave her? Jojas. Sali. Only around for a spell of time. Then, they're gone. Taken away. Sali was heaven knows where. Dead? Alive? Jojas? Dead. Iajim? Yet all these people, Asylon, her escape and her travels, all in a span of one year. In over one year she lived more than most did in one decade. How, or why this came to be her lot in life she would dwell on for years, she suspected.

The mattress was worn, but durable. The night's rest turned out to be fitful, and almost surreal. Even so, she slept long and well, wholly unaware she was suddenly in the crosshairs.

Her first few weeks consisted of seeking steady work, counseling Minna (who had become a non- presence. She was gone a whole day and a half, returning with fresh bruises. Tahina read into the girl for almost an hour afterwards), and adjusting to the Quarteyan palette. "It's not spicy enough", she complained. She found herself a fixture at Shel's. She became fast friends with Orrin, and even extended the olive branch to Mert, when she saw him again. Doing so made her feel bittersweet. She regretted, greatly, she hadn't done the same with Jeth. She was surprised when she met his wife, a strikingly rich brown beauty a decade his junior. She felt foolish about how much she misjudged him. This made her return to feeling bad about not parting on good terms with her former friend.

In part, it was why she avoided contacting Sam. She never really liked her to begin with, and it really was time to move with *her life,* no matter how much she loved certain parts of the past.

The streets of Quartey she came to know rather quickly. They were tight, straight, and the metro system was inept, but at least they had marked evverything well. Hefu Blvd, for example was in deep red letters atop a corner post. The city was sectored, Minna explained, in districts RED, YELLOW, PURPLE, GOLD and ORANGE.

"Why such a loud color scheme?", Tahina asked.

"I dunno", Minna replied. "We favor primary colors, I suppose."

Touring the city streets, Tahina immediately saw the disparities in wealth, privilege and position that was Quarteyan society. Minna told her about the High Hills, where the very affluent dwelled. "My parents...", Minna stopped herself, shame blushing her face. "My parents still reside there."

Minna told her, to change the subject, about the other parts of Port Alim, both above *and* underground.

"Were you aware that this ecumenopolis extends some seventy levels underneath the planetary surface? Or of the fact that it was built upon a crater left behind from a meteor strike?"

"Actually, I wasn't", Tahina admitted. She gleaned the pride that Minna felt from telling her foreign friend something she didn't know, in the manner Tahina usually spoke to her. Sharing information for the sake of doing so? Or some form of get back? Or a bit of both? Tahina couldn't truly decide; she just sat on the edge of the sill, listening.

"Underside is where the majority population lives. Most of them are rarely allowed to come up topside, even during the Festival. They create a strain on the social fabric, so it was deemed best to keep them "out of sight, out of mind."

Tahina was shocked by this societal truth, but even more so from the callousness in her commentary. *Does she not realize she's not far from being the very untouchable she smugly scorns?* Disturbingly, as intriguing as the Underside was, she was more interested in what was immediately in front of her. So, she pressed for information about "Overside." Where to go, where to avoid.

There was a large area in the north side of Port Alim called Tent Town, where a mass of visible homeless camped. Thin polyfibers of various colors was what stood between a raging sun and the invisible denizens that went ignored, until the political cycles began anew. Or in time for the Festival, where they were herded away to a relocation center miles away into the outskirt fringes called the "desert".

"Why aren't they restricted to this "underside?"", Tahina asked.

" For various reasons", Minna said. "But I'll say this. Even the poor need someone to look down upon. And they don't like those worse off than them around. It reminds them that they're not so far off.'"

Tahina just listened, keeping her opinions about how backwards this society was, to herself as Minna continued her run down on the many social classes and neighborhoods that made up Quartey. In between those extremes of rich and poor were neighborhoods like Alim's Cove, The Abyss (Minna warned Tahina emphatically about avoiding *that* part of town), Saturn's Eye and Ashanti Town (or shortened to Ashanti).

"A boy I worked with hails from this Ashanti Town", Tahina told Minna.

"Did you get along with him?", Minna asked, in a fit of laughter that confused Tahina.

"We didn't speak the entire time", replied Tahina.

"It was best you didn't", returned Minna caustically. "A lot of crazies live there." By that she meant the conspiracy theorists, the Pro Quarteyan "hypocrites" (her words), who made a living talking one thing and living completely opposite. "One of the biggest Planet Pride groups was a front, she asserted, for dealing Fek."

The thought came to Tahina to ask her how she knew about that, but she again curbed her tongue. Some matters she didn't need, nor want, to poke her nose in. Nevertheless, her new friend's lifestyle brought trouble, and it was only a matter of time before trouble found her.

Minna was a fek head, Tahina discovered. Fek was at first a contact drug. But other means for consumption evolved. By injection, or rubbing the chalky powder on an open wound, it first exhilarated the body, then brought it's user crashing down as if dropping from a skyscraper. It consumed its addicts, and the walking near skeleton that was Minna was a tragic testimony to its destructive power.

She was two years younger than Tahina, and came from a relatively wealthy family that disowned her. Doing things to herself that, in her right mind, would've brought great shame and rebuke on herself, to the point of Hara Kiri. But despite the lies (she was an expert liar) and the appearance of being a decade older, there was still a remnant of the sweet, approval seeking girl that she was. It was a matter of sifting through the dirt and the rock to uncover a diamond.

Tahina had found work, in a nearby cleaners. The pay was fair enough (covering the basics, leaving little extra), and she didn't have to worry about being late. The customers spoke in a heavy accent that she struggled to understand. "Uti", Minna had called it. By the first week she got the hang of it. It wasn't hard to apply the detailed administrative acumen she learned working for Geon elsewhere.

A couple came into the shop, dropping off a pair of five uni-suits apiece. Tahina took their garments, applied the digital label to each item (name, type of garment, price, etc.) and hung each one gingerly on the rack. By the time she turned, they were gone.

"They'll be back", the owner reassured her. "We have customers who do that all the time." Despite his reassurance, she couldn't help but feel uneasy. Though she was free of her past, that did little to nothing to free her of being a fugitive. *I'm being ridiculous,* she convinced herself. She went back to work, desperately focusing on the *now.*

"Was that her?", asked the woman, as they cut through the busy traffic. Cars purred and honked angrily at each other. Shadow hovering above shadow, foaming at the bit to get on with their day.

"Biometric scans don't lie", returned the man, leading her to the next intersection. "She and Tahina of Duriy share the same vital and biometric stats. It's her."

A lump of uneasiness formed in her throat, almost preventing her from speaking, but the female agent asked, "Why now? Why go after and capture her now?"

Her partner looked at her, then said, "Only the Colonel knows. We just follow his orders."

"When ...?"

"Sooner than later......"

"Do you think she's on to us?", his female compatriot asked, now looking back, seeing if their quarry was watching their motion.

"We'll find out soon enough", was the curt reply.

Days passed, then a week.

At lunch, nine days later, Tahina was sitting in a nearby garden park that consisted of a lined row of trees, flower beds, a semi -

irrigated stream that had a tiny bridge that one could walk literally ten paces to get to the other side, and a caravan of food trucks that could hover off into the evening after the end of the workday. She liked to come there, for peace if not quiet. At this time, in the burgeoning afternoon, the park was packed. People on break, like her, enjoying a sun- drenched afternoon, talking, eating, flirting. Being human.

She had her tablet in hand, half covered by the shade the tree limbs above provided. There were some benches that circled the whole of the park, a line of defense against the weary. She sat there for over five minutes, and the screen was still blank. Her shoes under the bench, she had legs and feet curled beneath, swallowed in the folds of her lime and crimson sundress. She'd taken to wearing sundresses lately. It made her feel feminine. Especially since life snatched her away from Duriy.

"Life……", read the only word she managed to type. In her mind, she wrote the following :

Jeth,

How is life treating you these days? How is Geon? Are you both well? If I know you, most likely you're still fixing that infernal engine of yours. You love it, and it loves you. If a machine could know love. But, I'm happy for you. In freedom, you've found a passion. And I hope that in your heart, you'll be able to forgive me for trying to come between you and what you love.

I suppose in a universe such as this, where left is now right, and wrong is now right, finding what and who you love and holding on to it, or them, is the most important thing you can do.

I think about Asylon sometimes. No, I think on it all the time. Its horrors will never go away, no matter how long ago it was. But the only good that came out of it was that I met you, and in turn, you and I escaped into the cosmos. Either for good or ill, that remains to be seen. But, enjoy your freedom for all your days.

Forever,

Tahina

The screen went black, and she turned the thing off. She never typed the letter.

The next day, Tahina came home early in the afternoon, to a vicious fight between Minna and someone.

The noise reached the hallway, and she quickened her pace. The smashing of glass (maybe that bulb shaped lamp she liked so much), made her open the door hurriedly.

"I'll have it tomorrow ! I'll have it ... Aiiee!". Minna was cowering, screaming, as a woman, burly and snarling, beat at her head. Blows were flying quickly, mercilessly. She was a giant, a little over six feet, built like a man, dressed like a hoodlum. Tahina felt the surging fear, saw the upturned bed and furniture. Her rucksack and its contents scattered everywhere. Fear became rage, fueled by Minna's helpless wailing. A door in the hallway had opened, then quickly closed.

"Fek using, bougie whore!", came from above as muscular fists wailed away.

The door slammed, and the woman, a crescent scar running on her right cheek, turned. Curled lips revealed a broken tooth or two.

Minna, peeking through fingers that protected her face, looked up in frozen fear. Fear and awe. If her jaw wasn't so pained, she would've yelled "Tahina, get the hell out of here!"

"The fuck are you?", She barked at Tahina. Her arms were swollen with hard muscle. She knew how to use them, obviously.

Steeling herself, Tahina said harshly, "I live here! Leave her alone and get the sluck out!" *I really, really hope I'm convincing her to get out of here. I'm convincing myself I can handle this.*

"Sluck?!", said the woman, who ignored Minna and began advancing on Tahina. "The Hell are you from?" An ugly smile creasing her horrendous face, a face recalling a horror monster from those old movie discs Geon kept as collectibles. But this was no movie.

"Doesn't matter, I'm here now", the Duriyan replied. *Really, convincing myself....*

There was scant time to duck, because the air was cut in half by that blow. Tahina immediately attacked the mid-section, which amused her well ripped opponent. She was grabbed by the hair and thrown back. Her head banged against the wall, came forward and she was slapped down . She almost landed, head first into the nightstand.

"Might make some money off you" , the muscle woman laughed. Hard, ice cold eyes were looking Tahina over. "Might sell you..."

Minna, grabbing the chair, crashed it against her tormentor's head. Muscle Woman staggered with the blow, then turned toward her with quick fury. Her hand lunged out, taking Minna by the neck. She squeezed. Minna was turning blue.

Tahina, still dazed, only gasped when the beam of blue flashed in the room. Minna lurched back as the arm severed from body, her assailant's scream shook the room. A hole in the door billowed, eyeing. Then it was kicked in, the laser rifles trained on Ms. Muscles.

And fired until what remained of her was a trail of blue vapor and a tiny pile of ash.

In the confusion, a quintet clad in black uniforms, silver striping the sides of their legs invaded the room.

On the floor, Minna shook nervously, as she was made to lie on her back and cuffed. Tahina was made to lie face down on the right side of her bed, suffering the same.

The dream is but ashes and vapor... A Dez Vulker poem once began.

The shot came through the door, Tahina realized too late. The wreckage that was the door was splintered, its jamb fractured beyond repair as the smoke choked the room and hallways. Curious spectators began to emerge, whispering, pointing fingers and trading perplexed, worrying glances.

"Clean operation, Lieutenant?" said an iron voice through a radio ear. Lieutenant Royst stood in the center of the room, overseeing the carnage.

"One casualty, sir. A non- entity. Another in custody. Our quarry has been captured."

She recounted the details into the radio, grimly satisfied.

"Begin clean-up and extradition", came a terse command that ended the communication.

Lieutenant Royst sent an officer out into the hallway, to get the bystanders out of their way. Another summoned their transporter to rendezvous with the team in less than a quarter hour.

Her head throbbing, her right cheek was bruised, and she felt the faint trickle of blood forming small drops. But all that paled to staring into the cold, vindictive gaze of Jalice Royst.

"Tahina of Duriy, she spoke just above a callous whisper, it's good to see you once again."

The dream is but ashes and vapor....

Chapter Fifteen

Warden Quinn, peering into the capsule, saw Tahina's expression as a mask of profound grief and sorrow.

But there was something else. She couldn't decipher if it was anger, hatred, confusion or a child of all three. She didn't even know what to truly make of this newfound development now. That really frightened her. For reasons she couldn't articulate, her greatest wish (half of it anyway), had become a gateway to some new form of horror. But she refused to dwell on it for now.

"That story was neither funny, nor worth the effort of retelling", she replied dryly.

Shaking his head, with a wicked half smile he asked her, "Did you ever have a sense of humor?"

She glared at him. Her feelings of revulsion grew stronger, even though he granted her this boon. Even with gratitude she found being gracious to him a difficulty. "I don't believe in gallows humor. But what of her friend?"

"She's being held and observed", Harudamapati shrugged. A gesture which was rather unusual for him. Then again, he had a different personality for whatever identity he wore. Like changing shoes, or an outfit, to fit a specific function.

"If you don't mind my inquiry.... "

"I do", he replied sharply. He began to walk away from his imprisoned guest. His stride suggested to Quinn that she should hastily follow. A sleek, shiny black door almost closed in on her.

"Try to keep up", he warned. "I have much to do."

As did I, she thought, feeling resentful.

They walked down a corridor. Turned another. The smooth black walls took some getting used to. Metallic marble. She wondered, half mindedly, at what manner of construction went into this vessel Harudamapati commanded. But she had more pressing concerns.

"I..I need to go back", she began, uncharacteristically nervous.

"You will", he assured her. Abeit not too convincingly.

"Any word on Akim? I, I would've assumed they'd be together."
The idea of one or the other remaining free, or even dead, was
troubling.

"You know what they say about assumptions", he said, half in
jest. Disquieted by the other half lurking under the surface, she
returned to the subject of Minna.

"That other girl...."

"What of her? "

"For what reason are you holding her? She's innocent."

Turning sharply, he faced Quinn. His face was tired, lined with
fatigue and what appeared to be an unending burdening of stress.
This was not the person she'd become, albeit grudgingly, accustomed
to. But his eyes were twin infernos of black fire.

Two of his officers walking down the opposite side of the narrow
space, nodded in deference and backed themselves to the wall so
their commander and guest could stride freely.

*They're in awe of him. In awe, and fearful in an almost paralyzing
kind of way,* Quinn noted. Wondering if it would be wise to assume
that same disposition. Then she shrugged it off angrily. She wasn't
some junior officer stationed on a star ship on some clandestine
mission. She was Warden Prime, the visual face of the Trans-galactic
Prison Industrial Complex.

"In this forsaken universe, Warden, no one is innocent." His brisk
stride continued, as the Warden was left stunned in her tracks,
mentally, pondering.

The mirrored walls reflected her exasperation, her frustrations,
and now, her open disgust over what he had just said. For the first
time in ages, she began to rethink the positions those professors and
activist types took the very first time she heard of this guy. *Were they
right all along?!*, she forcefully asked herself.

Walking in silence until he bounded three hidden steps (that
emerged when he came within vicinity. The biometric activation
sequences were incredible!), and pressed his right hand on a wall

panel. Unsurprisingly, a hidden door revealed itself, from seemingly nowhere.

Another smorgasbord of high technological advancement lay before her.

There were no bulky computer consoles, nor any awkward shaped system command terminals that stereotyped the concept of a star craft that could operate through interstellar space. Everything was smaller, almost organic in design. The viewing screen before them comprised the entire front wall. To her left was the ship's communications terminal; tiny, eye shaped, protruding from a thin stick of black steel that informed the crew effectively, and with crystal clarity of word and inflection.

His command bridge was tight, as tightly run as anywhere else aboard ship. One person was immersed in Data Receiving, another manned a miniature wall console that was comprised of many smaller versions. Each miniature featured a fellow officer performing some clandestine act. In the service of Humanity, naturally.

Navigations was mapping co-ordinates to False Star, the holographic trajectory before them in a haze of deep orange light.

Seeing all this impressed Quinn deeply. As deeply as it frightened her.

"What of Tahina? " she whispered. No one who was nearby acknowledged her presence with so much as a side glance. She was a ghost to them, less than an inconvenience.

The captain's chair was rounded, both arms held petite consoles through which he could issue directives, receive pertinent information and a news stream feed that put anything Quinn had previously known to shame. And it could turn in all directions, so the Colonel never had to rise out of place. He could run his bridge in the aristocratic leisure that men of previous eras could only have dreamed of.

"What of her?", he said, taking his seat. His arm console held several messages, in encryption. Nonchalantly, he read through them, finding a few amusing.

"You know what I mean. She escaped from ... my custody. I expect that you'll be leaving that prisoner here with me?" As foolish as it appeared, it fell upon her to ask. There was something very, very uneasy, something very wrong about all of this. She couldn't shake the feeling that she was a chess piece being advanced into position.

"Ednisa, he said, quiet and calm, enjoy the view. I have other matters to see to."

The screen came alive before them. Stunned, her mouth gaped.

They were moving fast in the deep reaches of space! Too fast for her to properly estimate. But she knew, instinctively, that she was miles from where she belonged.

She nearly shrieked indignantly, but she was led away by Officers Henkan and Roi.

"I'll be with you shortly", Harudamapati said. "I've more pressing matters now. They'll see you to private quarters. Get some sleep."

Somehow, he acquired a way to make an invitation to rest sound bone chilling.

I liked you better when I hated you for being an obstructive, intrusive and uber obnoxious lawyer! Quinn thought, being led down yet another hallway. *For how many times in, what was it, an hour and a half now ?*

Walking down the tight corridor was slow, ominous. Quinn was really fearful, openly fearful, of the danger this man radiated. She'd always been leery of him, but she wore a masque of annoyance, or outright animosity to hide it. She realized, fully realized now, what a dangerous position she was in. And she allowed herself to be placed there.

What have I become a party to ?

His underlings moved as he did. Brisk, efficient. Robotic. Without a soul.

"Where are we going? I have to get back to work ", Quinn said, immediately realizing how foolish she sounded. Again.

"You needn't worry, Warden Quinn", said the male officer. His name was Henkan. "The Colonel already informed your people not to expect you later today." He barely turned his head talking to her. As if he wanted to keep the rapid gait in his step.

Drolly, Quinn thought , *to be young again.*

"Tahina. I... need to see her", Quinn said, her voice echoed with a growing, gnawing sense of regret. Neither of them responded.

They came to a full stop. Roi placed her hand on the entrance panel. It opened swiftly, to an unexpected opulence of a bed, a king, and the extravagant fancy spiraling, blue crystal night lights atop two chiseled marble nightstands that belied the spartan polish outside.

Quinn thought she was stepping into a dream. One of hers, to be specific. Since a child she had always admired private rooms so grand, so affluent that it mocked the less acquisitive and less fortunate. *Was this yet another way of him mocking her?*

"The colonel's private quarters is being made available to you", Roi said, with a subtle hint of envy. Henkan smirked a little.

Though she was perturbed by the implication, Quinn was relieved, a little, that they were at least somewhat human.

"Thank...you", repiled Quinn. The sound of a gale of laughter was obscured by the closing door. It was gaudy alright. With the command "illuminate", she saw the room brighten. Well kept, very exquisite. The furniture was neo antique (mid twenty -fifth century craftsmanship blended with the retro stylings of long past eras.), and well maintained. There were actual oil paintings (long abandoned for virtual sculpting and plant- based painting), and they looked well preserved. She imagined it would be like living in a museum, or a walk through a collector's paradise. Anything from nineteenth century Earth that survived The Atomic Fall, would be worth billions today. Only Bevels could afford that. Twenty- fifth century antiques, especially around the time of the colonization era known as The Great Expansion, which followed the Star Rush, was gaining in popularity. If only...

A two-seater sofa, so out of place, sat in the middle of his suite. She sat on it, lulled by it's almost silken cushions. So soft and relaxing to the touch. As tired she was, she was fast asleep.

She awoke to an incomplete darkness.

When Tahina came to, she found herself strapped to a chair. She saw she was draped in what amounted to nothing more than a paper-thin set of pajamas. Her toes touched the hard, cold steel floor. Its frostiness made her bunch them for warmth. Her hair was matted and drenched. Ends stuck out like tiny prickly needles. Beads of both perspiration, and the inertia solution they placed her in, dripped onto the floor, the lap of her flimsy garments. The chair itself was by no means a luxury. It was basically welded in place. And the seat to this thing, as hard as bricks. She was a captive once more, which was horrible enough. That they were making it as uncomfortable as possible made it inhumane.

Uncomfortable, her stomach was upset, and she was achingly hungry. The steel ringlets that secured her wrists firmly to the chair didn't budge, and after five tries she ceased her futile efforts. Right now, she needed to clear her mind and recall everything that transpired.

Screaming, the smell of eviscerated flesh and bone. Blood trickling from face to hand.

Royst.

Royst. The last thing she remembered, before they electroshocked her, was the hard kick she gave her.

They lifted her up, her hands cuffed tight behind her. Minna was wailing on the floor. Blue smoke filled the room, the hallway. Sounds of gossip were growing louder. Royst stood in front of her, smiling. Her face a mask of vindication and iron hatred. The type that holds a grudge for decades after the offense, real or imagined. She gave her a hard, sound slap in the face. Tahina's injured cheek stung, blushed and bruised. The other officers were watching , noncommittal.

Tahina staggered back, steadying herself.

"This couldn't happen to a nicer person", she remarked. "Duriyan...."

Steadied, and with somewhat still lightning reflexes....

Tahina crashed her left foot dead into her nose, upper lip. Royst fell back, holding both.

Gasps, then a snicker or two. Open laughter.

"Hold her!", Royst cried, covering what was either a broken nose or busted lip. Blood dripped through the fingers of her cupped hand. Murder flashed hard in her eyes.

Another officer held her back, laughing hard.

"Royst loses yet again!", another said. Tahina burst out laughing. The ensuing jolt shocked her. Then, as everything faded to black, Royst's bloody face was her last embers of consciousness. That, and hearing Minna scream her name.

"Minna?", she asked weakly. *Was she here? Or still on Quartey?*

Where was she? Certainly not on Quartey still .

Her mind had become less groggy. She looked around, but everything was still so dark. She couldn't make out anything to tell her where she was. The tiny shards of lighting above was useless to her.

Fear. Desperation. Worry .Grief. Powerlessness. These five things created a tidal wave within her. They had her again. And they'd do everything, this time, to ensure that she was incapable of escaping their grip again. There was nothing she could do about it.

Except weep.

A deep, sorrowful wail; the pain of her soul flooding from her, it's release draining her totally. She was spent. At her most vulnerable.

Which Col. Harudamapati observed from nearby. And was counting on.

His terse command filled the room with light.

In confusion, Tahina turned sideways, straining to see what was behind her. She looked about at spiraling wire coils that ran from dark crystalline tube to red crystalline tube. Sixteen in all, lined side by side to the right of her. To the left were medical consoles (she recalled the infirmary on Asylon), which held running schematics on the human brain and neurological processes. One of which flashed a virtual simulation demonstrating the aftereffects of biotoxins on the human brain. A familiar name flashed underneath the simulation:

HEJIMMA.

Rapidly, sorrow and self- pity was shoved aside by bone chilling fear desperation.

Hard soles clacked hard on the cold floor. Each pace harder, more unnerving then the last. Then, it stopped. She could see him.

Finally, Tahina and the Colonel were face to face, in a manner of speaking. Deep within her, there was a sense of revelation. *No, not revelation. Reckoning,* she corrected herself.

"I was wondering when you'd wake up", he said. From a thin curtain of light, he fully emerged, in full regalia. Quickly, she realized he was the one in charge. Despite going by the tired, brown face, plain and unimpressive, she knew not to take him lightly.

He smiled, but there was no joy, not even a slice of mirth on his countenance. She shrank back as best she could, as he approached her, but knew there was no refuge to be found. It soon became apparent that he was assessing her, while she was doing the same with him. Like the beginning stages of a chess game, when both players study the board for advantage. Only thing was that she knew, going in, she was the one heavily disadvantaged.

Come what may, I'll have to play this until the end, she understood ruefully.

After considerable groping, she found her words. "Who… Who in all the levels of Hell, are you?"

Still smiling, he pressed a red button on his sleeve. A hover chair came out of the wall, nearing him. He took a seat. Face to face. Literally. He sat, obviously reveling in the roiling confusion he was stirring within her.

"You may call me Colonel, Tahina. Colonel Harudamapati."

"How do you know my name?!", she demanded. *Wondering why is his name so familiar?*

Ignoring the petulance of her outburst. He began.

"I know everything about you. Eighteen years old. From Duriy, of course. You last lived in the ill- famed Shakur Province. A very bright, promising student, academically speaking. Troubled home life. Despite it all, and personal idiosyncrasies aside, your future looked to be considerably bright. Then the riots happened."

She breathed hard, the paper thin plastic that covered her breasts fluttered lightly.

"Such a twist of fate I couldn't imagine", he replied dryly. His eyes were probing, more than simply curious. He was looking to see what made her work. Like a kid that takes apart a motor engine, or a computer panel, just to see. What buttons to push. Jeth came to mind. But Jeth, despite his many flaws, was just a benign bumpkin. This man was nowhere near benign. And by no means a goof.

"Are you to narrate my life story?", she asked him. Her insolent tone was an attempt, however futile, however desperate, to maintain a degree of control over herself.

"That's still being written, as your Dez Vulker would say. The thing is, who'll be doing the writing. I believe he puts this way:

"The pen of fate lay'd in my hand

Lay'd for days and days became

seasons. Seasons birthed eons of

time.

Only when, another snatched the pen,

Did I scream "Mine !!!".

She frowned deeply, saying "He says it much, much better."

He returned a short snicker, then smirked.

"But I, more succinctly. And succinct is by far more applicable to your predicament than eloquence, I'd gather."

Even his smirk was obnoxious. Pretentious. Like a mirror. She began to truly glimpse how others felt around her. And about her. *Am... Am I really this bad?*

"People dislike intelligent people", he spoke, divining her thoughts. "For one, there's not many of us to begin with, and the number dwindles with the passage of time. It's a prayer to Divine Intervention that the intelligent species amongst Man has yet to die out."

"Dulos Kulm", she said knowingly. "You're well versed in my... people's culture. Yet I'm not bound up here to discuss Duriyan poetry, nor elitist philosophies...."

"That you yourself subscribe to. And why not? You see the truth in them, even more so, I should think, since your short lived "freedom".

The condescension in his tone wasn't practiced, nor even forced. It was natural, she noted. Much like hers.

If I spit in his slime ridden face, will he strike me unconscious?, she pondered.

"What do you want from me?", she asked, feeling herself quiver.

"Heat, magnify by seventeen percent."

Tahina felt the floor get warmer, radiating heat tickling the soles of her feet. Against her own will she began to relax. Ever observant, he said, "The mind and flesh, forever at odds. The former ever at the mercy of the latter."

Silence.

"To answer your inquiry (as you'd say), of yourself nothing. That is, until escaping Asylon. Then, and he held a lanky finger before her face, wiggling it, you became very interesting. And important. "

The gesture was to goad her, she knew instantly. When her mother did it, when a teacher did it, she reacted badly. Sluck, Jojas did it, and provoked the worst fight they ever had. Only because they were with others who kept her from hurting him beyond a busted lip and bruised right cheek.

She breathed hard, then asked, "In what way?" She was exhausted, distraught, struggling to not panic. He laughed. She widened her eyes with disbelief. Then squinted at him with disdain.

Abruptly, he stopped, the smug, glacial mirth melting away. He settled in his seat, rocking slightly. In a deliberate manner honed over decades, Colonel Harudamapati began the "lecture".

"Tell me, do you wonder about the universe that you find yourself in? How, almost overnight, everything's so radically different than the one you rested your pretty little head in just hours before? Have you? I'm certain you have, but I want to hear it from you."

More than anything, right now, she wanted to tell this bastard off. Or just play silent. But neither was an option. Perversely, she was curious about what he had to say. He'd gone to so much trouble to bring her before him. Whatever his plans for her, instinctively she realized he was revealing himself for a reason. Perhaps through dialogue, she might discover some means to save herself. Theoretically speaking.

Reluctantly, she told him, "I have. Though not as close as I should have." She hated to admit an error. Yet, in this instance there was no face to save.

"Given your circumstances, it's understandable." The tone of conversation had changed, she noted. Not of jailor and prisoner. More like a dialogue between teacher and pupil. A very promising, albeit wayward student. "The fact remains that so very few people, and especially the political leaders on worlds like yours, realized how expansive the Thirteenth Law could become. And has become. Even the fools who run the GCW didn't see it's full, true potential. Most of them, at any rate. A growing few are just grasping it, even after all this time."

She didn't respond. She had no measure to contest him, and bringing emotionalism to a logic battle was an exercise in futility.

"So, I have to surmise that you do".

"Naturally. Rather, we do. The people who head this organization do. And others like it."

Others like it. The realm of political conspiracy was an area she never wandered in too deeply. For her, it was the stuff of over fertile imaginations. The fantastic talking points, only mere wordplay for excusing the failure in one's own existence. Asylon did little to change that train of thinking. But his admission here derailed it .

"The original intent of the Law 13 was to protect citizens from the overreach of extremists. Rather ironic then, that no provisions were made for the extremism of government, is it not?" He spoke with a fearless candor that scared her. *Why is he telling me this?,* she thought, feeling the anxiety gnaw at her insides.

"Do you expect me to answer you, knowing any counterargument I attempt will be met and beaten back by your infallible master logic?"

He smirked again, then answered blithely, " Your understanding, or the obvious lack thereof, is a minor amusement to engage myself while in the face of far more important matters."

She again restrained herself, knowing he was being both serious and provocative all at once.

"For now, it suits the purpose", he added. "From this point forward, there is no going back to what was. Only what shall be, of which we are only on the cusp of beginning to realize."

"An interstellar police state", she said. "A galaxy of oligarchs, which number in the hundreds while the enslaved masses are in the trillions."

"A condition as old as humanity itself, Tahina", Harudamapati sneered dismissively.

"The old saying goes, if it isn't broken, why fix it?", she returned. Faintly, the Colonel smiled. *At least he has an appreciation for witticism.* Rising, his hover seat returned to the shadows.

"Of that, you are correct", he acknowledged, pacing the obscenely glossed black metal floor. Echoing hard steps made it uncomfortable for her to concentrate, to think. Gazing upwards, she saw the arches that buttressed the ceiling. The arches were more ornamental in nature, as opposed to the austere functionality of what was around her. It made her wonder just how much this star craft cost. Its true cost. The cost in human life to make this a reality.

Adjusting herself as best she could, the thin paper plastic covering her rustled. "So what this comes down to is how many will suffer to make the life of a few more regal? And what happened to Hejimma?"

The last question gave him reason to pause.

"Such a limited scope of thought. I'm disappointed, however not surprised by this."

"I merely give you my analysis. Isn't that what you wanted?", she answered back, taking no care this time to keep the snark out of her voice.

"The time has come to give you full enlightenment, it appears." He ignored the last question.

"So, where do I fit in all of this?", she asked. She wanted to know why he was telling her all this. She calmly realized she wouldn't be leaving this room alive, most likely. Somehow, she wasn't disturbed by the notion. Perhaps she even welcomed it.

He stood over her, looking down . He reached down and adjusted a dial on the chair. The bonds loosened. Not enough to free her, just enough for her to feel less uncomfortable, if that were possible.

"Diagram fourteen. Nine tenths full capacity".

The hologram that appeared above her was the Human Diaspora, in the form of a chessboard!

"Ignore the astrophysical inaccuracies and focus on the sociopolitical, Trans-political, geological side of things", he instructed her.

She found it impressive that quadrillions of astro-kilometers, of so expansive an occupied space could be neatly fit into a fully realized, multidimensional hologram. Impressive, frightening in implication. This was the result of careful, skilled, diligent planning, now bearing its ruthless harvest. She suddenly thought of Jeth again, remembering the story of the Hikka root she told him when she was sick.

"It takes nine months to grow to ripeness, like a human", she said, through bouts of intense coughing.

"You don't say?", he replied. He found it an interesting fact, simply due to having nothing to compare it to.

Now sitting up, hands holding the tea, she told him about the extraordinary care that went into it. "You have to bury your seeds two to three inches deep, preferably in soil fertilized with cow's dung, because Hikka is a root that thrives in very rich, very fertile soil. The seeds themselves are almost microscopic, so you must handle them one by one, usually with a pair of tweezers." She laughed lightly when she saw the scrunched face he had made.

"After planting, you'll have to protect your field from the Sunbirds, who prey on the seeds." Sunbirds were native to Duriy, in fact it was the planetary mascot. They were bigger than an Earth pigeon, with a gold and orange plumage, sometimes speckled with tiny black dots. And they multiplied like rabbits. Tahina remembered coming across a nest with no less than thirteen eggs.

"By law, we can't kill them. But we use other means to keep the harvest productive...."

Not so gingerly, Colonel Harudamapati nudged her back to the here and now. "You need desperately to pay attention!", he snapped.

The dread of a dull class lecture had come upon her, only this time, moral terror overrode the ruination of intellectual stimulation. "Where's Minna?", she asked, feeling ashamed that her wayward friend had, ony now, just returned to the forefront of her thoughts.

"Well enough, for the moment" , he told her, turning his back. She welcomed it. His face, half shaded by the hologram's pixilation, was iron and compassionless. "Now, let's begin", he bellowed to her authoritatively.

Clanging, the familiar sound of fine china being placed upon the dining table roused Quinn from her brief, though fitful, sleep.

As she stood, and stretched, the pillows were filling out the imprint she left upon them. As if she had never sat on it, let alone getting a few hours rest.

She let out a brief yawn, then crooked her head towards the kitchen when she got a strong wind of the aroma.

Mint tea. Hot, and steamy. And coffee, with cream, cinnamon, and sugar added.

To herself, she mused *At least he's giving me a choice in something.*

An Infosynthesis stream, from a retro styled entertainment console, came alive with breaking news:

"The raid on False Star by GCW forces has turned up a wonderland of illegal tech..."

"Shares in IREL has risen substantially since the ascent of Herod Bevel...."

"The latest concern for a unified Human Diaspora is the new resurgence of piracy...."

"The latest woe to hit the former Far worlds, and particularly the young : Syathin-9. More on this next seg..."

"Off", Quinn said, wondering if voice command would work for her. To her surprise, it worked. She looked around. No one else was in the room with her. In silence, she sipped the tea. Peppermint. Earth peppermint, or a substance so close to the original, only seasoned taste buds could tell the difference. She had no choice but to admire this. This affluence. *This is a level of wealth only a Bevel could acquire,* she pondered, yet again, as she was staring out the porthole. Stars were moving; no, this sleek bird of a vessel was moving at speeds she only heard about. *How did he get to this point in life?*

The maid girl reentered the quarters.

She moved about so quietly, that Quinn didn't notice her bringing in a tray of food. The scent of breakfast fare made Quinn turn, realizing she was being stared upon for minutes on in.

She who brought in the food wasn't attired as the others. She wore an all-black dress that reached just past the knee. A white apron covered her torso and abdomen. Her hair, braided. And her feet were bare. Well cared for, but naked. A gold bracelet on her left foot held a glass oval that glittered green. On more than one occasion, it flashed.

Quinn took the imagery in, a slow distaste rising inside her.

"Your breakfast is here, Warden Quinn", she replied, in a voice so low Quinn had to make her repeat herself.

Side eying her, Quinn said self- consciously, "Thank You".

It was strange to see a maid in a setting like this. A young one, at that. Her face looked familiar. Black, expressionless, with the most vacant eyes she'd ever seen. Devoid of personality, bereft of life, she went about her duties robotically. More than the officers under Harudamapati. Quinn briefly wondered if she even had a soul.

The grand irony of irony, she thought, suddenly wondering about herself.

"What is your name, child?", Quinn asked her, unable to shake the feeling she'd seen this young lady somewhere before. Which is odd, she realized. She scarcely knew any teenagers. And this was clearly a very young woman before her.

"Sali", she said. A voice as hollow as her movements. Even her inflection was flat. Not much of a trace of a definable dialect.

Putting down the cup of tea, Sali interrupted her.

"Allow me, Madam Quinn", she said as she hastily took the cup and placed it on the sterling silver tray.

"Thank you, Sali." Suddenly, a wave of ill feeling came over Quinn. But it wasn't Gyddis. "Sali, where are you from? What planet?" Her face *looked* like she could be Duriyan. The way the girl contorted her face gave her a scare. Sali looked like she was struggling. In pain. Her face revealed anguish by some hidden, great source of distress.

What is deviling this poor girl ?

"They told me I came from Duriy. I..I don't remember anything about it though", Sali confessed, unashamed. Face was less strained, as flames of memory were extinguished. No visible signs of brain damage. On the surface, she appeared an open book with blank pages.

However, Quinn read hostility in her. Inarticulate and long buried, but it was there. Taking her by the hand, she told Sali to sit. The girl resisted, but Quinn repeated, with more authority. Reluctantly, the young lady obeyed.

"Don't you know how old you are?"

Sali nodded her head negatively. Face reddened; a tidal wave of shame threatening to consume her.

"What do you remember about ...anything?", Quinn asked her, none too gently. Her questioning was humiliating to Sali, who began stifling tears.

"I'm not allowed to sit on the Colonel's sofa. Nor should I..."

"It's...alright, Sali." Quinn was doing her best to sound comforting, even empathetic. She ended up sounding even more hollow to the tormented maid sitting next to her. She noticed the flash in the middle of her anklet again. *It was a medical device!* She forgot the actual term for it, but she had seen this jewelry during her therapy. A distributor of medicines, of drugs.... . *This girl is being drugged!*

Sali moved away from the woman. Her hostility was now finding a target, a face to direct its fury towards. Quinn knew it was her, but she had to know the truth. At least what this sad soul could reveal.

"Sali... what did *they* do to you?" Her words sounded incredulous, even unreal. She felt the cold regard in the stare, but she'd bear it. Perhaps it was the least contrition she could offer...

Against her will, she struggled to put a distorted fog of memories into words. Sali's tightly drawn mask quivered, as if readying itself to slip off. The lips twisted open and without a warning, she spat out, "Sold Me!" Getting up before Quinn could grab hold of her. And for her part, Quinn stopped herself, wondering how she'd react if she did anything more.

"Who...?", Quinn asked dumbly, preparing herself for violence.

Venomously, Sali yelled "YOU, YOU SLUCKFACED BITCH!!".

The porthole was nearby. *Could I fit through?* Quinn thought hurriedly. She opened a pandora's box of guilt, and lacking the ability, or will to shut it closed, throw it across the room, she forced herself to endure the unleashing of its horrors. Horrors she inflicted on this girl, and others. Knowingly, without care nor concern of ramifications.

Sali was screaming at the height of her lungs, heaving with fury.

" I...remember the bars! The beatings....my friend. They dragged her away.... and ....took me away from him. You caused it!! You!", Sali screamed, past the point of hysteria. An abrupt flash from the anklet. The thing beeped several times, and the girl quieted down, rage stifled. Eerily, she was soon calm and robotic once more.

Deep shame grew within Ednisa Quinn. Though she never delved into it, she had heard rumors about girls from Asylon being used as domestics, as maids. And... she shuddered. *How many Sali's have I created? How many did I send off to their deaths in the mines? How many more have I condemned?* Suddenly, Tahina was spitting in her face. Once again, it was that day on Asylon, that an insolent child, a haughty girl with green eyes and an unusual vocabulary did the most despicable act a person could do to another. So Quinn thought at the time. Her actions had proven to be even more vile, more soul rending, more eternally damaging. She knew she had fallen so far into oblivion to be redeemed. But at least...

"Sali, she asked weakly, contritely, would you like some tea? Coffee even?"

Fully composed, Sali said cheerfully, "I must go, Madam Quinn. The Colonel needs me."

"Harudamapati", she whispered. "Can you take me to him ? "

"I... I don't know, Madam Quinn. The Colonel.... doesn't like to be disturbed when he's working", the maid said, with lingering hints of hostility.

In a violent rush of anger, Quinn roared, "Take me to him. NOW!!" She hated herself. Not only her being, but what her life had come to represent. She wanted to claw his eyes out, smash him about the head with a truncheon (or some other iron tubing), anything that would smash that smug, swarthy brown face to a million pieces.

Cowed into submission, Sali complied, leading the way out.

"Hungry?"

"What does it matter?"

"It doesn't. Hungry?", he asked again, with a suffocating smugness she had come to loathe.

"Yes.... I'm very hungry. And I smell of foul chemicals. May... I have a bath and some food to digest?" She hated how she sounded. More, she hated that she was saying these things to him, of all people. It was like begging Quinn for hygiene products back at Asylon. In fact, until this very moment, she failed to notice just how *similar* the two of them were. *Two faces of the same, ambiguous, anthropophagic entity.*

"Perhaps, Harudamapati said, in due time. For now, stew in both your hunger and body funk."

Sluck you!!!, emblazoned her conscious thoughts. "So why the hell did you bother to ask me, then?!"

"Because I could, I can, and I will", he told her simply. It was another way of informing her who was truly the dominant party. Not just in these chambers, but in the universe she was a prisoner in. Like trillions of others, she was under this unimpressive man's thumb. And all she could do is squirm, malnourished and smelly.

Tahina stirred again, stifled by her bonds. Perspiration made the thin plastic stick to her skin. Amid a tedious flow of words, she fought against falling asleep. The map, in its harsh and resolute brilliance, made her eyes hurt.

"Is this how you torture people?", she asked, exasperated."By lecturing them to death?"

He smirked, then replied with his trademark smugness, "I've been told you've employed this same technique, from time to time."

She moaned as he continued.

"So, as you see, the cyclical theory of history is most accurate. Truly, there is nothing new under the sun. Or suns, to keep things true to our times." He spoke with the authority of a university professor. Backed with facts and statistical evidence. Yet, in her heart of hearts, his whole rationale, his reasoning for attempting to reach whatever his endgame was, he was most definitely in the wrong. Not just in the moral sense, but in the fact that it violated the very principle, the very inalienable nature of human spirit and dignity made all his history unnatural. Factually, she couldn't deny him; nevertheless she felt it, and him, were an abomination.

"How does past injustice qualify today's tryanny? Of which you're a guiding factor?" , she asked him, her voice was even. Even curious. "Why do you insist on repeating the same mistakes others have made in the past?"

Turning again, his face was half concealed in shades of red and gold. *Very much demonic,* she mused. "Are you familiar of the saying of George C. Santayana?", he asked, malice dripping from his words.

She nodded in the affirmative.

"Only know you're speaking to the learned. Now, shall I continue, *please?*" A most mocking statement for sure, and she could only fume. And she hated that he reveled in it.

"To bring things current, let's look at the past year. The aftermath of the food riots on your world, the spreading piracies reaching from the Karuki belt, and the civil unrest on Sefu Trius, and other dysfunctional Far Worlds drama made the great experiment of "Independence" a colossal farce, a grand exercise in futility. All fifteen worlds collapsed under the weight of sovereignty. And, despite the patriotic bleating you were surely indoctrinated with, even someone as nationalistic as you can see the eventuality of failure." He paused, waiting for a spirited rebuttal.

Nothing came.

"The truth, the harsh truth of the matter is that Humans are a living contradiction. The individual can only be such in a society that permits it. Thus, a person, or worlds of such people can only thrive in a system based on interdependence. Tell me, Tahina, why didn't Duriy conduct any trade with its neighbors after it won "Independence"? Or they with Duriy? All involved were free to do so."

Pacing before her, she strained her head upwards. She saw something on his holographic construct that was an inaccuracy. Behind the last planet in the Far worlds there were a series of grey spheres in unmarked space. *Inaccuracies, or is this what they are crafting this intergalactic dystopia for?*

She returned her attention to him. He had ceased pacing. Standing still made him look constipated, almost on the verge of bursting apart. Much of what he shared with her wasn't in any of the history books she read, nor the many info-discs or info-streams she'd been allowed to privy. And what she did know, this "lecture"was putting it in a new, extremely unpalatable context. Her notions on human nature, justice, and freedom were being dashed to nothing. Destroyed, or perhaps, as she began to fear, corrupted.

"Why didn't the people of the Far worlds learn to work together, to trust in each other? To ensure a mutual independence based on the necessity of each other?"

She twisted her head away. She had no answer that could contradict him. They both knew it.

"Nothing to say?", he asked her mockingly.

Reluctant, she whispered out, "No."

"I won't wait for a half assed answer", he replied. "You're still full with ideas of National pride, to see things objectively. And however bright you are, you're much too young to grasp the complexities of human dynamics..."

"And you'll teach me, no doubt !", she spit, finally weary of him. She squirmed, fully aware she needed to relieve herself. Plus, she was sad, scared, and most of all, enraged. She was insolent, far less tactful. Her anger, her now unbridled tongue were fighting for release.

Regarding her with amusement, he strode over.

Momentarily, she thought he was going to strike her.

Harudamapati reached, pressed a blue triangle on the side. A sudden flush of relief ran its course through her. She no longer had to go, but whatever he used left her with shuddering aftereffects. Her left leg shook nigh uncontrollably for almost a minute. He smirked, clearly amused by her, and she hated him all the more.

"Better? Technology is wondrous when kept in the hands of a few. But I digress. A word I'm looking for, which you can't provide, is distrust. Or pride. On a state level, the Far Worlds were a cosmic version of the nation states on Earth. Conceptually, that is. But the stakes are far higher, the consequence of folly far greater. Here, we are dealing with planets whose populations were either too short sighted, or too fragmented within to exist long term. As single entities. Yet, National / Planetary pride, and the misguided notion of sovereignty was given priority over common sense, as well as common interest. And your leadership lacked the courage, and intellect to guide properly. "

"That's not true!", Tahina heard herself say, unconvinced of her own words. She had no other defense than that. They both realized it. Nonplussed, he continued.

"Oh, of course it is! Look at what happened. This characteristic, xenophobia, was a natural and understandable consequence of colonization. And the subjugation that follows it hand in hand. Then after the hangover of "independence", reality should've reared its ugly face. The isolationist period is endemic to any human society, past to present. Prolonging it past its natural course has brought us to this point. As you're evidence of, the vestiges of planetary pride remain. But presently, that is being phased out. Now to my point. Back to the chief error that doomed this experiment before it could truly begin. Over time, that isolationism became a detriment. Economies faltered. Corruption set in. The populace of the worlds became corrupt, and complacent. Turning inwards, which would have been healthy for a period of only two generations, became cancerous. In short, the problems it produced festered, simmering underneath the baseless slogans of "Pax (insert name of shitty Far world) ", until the events, that awful display of uncivilization the whole universe witnessed, transpired over the past year. In your generation, "independence" exploded into full chaos. A disgrace before all Humanity!" He fell silent, waiting for her to respond. He read the fury on her riled countenance, knew an outburst was forthcoming. She didn't disappoint.

"Is this where I kiss your feet and thank you for saving us, the backwards savages of the Far worlds?", she asked, her sarcasm molasses thick.

"In time", he retorted snidely. "As it so happens, you've helped greatly as it is."

Confused, with a quivering voice she inquired "And how is that?" Instinctively, her mind went to the faces of Geon. Of Sam. Finally, Jeth. Fearful awareness grabbed her.

"For making opportunities possible!" The glee undergirding his words made her slink back in the chair. The futile gesture amused him further.

Harudamapati smirked. "You see, one thing that can always be counted on is the unpredictability of the young. At some point, a situation would come about to bring the Far Worlds back into the fold. It was on the table for some time to bring about "The Great Reunion", as you should've guessed by now."

"Which you and your ilk doubtlessly worked to make possible! How many lives did you destroy to make this nightmare a reality?!" She was fully consumed with fire. Hatred. Perhaps, for a fleeting moment, she thought it was better to be restrained.

"No more than necessary", he admitted evenly. "It's not healthy to engage in conspiracy theories. It makes one intellectually lazy. As I was saying, The Great Reunion was in the works for longer than you've been alive. At least as old as I am. Politically, it would've been suicide on both ends. But then..." he hesitated; for a moment he was uncertain. She saw it.

He was debating sharing a vital piece of information. Deciding whether to truly rob her of any lingering illusions.

"You may as well spit it out, Colonel ", she whispered, wanting nothing more than for this sordid episode to end.

From somewhere, his face beamed with devilish mirth. *Was he amused by me?* she thought, bewildered.

"Yes, you're right. You'd find it out at some point, at any rate. What metals are Duriy known for?"

"Gold! Silver We... Duriy has extraordinarily high deposits of both!", she answered. The question was stupid. That was as elementary as they come.

"And?" He asked as if goading her into realizing some great truth.

She didn't reply. *Why is his name so damn familiar?,* she kept thinking.

"See how it feels to not know?", he asked her smugly. "After everything mentioned, Duriy is a rich depository of not only AU, but also Cobalt Silicon (CSci), Turbranium Nine (Tur-9), and most importantly, Copper and Palladium. "As is Verdia, Solia, and Sefu Trius. And your neighbor Vembe has the richest silver deposits in the Far worlds. Among the other raw materials sitting idle, unused in your backwards neck of the woods. That's what sped up the timetable."

She was silent, letting it sink in.

"The ruling classes of your worlds came to the table, with the proverbial hat in hand. And for a price, part of which being the mineral rights to their worlds, and a steady labor force to extract them, they would receive the assistance they needed. The myth of Planetary Individualism is dead, has been for some time. On Duriy, the deathblow was the riots. On Sefu Trius, Trunza Square was the beginning of the end. By next year, Duriy will be exporting an estimated ninety tons of Tur- 9. Which will be mined by convicts like yourself. The leaders of your worlds will receive their share of the profits, and "The people" are already being put to work, earning their their keep. Observe the rapid costruction of the Globe prisons. After this latest dust up on your world ends, the security state will tighten, constrict the freedoms previously enjoyed even more. People will come, and go, only under state largesse. Like on Sefu Trius. As I speak, the infamous Karuki belt is following suit. Everywhere you go, individual freedoms will be a shadow of the long- forgotten past." He stopped, turning off the galaxy above them. He let her absorb it all. But still, he wasn't finished.

"And I *know* you spied it, did you not?" He half paced, then pointed at fading, nebulous space and unmarked planets. "Even more worlds, more minerals, untapped and just waiting to be extracted by a ....well oiled, efficiently run workforce. A new Great Expansion, no longer on the horizon. It's here."

She couldn't take it anymore.

"This is what all this is about? All this pain and suffering? Snatching people from families, their home worlds, for slucking rocks?!", she screamed. "People died in mines, family and friends were sundered, because of.... "

"Their own decisions!", he countered, cutting her off. "No one made any of you on Duriy riot, or people on Sefu Trius march on Trunza Square, instigating that bloodbath. Besides, under law, you're no longer a Duriyan national. Your fate, and the fate of those like you, falls under the harsh gaze of the GCW. Public opinion is *not*, since Polim Tef, in your favor. Sympathy is non-existent. A permanent source of cheap labor has been secured, and will be used to push human expansion further. Resulting in new markets being established, new venues to consolidate wealth and power for those who truly possess it. And most pertinent to you, *thanks* to you, the stiffest penalties imaginable will await those *caught in the act* of assisting and harboring fugitives. Imagine... your dear Mr. Geon spending his remaining twilight years rotting away in a cell, on a globular prison world. Would that nature be so kind."

Tahina exploded, unleashing a torrent of expletives she never imagined herself capable of. He looked amused, then laughed.

At that point, the entrance opened. The colonel smirked abruptly. Tahina's heart skipped a beat.

The stamping of bare feet made soft, squishing sounds that proved a welcome, minor distraction. Or so she thought.

"You sent for me, Colonel?", Sali asked sheepishly. A spark of recognition lit up in Tahina, a false sense of relief coming alive in her.

"Sali? Sali?!", Tahina cried. Unable to see her, she turned her head in vain.

Colonel Harudamapati motioned her to come forward.

Tahina nearly became ash white. Her face and the body were the same, even the braided hair style was still familiar. But the vacancy of eye, the absent spirit made her totally alien to the person who had been her closest friend. The outfit, the bracelet... her nightmare had become a horrific reality.

Tahina saw that flash of light in the eye of the bracelet. Fleetingly she looked around her. The image of Asylon's infirmary flashed in front of her. Before Harudamapati's history lesson, she glimpsed the faded out holo sketches of the human brain and neuro system.

HEJIMMA. Urgently, it became crystal clear to her what happened to Sali. What *was* to become of her.

"Sali, introduce yourself to Tahina."

"I'm Sali. I'm pleased to make your acquaintance." She was a robot, absolutely sickening to hear.

"May I....sir? ", Sali asked. After a terse nod, the Colonel watched approvingly as Sali gave Tahina a shoulder hug and a quick peck on the cheek. The act was meant as an insult, as that was how platonic girlfriends on Duriy typically greeted one another.

Tahina shrank from her, openly crying. "The hell? Why in the slucking hell did you do this to her?!"

Sali moved placidly by the Colonel, side eying Tahina suspiciously . The restrained girl was a curiosity. A distorted haze of mysterious familiarity.

"Sali... don't you remember me?", Tahina whispered in wild desperation. She was looking at the future, one where the past was clouded, held captive in a haze of oppression and exploitation. Her mind turned to her siblings. May this be a fate her sister may have to suffer? Her brother, to meet his end in the terra-mining schemes this madman and his ilk concocted?

Sali gave her a long, pained look. She struggled to think. Finally, she said, without feeling, "No, young madam. I do not."

Tahina's heart sank to her gut. Breathing felt heavy, harsh to her being. *If only this nightmare could end,* she thought sadly. *If only I had stayed with Jeth and Geon....*

Sali, remembering why she came, stammered, gaining Harudamapati's attention. For a sliver of a nanosecond, Tahina took this as a kindness.

"Colonel... Madam Quinn asked me to lead her to you", Sali said, her face suddenly filled with dread and confusion. The enraged mask of the Colonel was withering. Tahina clutched hard at the handles of the chair, bracing herself for an attack.

Harudamapati yelled. "The bloody hell?! Sali, where is she?!"

The maid shrank away from him. "Right there, Colonel." She pointed at the entrance.

"Quinn, get in here!", he yelled.

To herself Tahina thought, *How in the six suns can this get any worse. Quinn?! QUINN ?*

Quinn slowly came into the room, followed by Lieutenant Royst and a shackled Minna, who was under watch by another female officer. Her bearing was uneven, her clothing in damp tatters. Her mouth was bound by binding tape, she could only scream and weep inaudibly.

Not too gently, Lieutenant Royst gave Quinn a push forward. Though angry, she thought better than to protest.

Quinn had her hands at her head, the nozzle of a .375 caliber quick pistol hugging the small of her back. Behind Royst's left side, the chains swung lightly between Minna's wrist. Royst, her nose bandaged in transparent tape, glanced menacingly at Tahina.

Harudamapati was infuriated by the intruders, and completely ticked off with the show of incompetence now before him.

Tahina, for her part, all but disappeared in the clustering shadows of confusion. *Swallowed in the darkness,* the old Vulker jingle began.

"The meaning of this ,Lieutenant, is what?" He began calmly enough. Taking in the whole scene, he told her, slowly, "There'd better be an exemplary rationale for all this."

Quinn was about to speak when the nudging in her back changed her mind. Casting his hardened glance at her, then back to Royst.

"Well... don't everyone speak up at once!"

"I observed her going down the hallway, unauthorized, sir. I was..."

"The short version, Lieutenant!", he intercut. There was his trademark arrogance, and an uncharacteristic lack of discretion in Harudamapati, Quinn noted silently. *Was he being his true self, finally? Not the gilded slickster she only thought she'd come to know?* Though she dared not look, she felt the eyes of both the Duriyans upon her. She felt their anger, their bitter hatred. Their silent, unwavering condemnation. Condemnation she rightfully earned.

Royst explained spotting, following, then intercepting Quinn, activating the silent recording mechanisms all throughout the ship. And she acquired the Quarteyan along the way.

He listened, nodded, then said finally: "Rather overzealous, Lieutenant."

Royst was at first dumbfounded, then smoldering. But she dared not betray her feelings.

"If I should err, sir, I prefer to do so on the side of caution", Royst offered.

" And of her? ", Harudamapati asked, nodding to Minna.

"The doctors have finished their analysis, sir. Her neuro-system has proven too resistive to the effects of syathin- 9. Unlike that re……"

His abrupt glare silenced her.

The problem with people like Lieutenant Jalice Royst is that they are eager. And being eager, one becomes overanxious. And in becoming overanxious, one makes blunders.

Sometimes small ones. Sometimes blunders of epic proportions.

His continued stare, Quinn's gaping mouth, and the ensuing awkward silence indicated to her which one she just committed.

"Is that all, Lieutenant?" He remained calm. But now it was a dangerous calm. The calm of a tiger before he bites into his prey.

"Y-yes sir ", Royst stammered. It really dawned on her just how truly, how royally she messed up. Just how deeply...

"Take this young lady to a holding cell. Immediately. Then, escort Tahina to room number one twenty- six". After a few minutes, he followed up with, "Before you leave, apologize to Warden Quinn for your brutish treatment, and lack of protocol. Sali, attend to your duties ." The maid half bowed, turning to exit. Her eyes met Tahina's, and the sight of the teary eyed, slumping, defeated girl strapped in the chair stirred a flicker in her. Sali hesitated, looked back again, then left out, a profound hurt coming over her.

"Must I repeat myself, Royst?", he inquired sternly. He never repeated himself. Stiff penalties awaited those who didn't get it the first time.

Royst's eyes blinked, almost in disbelief. "I apologize, Madame, for my inexcusable actions. I hope you forgive my error."

Quinn, confused, said hurriedly, "You're forgiven."

Royst, burning with humiliation, lead Minna out of the room, the other officer in tow. Minna longed to reach Tahina, to at least give a squeeze of the shoulder for reassurance, however scant. It wasn't to be.

"Minna, Tahina said loud enough to echo the room, stay strong."

Minna, although gagged, mumbled something in return. Loud enough for the whole room to hear. Royst jerked her harshly out into the hallway. Chains jingled as steel hit steel.

"Hardly the touching scene, eh Warden?", Harudamapati sneered.

She said nothing to this, only shaking her head, openly disgusted. "Syathin-9?", she whispered over Tahina.

Syathin-9 was a mind- altering drug, a mind destroying drug. The latest scourge affecting the Far Worlds... *Sali*, Quinn quickly realized." The re...." flashed in her mind. She quickly understood it could only have meant...

"This is who you *really* work for, Quinn?", Tahina asked her .

Quinn, ignoring Tahina , turned to him. "What was the meaning of all that? And...what did she mean by testing?! Syathin-9?! My God, you're using drugs on people?! What did she mean by..." she stopped herself; she couldn't find the words to continue.

"Silence, Quinn! By rights, she should've put you in a holding cell! What the hell was so important that you feel the need to disrupt my work?!" , he returned her questions with a question, a near feral rage consuming him. *The mask is off, it is off fully,* she said to herself. She saw oblivion; the absence of a conscience, the lack of anything resembling a human being. But most sickening of all was that this was a mirror into herself .

"This is the devil you serve", Tahina said to her, half mockingly. "You've signed your soul over to .... Lucifer in glasses for a condo and credit rating?!" Breathing heavily, she felt sleep threaten to overtake her. "More than hating you, now I...pity you ."

Quinn again ignored her. "Well? What exactly *is* your work?", she asked accusingly.

"Bringing despotism to..."

"Quiet!", he yelled Tahina down. Then, "Bringing order to chaos, Warden Quinn. That is the work I'm engaged in. And enlisted many in this worthy endeavor, such as yourself."

"Tell her about the mineral rights, then!", Tahina shouted back. "Tell her about all the money you and your friends are going to reap. Tell her about the "history" you told me. Speak to her about the expansion past the Far worlds into......"

His thundering slap resounded across the room, easily bruising the bound girl's cheek further. She yelped, shocked at the blow.

Quinn stepped back from him, yelling in disgust, "You didn't have to hit her like that!".

"I've heard you've done worse", he responded viciously . At that, a duo of his officers entered. No one realized he silently called for their presence. *How ahead of everything and everyone this bastard is!,* Tahina thought, the pain from the blow mildly fading away.

"Place the good warden in a holding cell", he said. "I'm afraid she's become a detriment to us all."

Quinn kicked, clawed them away, and for a brief minute the effort was valiant. However, a minor taser shock from behind took her down. Horrified, Tahina looked sideways as she was carried out.

She felt drowsy, her jaw still reddened. The blow was cruel, though its sting had, by now, left her. The shadow of the Colonel was standing over her. Her head fell forward.

He drugged me, she thought sluggishly. *The bastard....* The thought ended suddenly, as her eyes closed on the blurred red and black.

"Sad", Harudamapati remarked ruefully. "But then, all good things do end." Alone with Tahina, he said, as if thousands of feet above her, issuing an unholy commandment, "Now, as for you ......"

It was a dream. It had to be. No... A nightmare. But Tahina couldn't remember... No. She could. That time on Geon's ship. Jeth came. And comforted her.

TAHINA !? TAHINA.... Do you know where you are?

No! I don't know where I am....

Tahina felt she was dreaming. If such a thing could be. *But dreams aren't THIS real, are they? She saw herself, looking down at herself, strapped to a gurney, a face mask filled with red mist gagging her. Choking, threatening. They were trying to take her mind away.*

Sounds. Noises. Whispers. A chorus of hidden confusion.

Voices were disembodied. Echoes surrounded, with no discernable direction. It was unfocused, loud, and rocked her beyond the fragile scope of her embattled senses.

In the dark, in the literal black she groped. Her thoughts were fuzzed, and she heard, now, static distortion. She groped around, panicking. She put the left hand before her, placing the right over it. The electric sting made her pulse race.

She couldn't see them, but their eyes were on her. Even unconscious, even helpless, she knew they were observing her. *He* was observing. *He who was the face of all the recent misfortune that had befallen her. Befallen her home world. The whole of Humanity itself. He gave a face to the darkness that dominated human existence. A malignant smirk that brimmed over with vile intent. He was peering over her, the stench of him forever present.* In revolted protest, her head began turning, twisting without either grace nor control. Her body quaked and heaved violently.

From a control booth, Harudamapati paced about, contemplating.

"Sir, a familiar feminine voice spoke through a private intercom, she's resisting!"

"As I knew she would", he said. "She has a strong mind, a useful mind. A shame we must reduce it to mush." Briefly, he shook his head regretfully. "A true shame. She would make quite the assistant."

"The dosage needs to be more potent to achieve your goals then. I estimate another fifteen milligrams."

"Even more so than Symmons? That may kill her!", Harudmapati protested.

"As I've said, Colonel, the doctor continued, she's very strong. Either way, she'd be as good as dead." Her voice, as ever, was hollow, uncaring. And even Harudamapati was momentarily offended by her callousness.

"As a medical practitioner, your alleged "concern" for the well-being of your patients is sorely lacking", he reproached her sternly.

To which she returned, "There's a universe of difference between a patient and a lab rat." She reminded him of that fact in a manner he had to respect. But the prospect still bothered him. He stewed in his thoughts for a moment. "Let it be for now."

Disbelieving what she just heard, she activated the skype screen. Her rich, brown face frowning, her eyes glazed with astonishment.

"Let it be!! For the moment, Doctor!", He thundered, then quieted down to a perilously restive calm. She knew well enough to obey the ludicrous directive. The dial slowly crept back to zero.

The assault on her discontinued, Tahina breathed slowly. The face mask flowed now with oxygen, not syathin- 9 vapors. Weak, she slowly began to recover herself.

She felt the mask being ripped off from her. But it hardly mattered. Barely conscious, and completely helpless, she was subject to whatever abuse they deigned to dish out. She again heard steps, felt the chill of shadow hovering over her prone being.

"A second wind doesn't mean a reprieve", the disgruntled woman whispered in her ear. She heard footsteps scurrying away.

That's rather true, Tahina was thinking, wandering between awareness and unconsciousness. *But I welcome it all the same.*

Her holding cell was no more than a closet with an electric grid shield. No room to walk, to pace, let alone sit down.Hardly. Just enough room to ponder this turn of events. There was no way she was leaving this place alive, she reasoned. After what she'd been party to, she didn't feel that she deserved to.

Her pity party was abruptly ended by an attack from Gyddis'. She found herself lurching over, almost being forced to vomit. *Shit! I forgot my damn medicine!* Quinn was almost on her knees. In great pain, she screamed. Her lips were overcome with bile laden foam.

The O.O.D (Officer on Duty) saw the woman frothing. Protocol was to alert the medic. Officer Renys Juh followed the call of her emotions. She instinctively went to the frothing, convulsing woman, and deactivated the grid.

At that time, the brig door slid open.

Lieutenant Royst shoved Minna through the entrance hard. The chains rustled, and the girl stumbled forward.

The welts on her exposed arms and the bruises on her face were fresh. As in minutes ago. The banding tape was removed from her mouth, where a deep red trickle of blood had begun drying on the left side of her battered face.

"Try to escape me...", Royst mumbled angrily. This shift was shaping up to be a bad one, three hours into it. Shamed for doing her job, then a fucking fekhead tries to escape her. The reason she didn't get assistance was that she didn't want that impossible Harudamapati coming down harder...

Juh standing over Quinn got her attention.

"Officer Juh? What the hell's going on?", Royst rasped, pushing Minna forward. Being distracted, she didn't see Minna reach into her deep left pocket. *If I can get it before she turns back to me!*

"Uh... Ma'am, she's, uh having a seizure", Juh said quietly. *Too quietly.* Naturally suspicious, Royst hurried over. *This day just keeps getting better....*

In less than a minute, Quinn, having Juh's pistol, fired past the kneeling officer's head. Royst responded quickly, ducking the finger thin beam. Her attention was now completely off Minna, who in turn used Tahina's light bomb to temporarily blind almost everybody. Quinn had seen her, and turned her head just in time to avoid the barrage of pain inducing, concentrated illumination.

"Uhh, you junkie bitch!", Royst screamed. Minna snatched her weapon, tempted to fire. Instead she asked her, "Where's Tahina?", relishing the sudden turnabout.

"And Sali?", Quinn chimed in. She had Juh on the floor, face down. She scanned around for any alarm, silent or otherwise. Such a discharge had to set off an alert.

"If there are any alarms, turn them off. NOW!"

Whatever resistance Royst would've put up evaporated when she felt the nozzle of her own weapon digging into her temple. Under duress, she went to deactivate the brig's alarm sensors. Which, to her great dismay, had already been shut down for a routine diagnostic check.

"Where's my friend? Where's Tahina?", Minna asked, giving her a vicious kick in the ass.

" Room one twenty- six", she said desperately. She was forced to lay face down, as was Juh.

"What about Sali? Call her", Quinn insisted, fighting back the disease's side effects.

"It'll raise...", Minna began to protest, but the look from Quinn withered her into silence.

"I don't care about that. Or that bastard!", Quinn said vehemently. "Now fucking do it!" Royst glared hard, and pressed down on the summoner pad on the left wing of her lieutenant's insignia. A small green light lit up, calling the maid girl to her. She was one of the few officers that the Colonel had allowed to handle her.

As she was doing Quinn's bidding, she felt Minna ruffle through her pouches. Securing the keys, she freed herself. The thought of beating Royst senseless with the chain came and went. First, she had to help Tahina, then they had to get out of here. Somehow.

"Get some cuffs" , Quinn ordered. "Quickly!" She was breathing heavily, sounding almost out of breath. She could only fight it off for so long...

Minna winced, but obeyed. Royst and Juh were quickly cuffed, and with binding plastic gagged (Minna got deep satisfaction at quieting Royst. And gave her a punch in the face, with the chain rolled around her small fist, as a parting gift. Not beating her senseless, but it was something), then shoved them both into a cell.

She saw Minna fingering a device .

"Good job with the light thing a bob, she said warily, but what are you doing?"

"Calling for help" , Minna said flatly. "Again." Quinn looked at her quizzically, then she got a closer look. A trans-galactic responder, but it wasn't anything she recognized. It ran on an energy signal that was unauthorized by the GCW. The False Star raids made much more sense now; all this black market, unregistered technology that went unchecked was a threat. One that needed to be crushed to achieve complete authoritarianism.

"You had this on you, and they didn't frisk you thoroughly?" Quinn asked, both incredulous and relieved at the same time.

"They weren't after me", Minna replied. "It's Tahina's anyway. I... I stole it. I feel bad about that ", Minna confessed. "They, her head nodding at Royst, just threw me in a cell. At first."

As Quinn figured out the controls, she mumbled "Nice to see incompetence is easily distributed in this new universe."

The electric grid flashed , its energy crackling violently . Royst and Juh were locked in, out of the way, moaning and screaming miserably.

Just then, the brig door opened yet again. Both Quinn and Minna had the newly acquired weapons up and ready, though Quinn's hands twitched nigh uncontrollably. Minna noticed, and she grew even more leery of Quinn than she already was.

When Sali entered through, she was alarmed by the shrieking, bound and gagged women in the cell. She was further terrified by the weapons drawn on her. She shrank, but gently, Quinn put a trembling hand over her left palm.

Anxious eyes flittered from Minna to Quinn. Sali wanted to snatch herself away, to flee. Quinn's tremulous grip tightened.

"I won't hurt you", she told her. *Any more than I already have.* Whether this calmed the girl, or intimidated her further, there was no time to decipher. Not knowing what else to do, Sali stayed put, scared and feeling Minna breathing down hard over her left shoulder.

Kneeling, Quinn struggled with herself, removing the anklet from the maid girl. The abrupt convulsions alarmed both her and Minna; they were at a loss at how to stop it. A trickle of spittle flew from her mouth. She was on hands and knees; slowly Minna grabbed her by the right forearm, helping her up. In the background, Royst and Juh mumbled and moaned in futile protest.

Sali had a disturbing resemblance to an addict suffering from withdrawal pains. Minna watched quietly, her failed bouts of cold turkey flashing in front of her.

Heaving for a few minutes, putting a hand over her forehead. She was now crying.

"Sali, Quinn said gently, we're not here to hurt you..."

"YOU!" , Sali began, her face distorted by rage. Murderous rage. She almost pounced at Quinn.

Leveling the pistol, Quinn cut her fury off. "Don't make me *use* this. We need to help Tahina. Where is she?"

Suspicious eyes went from Quinn to Minna. " Sali, I'm Minna. Tahina's roommate from Quartey. Please, she's in danger. By the same guy who did, whatever he did to you...."

"She..., she helped him!", Sali pointed a petulant finger at Quinn. "She helped him kill us!" Minna noted the glow of shame on Quinn's face. But at the moment Tahina was the priority.

"Right now, he's trying to hurt our friend", Minna pleaded. "Will you help us?"

Though her mind, and memory of her young life was clouded in the red fog of Syathin-9, Sali comprehended fully what the other girl was saying. She remembered her closest female friend, and that friend needed her help. She nodded weakly in the affirmative.

"Where can we find her? ", Quinn asked, feeling the onset of another attack.

For a moment, Sali regarded her coldly. "Room one twenty- six", Sali said finally. She hated Quinn, that was certain enough. But this girl, if she was a friend of Tahina's, she would be a friend of hers.

"It's settled", Quinn said decisively. The symptoms were getting out of control. She fought back another urge to vomit. She was barely able to hold her composure.

Stumbling over each other, Royst and Juh mumbled violently.

Opening the entrance to the brig, Sali took the lead. "Follow me", she said. Her voice became more human by the second. Privately, both Minna and Quinn wondered if that was a good thing, for them. It was obvious she was left unhinged by the experience of being a drugged up, debased maid girl. And was looking to lash out. Two things that could get them captured, or worse.

"Wait. How will we get to her? This ship is crawling with scum like those two", Minna spoke up.

"The service pathways I'm forced to take go relatively unused", Sali said. "They take you throughout the whole of this damnable ship." Words were coming easier to her, more natural. Her tongue was hers, once again.

"Let's get moving then", Quinn said. She was feeling worse by the minute. Soon, very soon she wouldn't be able to control the symptoms. Then to Minna, "Is that thing, that beacon working at all?"

"I... I don't know", Minna said, uncertain. "I hope it does".

The middle of a solid black wall panel suddenly parted. It was a servant's corridor, reasonably well-lit and clean. The floor girding was cool iron and steel. Minna wondered how Sali walked about this surface barefoot; her sandals flopped hard on the floor, her feet numbed by the coolness.

A right turn, then a compact hyper lift revealed itself. They crowded inside, Quinn last. Squeezing in, the room to maneuver was hair thin. Sali's left hand barely fit into the digital imprint reader. A faint blue glow, and then suddenly they ascended....

This must be a dream, she thought. It had to be a dream.

She was loose. No chair, no steel cushioned gurney, no bonds. She could move freely, but not without handicap. She found herself again cloaked in thick blackness.

Then, without warning, everything changed.

From the intense dark, black as space, it had suddenly become bloody red. At a seemimgly snail's pace, hard light dissipated in an ominous haze. Eeriness overcame her as the fog clouds vanished.

Tahina found herself in a room, with the only way out, from her vantage point, *miles* away into the horizon. There was no ceiling, only a misty red sky. And the *floor.* The floor was neither steel, or even faux tile. The floor was a legion of *bloodied* hands. She would've fled, if she could escape. She would've shrunk back as far as possible, but she was back to wall. Then, the noises. Moans and wails of agony echoing around her; unnerving her, weakening what little resolve she could muster.

With no other alternatives at hand, she began to sprint, hoping she could make it across in one piece. Failing that, a morsel of sanity she'd have to settle for.

She failed. And wound up where she started. And she tried again. And yet again.

Every time she tried to run across, blood painted fingers grabbed, gripped her ankles, the fury of the unavenged. Each time they got a hold of her, they would pull her down into the void of darkness...

"Retribution!!, the agonized chorus would chant. Justice!! Freedom!! " Their cries resonated within her, resounding over and over. Echoing, maddening. She would fight, kick, cry, plead. Nothing did her any good. Steeling herself, and wiping away tears with a left hand smudged with dried, flaking blood, she again dashed across the field of writhing hands. She went faster than she ever ran, went further than she did the last three (?) times. She could see it, the exit. Like a mirage (?!), it looked faded like a hologram, yet as real as oakwood. She felt it's pull on her, it's calling to her.

The door seemed closer, closer, closer still.

Then, she stumbled. *Not again? NOT....*

Hands were waiting. Welcoming, the blood smearing a grotesque purplish....

Abruptly, someone grabbed her....

He sat in his study, in near pitch blackness. He was most comfortable in this degree of darkness. So much he had accomplished moving in the shadows. So many more conquests he had yet to reach. Obstacles be damned!

Obviously, things had changed. Quinn needed to go. No longer a controllable entity, and she now knew too much. Too much of what she shouldn't know. As the cognac left his lips, he let out a rueful sigh.

She had to go. A mere firing wouldn't do. She had to be an example, a warning. Only to those in the know. How to get it done was the matter of contention. Then, that girl's face came to him. He smirked, beaming with equal measures of arrogance and ingenuity.

Tahina. She'll be the instrument of her destruction. How fitting. How brilliantly ironic that her obsession with that girl would be the means to her end. Playing things correctly, it would instill fears of resurging pirates and space gangs to an already cowering and fretful universe. Herod would understand. He'd have no choice. And after all, he persuaded him to keep her on. He thought on it, taking another sip.

He finished his drink, thoughtfully refilling only a splash. He needed to calm his nerves; he couldn't afford intoxication. At this point and time especially. His mind returned to the *untimely* demise of Warden Ednisa Quinn, and her would be murderer.

He finally justified to himself why he didn't kill the obstinate brat. Given time, all problems work themselves out. Yet, for new ones to take their place. Some proving more grave than others.

First, his ship suddenly found itself in the middle of a derelict field. Some three decrepit, old tanker vessels had somehow escaped the detection of state of the art radar. "Evasive maneuvers 101!", he scolded his suddenly ineffective bridge crew.

"A bridge of first year yeomen can do better than this!", he savaged them upon taking his seat on the bridge. Eyes fell away from him, back to the tasks assigned them.

"Navigator, ETA for our next destination?"

"Less than eleven hours, sir."

Admiring the past for a moment, he abruptly left his seat, left the bridge. Eleven hours. Quite a long time; a lot had to be done in the interim.

"Notify me should any emergency arise. A *true* emergency." He attempted to be affable, but the threatening undercurrent resonated. Out of earshot, the bridge crew sighed relief in unison.

"Crisis averted", he said sardonically, pouring a half glass of scotch.

Second was the sudden realization that Lieutenant Royst had yet to give a status report. Odd, she failed to deliver Tahina to room one twenty- six. This was most unlike her to fail an order. Or at the very least report she'd delegated that responsibility to another. But he'd been so focused on the Quinn/ Tahina Conundrum, among the long itinerary he needed to accomplish, all around him went absent.

Going forward, he'd do well to delegate to better trained, more competent persons. The skillful maintenance of all he worked to establish, as well as regain, depended on it.

"Lieutenant Royst", he repeated a third time. It was then he began to realize something in his perfectly structured world had gone wrong. "Royst, come in!" Her personal responder was dead. So he called his second most reliable officer.

"Lieutenant Crade!", he bellowed. He threw the glass aside, it's shattering on the ground adding to his annoyance.

"Sir, this is Lieutenant Crade, a smooth, masculine voice responded. He seemed, in spite of what should have been the hum drum, relative calm of space travel, preoccupied and harried. *Crade is never in a rush, nor completely absorbed.* Worry started to plague him.

"Report! And get Lieutenant Royst to the nearest responder and have her call me!"

"We've been trying to raise via...."

"Don't try, dammit, get it done!", Harudamapati raged. He felt horrible instantly. He was losing himself. His poise, his polish, his grace under fire. Only he wasn't under fire. He was merely managing manbabies and woman babies. *The nincompoops!*

"Will do, sir! But your presence is needed on the bridge."

Before he could utter forth dismay, or a string of profanities, the alarms began blaring and ringing throughout his ship.

"EMERGENCY!! EMERGENCY......!! EMERGENCY... EMERGENCY!!..."

He forced his way through his scurrying officers in the corridors. Red lights streaked through his walls, flashing deep, blood red. Danger was not imminent, it was now directly *facing him.*

How would he snatch victory from the jaws of defeat this time?

"Daddy?!"

A tidal wave of unabashed tears flooded from her unbelieving eyes.

Eyes that, excepting color, she inherited. That familiar look of parental bemusement and concern blended. A look she thought was lost to her forever.

Her father, long dead, was lifting her to her feet. Without reserve, the child hugged the parent. *This can't be real, she heard herself say in her mind. This can't possibly be real, but I don't care!*

"I missed you, daddy, I...

Looking up, it was no longer her father, but Jojas. She stepped back, confused and afraid. Behind her, the floor of writhing hands stopped moving, the wailing came to an abrupt stop.

Jojas became Iajim. Iajim became Sali. Sali became Jeth. Jeth turned to Geon. Geon to Minna... Everyone in her life that mattered. Her siblings for the briefest moment... then from Her siblings to finally, her mother.

Tahina gaped her mouth, but no words came forth. *What in all the worlds is this?!*

It lasted for just a few seconds more, but the fading image with many faces, said only one thing to her. "Life moves forward. And so must you..."

"W-What does that even mean?!", she stuttered in confused anguish. She was left alone, on a tiny isle of questions.

Whatever it was, it was now gone. Then, in her father's voice, she heard it say ,"Think about it".

The Control Room was full of charts and monitors. And a viewing screen half the size of the one on the ship's bridge. The woman in charge, Dr. Humfir, stood over the dials, shaking her short braids at the sleeping girl, in the next room over. Whatever else was going on, Harudamapati gave her the unenviable task of watching over this unconscious brat.

No problem, she thought absently. *I'm still being paid. But still .*

Daydreaming, she neglected to seal the entrance. Since few rarely travailed this path, it was natural for her to do. The natural thing proved to be her undoing.

The blow from the quick pistol's end was fast, hammering her head into the main console dial board. She was instantly knocked out.

"Get Tahina!", Quinn said to the girls.

Sali and Minna eyed each other, then looked at Quinn with deep uncertainty.

"Are..."

"GO!" , the woman yelled over the abrupt, loud cry of the siren. "Go Now!!" Her voice, heavy with a knowing urgency, knew what was coming. Sali stared, then took Minna inside room one twenty- six proper.

The pain gripped her, paralyzing her. *Not even time to make a face in protest.*

Giving a profound sigh, Quinn slumped hard and hit the floor headfirst. *Pain....* she thought as the dark of unconsciousness grabbed hold of her.

They saw her, twisting violently on the gurney. Minna took one side, Sali the other, removing the straps that pinned her down.

Tahina moaned, "Move forward!" over and over, as if reciting a chant.

Not so gingerly, Sali ripped away the face mask. Shards of horror stained recollection pierced her. Remembering when *she was* underneath that mask. Being robbed of herself...

Hard oxygen escaped into the room. Tahina coughed hard.

"Tahina!", Minna yelled, jerking her to her feet.

She struggled, so Sali came from the other side and propped her up. She still moaned, "Move forward."

"Is that your new catchphrase of the day?", Minna said to her, half joking, shaking her harshly. She recalled, not so fondly, when Tahina used to tell her, "Learning a word a day keeps an idle mind busy."

Motion snapped her back to reality. Where her head still throbbed, at migraine levels.Blaring alarms increased her misery. Her vision improved. Her stomach was queasy, but she'd overcome that. As she looked from Minna, and the quick pistol she was wielding, to the other side of her, where she saw Sali. And she smiled feebly. The look on Sali's face was almost what it was on Asylon. Warm, curious and intense. But now it was laced with fury and bitterness.

"Do you remember me, now?", she asked her.

Sali responded with a half hug, and a kiss on the cheek.

"How could I... forget? ", Sali replied, sadly. Her memory was still in pieces, a puzzle that would take years to reconstruct. But the most immediate, important things she recalled without trepidation.

"Quinn's coming in a few minutes", Minna said, feeling out of place. "We need... " She had to yell over the alarms.

"Quinn?!"

"She switched sides", Minna said hurriedly. "Something's happening."

The overbearing noises made it hard to concentrate. Then, all too abruptly, its blaring chorus of warning stopped. Followed by the power. The trio found themselves in pitch darkness.

Tahina freed herself from her friends, nearly stumbling. Her motor reflexes were still weak. That she was practically naked had gone unnoticed until now. Her pajamas were torn and tattered, she realized. "My clothes..."

"Here", Sali told her, tossing her maid's apron. "Until... "

Hard footsteps interrupted her. Even weakened, Tahina had no trouble recognizing his belligerent stride. Nor Sali, who felt an sudden, quick, icy surge of fear run down her spine.

"Down!", Tahina whispered fiercely, drawing the other two girls to her behind the gurney, the only hiding spot in the room. A still figure was now in the doorway, a weak finger of light pointing inside.

"Minna give me the gun", Tahina whispered, looking up from the end of the gurney.

"Why?", she whispered back nervously, overwhelmed by ominous portent.

"That's why", Tahina returned, as Colonel Harudamapati stepped into room one twenty-six.

Chapter Eighteen

Despite the imminent danger of three derelict ships surrounding him and closing in, Harudamapati had loose ends to tie up. Whatever else happening, Quinn couldn't leave this ship alive. Nor Tahina. And as her friend was useless, he would make it a trifecta of homicide..

"Evasive maneuvers!"

"Sir, they're moving in response! ", his navigator said, astonished. Sir... they're not just derelicts."

Do tell, Harudamapati thought to himself. *A trap... we... I've clearly walked into a fucking trap!!!*

An explosion rocked his ship sideways. They sailed by a detonating depth charge. Its concussive force took out a third of the state of the art, beyond what was considered uber modern navigational systems. The left rear of the outer hull was bruised, red sparks spitting into the cosmos.

"Sir... they're attacking us with...*ancient weapons!*"

From the responder Lt. Crade, half amused, alerted him to the whereabouts and hapless condition of both Lt. Royst and Officer Juh.

"Leave them! Report to battle center IX!"

"Aye, sir". As the transmission died out, he heard the indignant mumblings in the background.

Without his barking out the order, *someone* took the initiative, and began readying the laser cannons.

As his ship began to send out a volley, the left side of the hull was again attacked. Another assault, this time the target was the middle. Speed was quickly reduced to impulse, a snail's pace for an interstellar star craft designed for traverse light years within *days*.

Outwardly, Harudamapati was iron. A stoic, inflexible man that kept his relative calm in the face of a disaster. Inside, he was a glass statuette, suffering that one crack eventually shattered the whole thing to pieces.

"Lt. Crade, report to the bridge!"

Silence.

"Lt. Crade's unconscious, sir! He was caught in the blast!", a frantic officer screamed through the communicator.

"Sir... the enemy vessels are closing...".

The sound of the door behind him drowned out any curses his bridge crew sent his way. Astonished, beleaguered faces reflected on the metallic obsidian. He brushed aside the desperate men and women coming to him, looking for him to lead them, to save them from calamity. He pressed on, mental images of triple murder obscuring the chaos surrounding him.

"Colonel!", said someone who was met with an open hand slap. The crazed glare didn't even warrant a second's notice.

Light turned to dark. It didn't deter him. He knew the panel, pressing his print hard. To his amazement, it still worked. The hidden door closed behind him, the chorus of confusion temporarily silenced.

"EMERGENCY!! EMERGENCY!!" echoed through him, taunting him, prodding him dangerously as he eventually met his destination. The power systems finally failed, leaving him in the dark. Thinking quick, he activated the illuminator feature on his insignia ring.

Room one twenty- six.

He made out the two crumpled figures on the floor, immediately dismissing them. His stride slowed; the hard soles of his shoes clacked on the smooth metallic tiling. "Tahina!" , he called, his anger no longer raging, just smoldering. And that was him at his best, his most dangerous. Angry, yet rational enough to utilize it to deadly effect.

"Tahina. I'll make it quick", he said, for you and your friends." Sali came to mind suddenly. Intuitively, he called for her.

Sali held herself. Minna crouched close, keeping her from betraying herself and them. She fumbled in her pocket.

"This is foolish, little girls!", he called out in the darkness. "Make it easy for yourselves. "

Tahina felt the nudge. She turned, gripping the pistol in a vise. The ember of light was faint, but she saw the devious smile on Minna's face. She had it. Now, to get him into position.

Overhead, a new warning boomed. *"ALL HANDS, ABANDON SHIP. MAKE FOR ESCAPE POD BAY!! REPEAT..."*

In his mind, Harudamapati saw himself engulfed in flames. Its imaginary sulfuric stench and brimstone choking, distracting. Paralyzed, he froze with indecision. Sensing his weakness, Tahina quickly took the offensive.

"Having a bad day, Harudamapati? ", Tahina called out, in the most mocking tone she could muster.

Overhead, the warning bleated again and again. *"ABANDON SHIP!! REPEAT, ABA...."* The intercom went dead. Somewhere nearby, a small explosion spit out smoke.

"It's over, Colonel...."

Silence. Angry silence.

"How does it feel?", she taunted him. "All this effort, just for a handful of ash! I'm certain your powerful friends won't brook so colossal a failure, assuming you leave here alive!", she laughed hoarsely. She kept goading him. Make him sloppy. They heard another explosion from somewhere.

Rough trembling. For a brief microsecond, lights blinked on, then off. Enough for them to see him. As he saw them.

Get the damn bomb ready, Minna! Tahina's face read. Sali... Sali's face read something else. Utter hatred.

He was drawing closer, weapon drawn....

"Colonel Harudamapati, for God's sake...!!", someone screamed overhead, where in hell are...."

Furious torrents of laser fire abruptly ended the plea for absent leadership. He stopped dead in his motion, rudderless and lost. Not so for Tahina.

"Now, Minna, Now!!!"

Without hesitation, Minna threw the light bomb at him.

He screamed as the light exploded in his face. In pained reaction, his head jerked forward. Off guard, he fired. The volley stained the wall. Minna and Sali ducked, dove out of the way, just in time.

Tahina aimed, but she....couldn't. Sali snatched the weapon, shot Harudamapati in his left leg. The flame that consumed his limb, his pants leg was hideous to behold. But incredibly satisfying. The blinded man rolled on the floor, howling in horrible, bloodcurdling anguish.

Tahina looked at her friends, then at the door. The macabre scene was... inviting in a way that she couldn't define, *and yet....*

Minna yelled "Tahina, let's go!"

Almost absently, she nodded. "You're right. Sali, lead us out of here."

Sali was preoccupied. She wanted to kill this quivering cretin howling in pain. It took Tahina pulling her away to snap her back to reality.

Faintly smiling , Sali whispered, "This way." Her anger was far from satisfied, Tahina noticed anxiously. *Sali, what in the suns did this demon do to you?,* she wondered.

The control room was empty, the only signs of struggle being an overturned console chair. Smoke was strong. Sparks spit feebly from the walls.

Quinn was gone, without a trace.

Sali took them back through the service door, Harudamapati's wailings died against the raging chaos. This service corridor was dark, long. It was silent. Eerily silent.

"How much longer before we reach a shuttle pod, Sali?", Tahina asked. She tied the end of the apron Sali gave her to cover herself. Drafts of fleeting cold made her acutely aware of her nakedness. Yet, she didn't care.

"If there's a shuttle left", Minna said morosely. Her craving for fek was absent, for some ill understood reason. *What did they do to me?,* she wondered quietly. Half grateful, half frightened, her dependence on Fek was broken. She felt liberated.

What now?, Tahina thought, arms crossing her breasts.

From the ventilator a few paces ahead, sounds of laser fire crackled in the background.

"Who do...you think did this?", Sali asked. She was a cauldron of anxiety over the unknown and of gratitude the horror of the past, *her past especially,* was fading into memory. The cruel irony notwithstanding.

"A raid. Probably pirates." Tahina let the rest die in her mind. She suddenly wondered what Sali, who was leading them, was thinking. Minna as well, for that matter. *Was she a coward to them? She was certainly feeling that way about herself. After all that bastard admitted to, she still couldn't....*

Ahead, just ahead of them, a flurry of orange light suddenly glimmered, flickered, and rose upwards. They came to a full stop. Tahina, taking the quick pistol, immediately pulled ahead of Sali.

Though feeling foolish, still she spoke into the light, "We're armed, and ready to shoot! So, try us, if you like! But we refuse to go without a fight!!" Her words were steel.

Radiant orange grew stronger. A figure, then two of them emerged in the ambience.

Tahina's mouth fell in disbelief when recognition slapped her.

"We figured as much", said Jeth hoarsely. "That's why we came after you ourselves."

And Iajim, beside him, said "We go after our own."

Jeth! Iajim! The sight of them, together, made her cry silently. At first.

"Jeth?", she hugged him deeply, then Iajim, then Jeth again. Stronger this time, and said, head buried in his chest, "What are the two of you doing here? How did you find us?!"

"A homing beacon Geon gave you, fixed your location. We heard from Sam... what happened." This made Tahina blush, ashamed she regarded that woman so low.

"Is he here, with you two?", Tahina asked, wondering. *What in the Founder's name is going on?*

"He's around.... Jeth said tersely. He was affable, as usual, yet there was something markedly different. "We're taking you all to him and the others."

Others?!

Gingerly, Iajim took Sali by the forearm. For a second, she squirmed, almost confused

"Sali... you okay?", Iajim asked quietly. Sali squinted in the light, struggling to recollect. And when she reconnected with the past, she said, very quietly, "Yes. "

"Do you... remember me?", he asked her gently. Nodding, she buried her head in his left shoulder, weeping. "Yes... though not like I'd like to."

Tahina turned from them back to Jeth.

Many thoughts ran through her mind. *Jeth and Iajim are... a part of whatever's taken place. What's going on? Their manner of dress, paramilitary and they're brandishing weapons and ...I just want to know what the sluck is GOING ON ?!*

Feeling left out, Minna moved back a little, only for Tahina to take her by the hand.

"Jeth, Iajim, this is Minna, my, our friend. She's the reason you guys found us. But..."

"Let's go, Jeth said firmly, there's a lot of explaining to do. And after that, there's some things I need to ask you."

She frowned in consternation as he led the way into the light.

Tahina's Journal :

To whom this account may be discovered by, this is a chronicling of the earliest days of the struggle. The beginning of the fight for freedom. From my eyes to yours, this is the story as how I lived it:

As I was getting comfortable in the rickety chair, I realized how quickly I was past the shabby clothing they'd given me. The conference room of the former S.S. Durton was large, extremely grey and unbearable due to overheating problems with air temperature controls being rotted beyond repair.

I sat on one end of that steel rectangle, and Geon, Jeth and a one-eyed guy named Korlos on the other. "Johnny (I thought of him as a Johnny)", one long scar running where his left eye and cheek USED to be, was a pirate from the Karuki belt. And come to find out, he was the one who rescued Iajim and others from the mines.

They talked, and I listened. Jeth stared at me, then away, then at me again. I noticed the oiled stained tips of his fingers, poking out from heavily gloved hands. I wondered, in the back of my mind if that oil came from an engine, or from replacing a laser blast cartridge.

They were there to vouch for me. Whether I could be trusted.

This was The Sovereign People's Revolution, I was told, in a tone so flat and bereft of welcome that I grimaced with dismay. If this was the invitation speech, this whole thing was in big trouble. Enough frivolous thoughts, for now. They were serious, and so was I. They explained it succinctly :

"We're not out to be heroes, nor are we fighting for the grandiose notions of peace and justice, Tahina. We're fighting to survive, no, not just survive. To live. And we'd rather fight and die than roll over."

Simple as that. From the bowels of society, disenchantment had become open defiance and rebellion. And it was thankless, non-

glorious, and without any "noble" pretenses that human beings used in the past to justify anything.

So, it came to Jeth to ask me: "Are you in. Or out?"

"In", I replied, no hesitation involved.

The discussion then turned to Harudamapati, and everything he told me. In length, I gave a vivid account of his "history lesson". Of his future goals for humanity. Of his view of "progress".

When I finished, Geon looked at me. I sensed something was amiss.

"Tah, he said slowly, I don't doubt the truth of what he said, or if he was being sincere. But the Harudamapati name is as dead as the family itself."

I felt a veil of disbelief come over my face. After Geon (who else?) recalled the infamous merchant clan, and the uprising in the Far worlds that wiped them out to the last member, and thus from history, I wanted to kick myself for not remembering.

"Then..." I stopped myself. The mystery of this man swirled inside my head. All that he told me, shown me, could only have come from one with deep inside knowledge.

"Whoever he really is, by no means is he a Harudamapati."

"Then ask Sali. She...served him." The images of what atrocities he may've forced upon her made my skin tremble in revulsion.

"We did", Johnny said blankly. "She's less informed about him than you are."

I shook my head, now weary of it all. Weary, and confused. Why did he spare me from a fate like Sali's? And what of Quinn? Did she....She appeared so contrite. Questions without answers, begetting even more questions. An endless spiral downwards... like a rabbit hole.

Almost awkwardly, Korlos (Johnny. I'll never stop thinking of him as named otherwise) stood up, the chair screeching loudly. My concentration into myself was broken.

"We're done here", Korlos said finally. Perhaps tired himself (his long, scarred face, I noticed, never lost its gnarled, languid expression), he extended his right hand (the left reduced to a nub. The hazards of pirating, I was certain. But was too polite to ask) and said, "Welcome to the future."

Shaking it, I merely said, "Thank you."

As he left, Geon and Jeth (who got up to close the door) both said,"Let's go home. There's a lot we have to talk about."

As eager as I was, there was a turbulent undercurrent brewing under the bouquet of pleasantries.

"The hell you say!", I was beside myself. I had to resist the urge to hurl the chair at them.

They told me the reason they "nudged" me off the ship. They thought they would be dragging me into a mess I couldn't handle.

"Tah, you had the best chance to lead a decent, normal life", Jeth said. We didn't want to ruin that for you." He was passionate and sincere. And still wrong as hell .

Rolling my eyes, I said, "What I'm hearing is that you didn't think I'd make the cut!"

"That's the anger talking", Geon said, calmer than I'd ever seen him in a heated argument. "You know everything I told you in those last days were true. You know, now, what we're saying is true. And yes, maybe we could've, should've done it in a better way, but you can't deny our intentions weren't in the right."

Then, I simmered, sighed, and sat down. Like old times. "I... know. It's just... just that with everything that's happened, is happening, I don't want to be left in the shadows anymore. In anything."

While I was still mad at them, I was grateful that they cared. Cared that I had, at least, an opportunity to live a life different from this. I wish I did too.

When it was apparent that I wasn't mad, or about to throw anything at him, Jeth came to me and said, "Let's walk."

So, we did.

This place was so much like False Star, with its hulking, gutted interior, eternally static grey depressing everything and everyone under its gaze. People were huddled by large cubicles, either entertaining or being entertained by the brusque and semi crude actions of others. People need so much to stay human.

Taking a closer inspection, I recognized that some of the vendors here were from that now besieged space station. Before I could ask, Jeth volunteered that, "It was a nightmare moving our brethren from there to here."

I was full of questions, and yet I lacked the words to form a sentence. Jeth , for certain, wasn't helping matters. He led, not looking back once.

My mind turned to Sali. It would take years for her to make a full recovery. But she had me. And Iajim. I had no idea they were lovers during our time at Asylon. He's been with her ever since they found us.

As for that sneak friend of mine, she'll have no problem fitting in. Her addiction seems to have been nullified by exposure to Syathin-9. And she's already made herself valuable. She has a perfect memory, and she recalls with perfect clarity the weapons the Galactipol crew used on the raiding team. Royst dragged her by a training room while bringing her to...

Amid a great throng of people, they were torturing the officers they captured, Royst among them. Held in brass ball cages, they were subjected, all five of them, to taunts, rotted fruit and vegetables being thrown their way, and most shuddering, the threats of bodily violence.

For a millisecond, I felt Royst's eyes lock in sync with mine. The look of a broken, scared woman, smudges of brown banana and spit staining her cheeks. Disgusted, I looked away, hurrying to catch up with Jeth.

"No different at all", Geon said once, when I told him about people. I asked, "What makes us any different than what we're running from?"

Cigar smoke billowing, he sat on the hard, plastic chair. "People have this notion of good vs evil. As if one opposes the other..."

I opened my mouth to voice an objection, yet I kept silent.

"I mean to say, he continued, as if we're not both. It's not a matter of one against the other. But of one co-existing WITH the other. Balancing what you know to be good and controlling what you see as evil. Human Beings are the only beings in the universe that can be awe strikingly beautiful and perversely ugly at the same time."

In the ceiling there lay an octagonal porthole. Briefly staring, I saw how beautiful space truly could be. On infrared setting, it displayed the many shades of colors the obvious keeps hidden. Glimpsing the sublime that surrounds us gave me a new and greater appreciation of the Great Expanse. Only we make it ugly. Yet we can choose to enjoy it's beauty, make our works of art from the infinite canvas known as Creation.

We finally found somewhere to sit, under the pirated (a pun most definitely intentional) Holo stream tower. From the tower across from where we were sitting, the latest developments...

"Mourning the passing of Jet Symmons, who died in her sleep this...."

"The latest round of protests beginning in the Far worlds has spread rampantly...."

"The latest pirate attack has claimed the life of Ednisa Quinn, head of...".

Jeth and I stared at one another, then at the screen, absolutely dumbfounded.

Our eyes were bound to the screen, as HE appeared.

"The private vessel of Anwar Anwari, a lawyer for Galactic Trust was raided several days ago. In the melee, Warden Ednisa Quinn was viciously gunned down by this individual..."

My eyes. My nose. My face was flashed before Pax Humanity.

The sight of seeing myself on the holo stream, committing a crime I didn't actually commit, and all the surrounding eyes fall on me, made me realize what the dream was telling me. "Move forward."

I felt Jeth tighten his grip on my forearm. A pittance of comfort.

I can only move forward now, because I can never go back.

Though he was in great pain, at least he could suffer in comfort.

The healing suite they gave him in the Medical Dorm at the Great Hospital of Quartey was nothing short of resplendent. Dr. Humfir herself commandeered it. An entire two floors, with the most advanced healing technology at Humfir's disposal. Spacious, and with him being the only patient there, it was more a penthouse suite. Especially with his own maid girl to answer his every beck and call.

He was getting back to form. Back to himself.

Despite the advice of his personal physician, he felt he *had* to make that appearance. *For Quinn's sake.*

His leg would take months to heal fully. Almost reduced to a stump, the muscle, tissues and skin had to be regrown. Bones treated with nanite covering, to ward off infection. Eleven months to make a full recovery, she told him. *ELEVEN MONTHS!!*

In the meantime, he'd amuse himself with the knowledge things were still proceeding according to schedule. No setback could stop that. His grip on the universe was, by now, a stranglehold. The protests would come and go. The opposition would fall to the wayside. And that smart yet silly little girl, he laughed, will be running for the rest of her days.

Especially when the reward for her capture is announced.

That he lost such an expensive, experimental spaceship, wasn't looked upon kindly. But his ability to spin it into a victory was never doubted. In fact, it solidified public support for the next phase: The War against Intergalactic Piracy and Terrorism. Already, the demand for justice squads capable of meeting this threat had quadrupled. The loss, of both vessel and crew, was obscured by the gains that he stood to reap in short order.

And of those crew members who survived, they, along with the girl who gushed over him at the Globe, were already undergoing mandatory "psych evaluation". There would be no trace of him in their memories. Or the incident. Their careers would continue as if nothing happened. And based on their further trajectories, he'd have the pleasure of selecting those like Lt. Crade who served with capability and intelligence. "The future", he mused. But for the present, back to the shadows, doing what he did best.

"Namesh", his father began, as their customary lesson during a game of chess was commencing. His father taught through strategies, through subterfuge. "Always size up any and all options before you make a move..."

In his resting chair, he lightly touched a button. A seventh dimensional chessboard appeared before him. He selected Black.

White opened the game with pawn to E-5. He countered with pawn to D-4

It took him almost a quarter of an hour. Checkmate.

"Problems solve themselves if you get out of the way", his father advised him repeatedly.

Finally, He learned that lesson painfully. Eleven months of rumination, of therapy. Of watching it all come to harvest, seeds of dreams planted long, long ago in fields of blood. He smiled grimly, contemplating whether or not to play another round of chess.

Right now, he needed a glass of cognac.

"Maid!", he yelled imperiously, as he pressed the summons bell. He drew a sadistic smile anticipating her arrival. It never failed.

When the door opened, the first thing in view was the two anklets she wore. One for the medicine needed to prolong her life (such as it was now) and the other to administer syathin-9. Ednisa Quinn shuffled into the room, carrying his drink on a tray, passing a large wall mirror. Once a neat and prim woman, her maid's uniform looked filthy and disheveled on her. Her formerly proud, erect posture was now slightly stooped and defeated. A haggard, remorseful face looked at her. Languid, fearful eyes stared back, into a face she no longer recognized.

THE END

RODNEY HOLMES

BALTIMORE, MARYLAND

2017

A thank you for all of you who have purchased this book, or have borrowed it from others to read. Thank you.

I would like, at this time to give a thought or two of gratitude for the people who have come into my life. Whether living or deceased, you have helped to shape me into the person I am today. Thank You.

And to anyone who's whited out a mistake, ripped up paper from the typewriter or deleted a whole paragraph because of one misplaced word... You Understand.

ELECTRIC HAZE PRESS

"Telling our stories in our own words, in our own image."

Contact Info:

electrichazepress2020@gmail.com

Twitter: ElectricHazePress@PressHaze

Instagram: electrichazepress_2020

Website: www.electrichazepress.net